I0671860

Kitab Kabbani

THE KABBANI BOOK

by Mike Mitchell

Black Sea

★Ankara

ARMENIA · Baku ★
★ Yerevan · AZERBAIJAN

TURKMENISTAN

TURKEY

Chaldiran

Caspian
Sea

★ Ashgabat

Konya ●

● Tabrīz

● Adana

● Gaziantep

Mosul ●

Mashhad ●

Nicosia

● Aleppo

Erbil ●

★ Tehran

● Herāt

PRUS ★

SYRIA

Hamadan ●

AFGHANIS

Beirut ★
Sea LEBANON ★ Damascus

Kermanshah ●

Qom ●

● Eşfahān

Kandahār ●

ISRAEL

★
Baghdad

Dezful ●

Tel Aviv-Yafo ●
Jerusalem ★ ★ Amman

● Shush ● Masjed
Soleiman

● Yazd

IRAQ

● Ahvāz

IRAN

exandria

JORDAN

Al Başrah ●

o ★

KUWAIT

Zāhedān ●

● Shīrāz

★ Kuwait

PAK

Persian
Gulf

T

BAHRAIN
Dhahran ● ★ Manama

OMAN

Al Hofuf ●

★ Doha
QATAR

Abu
Dhabi ★ DUBAI

Aswān ●

● Medina

Riyadh ★

UNITED
ARAB
EMIRATES

Gulf of Oman

Muscat ★

Port Sudan ●

Red Sea

SAUDI ARABIA

The Empty
Quarter

OMAN

● Jiddah
● Mecca

Arabian
Sea

● Najran

YEMEN

rman ●
rtoum ★

Kassala ●

ERITREA
Asmara ★

★ Sanaa

N

Socotra
(YEMEN)

● Aden   Gulf of Aden

This work is literary fiction and is informed by the author's study of and travel in the Middle East. He would insist that by no means is he an expert on this dynamic region of the world, but it is one of his express goals to own a flat in Jubayl جبيل (Byblos) Lebanon one day and continue his study and writing. Several prominent Middle Eastern families, historical individuals and facts, documents, and recorded events are featured in this novel. Where concrete evidence about these fascinating people and events are available, they are included where appropriate in this work. Some words are, of course, purely fictional. Several of the world's most prominent religions are also featured in this novel. Scripture and sectarian doctrine are left unaltered. Commentary by the novel's characters is informed by historical and contemporary sources as well as the thoughts of the author. The author has no religious agenda other than to ask how all might somehow, someday find room for each other in the field Rumi mentions and is prominently displayed as the subtitle to this work. Any negative reaction to this work is due to the author's weakness in communication, not because he expressly attempted to create that reaction.

Byblos Press
Newark, Delaware

Copyright © 2015 by Byblos Media. All rights reserved. This book, or parts thereof, may not be reproduced in any form without permission, except by a reviewer, who may quote brief passages in a review.

ISBN10: 0-9746003-8-5
ISBN13: 978-0-9746003-8-3

Printed in the United States of America
First Edition
Cover design and layout by Kent Bingham
More by this author at *www.mike-mitchell.com*

BYBLOS
p r e s s

Part I: Turkey

Black Sea

★ Ankara

TURKEY

ARMENIA
★ Yerevan

Baku ★
AZERBAIJAN

TURKMENISTAN

★ Ashgabat

Chaldiran

Caspian
Sea

Konya ●

Adana ●

● Gaziantep

● Tabrîz

Mosul
●

● Aleppo

Erbil
●

● Mashhad

Nicosia
★
/PRUS

SYRIA

★ Tehran

Herât ●

Beirut ★
LEBANON

Hamadan ●
Qom ●
● Kermanshah

AFGHANIS

Sea

Damascus
★

ISRAEL
Tel Aviv-Yafo ●
Jerusalem ●

★ Amman

Baghdad
★

Dezful ●
● Shush Masjed
        Soleiman
● Ahvâz

● Eşfahân

● Yazd

Kandahâr ●

IRAQ

IRAN

Zâhedân ●

JORDAN

Al Başrah ●

Jexandria

KUWAIT

ro ★
●

★ Kuwait

Persian
Gulf

Shîrâz ●

PAK▶

T

BAHRAIN
Dhahran ●★Manama

OMAN

Aswân ●

Al Hofuf ●

★ Doha
QATAR

Abu
Dhabi

● DUBAI
★

Gulf of Oman

Medina ●

Riyadh ★

UNITED
ARAB
EMIRATES

Muscat ★

Port Sudan ●

Red Sea

● Jiddah
● Mecca

The Empty
Quarter

SAUDI ARABIA

OMAN

Arabian
Sea

● Najran

urman ●
artoum ★

Kassala ●

ERITREA
Asmara ★

YEMEN
★ Sanaa

Socotra
(YEMEN)

N

Aden

Gulf of Aden

Chapter 1

"...*Akil,* how do you say it in English, *wise*? It would be wise for you to keep this to yourself or there will be *a kill* on your shoulders. Ha ha ha! You understand my joke? It is no joke!" And the phone went dead.

* * *

MY MORNING HAD STARTED OUT like most days. Up by six-thirty. Workout until seven-thirty. Shower and dressed by eight. I know I should eat breakfast—most important meal of the day and all that—but I usually skip breakfast. This day was no different. I was about to leave for work where I am a short-order cook at a small truck stop off Highway 99 between Chowchilla and Merced. Really awesome apple and gooseberry pies if you find yourself traversing the Central Valley of the Golden State. Just as I shut the door of my little two-bedroom rambler in Madera, my cell phone rang. I was surprised because I don't give out my number to many people. I am on most don't-call spam lists, but I expected it to be an offer for pest control, or a refinance loan. The phone didn't stop ringing by the time I opened the door to my robin-egg-blue 1962 Chevy Impala SS. I know, totally cool. I answered the call.

"Hello."

"Mr. Allen?" a voice asked in a heavy accent.

"Yes. Who is this?" I half expected it to be a friend from work joking around.

"It is not important you know that. What is important is, we have your sister and she will not live to see the New Year unless you do exactly as I say. Do you understand?"

The accent was too good to be a fake, but I couldn't place what kind of accent it was. Not Hispanic or Asian. Not British, French, nor German. No clue. I was still not convinced this wasn't a prank.

"How do I know this isn't some kind of joke?" I replied. "Can I talk to my sister?" I figured I had him there. My sister had recently moved to New York City to teach English as a second language. She had started her own business in Fresno, and it turned out she kept getting requests from contacts in New York City to relocate her company there but had few clients in Fresno. I didn't even know exactly where she was living yet.

"Make no mistake, this is not a joke," the voice said.

"If you want me to do something you will have to prove to me that this isn't a joke." Sounding serious on the phone is not all that credible. "Put my sister on the phone."

"Unfortunately, that is not possible at this time. You see, she is in transit to Istanbul at this moment. She believes she is going there to meet her husband who is in trouble. In fact, her husband is in trouble. He just doesn't know it yet. He may have what we want and that makes his life a—how would you say? —a less than long-term proposition, ha ha," the voice chuckled. "Do not contact him if you want your sister to live. This may sound like a joke to you or overly dramatic, like one of your American movies, but this is real life—and could be real death."

"Okay, I'm listening," I said, still trying to sort out what was really going on.

"This is where you are hoping I will say, 'just kidding,' but I am not. I have done this before, and I know what is in your mind. There is no way to make this go away or solve it, without doing exactly what I tell you to do. Now are you really listening?" the voice asked in a friendlier manner—if you can sound friendly and threaten death in the same breath.

"Yes, I am really listening," I said, wondering for the first time how he got my number if not from my sister.

"You must be in Istanbul within twenty-four hours. How you get there is your problem. Drive your old blue car if you think you can make it. Ha, a joke. We will find you when you arrive. Bring enough to look like a tourist, but you will not need anything. What we would like is in your memory. You carry very important information of which you are unaware. You have in your mind a blessing to millions, or you could become known as the reason for tragedy to millions. Do not warn anyone. Not the police, not friends, not relatives, and again, especially not your brother-in-law. Go to work and tell them you are sick or whatever you need to do. You will be gone a week at the most, and then you can return to your mundane existence that you call a life."

"Wait, you're talking about the Istanbul that is in Turkey, right? There isn't an Istanbul in Texas or Ohio or somewhere I don't know about?"

"Istanbul, Turkey, Mr. Allen," the voice said impatiently. I could almost see him rolling his eyes as he clarified the destination.

"Don't I have to have some kind of visa or something to travel? I can't do all that and be there in twenty-four hours! And I don't know anything important! Could it be you have the wrong guy?"

"*Jahech!* You are an idiot. You are already questioning me and putting your sister's life in extreme danger. She is of no importance to us, and she is only living because we would like your cooperation. If you do not want to help us or are not fully cooperative, it will slow us down, but we have hundreds of years of patience behind us and will yet be triumphant. You are of no significant complication to us. If you wish, your sister will die, and you can go back to your burgers and fries. Decide now, this very instant. What will it be?"

"So much for being the friendly neighborhood extortionist," I thought to myself.

"Of course, I am ready to do what you say, but please understand, I am not a world traveler like my sister. I don't know how to do this. And you must know that I have no idea what you are talking about."

"You and your sister can yet live a happy life. I do not mean to sound so dramatic. But, I will not be holding your hand. Go online. You can purchase a tourist visa for Turkey. Be at the Sabiha Gökçen International Airport within twenty-four hours. Tell no one. Be…*Akil*, how do you say it in English, *wise*? It would be wise for you to keep this to yourself or there will be *a kill* on your shoulders. Ha ha ha! You understand my joke? It is no joke!" And the phone went dead.

I sat in my car still holding my cell phone to my ear, frozen. Turkey, my sister Anna, her husband—my brother-in-law— Badri Kabbani. "This is insane! This is not really happening! I can't do this. Even if I wanted to, I don't know how." My phone started ringing again. It was extra loud. "Are my senses in some kind of ultra-sensitive state?" I wondered; then I realized I was still holding it to my ear.

"Hello?" I said, fearful of the voice on the other end.

"This is your lucky day! You have been selected from over five thousand residents in your area to install solar panels at no cost to you! That's right, no cost! Only an affordable monthly payment and you can be one of the wise ones that are taking charge of their monthly electric bill…" I didn't hear the rest. I dropped my phone on the seat with the sales guy or automated advertisement still talking.

"One of the lucky ones? Wise… I have got to get going if I am going to figure this out." I started my car and drove directly to work where I told them I quit because I got a better job in Arizona. The manager and my fellow employees were as stunned at this news as I was. I left Mable's Table Truck Stop and continued on to Merced. I stopped at the Chase Bank and withdrew all my savings, nearly seven thousand dollars. Sad how little money that looks like in one hundred dollar bills. My life's savings. That trip to New Zealand and Australia will have to wait. In the local shopping center, I located Merced Travel and walked in. I could feel the sweat running down my back. It was November 13th. The temperature was about 67 degrees.

"I was wondering if I could purchase a ticket for Turkey, er, the country. Can I do that here?"

"We can help you with that, sir. Please, have a seat. Is this for a holiday or special date in particular? And will you be traveling alone?" the kind lady asked.

"Umm, well I will be traveling alone, and I need to be there as soon as possible. Tonight, if possible. Can I do that?"

"Oh my, it will be impossible to get there tonight. You see, it is already tonight in Turkey. Let's see what we can do."

Within twenty minutes, I had a ticket from Sacramento to New York City on a United flight and a one-stop flight through Frankfurt, Germany on Delta Airlines to Sabina Airport, or whatever that name was. It would take nineteen hours. I had only four hours to make the flight out of Sacramento. I was also $1,237 poorer. Even with this purchase, I was still hoping someone would tell me this was all a joke. The travel agency also got me an e-visa. They thought it odd that I didn't need hotel accommodations. Thank goodness I had a passport. "Did The Voice know that too?" I wondered. It was hard to believe this would be the first time I would use it.

I pulled into my driveway forty-five minutes later, aware the time was ticking away. Even before I opened the door, I knew something was wrong, really wrong. The miniature lemon tree in the pot on my little front porch was knocked over, and the door was not fully closed. "I did lock it when I left this morning, didn't I?" I couldn't remember.

Inside, the entire house was torn apart. My shelves of books were tossed everywhere. It appeared my collection of books on the Middle East had been of particular interest. Even the cushions on the couch were torn up and the cabinet drawers in the kitchen were lying on the floor. Absolutely nothing was where it should be, except my weights set and barbell which sat where I left them this morning. "Did the voice on the phone do this?" I wondered out loud. I quickly grabbed a few clothes from the floor, a toothbrush and shaving gear, and stuffed them in a duffle bag. I hadn't gotten around to buying actual luggage yet for that trip to Australia. I stopped and looked around one last time before I stepped out the door. That is when I noticed a piece of paper tacked on the back of the front door. I took it off the door and read a note written in red ink block letters.

MR. ALLEN, YOU ARE IN GRAVE DANGER. WE HOPED TO REMOVE THE THREAT TO YOUR LIFE BY FINDING THE BOOK. IT IS OBVIOUS YOU DON'T HAVE IT WITH YOU. GET US THE BOOK AND WE WILL TAKE CARE OF YOUR LITTLE PROBLEMS. YOU MAY BE ASKED TO TRAVEL. YOU CANNOT TRUST THAT GROUP. BRING THE BOOK WITH YOU AND WE WILL MEET YOU AT YOUR DESTINATION. WE ARE WATCHING, FOR YOUR SAFETY AND OURS. DESTROY THIS NOTE. NO ONE CAN KNOW WE CONTACTED YOU.

FURQAAN

I didn't have time to think about this now. I was sure I would have more than enough time on my flights to the other side of the world. I stuffed the note in my pocket and walked out the door, not bothering to lock it. The drive to the Sacramento Airport was uneventful, except for all the emotional and mental gymnastics going on in my head. This Furqaan guy didn't sound like he was part of The Voice, as I had begun thinking of the person on the phone. Only, like The Voice, Furqaan sure knew how to mix almost friendliness with downright terror and meanness.

"And what is this about a book?!" I asked out loud, almost yelling. "This is nuts, or I am nuts."

"Could I be going crazy, schizophrenic—just hearing things?" I asked myself. "Well, my mind didn't tear up my house while I was gone, so something is happening!"

I pulled into airport parking and found a spot on level three, half wondering if I would ever see my car again as I got out with my bag. It was then, for the first time that it hit me. This was real; my sister and brother-in-law were really in great danger, and I was just a pawn in something much bigger than my petty little worries. I started shaking and leaned against the car. It took me a couple minutes to get control of myself. With a painful effort, I straightened my back, tried to relax my jaw, which I realized was clenched tightly closed, took a deep breath, and almost passed out from inhaling the exhaust from a passing diesel pick-up truck. I made it through airport security with thirty minutes to spare. I thought I might get pulled out at the security check because I was so nervous. Luckily, they must have assumed I was just a nervous flier—which I am. My flight was called on time, and I had just settled into my seat when I started shaking again. I could hardly connect my seat belt, and I am sure the lady next to me was wondering whether I was sick or simply nervous. Before the aircraft doors were closed, the lady had exchanged seats with an older man. I was glad that my five-foot-ten-inch frame fit comfortably in economy class. I closed my eyes and wished I could fall asleep. I knew I wouldn't, but I didn't want to talk with anyone.

Chapter 2

THE FLIGHT TO NEW YORK was uneventful—unless you count that the only food I got was a small bag of pretzels and a soft drink. I wasn't all that hungry, but it would have been something to do. I didn't watch the movie because there was this long, tall Texan, who insisted on wearing his cowboy hat the entire flight in the seat in front of me. I couldn't see the screen three rows away. It was some animated flick anyway. It seemed inappropriate, even irreverent, to watch a cartoon when my sister was by now a hostage, my brother-in-law was in grave danger, and I had quit my job as a short-order cook.

"Please fasten your seat belt, sir. We will be landing at JFK in just a few minutes," the flight attendant said. I fastened my seat belt. I wasn't shaking too badly this time.

"Wait a minute," I said to the passenger next to me—a businessman I assumed. Who else would wear a suit on a coast-to-coast flight? "Did she just say we were landing at JFK?"

"I hope that is what she said. I have a meeting in about two hours in Park Slope. I shouldn't have tried to cut this so close," my seatmate said.

"But my connecting flight leaves from La Guardia in less than three hours, and it is an international flight!" I said in a panic.

"It's a pretty direct drive up the Van Wyck to the Grand Central Parkway. It's a little less than fifteen miles and should only take you about twenty minutes this time of day. What will take time is getting your bags, getting a taxi, and at the other end getting through security at La Guardia. The regular shuttle is out of the question."

"I have my bag with me, but I have never been to New York before. Heck, I have never flown internationally before either," I said, hoping he would tell me it would be no problem.

He looked at me for a moment and said, "I have my driver meeting me. I think I can drop you off and still make my meeting. It would be the quickest solution, and it would save you a few dollars. Would that work for you?"

"Well, yes, that would be great! I would be happy to pay, though, and I don't want to cause you to be late, but then it is a matter of life and death, so-to-speak, that I make my flight. I guess the travel agency made a mistake, or I did in my explanation."

"Let me see your ticket. Maybe you are actually leaving from JFK. You wouldn't want to get to La Guardia and find out you were really supposed to be where you landed."

I showed him my ticket, and I had it right: I was departing from La Guardia.

"It really is no problem. I am glad to help out. No matter how my meeting goes this evening, I will feel like I did something useful today," my now-best-friend said. "You seemed pretty pre-occupied on the flight, so I didn't want to bother you. My name is Mack, Mack Albright."

"Good to meet you, Mack. I am Thad Allen." I offered him my clammy hand.

"Yes, I saw that on your ticket. Off to Turkey for your first foreign adventure. How exciting. But a matter of life and death? That sounds pretty dramatic to leave in the hands of notoriously late airlines and possible weather delays this time of year."

"No choice," I said and left it at that.

"There is always a choice, but the distance between stimulus and response is sometimes so constrained it feels like there is no choice. I have had to remind myself of that fact many times in business negotiations. I am sure you will work things out," Mack said. "It looks like we are at the gate. You said you carried on your luggage? Let's see if we can get off this plane as quickly as possible."

"What about your luggage?" I asked Mack.

"I don't have any to speak of. Change of underclothes and a toothbrush in my briefcase. Ever since all the security demands at airports, I just keep clothing at our West Coast office. Makes the travel just a little more bearable. I used to love it when the airports were easy and the airline food was something to look forward to," Mack explained.

Mack was a big man, older, maybe fifty-five or sixty, muscle, not flab and something over six feet I guessed from his sitting height, and I felt sorry for him cramped back here in economy class. He seemed like a person that would be in first class. I don't know what my expectations were for a first-class passenger, but not being much of a traveler myself, I dismissed the thought.

"Excuse me, Mr. Allen, you okay?" Mack was asking.

"Oh, sorry. I was thinking about this whirlwind trip. I didn't know this morning when I got up that I would be traveling to Turkey this evening," I quibbled.

"Wow, maybe I will retract the 'too dramatic' statement I made. You can tell me about it if you like on the way to La Guardia," Mack said.

We were off the airplane fairly quickly, thanks to Mack explaining to the flight attendant my tight schedule. I am not shy, but I probably would have just gone with the flow, not knowing I could take charge somewhat. Maybe there were more choice options between stimulus and response than I thought. I couldn't see any options, but just this little bit of efficacy made me feel so much better. I also noticed the lady Mack had traded seats with sitting in first class. I was glad the trip had worked out for her.

We were in Mack's limo less than ten minutes after the aircraft doors had opened. "This is going to work," I said as we pulled away from the curb.

"Of course, it is," Mack assured me. "How's the traffic looking, Hussein?" Mack asked his driver after explaining the detour to La Guardia.

"No problem, sir. We should be there in twenty-five minutes," Hussein answered.

"I have never been in a limo. Lots of firsts for me today," I said. "Thank you again, Mack. This really means a lot to me," I said.

"My pleasure. So tell me, what is the life-or-death matter that takes you to Istanbul? It is an amazing city, but can be overwhelming for a first-time visitor," Mack explained.

"I am supposed to meet somebody there, a family matter," I said, trying to stay generic with my answer. "A big city, you say?" I was getting a knot in my stomach again.

"Well, maybe I am being a little dramatic myself. Sabiha Gokcen Airport is about twenty miles to the south of the main city. It's newer and isn't as busy as Ataturk International Airport on the European side of the city. You shouldn't have any problems. Someone, a family member, is meeting you, or do you need transportation into the city?" Mack asked.

"I think I am being met by an associate of the family. I will find out when I get there, I guess," I said.

"And if no one is there?" Mack asked.

"Then I wait. I am sure I will be okay," I assured Mack. This conversation was rapidly getting to the point where I was going to get sick, in a limo no less, and where I would have to explain things I knew I shouldn't. I looked out the window at some kind of flying saucer tower and then a big stadium in a park. I was about to ask to change the subject when Mack continued his questions.

"You're right; I am sure it will be fine. So you have family in Turkey?" Mack asked.

"No, but I have a brother-in-law from Lebanon," I explained. "He will probably be the one meeting me." I thought, "I should have said that from the beginning, and this conversation would be over."

"Sorry for all the questions. I do have a reason. Let me explain, as we are almost to the airport. It just so happens I may have an associate flying to Istanbul tonight; at least, that was what was on the schedule last week when I reviewed it. Crazy coincidence, I know. We have an important satellite office in Turkey, so it isn't so odd we have to-and-from travel to Istanbul. Call it being an overprotective boss, but I wanted to ensure you weren't someone that would cause problems. I wanted to make sure—as best I could within a short drive—that you were a good person. My associate could answer any questions about Istanbul during the flight. Most of her family is from Turkey, and if your friends or family don't show up, she could probably ensure you find a safe hotel," Mack explained.

We were pulling into the airport. The sign said Terminal D, and I couldn't think of any reason to say no, without being rude to this person who had been so helpful.

"That would be wonderful, Mack, but if that is a problem for your friend, don't worry about it. Like I said, I am sure everything will be fine."

"I will give her a call after I drop you off to see if her travel is still set for tonight. She has important meetings there in a couple of days, so I am sure she is traveling, but it might not be tonight or on your flight," Mack was explaining. "I apologize in advance if I've given you some assurance and then can't follow through."

"Well, it looks like I am here, thanks to you, ready for the next leg of my adventure." I was trying to sound more positive than I was. I grabbed my bag and began to get out of the limo. I offered my hand to Mack.

"It was a pleasure, Thad. *Bon voyage*, or should I say *güvenli seyahat*? Oh, my associate's name is Leyla. She will probably find you. Here is my business card. On your trip home, give me a call. I would love to hear how things went."

"Will do, Mack. Thank you again. I'd better get going. Two hours before an international flight, right?" I walked away feeling like I was leaving a longtime friend. Was I actually going to miss a guy I had barely met, or was it that I felt like I was drowning, swimming away from the only lifesaver floating near me?

I walked into the terminal and found the Delta check-in counter. My knees were shaking. I had to use one of those self-serve computers, and when I scanned my passport, it told me to go to the counter. I waited in line, and when I got to the counter, a nice man named Jim asked me if I would be willing to take a later flight as the aircraft was already full. My blood pressure must have spiked to three hundred. "Three hundred what?" I momentarily wondered—pounds, inches, teaspoons?

"No, I can't take a later flight. I have to be in Istanbul by tomorrow morning!"

"We can offer you a $200 voucher and a hotel room for the night. Pretty good deal, sir," Jim countered.

"Listen, Jim. I really need to be in Istanbul as soon as possible. I would love to take you up on your offer, but there is absolutely no way. Please give me a seat," I pleaded.

"I am afraid the best I can do is to give you a pass to proceed to the gate, and we will see what we can do. Do you have a bag to check?" Jim asked.

"Just one carry-on," I said, hoping that would make it easier for them to get me a seat.

"Okay, Mr. Allen, here is your pass to the gate. We will call your name there when we find you a seat or another flight," Jim said with a smile like this was no inconvenience at all.

I walked away in a daze. Surely this wasn't happening. I was so numb I didn't even feel nervous as I went through security. I found a seat at gate D6 looking out at a Delta aircraft that I prayed was going to take me to Istanbul, a place I had never been to or even thought about before. I watched the other people sitting near or walking by. Each one had a story and a reason they were here. Were there people with as crazy a story as I could share? I doubted it, but who knows? Some are traveling because of a death in their family, some for new births, some for weddings, some because of a breakup. Most were probably just traveling—getting from point A to point B. Although their physical bodies were in this terminal, their thoughts, their presence, were somewhere else: in a book, at home with loved ones, on their computer doing business or trying to find something meaningful on social media. That was the real difference between these people and me. It wasn't the uniqueness of my story, but my presence. I was one hundred percent right here. I didn't know where I was going, and there really wasn't that much I was leaving behind.

"Thaddeus Allen. Mr. Thaddeus Allen, please report to the D6 gate," I heard the public address system announce.

I thought, "Someone else has the same name as me?" I looked to see who it was. It took me a moment to register that they were calling me. I jumped up and walked over to the counter. "Yes, I am Thad Allen."

The lady at the counter, Alicia, must have attended the same customer service class as Jim at the ticket counter. Same plastic smile. Or was it just me expecting the worst? "Mr. Allen, I am afraid we have had to make some changes in your travel to Istanbul," Alicia said.

My knees almost buckled. "Oh please, don't tell me I have another flight but that it is okay because you have a two-hundred-dollar voucher for me," I stammered.

"Oh, nothing like that, but would you rather have the two-hundred dollar voucher?" Alicia asked.

"No, I need to get to Istanbul as soon as possible. I can take another flight if it can get me there as fast as or quicker than this one," I explained.

"This is your best option for the quickest arrival. The flight is overbooked, however, and we are having trouble..." Alicia's voice was drowned out by a "last call for Paris on Air France flight 2797 operated by Delta" announcement. Alicia was continuing to talk. "So if that would work for you, I can make that change right now."

"I'm sorry, could you repeat that? I missed some of it," I explained, wondering if I had been offered a three-hundred-dollar voucher and dinner at a hotel.

"I am sorry. It is pretty noisy in here. I almost don't realize that anymore. I was explaining that you have been upgraded to business class on this flight. It must be a promotion or something, because it was taken care of at Delta, not here at the airport. Here is your ticket, seat 21A. If I could see your passport, I will complete your check-in," Alicia continued. "We have fifteen minutes to boarding."

I literally floated away from the counter. Not that I am super religious, but it seemed appropriate to go somewhere and say a prayer of gratitude. I settled for the seclusion of the men's restroom. I hoped that wasn't sacrilegious, but it felt good to wash my hands and face and relieve my stress. I tried to comb my dark curly hair that had some unruly bends in it. "Next stop Istanbul, Turkey," I said to my reflection in the mirror.

"He that endureth to the end shall be saved."

Startled, I turned around and saw an old gentleman with a kind smile—it seemed more genuine than Jim's and Alicia's, but I couldn't have said why I thought that. "I'm sorry, were you talking to me?" I asked.

"You sounded like you are on an arduous journey. It's from the Bible, the Book of Matthew. 'He that endureth to the end shall be saved,'" the older gentleman said.

I looked closer at him. He had on a black nametag. "Elder Foster, Church of Jesus Christ of Latter-day Saints."

"It seems everyone with a smile today has a nametag. Thank you for your thought, umm, Elder Foster. My first trip outside the United States," I said in partial explanation.

"Well, have a wonderful trip, wherever your journey takes you." He shared another broad smile and walked out of the restroom.

I actually did feel better. As I left the restroom, my flight was announced. I walked to the gate, gave Alicia my ticket that she had just recently given me and walked down the jet bridge. What a cool name for a square tube that leads you to a round tube. I was directed to my seat by a busy flight attendant. I didn't catch her nametag, but no matter, she wasn't smiling. The plane smelled good, like lavender, I guessed. I sat down and buckled my seat belt without shaking at all.

Chapter 3

I SAW HER AS SOON as she entered the aircraft. It never entered my mind that she was possibly Mack Albright's associate. She was young, maybe 24, and exotically beautiful. Long dark hair framed a face that made Angelina Jolie look plain. Olive skin, high cheek bones, eyes that looked like the color of sand at sunset, a perfect nose sitting just above rosewater lips, and a sparkle that lit up the plane. Even those who had their back turned to her seemed to look around to figure out what had changed. I see a lot of interesting people passing through Mable's Table where I work, I mean where I used to work, and I am pretty good at picking out ethnic backgrounds. She was indecipherable. She was looking at seat numbers and smiled when she discovered I was in the seat next to her. My heart stopped.

"Good evening, Mr. Allen. My name is Leyla," the goddess said. "I hope you don't mind, but when I got the call from Mack that a new friend of his was traveling to Istanbul tonight, I called Delta and changed your seat next to me so we could talk. The upgrade is on Mack. With all the travel our company does, we probably have a mountain of miles for seat switch. Mack said you might have some questions about Istanbul and Turkey. If you just want to sleep, or read, or something, that is, of course, fine, and I won't bother you." She sat down and tucked a small leather case under her seat. Her hands, no jewelry, also didn't shake when she connected her seat belt.

"Oh, no, talking is good," I said. I had no idea what to say next. "I may name my first child after Mack, though," I said under my breath.

"How interesting. *Heterochromia Iridum*," she said looking at me with those sparkling sandstorm eyes.

"I'm sorry, is that a foreign language? It sounds Latin. If it is a code, I am afraid I don't know the secret reply," I joked.

Leyla hesitated for less than a second then smiled and said, "No, not a secret code. It's your eyes. One is light amber, almost green, and the other is dark chocolate. A long-ago relative of mine had the same thing, so I know the official name for it. You have never heard that term?" Leyla asked.

"No," I said. "The terms I have mostly run across, or better said, that people have shared with me, include geek, dork, mutant, and freak. Some people sense there is something different with my face, but it is hilarious to watch them trying to figure out what it is. You are pretty quick to pick that out," I said, trying to stop my nervous speech.

"You must run in a very tough crowd, and," she hesitated, "you don't look like you would be the type to get picked on. I think your eyes are unique and special, certainly not weird or strange. I read once that only about two hundred thousand people in the United States have two eye colors, but many accomplished and famous people do," Leyla said.

"Well, thank you for that nice thought. Since leaving high school, I have established a rigorous workout schedule. Leyla, right?" I said as I offered my hand.

"Oh, sorry, yes, Leyla. Leyla Celebi." She shook my hand, and I didn't want to let go, but I did.

"Celebi? That is interesting," I said without thinking.

"You know the last name?" Leyla asked, slightly on guard for the second time.

"Well, no. At least not as a last name. When I was young, I used to collect Pokémon cards. A time-traveling green fairy creature was named Celebi. I guess I really am a geek to remember that," I stammered.

"Yes, I actually have been told that before. I wish I could do the time travel thing, but I am glad I am not a little green alien with blue tipped antenna," Leyla said with a smile in her eyes.

"Yeah, me too; I mean, wow, you know your Pokémon," I said and began to blush.

"Just that creature, I am afraid. I grew up mostly in Turkey, and we didn't have Pokémon there, at least as far as I know," Leyla said.

Just then the flight attendant interrupted on the public address system requiring that we watch the safety briefing on the screen in the seat in front of me. It was hilarious, I thought, but I am easily entertained. I also stole a couple of glances at Leyla. She smelled like rose water to match her lips. When the video was over, I said, "I hope this doesn't sound weird or anything, but that is a nice perfume you are wearing," attempting to start up a conversation again.

"Thank you, Mr. Allen. It's Quelque Fleur by Hubigant. They don't make it anymore, and I don't know why. I get more compliments when I wear it than any other perfume," Leyla replied.

"I understand your frustration," I explained. "My favorite candy bar is the MARS Bar, and one day it was just gone. There is this Snickers Almond bar, but it isn't the same."

"Ah, I think I can help you there," Leyla said with an impish smile. "Mars bars are still alive and well in France and a few other countries, perhaps where you are traveling, as well. I don't know if they are exactly the same as the American version, but you should keep your eyes open for them. Maybe you are a geek, Mr. Allen, and I mean that in a complimentary way."

"I guess I need to travel more," I said.

"Well, here we go," Leyla said.

As if on cue, the pilot announced that we were number one for takeoff and asked the flight attendants to take their seats. We were on our way. "In case we don't make the take-off, my first name is Thaddeus—Thad," I shared with Leyla.

"So I should only call you Thad if we crash on take-off?" Leyla asked, deadpan.

"Well, no, I didn't mean it like that. I wanted you to know my name, so please, call me Thad. I hate take-offs, so I wanted you to know my name before I clam up," I attempted to explain.

"Okay, Thad, but I think I will call you Thaddeus. That is an awesome name. I believe that you are the first Thaddeus I have ever met. Are you named after someone, or did your parents just like it?" Leyla asked.

"So, don't laugh, but I am named after one of the Twelve Apostles during Christ's time. My dad was Catholic when he was young and remembered it from school. He lost interest in organized religion, but not the name," I explained.

"Fascinating," was all that Leyla said as she looked at me.

I was a little uncomfortable with her stare. I was afraid she would tire quickly of my plain face, even if I have two different colored eyes. "So what does Leyla mean, or was that just a name your parents liked?" I asked, attempting to turn the table on my seatmate.

"It has a lot of history behind it, but that is for another time, maybe later on the flight. It is a long story. By the way, you survived the take-off," Leyla said.

I couldn't believe it. We had taken off, and we were over the water, the Atlantic Ocean, I guessed. "How did that happen?" I asked no one in particular.

"I am a seasoned traveler, and I have gotten to the point where I don't even think about it," Leyla began to explain. "I will admit there have been a few times that I have glanced out the window and am surprised to be at ten thousand meters—err, thirty-five thousand feet, and I thought we were still taxiing toward the runway."

"Wow. Can I hire you as my take-off coach? I usually don't even realize I am holding my breath, and I start to get dizzy about the time the wheels leave the ground. I don't mind the flight itself, though. Like my grandfather used to say, it is like a tractor stuck in the mud. Lots of noise, but it doesn't feel like you are actually getting anywhere. He was a farmer," I said.

"We make an interesting pair, Thaddeus," Leyla began. "Sometimes en route, I get pretty flustered going through bad weather. Airplanes feel so powerful and big on takeoff and even landing. They were built to get airborne. But, they feel so tiny, insignificant, and helpless—so alone in the midst of Mother Nature's power. The plane is like a dot in the clouds—just another molecule rising and falling like the water molecules around it. It is a speck, a particle in the big world of things."

"I feel like a dot sometimes," I admitted with a smile. "I only have one sister who lives on the East Coast—New York actually, with another home in Lebanon, and both of my parents have passed away. I live alone. I have friends at work, but I am pretty much a loner. I wonder sometimes if people remember me. Do they ever even think about me? Here is my theory: I exist, so I suppose that makes me a dot. There is hope, though, I think. When somebody loves me or is even just thinking about me, that creates a line from them to me. I am no longer a dot, but at least a two-dimensional line. Then when a third person is added, I become three-dimensional! Family is three-dimensional, a shape, tangible. One of the powers of religion is that it creates shape. I have thought about these lines coming into me, but I can create lines going out from me, too. Doing things for people, you know, like service, make us more than dots. And I can't believe I just told you that. I will stop before you come up with a reason to find another seat." I noticed Leyla's mouth had kind of dropped open. She must have realized it and clamped it shut.

"All the seats are taken, Thaddeus," she said after a few seconds. "This is a full flight. I do believe this will be a full and delightful flight."

I wasn't sure what she was talking about, so I just smiled and reached for the in-flight magazine in the seat pouch in front of me.

"So, is there more to this theory?" Leyla asked.

"Yes, but like you said, that is for another time, maybe later on the flight," I responded.

"Very good, for later. Do you have any questions about Turkey, or did you want to read the magazine you are holding upside down?" Leyla asked.

The flight attendant came by with hot moist towels. (I wondered when they stopped being stewardesses and stewards?) She handed me one with tongs. It smelled like lavender. Leyla took one, opened it and rubbed her hands. I wanted to be the towel until I saw her discard it on the tray the flight attendant was holding. I quickly cleaned my hands and turned back to Leyla. "I have never been outside the United States, so I have a million questions. I have read a lot about the Middle East, but sadly have not included Turkey in my personal studies."

"Why are you traveling to Istanbul?" Leyla asked. "That would help me focus on what you need to know."

With that question, reality returned like a lightning bolt. I was on a mission to save my sister's life, and I didn't have a clue what value I was in this insane situation that required me to fly to the other side of the globe. I couldn't tell Leyla any of this, of course, and I felt guilty for enjoying the last twenty minutes of conversation with a very interesting person.

"Is everything alright?" Leyla asked with concern.

"Just family issues. Your question reminded me that I don't have a clue what to ask you about Turkey because I don't have a clue what waits for me when we land there. I am just a pawn in some complicated family issues that require me in Turkey. I may not even get a chance to see the country," I explained, hoping that would appease Leyla.

"Ah, yes, family matters. I have those as well. I have no advice for you in that category," Leyla replied.

"I hardly know anything at all about Turkey or Istanbul, so maybe you could start with the basics. It will help me keep my mind off of the mysteries at the other end of my travel," I suggested.

"The basics. Well, Turkey is a country of nearly eighty million people. Most are of Turkish origin, and the largest minority is the Kurds, who are located mostly in the East, on the border with Syria, Iraq, and Iran. We are bordered by eight countries, in fact, and have one foot in the Middle East—we call that part of the country Anatolia, and one foot in Europe—that is called Thrace. We have been an international crossroads for most of human history. The vast majority of the population is Muslim, but I am getting ahead of myself," Leyla began.

"So, Turkey sounds like a really big country," I interjected.

"Relatively speaking, I suppose so. It is small compared to Russia, China, the United States, Canada and Brazil. It is about the size of California, Nevada, and Arizona combined. I think I read somewhere that Turkey creates about the same amount of products and services as Illinois. But Illinois doesn't have an Istanbul. Nothing against Chicago, but no city in the world compares to Istanbul. I am biased, of course," Leyla said with a quiet laugh. She was enjoying this geography lesson, and her enthusiasm was infectious.

"I am a cook back home," I said. "How is the food in Turkey?"

"Heaven on earth. Some say it is the best in the world. That is due to all the civilizations, cultures, and empires that have claimed our land through the millennia. We have coastlines on the Mediterranean, the Black Sea, and the Aegean Sea, plus The Sea of Marmara, the Bosphorus and the Dardanelles that bring in foreign influences from all over the world. You must try the kebabs, kofte, dolma, and borek, even if you stay only a few days," Leyla continued hardly taking a breath.

"You will have to write those down for me, although I have heard of kebabs," I said, to give her time to inhale.

"And you will want baklava as a treat or for dessert," Leyla added.

"Oh, I know baklava. My brother-in-law is from Lebanon. He has brought me some direct from Beirut. Much better than the stuff at Costco," I said a little too proudly.

"If your brother-in-law is from Beirut, you have probably eaten many things that compare closely to Turkish cuisine. Is he who you are going to see in Istanbul?" Leyla asked.

"No, but maybe someone he sent to meet me," I replied in half-truth. "So, what are the people like? Do they dress like in America, or do they wear the Muslim clothes like in Afghanistan and Saudi Arabia?" I asked to get off the family subject.

"Mostly the clothes you are thinking of are more cultural than religious. Most people in Turkey wear clothes just like you and me. In some areas, clothing becomes more traditional, and yes, some women cover their hair, or wear the hijab or burqa —you know, where most of their body is covered except for part of their face and their hands. Turkey is a secular country, so in some public jobs, for example, wearing religious headscarves is actually banned. It is a big issue in our country, the clash between modern secularism and traditional, conservative religion," Leyla explained.

"Lexus and the Olive Tree," I interjected.

"Oh, you have read that book? Thomas Friedman, right?" Leyla said, surprised.

"I read a lot. Trying to make sense of the Middle East since my sister used to live there when she first married Badri. Now it is a habit," I explained. "Pretty much all I do after work is read and work out. I am afraid I haven't read much about Turkey, though."

"You are full of surprises, Thaddeus," Leyla said. "Religious freedom is practiced to a point, but with such a large Sunni Muslim population, practice is not always perfect. For example, I belong to a sect of Islam that was banned for about half a century."

"Recently banned? What sect?" I asked. "I understand the difference, well, I sort of know there is a difference, between Sunnis and Shias. 'Understand' is really stretching the truth."

"I have been a Muslim from birth, and I wonder at times if I understand. I am Sufi. Do you know that word?" Leyla asked.

"I have read the term, but I don't know much anything about it," I said.

"Some say it is an offshoot of Shia through the Prophet's cousin, Ali. Others trace the origin through the first Sunni Caliph, Abu Bakr," Leyla said.

"What do you believe?" I asked.

"That Sufism was revealed by the angel Gabriel to the Prophet Mohammad and that we are the proponents and practitioners of the pure original form of Islam. That can get me into some big trouble in most parts of the Middle East," Leyla said with a confident smile.

Just then our dinner was served by our flight attendant, Susan. I got the beef; Leyla got the chicken. Both looked pretty good, but then, all I had eaten all day was a bag of peanuts and some ice from my soft drink. After a few bites, I asked, "So, do Sufis have the same food restrictions as other Muslims?"

"Yes, it is the same, and we follow the Five Pillars of Islam. We do see many things from a more inward perspective, though. And we have other practices that are unique," Leyla said in between bites.

"I have been looking into Mormonism for about a month. They have some of the same restrictions, on alcohol anyway. So what unique things?" I asked.

"I am a member of the Mevlevi order. Have you ever heard of the whirling dervishes?" Leyla asked.

"Yes, I have, but I am sure I have heard half-truths and urban legends," I said.

"If you are in Istanbul for any length of time, perhaps I can take you to a *Sema*—a Dervish dance. It is much easier to explain seeing it than trying to explain it over dinner," Leyla offered.

"That is very kind. I have no idea what my schedule will be like, but it sounds really interesting," I said. "Not to set religion aside, but anything else I ought to know about Turkey?" I asked.

"Food, religion, culture, all can only be understood when looking at our history. So here is the brief tour of Turkish history that every elementary school pupil in Turkey learns." Leyla stopped and smiled, and then launched into a verbal timeline. "Alexander the Great brought Hellenic culture to the Anatolian and Thracian peoples and, in a sense, unified for the first time what would one day become Turkey. Then there were the Romans and their conquering armies which, in the East, became the Byzantine Empire, and their capital was Constantinople— which would one day become Istanbul. Seljuk Turks migrated to the crumbling Empire in the eleventh century. I trace most of my heritage from this group," Leyla said with some pride.

"That is incredible," I said. My head was swimming with this condensed history. "I can't trace my heritage beyond my great grandfather. He was a Thaddeus, too."

"The Turks brought with them the Persian language, administration, new foods, and art. The Seljuk Sultanate of Rum ruled until the Mongolian invasion two hundred years later, and Anatolia was broken up into small principalities. Eventually, what was left of the Byzantium and the Seljuk principalities fell to the Ottoman Turks whose origins can be traced back to the Seljuk Sultanate of Rum."

"Your family, right?" I asked.

"Well, they were a part of it all, but this was hardly a single family affair. Over the next two hundred years, the Ottoman Empire expanded and encompassed much of South Eastern Europe, most of the Middle East, North Africa, and West Central Asia. The Ottoman Empire was the crossroads of the world for nearly four centuries. The empire began to crumble in the 1800s and dissolved and grew into the Republic of Turkey in 1923 under the leadership of Mustafa Kemal Atatürk. It was in these tumultuous early years of the Republic that the Mevlevi Order was outlawed, but that is a story for another day."

"I hope we have another day," I let slip out without thinking. "Leyla, you just boiled down two thousand years into five minutes. That is amazing," I said to refocus the conversation.

"Well, now that I have raised the historical dust, I will let it settle. If you will excuse me, I am going to use the restroom," Leyla said as she unbuckled her seat belt and got out of her seat.

Chapter 4

THE SEAT NEXT TO ME still had the lingering scent of Leyla's perfume. What a crazy day. When I got up this morning, I had no idea what was in store for me or my family. A scary phone call and an eerie note. I quit my job. My house was almost destroyed. I am actually on my way to Istanbul, Turkey. My sister has been kidnapped. I have these crazy people threatening me and my family. There is a book that I don't know anything about. I have met an amazing young lady. And all of a sudden I am exhausted. I decided to get up and stretch my legs. Leyla had gone to the restroom in the front of the aircraft, so I took the walk to the back. I didn't want her to think that I was stalking her. It was a nice walk. Most everyone was asleep. A few passengers were reading or watching a movie. One or two people were not happy with me walking by—probably upset that they were stuck in economy class while I was enjoying the comforts of business class.

"Did you have a nice walk?" Leyla asked when I got back to my seat.

"Yes, it feels great to stretch my legs. It has already been a very long day, and we aren't even to Germany yet. How do you do these long flights?" I asked as she let me scoot by her to my seat.

"Drink plenty of water, move around if the flight allows, and get some sleep if you can," Leyla answered.

"Well, I have been doing pretty good with the first two, but I should probably try to get some sleep. How much time until we get to Frankfurt?" I asked.

"I am guessing about two hours," Leyla said. "You can watch the flight progress on the screen in front of you. I usually don't bother. It only reminds me of how much longer I have to be that dot we were talking about."

"That's time enough for a little sleep, I guess. I want to know a little bit about you, now that I am an expert on Turkey," I said with my most mature smile. "Promise you will be here when I wake up?"

"I am afraid you are stuck with me all the way to Istanbul, Thaddeus. Sleep well," Leyla said.

The next thing I knew I was jolted awake as the landing gear came down as we approached the runway in Frankfurt, Germany. I was disoriented until I saw Leyla watching me. "Wow, I really slept. I hope I didn't snore," I said with a thick tongue that made me sound like I was drunk.

"I am impressed. You were out in less than thirty seconds. I wish I could do that," Leyla said. "I let you sleep through the small breakfast that was served. I hope you don't mind."

"I don't have many talents, but I can get to sleep pretty fast," I said.

"I am sure you have other talents," Leyla said and was drowned out by the pilot announcing our clearance to land and for the flight attendants to take their seats.

The approach and landing were uneventful unless you count that it was raining, and I couldn't see the ground or the runway until the pilot began to flare the aircraft. We taxied in and were at our gate in minutes. I was looking forward to stretching my legs and maybe getting something more to eat. I had to take my bag as I was changing aircraft here.

"I will see you at Gate 2E in about an hour," Leyla said. "We are fortunate. Typically, I fly Turkish Airlines from here, and they leave from the other terminal. You don't mind me abandoning you, do you? I need to make a few calls. Most of the restaurants in this terminal are more toward the D gates. I think there is a Starbucks by the E gates. Try *Sense of Taste*. The food is pretty good for an airport."

And with that, Leyla was out of my life, for an hour. I was looking forward to the flight to Turkey, but I wasn't. I walked straight to the restaurant she suggested. The menu said it was Mediterranean cuisine, but I chose the German sausages. When in Rome, I figured. It was great. After my meal, I walked around and then found the restroom near my gate. While standing at the urinal, I was approached from behind and told in a very stern whisper, "Do not move, do not attempt to turn around."

I could feel what I guessed was a knife poking me in the ribs. I could smell tobacco and clove on this stranger's breath. I froze and stared at the wall. I could only make out a dark blob of a reflection on the shiny white tile on the wall.

"You were fortunate to make your flight from New York, Mr. Allen. We have been watching you on both legs of your adventure, and there will be eyes on you on this last flight. Your Turkish history lesson was also very interesting. Do not tell the Sufi woman anything, or you will both die, as will your sister. This Mevlevi, no matter how beautiful or helpful she may appear, is not your friend. You have no friends right now, Mr. Allen. As I told you on the phone, we will meet you at the airport upon your arrival in Istanbul. Just exit the aircraft, and we will find you."

I knew I recognized the voice; it was The Voice. "Count to ten before you move a muscle. Remember, we are listening and are only a few steps away, to protect you or to harm you."

I stood there quietly as others came into the bathroom. I had forgotten to count, so I started at four and counted to fifteen for good measure. I washed my again-shaky hands and walked to my gate. Where was Elder Foster when I needed him? I boarded the aircraft when called and felt like a sheep going to the slaughter. Leyla was not in her seat. I began to wonder if she was alright. The doors were closed and still no Leyla. 'Maybe she is in the restroom,' I told myself. We began to taxi and no Leyla. The flight took two hours and fifty-two minutes, and I counted every second. I felt like a dot and realized I needed to adjust my theory. If you are connected to evil, you are still a dot. That is the big lie; there is no real meaning in our choice to connect to evil or in our connection against our will to the wicked, dishonorable, vile, or corrupt. Darkness has no substance. It is the absence of substance. When we are in a lighted room and open a door to the darkness, darkness does not spill in; light pushes out. I wished I could share this new insight with Leyla.

I had trouble keeping my breathing normal as we landed in Turkey. I couldn't remember a single thing that Leyla had told me about this country or what to do if no one met me here. I followed the lines through passport control and customs. The sign above the doors at the end of this line said "Arrival," but it should have said "Departure." I felt like I was being processed for my immediate demise that lay just outside those final doors to the rest of the world. I stood there for a brief moment before pushing through the doors to the outside. It was like a bad dream, and I couldn't wake up. I was the actor, just off stage, and the curtains were about to open, and I couldn't remember my lines. In fact, I had no idea what play I was in. Who was the audience? They seemed to know the script. Or there was more than one audience, and they each had their own version of the script. Yes, that felt more like it. There were competing scripts. Somehow that made my stage fright more bearable. At least for the moment, there was no one right answer, which left room for me to improvise. I stepped out on stage.

Outside ended up being still inside. There were many people waiting for friends, loved ones, and business associates. No one seemed to care that I had taken this courageous step. The bright lights—it was mid-morning—and the smells of sweat and car exhaust slammed into me. I wasn't in Kansas anymore. I had never been to Kansas, I reminded myself. I took slow and cautious steps like I was in a minefield. I was trying to remember every face and find someone that was looking at me or moving toward me, but everything was bouncing off my forehead.

"Ah, Mr. Allen," a large man in a chauffeur uniform said as he greeted me and took my bag from my hand. "Your car is waiting as you ordered. I trust you had a pleasant flight. Please follow me." His accent was thick, but not hard to understand. It almost felt comforting that someone here knew my name and cared about whether I had a nice flight.

I didn't attempt to say anything but began to follow him as instructed. About ten yards from the door leading to the street outside, a commotion began to my left. An old lady began shouting at a young boy who had attempted to grab her purse. I didn't understand what was being yelled, but everyone was looking their direction, and within seconds some kind of police officer or military soldier was at the scene. I had slowed to watch and then began looking for my chauffeur, my only friend in Turkey. He had disappeared, along with my bag.

Suddenly my arms were grabbed at both sides by two men moving very fast. They said nothing but pushed through the crowd toward the door. My feet were barely touching the ground. A silver Mercedes pulled up to the curb, just as we exited the building doors. The passenger door opened, and I was literally tossed inside. The men holding me just walked away in different directions. An old man sat in the back seat where I had landed.

He was slim, with a business suit on that looked like it was from the 1940s. He had a thin gray mustache and a comforting smile. "Welcome to Istanbul, Mr. Allen."

I said nothing. I looked for my seat belt out of habit. "I am not sure that seat belt has ever been used, Mr. Allen. Please feel free to use it if it works. You may call me Efe. It means elder brother, and I hope we can develop that kind of relationship during your short stay. May I call you Thaddeus, or do you have another name you prefer?"

"Thad is fine. Thank you," I said. I wanted to ask a hundred questions, but this was his script, so I kept my mouth shut.

"Good. Good. I like the name, Thaddeus, even though it is Greek," Efe said.

I looked at our driver and realized it was not the person who had first met me. I took a chance and asked, "What happened to the other chauffeur, the one who met me?"

"I am afraid that was not our chauffeur. He must have mistaken you for someone else," Efe said. He looked out the window and seemed to be in deep thought. I followed his lead and looked out the window and waited. A few minutes later, I read the road sign stating we were entering the E80. "This expressway begins at the foot of Mount Ararat on the eastern border of Turkey and follows the same passes and valleys of the original Silk Road from China to the medieval courts of Western Europe. You are now a part of this history, in more ways than you realize," Efe said while still looking out the window, but with his mind very much on the situation in the car.

"I honestly have no idea what you are talking about. I have no clue why I am here and what you want with me or my family," I said as evenly as I could.

"You will understand soon enough," Efe said. "Have you read the Qur'an, Thaddeus? Your brother-in-law is Muslim, so I am assuming it may have entered conversation at times."

"I have read parts of it, but I am no expert, not even a novice," I said. "I don't speak or understand Arabic, and Badri, my brother-in-law, told me all translations from Arabic should be suspect."

"He has spoken with wisdom. Just as the Bible of the Christians has many translations that change significant passages and many nuanced thoughts, the Holy Qur'an is not subject to our will, but to the will of Allah," Efe explained. "Even still, I must offer you a translation in English for your benefit. There is an eleven-verse passage called the Surat Al-Furqān. It is the twenty-fifth Sura. In English, that is traditionally translated as The Criterion or The Standard. I think discernment is a closer meaning. These verses speak of the entire Qur'an as the standard for judgment and emphasizes that there is no sin, however great, that cannot be forgiven if sincerely repented. However, the Al-Furqān final verse states decisively, "But they have denied the Hour, and We have prepared for those who deny the Hour a Blaze." I am afraid the world has arrived at that final hour, Thaddeus. You have a chosen part to play in this important hour."

"So you are the ones who ransacked my house and left the note on my door?" I asked.

"Interesting word, ransack. I believe its roots are simply house search," Efe said. "I do apologize for the mess that our overzealous brethren left in your abode. If you help us with what we are searching for, I will make sure your home is cleaned and any damaged items replaced. If you do not help us, well, there is a possibility your home will accidentally be burnt to the ground."

There it was again, the "nice demon" approach. "Efe, your carrots and sticks don't motivate me. I would gladly share with you or any of the other groups chasing after this mystery what I know. I just don't know anything. I really don't."

"You don't know what you don't know or what you might know," Efe said turning to look at me squarely in the eyes for the first time. "As for any other groups looking for this information, it is fortunate you believe you don't know what you know. Your life depends on you only sharing information with us."

"And my family? What about their safety?" I asked.

"Your brother-in-law is Sunni, no? We do not harm Sunnis except in self-defense. You do, however, bring up a good point. Some in our organization believe this entire matter is simply self-defense."

"No, you do not understand. There is a group that is holding my sister hostage unless I talk. I am guessing the chauffeur that disappeared at the airport is from that group, that is if you are not that group. They called me on the phone and then threatened me again in the airport in Germany. Now you guys take things into your own hands, and they are probably thinking I have gone rogue. My sister could be in grave danger because of you and your thugs," I said, losing control.

"The other group would have simply tortured you, got what they could from you, and killed you and your sister without thinking twice. I am sorry to say, but your sister is most likely already dead," Efe said matter-of-factly. "We are the guardians of truth and purity. We are the rightful owners of what you have, and what your brother-in-law's family has."

"What is it you think I have and that my brother-in-law has?" I asked.

"Ultimately you hold the secrets of the book, Thaddeus. We are fairly certain that your brother-in-law does not have what we are looking for. And unfortunately, we have not been able to locate your brother-in-law, or we would have confirmed this. I will be honest with you; we are not sure what we are looking for, but we cannot afford to simply assume it does not exist. You see, it is *hadith*, that is, 'tradition,' that there is a book of many secrets. In Arabic, it is the simple root k-t-b from which come the basic meaning of marking, inscribing or writing from which the words book: *kitâb*, books: *kutub*, the act of writing: *kitâba*, writer: *katib*, he wrote: *kataba*, and many others. Tradition holds this book, if it really is a book, a letter, a scroll, or metal plates, originated on 13 March 624 CE at the Battle of Badr. The original author, the *katib*, was an ancestor of your brother-in-law Badri Kabbani. In fact, it is called the *Kitâb Kabbani*. Don't you find it interesting that your brother-in-law is named in honor of one who took part in the Battle of Badr?"

"So there is some ancient book? That is what you are looking for? And you think I have this book?" I asked.

"We have pretty much ruled out that you have the book. We will make certain of this, of course," Efe said with a thin smile that caused a chill to run through my whole body. "But we believe you may hold a key to finding this book."

"Me? I hold the k—?!" I began to ask, just as we were rear-ended hard by another Mercedes. This Mercedes was an Antos delivery truck, and all I could see was the huge Mercedes-Benz logo covering the entire back window. I knew the three-pointed logo stood for sea/land/air, but at this moment it looked like an upside down peace sign, and that seemed pretty appropriate. The world was coming apart.

Chapter 5

I WAS THE ONLY PERSON in the car wearing a seat belt, so I was held secure, and everyone else went flying. Efe was thrown into the front seat. The driver was thrown into the airbag which deployed flawlessly. Good old German reliability. The car was filled with smoke and dust. I could hardly see. Someone from outside the car tried to open the door closest to me. It was jammed. I could tell the person was yelling, but the noise of the crash, the airbag deployment, and the horn, which was blaring steadily, kept me from understanding what was going on. The window by the front passenger side of the car burst into pieces.

"Cover your face with your arms. Now!" the young man yelled. "Bam!" the window next to me exploded just as I got my arms around my face and began to bend over.

"Unbuckle your seat belt. Quickly!" the young man yelled. As I undid the belt, I realized the car was still moving. The young man was jogging alongside the car as the truck pushed it off the road. Cars and trucks were whizzing by at high speeds, and I was afraid the young man was going to get hit. He grabbed me and began to pull me from the car. I was halfway out of the car window when the truck stopped, and I fell toward the pavement on the side of the road. I ripped my pants on the shards of safety glass still stuck in the broken window, and I hit my shoulder on the pavement. My head hit the stomach of the young man who had fallen backward onto the road. We probably looked ridiculous from the perspective of those driving by.

"Get up and come with me. Hurry!" the young man said. I began to think that this guy completed every sentence with a transitive verb. I wondered how many he had in his vocabulary before he started over again with "now," or "quickly." I stumbled to the truck, now beginning to be concerned if this was the group Efe had been talking about. I am not sure I could handle The Voice right now. Efe was not a nice guy, but The Voice was evil personified. Maybe that was just their scripts, I thought. I really knew nothing about either group. Perhaps they were all just as bad.

"Give me your hand," a voice yelled from inside the cab of the truck. I felt like a puppet, but I offered my hand and was quickly jerked up, and before I could even look at who grabbed my hand, I was pushed to the left by the young man.

"Good heavens, man, scoot over. Move!" I smiled in spite of the situation.

"I am glad you are enjoying this," the person to my left said. The truck was pulling into traffic in reverse. Being much bigger than the cars had its benefits. Before I could turn to see who had spoken to me, the front window shattered. Then the sound of a gun firing registered. The driver of the car I was just in was firing from close range. He hit the truck driver, who screamed out, but the driver kept driving backward, playing blind chicken with the cars streaming up E80. When the injured driver had enough fun, we pulled forward onto an exit that read something like IMES Cikisi-K1. We circled around on this exit, and just as we were about to enter another road, we took another exit and circled again onto E80 heading in the opposite direction. I knew this only because I could see signs for the Sabiha Gökçen International Airport.

"Ahmet, how are you doing?" the person to my left asked.

That voice sounded familiar. I finally thought to turn and look. I noticed first the bloodied arm of the driver. The person next to me had turned in the seat to attempt to treat the injured arm.

"This isn't life threatening, but we will need to stop soon and let Hande drive."

"Tie it up and let me get us out of the city first. You are right; I don't think I can make it to the vehicle switch point in Izmit," the driver said.

"Anyone else injured? Hande? Thaddeus?" the person next to me asked.

When my seatmate said my name, I knew who this person was, my seatmate across the Atlantic. "Leyla? What are you doing here? What is going on?" I asked incredulously.

All three of my cab-mates continued as if I wasn't there. "İyiyim."

"English, Hande. For our guest," Leyla commanded.

"Sorry. My back might be a little scraped, but I am fine. That was crazy, but what a rush," Hande said.

"Alright, Ahmet, take the next exit, and you can switch with Hande," Leyla suggested.

I was still staring at Leyla. "You really are enjoying this, aren't you?" Leyla said as she studied me for the first time since I stumbled into the truck.

"Why do you say that? I—we were almost killed back there," I said.

"You have this dumb smile on your face. I would take that as a compliment except that you were smiling as you climbed into the truck," Leyla explained.

"I was impressed with Hande—it's okay if I call you that?" I said as I turned to Hande on my right.

"Okay with me. You liked my rescue?" Hande asked with his smile. He was in his mid-twenties, strong, about five feet eight inches, I guessed, a strong square jaw and short messy hair. "You are right, Leyla. Our guest is a pretty cool guy," Hande said, trying to sound American.

"So you said I was cool?" I asked Leyla.

"I could have been wrong. We have a nine-hour drive ahead of us. I should know by then," Leyla said.

"Who are you? Really, what is going on? Was all the convenience of our seats just a setup? Mack? A setup, too?" I said as I sat back in the seat feeling deflated.

"Not a setup, Thaddeus. Not like you are thinking anyway. It was a necessary precaution," Leyla explained. "Pull off here, Ahmet. Hande, you ready to take the wheel?"

They made the switch, and I stayed silent, not sure what was going on. We drove in silence for about five minutes, no one offering to explain the situation. Then Leyla's cell phone rang. "Yes, we have him. It went well except that Ahmet was shot in the arm. Not serious, but I have Hande driving now. We will be at the vehicle switch point in about thirty minutes." Leyla listened to the conversation on the other end and then said, "Yes, he's fine. I think he is actually having fun. Yes, see you then."

Leyla turned and just looked at me for a full minute. I felt like I was under a microscope. I finally got up the courage and turned to stare directly at her. She turned her gaze forward, through what was left of the windshield. "Commanding rescue operations is not my day job," Leyla said. "We are risking our lives for you, and you are in this mess whether you want to be or not and whether we are involved or not. And by the way, this is much bigger than all of us combined. This could change the course of life for literally a billion people and many of the governments that affect every corner of the globe." No one in the truck said another word until we got to Izmit.

"Exit here, Hande. Drive by the clock tower," Leyla said.

We exited the D100 and followed the exit under the express-way we had just left onto a road that paralleled a beautiful little park. It had a large clock tower in one corner. I assumed that was the tower Leyla mentioned. It was early afternoon, but I was ready for a nap. The wind blast from the partially shattered windshield had kept me awake, but the slower speeds and the peaceful city built on the hillside next to the water were lulling me to sleep. We pulled into a hotel or guest house called the Ordu Evi Misafirhanesi and parked.

"Alright, everyone out," Leyla commanded. "Hande, you clean up the truck. Make sure there is no blood, fingerprints, clothing, information—nothing that is traceable to us. Then leave it. Here are the keys to your car."

"I am okay, Leyla," Ahmet said. "We are good to go."

"Hayır, no," Leyla said. She launched into a brief but heated conversation in another language. I assumed it was Turkish.

"Hoşca kalın," Ahmet said, looking at Leyla, and then, approaching me, he said, "Allahaısmarladık. That is a Turkish goodbye, but it literally means 'I leave you to God's care.'" He turned and walked over to Hande, who was just finishing up the truck cleaning.

"Güle güle," Leyla said to both her companions, turned, grabbed my arm and walked away.

"May I say goodbye to Hande? He literally pulled me from the clutches of that man named Efe," I reminded Leyla.

"You will see him again. We must go. We still have many hours to travel before we reach our destination." She walked to the other end of the parking lot mostly filled with cars. She put the keys into the passenger door of a black sedan, a Renault Fluence, the chrome markings announced, and motioned for me to get in. She went around to the driver's door and hopped in. She started the engine and pulled out of the parking space.

"Ahmet and Hande have another car and will travel a different route to our final destination. They also have other business to attend to before their day is done," Leyla explained. "Sit back and relax, Thaddeus. We still have six or seven hours left in our travel day."

We pulled out onto the main road, and Leyla noticed me looking at the clock tower. "Beautiful tower, isn't it?" Leyla asked. "You know, your brother-in-law's great grandfather indirectly influenced the building of that tower."

"Badri's great grandfather? You know Badri?" I asked.

"I know of him. And his family," Leyla replied. "The Kabbani name is well known throughout the Middle East and former Ottoman territories. To celebrate the anniversary of Sultan 'Abd al-Hamid II's ascension to the Ottoman throne, Shaykh 'Abd al-Qabbani, your brother-in-law's great grandfather, decreed the construction of the clock tower in Beirut a few years before the turn of the century. It stands by the Parliament building today in downtown Beirut. It made quite the impression in the Ottoman court. A decree was sent to the provincial governors to commemorate the 25th anniversary of Sultan Abdülhamid II's ascension to the Ottoman throne a few years later. The Izmit Clock is one of many clock towers built throughout the Ottoman Empire as a result of that decree."

"That is amazing. Not only did it happen, but you know about it. I am so new to this part of the world, even with the reading I've done," I admitted. "Sometimes it seems like this area of the world is a single village and everyone knows everyone else's history or at least their spin on that history. Some neighbors get along, some don't. Some truths endure, and some get lost or skewed and leveraged by this power-hungry group or that despot struggling with self-esteem issues."

We entered the O-4/E80 toll road. "Next stop Ankara," Leyla said. "Your description of the region is insightful, but you may be describing the world, not just this corner."

"We are going to Ankara? Why?" I asked. "I really need to be clued in on what in the world is going on, Leyla. I feel like a ping pong ball, and it appears there are three paddles in this game."

"Ankara is just a pit stop," Leyla said. "Our final destination tonight is Konya. I will explain along the way. It will help keep me awake."

"It's not the biggest question I have, but what happened to you on the flight from Germany to Turkey?" I asked. "You know, I was accosted at the airport and warned not to talk to you. It was this guy I have nicknamed The Voice. He was the one who called me on the phone that got this whole adventure started." The words were pouring out, and it took effort to stop. I had so many questions. So many points that I couldn't connect. "Wait. First, tell me. Who you are? How are you connected to all this?"

"Who am I?" Leyla repeated with a smile. "I am just a young Turkish girl, caught up in an affair of global proportions."

"I hope we have become friends, but I would hardly term that an affair. We haven't even had a first date," I said in an attempt to lighten the conversation and to hint to Leyla that becoming friends was my desire.

"I didn't mean that kind of affair, Thaddeus," Leyla said with an uncomfortable laugh.

I was glad there was still some daylight left because I was able to see that she was blushing. That somehow made her all the more alluring, and it told me she was much more than some hardened foreign superhero commando special agent that I had come to know and maybe fear a little. I left our relationship, whatever it was, in the air. "So tell me, really, who are you?"

The countryside was drifting by, well, streaming by at one hundred twenty kilometers an hour. It hit me that Turkey was the most beautiful place I had ever been. The setting sun was creating lazy shadows on the ancient trees. They looked a lot like the oak trees in California. The small fields had already been harvested but looked well-cared for. It looked, well, Jeffersonian. Crazy I thought that, but I guess we reference what we know on situations we don't know. I was still very worried about my sister, Anna, and Badri, but I was grateful at this moment to be in this car, in this country, with this driver. Both of us had our seat belts on.

"My first name, Leyla, in the Arabic language, means 'night,' and can also mean 'one who works in the night,' which brings me to my work. I am part of a group that is charged with bringing light and truth to the world." She glanced over at me to see my expression.

I would have had an expression, but I was too tired and too numb from so many incredulous things already, that this sounded almost normal. "I was a Boy Scout some years ago. I pledged to be trustworthy, brave, and help other people," I shared with attempted enthusiasm.

"Cute, Thaddeus. Our organization is not the Boy Scouts. We are called Al-Ĥujurāt. That means rooms or dwellings and references the Qur'an, Surah 49. Verse four speaks of rooms and those who shout from outside that do not have understanding. And what do they not know? Verse thirteen says: *O mankind! We created you from a single (pair) of a male and a female and made you into nations and tribes that ye may know each other (not that ye may despise each other). Verily the most honored of you in the sight of Allah is (he who is) the most righteous of you. And Allah has full knowledge and is well-acquainted (with all things).* This is not too far from the Christian verse in the New Testament gospel of John 14:2 which states, '*In my Father's house are many mansions: if it were not so, I would have told you. I go to prepare a place for you.*' We have been in existence for nearly one thousand years.

We are devoted to the One God and to finding, nurturing, and protecting truth wherever it is found. We believe in inclusion, not exclusion, and knowledge and understanding. Al-Ḥujurāt is the searcher and sentinel of truth."

"So you are like the Universalist Church, only Muslim?" I asked.

"No. We aren't a church," Leyla corrected. "We aren't really a religious organization, but we are made up of religious people. Most of our group is Sufi, but we have some Sunni, Shia, and Ismailia Muslims, as well as a Zoroastrian and a few Jews. In all, we are only about one hundred people. There has almost always been a member of my family in Al-Ḥujurāt since its beginning."

"So you are saying you can trace your family back almost a thousand years?" I asked.

"Oh, yes. Even farther back than that," Leyla said. "Remember, my last name is Celebi," she continued as if that answered the question.

"Okay, we already established that you are not a Pokémon," I reminded her.

"What we didn't establish is that name denotes me as a descendant of Jalāl ad-Dīn Muhammad Rūmī. Do you know the mystic and poet Rumi?" Leyla asked.

"Yes, of course," I said. "You can hardly study the Middle East and not get a dose of Rumi. I read somewhere that he is the most popular poet in the U.S., too."

"I am the twenty-third generation granddaughter of Rumi," Leyla said with solemnity. "In Ottoman history, the Mevlevi became an important part of the Ottoman Empire, and many sultans are my ancestors. When Devlet Hatun, one of my many-greats grandmother, a descendant of Sultan Veled, married the sultan Bayezid 1st, they had a son. His name was Mehmed Çelebi, and he became the next sultan. My family has carried the Celebi name ever since."

"So you are also royalty?" I asked. "I am so far out of my league," I thought but didn't say.

"The Mevlevi Order and the Celebi family have in-part survived because we are non-political," Leyla explained. "Al-Ĥujurāt is also non-political, although we sometimes rattle the cages of the political establishments in this region. I started this conversation by explaining my first name. I don't work in the darkness of night, but rather I expose hidden things to the light, which sometimes takes me to dark places where these hidden things cower. Places that some power brokers also want to keep hidden. The world is made up of people that are mostly just trying to live their lives, make meaning out of their day and out of their years. They ingest the moldy lies along with the light and truth. And sometimes the mold kills them or brings them needless tragedy or sadness. When those things are brought to light, people can make better choices and find long-term happiness."

"So your motto could be, Ye shall know the truth, and the truth shall set you free?" I asked, quoting the Bible, I thought, but I wasn't sure.

"Yes, the Jesus Christ of the Bible teaches that as does the Qura'an," Leyla replied. Man has the choice. The Qur'an teaches that Allah makes truths and falsehoods clear. There are deceivers that turn man from truth, and thus, how can man choose to accept either of them?"

"Okay, okay, we are solving the challenges of the millennia, but you still haven't told me about you," I said with a little impatience. "Tell me about your family, about your life. Do you have any other goals than bringing truth to the world? What is your favorite color, your favorite food, your favorite music, or movie? You know, share some shallow things with me."

"Why would you want to know any of that?" Leyla asked perplexed. "As you said, we were just shot at. Your sister's life is in danger. The evil in the world is conspiring, and you are their target. In the midst of this, you want to know my favorite color?"

"The real answer, Leyla: I need a little simplicity and normalness right now. I need to know you are a regular person, that you are approachable, and that we can talk about things other than the history of your family ruling a big chunk of the world and starting a religious order and saving billions of people from darkness."

"That is kind of sweet, Thaddeus," Leyla said.

I felt shallow with that explanation, so I added, "Well, the deeper reason would go something like, I need to understand the human you, and that requires context, identity, and practice. Being human is analog, not digital. Qualitative, not quantitative. We are made up of matter and atoms, not ones and zeros. It's the little blemishes that remind us that we are not alone in our imperfections. Life is like a dimmer switch, not an on/off switch. The essence of life, that is, what we learn, experience, accumulate, and carry with us may be knowledge, but 'zero and one' data is not synonymous with life. To be alive, we not only hold information, but we have to process and use it in all its variances and varieties. It is the practice, not the passive storage, which constitutes life." I knew I was failing in my explanation, so I stopped talking.

"But there is perfect, flawless truth, and then there is everything else," Leyla countered. "Everything else has varying degrees of darkness, shades of lies."

"I won't argue the fact that some people create meaning by comparing opposites. But wasn't it Rumi who suggested, 'Out beyond ideas of wrongdoing and right-doing there is a field. I'll meet you there,'" I said, pretty proud of myself that I came up with that quote from her twenty-third great grandpa.

"And the next line says, 'When the soul lies down in that grass, the world is too full to talk about,'" Leyla added.

"I never heard that line before. Rumi may be a very popular poet, but we only get him in sound bites. Digital. Something you can print on a marketing poster. Maybe the world is too full, or we are too full of the world," I would have to think about that, "but that proves my point. Context is key. Half the problems blamed on the Bible and the Qur'an I suspect come from taking a verse out of context. Understanding the importance of etiquette in the ancient Middle East, or the significance of the cost of a slave two thousand years ago, or the annual cycles of a fig tree, make a big difference in understanding scripture or literature in general. Identity defines perspective, group allegiance, values, norms, and expressive symbols. And practice comes in the form of habits, intuition, repetition, emotion—very human events and feelings. Practice, the doing, reminds us that meaning making is possible. We connect the dots, discover patterns, symbols, metaphors."

"You are a cook at a fast food restaurant in a small town?" Leyla asked.

"Yes. And I read a lot, and I think a lot," I said. "But sorry, I don't talk to many people—actually no one, about those thoughts. No one I know is interested."

Leyla drove the car in silence for a few minutes that felt like much longer. I was about to apologize for sharing my disjointed thoughts, thinking they had offended her. "You have me, and I am interested," she said at last. "Magenta and Cinnabar."

"What?" I asked, wondering if she had slipped into Turkish.

"Magenta and Cinnabar. They are my favorite colors," Leyla said.

"Those are colors?" I said without thinking. "I mean, wow, those sound exotic."

"They are both variations of red, magenta being more purple and cinnabar being more orange. Red symbolizes unity with God and departing worldly life for spiritual life. Magenta is the sunrise, and cinnabar is the sunset, my two favorite times of the day." Leyla said.

"I like yellow. It reminds me of bananas," I said and then added, "and the middle of the day."

We turned to our own thoughts, and I enjoyed the cinnabar sunset as the hills turned into mountains.

Chapter 6

WE PULLED INTO A GAS station on the outskirts of Ankara. I was tired and hungry and needed to use the restroom. At the airport in Germany I had picked up a fear of restrooms, and it took me a moment to get the courage to go in. My fears were reinforced, but for an additional reason, as the bathroom was only a porcelain hole in the ground that looked like it hadn't been cleaned since the Ottoman Empire fell. On the other hand, it was probably more hygienic than the one I visited in Germany because the only thing I touched was with the bottom of my shoes. No gross commode to sit on. There was a plastic bottle with water in it, sitting under a spigot, so I poured that in after and filled it again for the next person. I had no idea if I followed correct protocol, and there was no way I was going to ask Leyla. I must not have been far off, as Leyla offered me a wet wipe and sanitizer for my hands when I got back to the car. I felt practically local.

Leyla filled up the tank and bought us some *dolma* and *börek*. I didn't ask what that was because about an hour before we arrived at this pit stop, I was considering gnawing on the leather seats. They ended up being stuffed grape leaves and a thin pastry stuffed with cheese and topped with sesame seeds.

"This stuff would put McDonalds and Kentucky Fried Chicken out of business if I brought this to the States," I commented to Leyla after ingesting just one of each. Leyla chuckled and excused herself to use the *tuvalet*. That sounded more French than Turkish to me, but then, I don't speak French either.

When Leyla came out of the restroom, she was talking on her cell phone in rapid-fire Turkish. She switched to English when she approached the car. I was outside the car doing some light calisthenics to wake up. "We will be at the Mevlana Turbesi by one in the morning, maybe earlier. We will expect you by daybreak, in time for…" Leyla looked at me and whispered, "…morning prayer." She continued, "Okay, travel safe, dear friends." She pocketed the phone and jumped into the driver's seat.

"Is everything alright?" I asked, wishing I had her energy.

"All is well," Leyla said with a smile. "It looks like Ahmet will be fine, thanks be to God. They were also able to pick up the things we will need when we get to Konya. They are pretty sure they weren't followed, which means Efe, as you call him, is either not on our trail or we have lost them for now. Are you ready for the next leg of our journey?"

"I assume you are going to explain all this to me soon," I said hopefully. "We have surveyed the forest, the big picture of Turkey and your family. Now you have got to tell me about the trees that I keep bumping into and which ones may fall on me."

"I can do that. I am just glad you lost interest about why I didn't make the flight with you from Germany to Istanbul," Leyla said with those amazing eyes twinkling.

"If it matters, I want to know, but frankly, I am on information overload," I said with a frustrated yawn. "If I am just a pawn, and you were being nice to me for some unknown reason, I accept that. I will be disappointed, but it's not the first time I have been used."

"Listen, Thaddeus. You are not being used, and this isn't just about you," Leyla said. "Ahmet and Hande risked their lives for you and also for a bigger reason. You are important to this whole crazy situation, but some believe you are expendable, a means to an end. We, Al-Ĥujurāt, think you are more than that. You are lucky we even exist. You would probably be dead by now otherwise, along with your sister." Leyla was rapidly accelerating to 120 kilometers per hour, and she was irked.

"Sorry I ruined your happy mood," I said after a few minutes of reflection. "I know your intentions are grand, and I do appreciate you saving my life, and by the way, I know you risked your life for me as well, but I am as clueless at this moment as I was driving to the airport in California. Was that just yesterday?" I asked myself out loud and amazed.

"We needed to know you just a little better, Thaddeus," Leyla said as she put on the cruise control. "If we were going to risk our lives pulling you from the clutches of the Furqaan and your friend, The Voice, we wanted to know if you were legitimate. That is, a serious and honest person, not someone easily enticed by these evil people. That was my job. It was Mack's job to get you to the right airport in New York safely and make a brief assessment. It was my job to get to know you better."

"So I passed Mack's brief assessment, and they sent in the beautiful and mysterious young woman to lower my defenses," I said, rolling my eyes in the dark. "I am such a chump. What did you learn?"

"That is very nice of you to say about me, Thaddeus," Leyla said. "And a mean thing to say about yourself. I really enjoyed the flight and the conversation. I learned that you are much more than any of us suspected, and you are anything but a chump, if I understand that word correctly. We are honored to join with you if, after I explain your role, you want to work with us. One other thing, for full disclosure. I looked through your bag while you were sleeping. I needed to make sure there was nothing planted there that would cause a problem in customs when you arrived in Turkey. That would have been an easy way to capture you with only a minimal payoff of a customs agent."

"I would have never thought of that. Did you find anything?" I asked.

"No. But I wanted you to know I didn't like doing that," Leyla answered.

"Heck, I don't even know what I packed. The Voice told me to bring a bag so I didn't look too odd," I said.

"No matter," Leyla began, flicking her hand in the air. "We can get you the clothes you will need, with a more local look. I do need to explain one more big picture forest item before getting to your individual trees if that is alright with you. It is short and will help explain how you fit into all this."

"Okay, shoot," I said.

"I have always thought that to be a curious expression that is uniquely American. I would be afraid someone would take me literally," Leyla said.

"After today I may work on keeping that out of my conversations," I said. "So, one more forest item, then specifics—go."

"Before I was born, in the 1980s," Leyla began, "when the City government of Konya was doing some badly needed road reconstruction, the plan required moving the tomb of a close associate of Mevlana, that's our name for Rumi. Her name, Rumi's associate, was Fahrunissa Suleyman Dede. The Mevlevi Sheikh of Konya and a dear friend of mine—so I can speak for his total honesty—was asked to attend the repositioning. He told me that after seven hundred years, when the archeological experts opened her grave, her body was still there, although withered, and the fragrance of roses filled the air."

"That could happen," I said, eager to share my knowledge. "Some lipophilic compounds do not go rancid with time. Tombs with frankincense, clove, and, I think, rose oil have been found in the ancient tombs in Egypt. Rose oil was useful as an embalming fluid, I believe, and could retain some odor fraction."

Leyla turned and looked at me, I guess to gauge whether I was being serious. After a few seconds, she turned back to watch the road, much to my approval, and continued. "The beautiful fragrance drew others who were there to peer into the tomb. One person there was a member of our group, although others there did not know of his affiliation with us. Al-Ĥujurāt is more myth than reality in the Middle East and not even heard of elsewhere. All our members are unknown to those outside the group. Our member saw two scrolls next to the body of Fahrunissa. Both were taken into custody by the government archaeological expert. The non-governmental archeological expert was our member, so he got a first-hand view of both documents. One was a beautiful copy of several verses of the Qur'an. The other one was written in the hand of Mevlana. That alone is a find of the century. You know, most of his works were dictated. What it said, however, was a find of the ages. It references the books that Shams tossed in the water. One of those references is to the Kitab Kabbani, your brother-in-law's family.

"Shams? Books in water? I don't know that story," I admitted.

"When *Jaad-di*, Grandfather Rumi, was about twenty-four years old, he was sitting by a fountain in a small square in Konya reading to students the Maarif, his father's personal spiritual diary. Shams Tabriz, a wandering mystic, stepped into the group and asked, "What are you doing?"

Rumi replied pridefully, "Something you cannot understand."

When Shams heard this and felt the ridicule in Rumi's voice, he threw a stack of four books into the fountain of water. Rumi hastily rescued the books, and to his surprise, they were all dry. Rumi then asked Shams, "What is this?" To which Shams replied,

"Mowlana," ("that is Rumi's first name," Leyla interjected) "this is what you cannot understand."

"Wow, that was a lesson in humility," I said.

"Yes, it was," Leyla said as she maneuvered around a slow moving truck. "Rumi learned much from Shams. The point here is, those books in the thirteenth century were rare and very valuable. More than that, one of those four books was the Kitab Kabbani. The scroll found in Fahrunissa's tomb tells this story and suggests the Kitab Kabbani holds great secrets that will not find light until there is great darkness. Because of this scroll, several groups are searching for the Kitab Kabbani, the Kabbani Book. That is the book mentioned in that threatening phone call to you and why your house was searched."

"Wait, how do I fit into all this?" I asked. "I have never heard of this book."

"Now we get to the individual trees, Thaddeus," Leyla said. The Fahrunissa tomb scroll predicts, *One sharing the same name as the Brother of Jesus the Prophet will be the bearer of the key to reclaiming the Kitab Kabbani.* Since discovering the Fahrunissa Scroll, several groups, Al-Ḥujurāt included, have been looking for a James or Jude that might somehow be connected to the Kabbani tribe. We failed in our search, and many began to believe that the word brother could have meant any of his spiritual brothers, fellow believers."

"And, how do I fit into this?" I asked again, still not understanding.

"Without getting too deep into varying views of the history of Jesus, Muslims believe he was a great prophet and that his traitor was Judas Iscariot. In fact, many Muslims believe it was Judas that died on the cross and that Jesus was taken to heaven. Christians believe Jesus was the Messiah, the Savior of the world, and that he was betrayed to the Sanhedrin by Judas. In either case, the name Judas was synonymous with evil. Thus, the scribes of the Bible would often take pains to separate others named Jude or Judas from Judas Iscariot."

"I don't know if you realize it, but every time you say you are getting to the point, you offer preambles that would make only a history professor smile," I interjected. "How does this involve me?"

"My father says the same thing about me," Leyla said. "Alright, here is the short story, and don't blame me if it doesn't make any sense, because I haven't provided the full context. One of the brothers of Jesus was named Jude and was also the Apostle Jude Thaddeus."

"So you think I have some key to this Kabbani Book because my dad named me Thaddeus?" I asked in disbelief.

"It really doesn't matter what you or I believe. What matters is, there are those in the Kabbani family that believe it. This has also put a price on your head because there are others who will stop at nothing to keep the Kitab Kabbani from ever seeing the light of day. If there is even the slightest chance that you could help retrieve that book from some forgotten room of history, then it is worth pursuing, and your death and the death of your sister are a small price to pay."

"This is nuts, Leyla. This isn't even mistaken identity. This is twisted wishful thinking."

"There is one thing more, Thaddeus," Leyla said.

"The short version, please," I pleaded.

"The Fahrunissa Scroll states that just as your namesake did, you—if in fact the scroll really is talking about you—will die in Beirut. I don't think any of the people chasing you care about fulfilling that prophecy. They will be happy to kill you wherever it is convenient for them, but I thought you should know this."

"Thanks for that extra bit of knowledge, Leyla. This is totally nuts. How do I get off this train?"

"I think you will have to ride this train to the end of the line, Thaddeus," Leyla offered. "And the train's first stop is Konya. We will be arriving at that station in a couple of hours. You might want to get some rest. Things are going to be busy."

Chapter 7

"TIME TO WAKE UP, THADDEUS," Leyla said as they pulled into a dark parking lot. There were some low buildings in front of the car and beyond that a cathedral—no, more like a Wizard of Oz tower that was the most beautiful structure I have ever seen.

"How long was I out?" I asked as I tried to get my bearings.

"About an hour. Maybe a little longer. We are here."

"Where is here?" I asked.

"To the world, this is known as Mevlâna Müzesi, the Mevlana Museum or Green Mausoleum," Leyla began. "It is the burial place of Rumi and his father. The museum used to be the headquarters of the Mevlevi Sufi Order. Today it has a tekke, that is, a lodge, a *semahane*, where the ritual *sema* or whirling ceremony takes place, a *sadirvan* for ritual ablutions, a library, and living and teaching quarters."

"That turquoise tower is amazing! It is so spectacular at night with the lights highlighting it. That may be the most beautiful building I have ever seen."

"There is much wealth in this museum," Leyla said as she got out of the car and shifted effortlessly into tour guide. "The main tomb is enclosed by a silver gate crafted in 1597. There are musical instruments and robes belonging to Mevlana, along with Seljuk and Ottoman objects like gold-engraved Qur'ans from the 13th century. My favorite objects are the ancient prayer rugs and the most valuable silk carpet in the world."

"Wow, I wish I were here under different circumstances. It would be great to see the insides. The thing is, Leyla, I am in no mood to be a tourist. Not when my sister and brother-in-law are in mortal danger."

"We are not here as tourists," Leyla continued. "Far underneath the tomb of Mevlana is a cellar that is unknown to the world. This is the headquarters of Al-Ḥujurāt. Come, we will enter through a tunnel that surfaces in the basement of this house." With that, Leyla walked forward to a non-descript door of a non-descript house about one hundred meters outside the wall of the Mausoleum complex. Leyla pulled a key from her pocket and opened the ancient door. I admit that I was let down that it didn't squeak or make some kind of ominous noise.

The inside of the house was just as nondescript. The furnishings felt exotic to me, but I guessed that they were typical of the area. The couches were lower than normal, and the rugs and pillows were beautiful. The front room smelled of coffee and something else. "What is that smell?" I asked.

Leyla stopped and smelled. "Coffee, I think. Oh, you probably smell the, what is it called in English? Crushed cardamom seed? Come, this way. Be careful not to hurt yourself. I know there isn't much light, but it is best to keep it that way tonight."

We walked through the living room and small kitchen and turned to a door. Instead of opening the door, Leyla moved the chair sitting by the wall to the left of the door. She slid a wood panel that looked like part of the wall, and there was another door knob. She turned it and opened another door that was part of the wall. "No secret buttons or revolving walls?" I asked in jest. Truth be told I was a little disappointed.

"This has served us for nearly one hundred years," Leyla said quietly. "Sometimes technology is not needed." We walked into a dark hallway, and Leyla shut the door. She then flipped a light switch, and the hallway and a series of rooms were illuminated. Leyla walked to an array of flat screens that she turned on with one switch, and six different views of the outside of the house and two views of the inside of the house came into view. "Sometimes technology is useful," she said. Next to the eight screens was a communications system and what I assumed were three computers. "These servers operate our secure communications and our worldwide access to the internet, untraceable to anyone trying to track where we are physically."

I walked past Leyla, who was still studying the remote camera views and looked into the other rooms. Some were simple rooms, like small libraries, and some looked more like bedrooms. I began to yearn for one of the beds, but I didn't ask if we were going to sleep here. I hoped I was sending Leyla a subliminal message that sleep would be a good next step.

"Yes, we are going to get some sleep after I am sure we were not followed," Leyla said while still studying the screens.

"How did you know I was thinking that?" I asked, a little unnerved.

"It could be my incredible mental powers, or it could be that you are looking at the bedroom like a little boy in a candy store. We will not be sleeping here, however."

"Oh," was all I could muster.

"Alright, it looks like we are safe for now," Leyla said. She stood up and walked past me to the corner bedroom. "This way." As I walked into the room, I saw her lay her hand flat on the glass table beside the bed. An entire wall panel began to move silently to the right. Another dark room or hallway was revealed. The light from the hallway we had just left seemed to be absorbed and lost in this new passageway. "Sometimes technology is really cool," she said to me as she took my arm and we walked once again into the darkness. "Trust in God—but tie your camel first, my brethren in Arabia say."

The door automatically closed behind us, and lights automatically came on. We were in a stairwell that descended steeply. "Watch your step, Thaddeus. These stairs sometimes get a little moist and slippery. We descended for about 30 steps and came to yet another door.

"Let me guess, a retina scan?" I said.

"Right," Leyla said rolling her eyes.

"Voice with a password?" I guessed as she reached for the door.

"Yes, it is a password," Leyla said. "Open says-a-me," she said in a genie voice and turned the knob. The door opened to a very large and ornate room. It was round, about one hundred feet across the floor. The ceiling was about twenty feet high, and to my right was an alcove near the ceiling that looked like it could seat about eight people. The floor was beautifully burnished wood. The sides of the room had various alcoves at floor level and deep enough for one row of chairs. Two portions of the walls were draped with ancient-looking silk carpets. Leyla walked to one of the carpets and pulled the edge of the carpet from the wall, revealing yet another door. "This is your room for the night, Thaddeus. There is a small bathroom connected to your room. You will also find some fresh clothing that I hope is about your size. There is also a small refrigerator in your room that has bottled water, juice, and a special treat. Sleep tight. I will wake you about six. Sleep fast; that is only five hours from now."

"Thank you for everything, Leyla. I am sorry I have been difficult. I don't know where I would be without you." I reached out my hand to shake her hand. Leyla smiled, ignored my hand, and gave me a hug. She closed the door behind me, and I assumed she was going to her room somewhere in this menagerie. I would find out the next morning that she went up to the closed circuit screens and watched for anything for another thirty minutes before retiring to one of the rooms in the first underground level.

My room was decorated in prime Ottoman style. The bed was covered with overstuffed pillows, and the floor was wall-to-wall oriental rugs. There were pictures of people in what I guessed was Sufi clothing and tall hats on the walls. The bathroom was simple, but I had a welcomed shower and put on actual pajamas. I hadn't slept in pajamas since I was eleven, but they felt great. I checked out the refrigerator, and there was a MARS Bar with a note that said "sweet dreams." I was about to tear into the candy bar when I thought of my sister who was in who-knows-what kind of terrible situation. I set the candy bar on the nightstand, turned out the light and went to bed.

* * *

The words were floating in the air above my head. I am pretty sure I was sitting in my backyard in Madera under my oak tree. The breeze was rustling the leaves and the words were falling like fruit, but light as feathers.

The breeze at dawn has secrets to tell you.
Don't go back to sleep.
You must ask for what you really want.
Don't go back to sleep.
People are going back and forth across the doorsill
where the two worlds touch.
The door is round and open.
Don't go back to sleep."

"Don't go back to sleep," I found myself mumbling as I felt someone nudging my arm. I opened my eyes and looked into the eyes of a familiar face. I couldn't quite remember who this was, however.

"Thad, this is Hande. How did you sleep? It is time to rise. Rumi said, *The breeze at dawn has secrets to tell you. Don't go back to sleep.* Up!"

"Hande, it is so good to see you, man," I said in the most-awake voice I could muster. "Honestly, I felt like I just closed my eyes. Did you and Ahmet drive all night?"

"No, of course not. I dropped Ahmet off at a house of a relative who can treat him, someone that will ask no questions. But I drove all night. I will be fine. My part in this is nearly over for a time. I will get some rest soon. For you, the day is just beginning, my American friend. Get dressed quickly and come into the *semahane*, the big room on the other side of your door. Quick."

I pulled myself out of bed and began to shuffle to the bathroom. My legs felt like they were single stiff appendages and twice as heavy as normal.

"Nice sleeping clothes, Thad," Hande said, as he exited the room. "Perfect start to a day, waking up in such nice sleeping clothes. Smile!"

Despite feeling like a cardboard cutout, I chuckled at Hande's enthusiasm. I washed up quickly and put on the clothes left for me. They were not that much different than what I had worn yesterday, except I noticed the collar of the shirt was a little wider, and the pants had square pockets. It felt good to have on clean clothes. I walked to the door of the room and paused, wondering if I was ready for the day. The answer I came up with was, it really doesn't matter because the day is here, and it will take me along whether I want to go or not. I opened the door and peeked around the carpet hanging on the wall above the bedroom door. Six or seven people were waiting in an alcove on the far side of the room.

"Good morning, Thaddeus," Leyla said. "Come on over here, and I will introduce you to our rescue team."

As I walked across the room, I had to remind myself that we were underground. I realized the ceiling of this large room was a dome that had a blue tint to it. It had gold lettering that I guessed was Arabic. It was like the words were guarding me or smiling down on me. It was very comforting. I thought Leyla was the only woman in the group until I noticed one other woman with short cut hair and less than flattering clothing. The four men looked serious as they watched me approach—well, three looked serious. Hande was smiling like he had just heard a great joke.

"Everyone, this is Thaddeus Allen. He likes to be called Thad. You know his situation, and it speaks very highly of him that he is here with us," Leyla began. "More specifics in a minute. First, Thaddeus, let me introduce you to the rescue team."

And with that Leyla began to introduce the other members of the group she had labeled the rescue team. I wondered if Leyla was in charge or just my hand holder and this was one of her assigned duties. The team appeared to be all in their mid-twenties and looked relaxed, while also leaning forward in their seats. Sort of a casual confidence.

Leyla first introduced Lydia Nabat from Iran and a Zoroastrian. She was dressed in jeans and a flannel shirt. She had short dark hair, a square face, and olive skin darker than Leyla's. She looked serious and confident but with just a touch of melancholy in her dark eyes. I liked her immediately for some reason.

Sami Mansur was next introduced. He was a Sunni from Saudi Arabia and looked like a desert prince. Prideful eyes, a kind smile, but a tenseness that did not fit the moment—unless he knew something I didn't, which of course was the case.

Karim Arkoun, an Ismaili from Tunisia, looked like a young college professor. His eyeglasses perched on his nose below his eyes that looked like he had been reading all night. His hands were delicate for a rescue operations soldier. He wore a traditional-looking long brown robe that appeared really comfortable.

Hande Soroush, who I already knew, a Sufi from Turkey, had a big smile and sparkling brown eyes. He looked athletic and bursting with energy. His black hair looked like he had just been shocked with a couple of hundred volts. He was wearing the same thing as when we were first introduced with the smashing of a car window in Istanbul: a long-sleeve gray t-shirt, jeans and tennis shoes.

Irshad Nisan, another Sufi from Turkey, was the final member of the team Leyla introduced. He was muscular and reminded me of a Turkish version of Kirk Douglas, complete with square jaw, interrogating eyes, and cleft chin. His hair was lighter than the rest of the members and cut short.

Everyone was very polite and stood and shook my hand except Irshad, who just glared and nodded his head in my general direction. No one seemed to notice, so I figured he was just a serious guy.

"This group was selected partly for their skill sets, willingness to put their life on the line for this project, their physical and mental strength, and because they all speak English," Leyla said.

"The English part is how I got into the group," Hande interjected with a laugh.

"Right, I saw your *English* as you rescued me on the road yesterday," I said. "Thanks again, by the way." I noticed Lydia smile at him, maybe hoping he would notice her acknowledgment of his courage.

"I have briefed everyone on the events of yesterday, and as an update, Ahmet will recover just fine. No serious bone or internal injuries are apparent. He will be back with us in a couple of months." Leyla stopped and looked at each person. Then she continued. "Unless you have any questions, I will turn the floor over to Irshad, our team leader."

Well, that answered my question. Leyla is just my assigned supervision. I believed what she said last night in the car, but I still felt a little used. I had a thought: maybe I am the bait? Maybe I really don't know anything about this Kabbani Book, which is the truth as far as I know. Maybe keeping me close allows Al-Ḥujurāt to be in the driver's seat on this book quest. Irshad, interesting name, stood up and cleared his throat.

"Very good team, you have been briefed on our plan, but in quick review let me repeat the highlights. Thad's sister, Anna Kabbani, is being held in Göreme," Irshad said. Then turning to me he explained, "That's about four hours from here, Thad." Turning back to the group, he continued, "Hande confirmed last night from our contact there that she has not been moved. After dropping off Ahmet in Ankara, Hande was also able to arrange the delivery of the package to Aksaray today. We will travel to Göreme in two vehicles. Sami, you take Lydia and our friend Thad. The rest will travel with me. Hande, you get some sleep and handle communications and coordination from here. We leave in thirty minutes. Any questions?"

I could see that Irshad was very much in charge. If there were any questions, I guessed no one wanted to ask them. Hande came over to me and wished me well and said he would be waiting when we got back. "Is anyone going to actually explain to me what is going on?" I asked Hande.

"You are going to get your sister," Hande replied with enthusiasm." It is a trade. Something the Hashshashin want almost as bad as they want the Kabbani Book, in exchange for your sister. Be careful, the Cappadocia area is small. I mean, everyone knows everyone. There will be a few tourists, but not many this time of year, so it will be hard to blend in. It is also a conservative area, so the women will have on scarves. Oh, and I hope you don't have trouble breathing. It is starting to get cold there, and they burn coal for warmth, so the air is pretty bad. Probably if you don't have to run, you won't even notice. But this is a good thing, no? You will be reunited with your sister soon! You have Leyla to thank, you know. Be grateful!"

With that parting command, Hande left the room through the stairwell leading to the upper rooms and communications equipment. Leyla was nowhere to be seen. What did he mean I have Leyla to thank? For my rescue? Hande and Ahmet did the lion's share of that caper. And what does that group, The Voice, want almost as much as the Kabbani Book? Why wouldn't they just take what the Al-Ḥujurāt are offering, and me? They have certainly seemed ruthless enough. Memories of the bathroom encounter in Germany flashed before me. I saw Sami and Lydia talking, so I walked over to them, hoping to finally get some answers.

Chapter 8

"SAMI AND LYDIA, RIGHT?" I began. "Is it okay if I call you by your first names?"

"Yes, I think that would be appropriate, Thad," Sami said. "In our culture, we usually dedicate much more time to get to know each other, our families, our background, before we launch into business. This is an odd situation, but I think it works for both our worlds. We already know a lot about you, and although it lacks the personal exchange, we are ready to go to work. Being American and knowing that your sister is in grave danger, you are ready to get to work without all the preamble. Am I right?"

"Yes," I said, "except it feels like all I have done for the past 36 hours is preamble. When do we leave? I assume we have time to talk on the way."

"Great," Sami said. "Did you get anything to eat? It will be a long day, and I am not sure a meal break is on the schedule."

"No, but I have a candy bar in my room," I said. "I would be okay with just some water, though. Let me get a bottle from my room, and I am ready."

"We have water in the cars, Sami said. "We are all going to meet up in Aksaray at eleven this morning, so we may have time to get a snack there. *Yallah!* Let's go."

We ascended out of the Al-Ḥujurāt catacombs to a brisk morning. Hande waived a goodbye as we walked past the closed circuit monitors. No words were spoken. The team was getting their game face on. I didn't see Leyla anywhere. I would have liked to have wished her good luck, or something, but I knew I was going to see her when we all got together later. The sun felt good as we left the house on the ground level. We hopped into a non-descript Peugeot four-door. I was in the front with Sami. Lydia got in the back seat. We were out of town and in the countryside before anyone said anything.

"So what's the plan?" I asked to break the ice.

"Irshad and Leyla will meet in Göreme immediately after Asr, afternoon prayer, with the Hashshashin," Lydia said from the back seat. "We will stay out of the way, but they will know we are in the area to intervene if there is any problem, unwillingness to complete the exchange, or if they try to take you."

"Why am I even going? Of course, I want to be there, but if you are so worried about these guys getting to me, don't I pose a bigger risk to everyone just being there?"

"That was a big discussion point among the team before you arrived," Sami said. "We decided, well, Irshad decided, that it would be best to have you available in case there was a need to confirm your sister is really your sister and to help negotiate if there was a problem. You know, your sister is of no interest to us, other than being another human being in danger. Putting our lives on the line is one thing for the Kitab Kabbani, but another thing for someone simply caught in the crossfire."

"Sami!" Lydia shot back. "That is a crude thing to say. Those feelings were never part of the discussions. Why highlight your personal pettiness now? In front of Mr. Allen, I mean Thad." Lydia turned to me and added, "That is what we were instructed you like to be called," in an attempt to warm the chilly turn in the conversation.

"I just want you to know, Thad, that the Hashshashin are ruthless, and we are less than prepared to meet them at their level of devious warfare," Sami said. "These guys kill for sport or without thought like a civilized person might swat a fly."

"Well, that certainly shores up my confidence," I said. "So I am a pawn—no, bait—for a timid group with a half-baked plan. Leyla forgot to mention that."

"Hardly," Lydia said. "Every member of this team has been through a year of intense training and at least two operations of one sort or another. We are well practiced, educated, and very courageous. As for Leyla, she is the reason this whole operation might have a happy ending."

"Yes, Hande mentioned that, too. What is Leyla's role here?" I asked.

"Go ahead, tell him, Lydia," Sami said. "You were the one who brought it up. It isn't like it is an operational secret."

"Leyla asked us not to tell you this, but Sami's right, I can't see the harm in it. First, I have to tell you who we are dealing with," Lydia began.

"The Hashshashin, the Assassins, as some call them, are a pretty famous band of murderers founded in the eleventh century. They were a small order of Nizari Ismailis governed by a grandmaster. They were feared across the entire Middle East and at one time were a threat to the Seljuk authority in Persia. The Hashshashin disappeared in 1256 when the Mongols conquered the order's headquarters, the mountain fortress Alamut. Alamut had a grand library of the order's history, as well as rare relics, but was destroyed when the Mongols took the city. In reality, the Hashshashin did not totally disband and are still a dedicated Shia Ismailia group fostering preeminence of Persia in Islam."

Just as I began to think that all the women in this group answered questions with long historical diatribes, Lydia got to the point.

"The Celebi family, Leyla, in fact, has been the secret owner of one of their books from the grand library and also the dagger of the founding grandmaster. These apparently fell into the hands of Rumi through a Hashshashin he converted and have been kept in the family ever since. The Hashshashin will do anything to get their hands on these items, even trade away your sister who is only a means to their end of getting their hands on the Kitab Kabbani—which they would then destroy."

"Wait. I have read a little about the Hashshashin. I thought they were all killed in the Mongol invasion like you said. So there were some that survived, or that restarted the group in Persia? How could there have been a convert that met Rumi?" I asked.

"The Mongols took Alamut in 1256. Rumi didn't die until 1273. Rumi and the Hashshashin were contemporaries," Lydia explained. "There are many myths about the Hashshashin that come from the writings of Marco Polo, who visited the Alamut area in 1273, the same year Rumi died. Interesting isn't it that the stronghold was supposedly destroyed two decades earlier? No, there were many Hashshashin still practicing their wicked arts during Rumi's lifetime, and still today, in many places."

"Now wait, I thought you were an Ismaili," I said turning and looking at Lydia.

"No, I am a Zoroastrian," Lydia explained. "Karim Arkoun, he is traveling with Irshad and Leyla, is Ismaili. There are over twelve million Ismaili of various sects. Probably less than one hundred are Hashshashin. Karim is a Nizari and a member of Al-Ĥujurāt in part because of the bad name the Hashshashin gives all Ismailis. That is his personal battle."

"Why are you two members?" I asked.

"We have all seen too much violence, suffering, and death within Islam and outside Islam perpetrated in the name of Islam," Sami said. "We learn through Jami at-Tirmidhi's collection of hadiths, customs of the Prophet, that the Prophet, peace be upon him, said, 'The Muslim who calls another Muslim an apostate is himself an apostate.' We, Al-Ĥujurāt, are dedicated to peace and community of all who believe in the one God."

"Yes, Leyla explained that to me, but I am still surprised at the diversity of Al-Ĥujurāt," I said.

"I have not met every member, but as far as I know there are no Christians. Perhaps you could be the first," Lydia said.

"Let's just get my sister back safely. I don't think I am cut out for these types of rescues and international intrigue," I said.

"That's not what Hande told me. He said you were a cool operator, to use his words exactly," Lydia said.

"You are kidding me," I said. "Hande was Mr. Amazing. I could not believe what he pulled off. He is one of those rare people who can not only handle super high-stress environments, but he can keep his head about him at the same time."

"Don't let him hear all that, or he won't be able to get that cool head through the doorway," Sami said.

"I will tell him," Lydia said. "He would appreciate the compliment. We don't tend to compliment each other much—it's just our job after all, and no one knows about us outside our little circle, so we can easily forget just how amazing our AlHuj brothers and sisters really are. Thanks."

"I hope I am not overstepping my bounds here, but I notice you think Hande is more amazing than most of the other people in this group," I suggested.

"It's alright, Thad, we all know Lydia has a thing for Hande. Well, everybody but Hande knows anyway," Sami said. "But we have a rule in the operations group, no romantic entanglements. They could jeopardize missions or get somebody killed."

"Yeah, right," Lydia said looking out the side window at the dry, hilly terrain. "How do you explain Irshad and Leyla? Different rules for Celebis?"

"You know we all approved Irshad coming into the group. I can't say it is operationally sound, but it was approved," Sami countered.

"What are you guys talking about?" I asked.

"Oh, Leyla didn't tell you?" Lydia asked. "Irshad and Leyla have been betrothed for many years, since Leyla was ten or eleven, I believe. It is an arranged marriage. I think there was some ancient connection between the families or something."

"No, she never mentioned that," I said, now looking out my side window and the barren hills also. "When is the date for the wedding?"

"No date that I know of," Sami said. "That will be another bridge to cross. The Al-Ĥujurāt operations group has never had a husband and wife team. They may need to move into the research and analysis group or our other group—retired advisors."

I was surprised how much this news saddened me. In an attempt to get the conversation off this new revelation, I asked, "So if the Hashshashin got their hands on the Kabbani Book, why would they then destroy it?"

"Oh, wow, you really are in the dark," Lydia said. "Maybe you should have Leyla explain that to you."

"You mean it has a lot of Middle East history that will require several hours of explanation before I get an actual answer?" I asked.

"Something like that," Lydia said. "But also because it is your family, your brother-in-law's family. Not our place to tread."

"But it is okay for Leyla to tread there?" I asked.

"It was her idea to offer up her family treasure and bring you into the team," Lydia said. "You would be dead by now other-wise, to be sure, but this is her plan, and her great respect for the Kabbani tribe gives her more of a right than the rest of us."

"So you know what makes this book so special but are going to make me wait for the answer?" I clarified.

"Yep. That is it in a nutshell," Lydia said.

"We are just pulling into Aksaray. Keep alert," Sami interrupted. "I doubt the Hashshashin have scouts this far out of Göreme, but you never know. I am sure they wouldn't bother us, but best that they do not see our pick up of the relics. There are plenty of ambush opportunities between here and Göreme."

"We have time; stop up there and pick up some yufka, Sami," Lydia suggested. "I'm hungry, and it would be a treat for Thad."

"Good plan. We can eat that in the car," Sami said.

Sami pulled up to a roadside stand with the name Yavuz Yufka. A short, portly man talked with Sami in extreme animation as he toasted something on a hot griddle that was ready within minutes and placed in a brown paper bag. Sami delivered the bag to Lydia as he hopped back in the car. She handed me a stack of thick filo-pastry filled with meats and what I guessed were ground vegetables.

"I cannot believe how good the food is!" I said after my first bite. "It helps that I am starving by the time I get to eat, but really, this is as good as the *borek* I had yesterday. I am a cook back home, and I really think this could catch on in the States."

"Yes, yes, there is much good here, but let's not get too relaxed," Sami cautioned. For some reason, the hair is standing on the back of my neck. I don't think we are alone."

"Sami, you always think that," Lydia said. "But better safe than sorry, I agree. Let's eat this in the car while we drive by the rendezvous point."

I switched places with Lydia and got into the back seat, feeling better at becoming necessary baggage rather than part of the operations team. "Do you guys carry guns?" I asked as we pulled back onto the road.

"Some of us do, some of us don't," Sami said. "You are an American; do you feel the need for a gun?"

"No, just curious," I said. "I was wondering how this meeting was going to be balanced since it sounds like the Hashshashin are pretty ruthless. What keeps them from just shooting everyone once they get what they want?"

"First of all," Lydia began, "they prefer the old ways—a cultural thing—and they believe it instills more fear possibly being killed by a dagger, a sword, poison, or a garrote. But yes, they do use firearms. These modern Hashshashin also use snipers at times, but they consider that somewhat of a coward's trick. Close range and personal is how they prefer to meet their target."

"There is our meeting location," Sami interrupted. He motioned to a leaning tower that I would have been afraid to even get close to. "It is called the Eğri Minare, the Leaning Minaret of Aksaray. We still have about thirty minutes until we need to act as backup to Irshad for the relics pick up. Lydia, this is where you get out. Thad and I will drive around like tourists for a few more minutes. Once you set up surveillance on the roof of that apartment building, let me know, and Thad and I will park across the street with those other cars."

Lydia got out, grabbed a backpack I hadn't even noticed on the floor of the backseat and was off. Sami drove away watching his rearview mirror. I was still in the back seat feeling like another unnoticed backpack. We drove around the small city for ten minutes, and then Lydia reported that she was in place, and the meeting place appeared safe. We parked the car on a side street on the opposite end of the small park adjacent to the minaret. Ten minutes later Sami's cell phone rang. I assumed it was Irshad and Leyla. I looked out the window and saw them walking toward the Minaret and then into the adjacent building. Leyla had her cell phone to her ear. Irshad was holding her other hand. About thirty seconds later I saw Karim walk into the building from a different direction. He also had his phone to his ear. Other people were also walking into the building. Over the past three or four minutes, I had counted nine or ten people going in and four coming out. I was not sure why they were making this exchange in a public place and why it was such a big deal operation. Sami was still on the phone, so I didn't ask him, but why didn't they just pull off the side of the road somewhere and grab the box or bag and press on?

"Okay," Sami said on the phone. "Be careful on that roof." He turned to me and said, "Let's stretch our legs, maybe take a short walk."

I gave Sami a quizzical look but didn't say anything. We got out of the car and walked toward the Minaret, but on the other side of the street. I noticed most everyone was dressed more conservatively. Most of the women wore headscarves and long dresses. Many of the men wore fez caps. My new clothes fit in, but I still felt a little undressed without the cap and a beard. Sami stopped and bought a newspaper at a corner stand. His phone rang again, but he made no attempt to answer it. He turned and began walking back to the car.

As I turned to follow Sami, thinking my name ought to be yo-yo, I noticed a man staring at me from across the street. He wore a gray robe and white turban but was certainly not out of place on this street. He was older, but clean-shaven, which did seem out of place. He made no attempt to hide his study of me. I felt compelled to stop. "If he needs to stare me down, I won't cower," I thought, so I stopped and stared back at him. After a brief moment, he nodded to me, turned to the building that Irshad and Leyla entered and nodded. He then turned and walked to a car I hadn't noticed and got in. The car left in seconds.

"This is so bizarre," I said out loud. "Sami, what is the game here? All the mystery, all the secrecy in public? I feel like the next thing I will hear is, it was Colonel Mustard with the candle stick in the library."

"What are you babbling about, Thad?" Sami asked with a slight smile. "I think you are losing it, my young American friend. Time to get in the car, and we can go for a short drive."

I got in the car, planning on asking what just happened, when I heard a small explosion coming from the general direction of the building that the man in the robe had just nodded toward. "Did he just authorize an attack?" I wondered. "Was that part of the plan?" I asked Sami.

"NO! We've got to get out of here right now," Sami said. As he pulled onto the street, his phone rang.

As he put the phone to his ear, I heard Lydia's voice on the radio. "Get out of here right now. Pick me up in ten minutes on the other side of the building. Furqaan!"

Sami was simultaneously listening intently to his phone. "Yes, we are gone. Lydia is still available for backup. Celebi Enfendi is gone and presumably safe." Just then our side window burst, and a split second later I heard a shot. Sami turned the corner and accelerated down a tiny side street—maybe it was an alley. That is when I realized a person on a motorcycle was chasing us.

"Let him get closer," I yelled to Sami. "Slow down just a little so he can get close," I repeated, "then accelerate with everything you've got. Do it! Now!"

Sami looked at me like I had two heads, but I had spoken with such authority that he complied. The motorcycle was accelerating to stay close. "Now! Slam on your brakes as hard as you can," I screamed.

Again Sami complied, and the motorcycle crashed into our back bumper. He flew forward over our car and landed just in front of us. Sami had to swerve to not run over him.

We had been so focused on the person chasing us, we had not noticed a motorcycle coming at us down the narrow alley. He certainly was brave, playing chicken with a car in a narrow alley with little room for escape. Then he pulled out a gun and started shooting at us. "He is shooting at the engine I think," Sami yelled. "Either that or he is a terrible shot. Now watch this!"

Sami slammed on the brakes and turned the car hard. I thought we would flip over, but we didn't. We did scrape the wall of a cinderblock building, leaving gashes and an artistic splash of our car paint. Our pursuer stopped shooting and kept his distance. As soon as we were out of the alley, he turned the opposite direction from us. Then I saw Irshad, Leyla, and Karim approaching at high speed in their car. They slowed when they approached us.

"Well, that was fun," Irshad said as he pulled up alongside our car, or what was left of it. "We have a schedule to meet, and we can still make it if we leave now. Thad, you come with us. Sami, toss me your secure radio and go pick up Lydia and find a new vehicle. Continue to Göreme as quickly as you can and keep to the plan. Keep us informed by phone if you run into trouble outside of radio range."

I thanked Sami for the Mr. Toad's Wild Ride and left him with a quizzical look on his face. I jumped into the back seat of Irshad's car, and we were off. We weren't ten meters down the road when I said, "Okay, explain."

"What's to explain?" Irshad said. "We picked up the relics, and we are on our way."

"I wasn't asking you, Irshad," I said, ready to explode. "Leyla, I will ask short questions, I want short answers. Who was the old guy in the priestly garb outside the building back there?"

Leyla looked at Irshad, and he nodded almost imperceptibly. Leyla turned to me and said, "That was my great uncle." She was taking me at my word, keeping her answers short, and giving me the least amount of information possible.

"Interesting guy. I think I would like him," I said. "Why the big operation just to pick up some relics?"

"You talked with him?" Leyla asked.

"I'm asking; you are answering," I reminded her. "Why the big operation just to pick up some relics?"

"In the Celebi family, we do most things of importance by vote. The Maqâm-i Celebi, the head of the worldwide Mevlevi order is chosen by the members of the Celebi family, for example. I could not obtain and then give away the relics without family approval. The family gave my great uncle final approval to pass the relics into my care and to eventually exchange them for the freedom of your sister. It was his stipulation that we not tell you he would be watching you during the collection of the relics. He approved. I knew he would."

Much of the steam of my indignation was cooling, but I still had a few questions. "That still doesn't explain why the big operation. Lydia on a roof somewhere, secure radios…and don't use the attack as the reason. That was not planned. That will be my next question."

"It was partly to ensure the safety of my great uncle. Also, we would not put it past the Hashshashin to pull a stunt to take the relics without having to give up their hostage. As it ended up, answering your follow-on question, the Furqaan decided to intervene. They staged the explosion you might have heard as a diversion in an attempt to grab the relics as they don't want them to get into the hands of their enemy, the Hashshashin."

"How did you know it was the Furqaan and not the Hashshashin, or heaven forbid, another group altogether?" I asked.

"Sami and Lydia both recognized one of their people," Leyla began. "Plus it is their…how do those American TV shows say it? Their M.O.? Their pattern of behavior. They like to blow things up, like the Hashshashin like the up close and personal attack."

"Sami and Lydia told me a little bit about the Hashshashin. What exactly is the Furqaan?" I asked. "The Cliff Notes version."

"Who is Cliff?" Leyla asked.

"Just stick to the short version," I clarified.

"Their name, Al-Furqaan, or "The Criterion" refers to Surrah 25:1-11 and to the Qur'an itself as the decisive factor between the Good and the Evil. They are a Sunni group that guards the separation of sects and believes in a zero sum game—that is, in order for me to win, you have to lose. They are driven by a scarcity mentality that there is only one pie and thus a limited amount of pieces, and everyone should get a piece, albeit the Sunnis should get most of it. They think they are the good guys. The Hashshashin proudly proclaim themselves the bad guys. The Furqaan hates the Hashshashin because they are nominally Shia, and they support Iran over the Sunni world, not because they are evil. I'm not sure where they stand on the Sunni fundamentalists and extremists like The Islamic State and Al-Qaeda. They don't want the Kitab Kabbani to see the light of day for fear of what it might say. I don't know how they knew about these relics, but they would happily stop this exchange and take you into their custody again."

Chapter 9

WE DROVE IN SILENCE FOR fifteen or twenty minutes. The landscape was becoming strange, like out of a science fiction movie. Odd stalagmite-looking hills were emerged from the ground like sign posts and hills out of a Dr. Seuss book. The silence was broken by Leyla.

"We are coming into the area of Anatolia called Cappadocia. It was famous during many eras, including the Jewish Talmud and Christian Old Testament—this is where the Kingdom of the Hittites was centered. Early Christians flourished in the area and survived Roman purges by hiding in the caves all throughout this area. The Armenians conquered the area, followed by the Muslims, starting with the Seljuk Kingdom and eventually becoming part of the Ottoman Empire. Today tourists from the Middle East and Europe come to the region to see the interesting landforms—the fairy chimneys, the Valley of Love, and the cave cities—one of which is Göreme, our destination this afternoon."

"Okay, the site is historical and a geologist's paradise. Why are we meeting the people that have my sister here?" I asked.

"Besides the Christians who found refuge in the cave towns, there are ancient rumors that when the Hashshashin were defeated by the Mongols, many traveled to this region and have operated from here ever since," Leyla explained. "This is where they are holding your sister. This is where they demanded we travel to make the exchange."

"So, is there a plan I am allowed to know, or am I on display again?" I asked.

Irshad pounded his hand down hard on the steering wheel. He held his breath for a few moments like he was counting to ten. Leyla was glaring at him. I was watching both from the back seat. "That is enough, you sorry *mızmız*. It isn't enough that we have expended tens of thousands of American dollars to get you here, that we have risked our lives for you and for your sister. It isn't enough that the Celebi family risks the life of Leyla's great uncle and that they are parting with historical relics that are priceless and that may help fuel the goals of the Hashshashin. And it isn't enough that we have brought you inside our organization and have attempted to be as transparent as possible by always speaking English in your presence."

"That is enough," Leyla interjected. "You know he deserves to know what the next step is." Leyla turned to me and explained, "Irshad is concerned about operational security and the safety of the people depending on his leadership. If you were captured, you would know more than is good for you to know. And like with my great uncle, there were agreements of confidentiality we had to make in order to move forward. You and I have had this conversation; Irshad has not." Leyla turned to Irshad again and punched him playfully in the arm and said, "Now play nice!"

Her effort at bridge-building wasn't working. I could hear Irshad grinding his teeth from the backseat. Maybe I needed to make an effort. "I am not trying to be a mizmiz, whatever that is. Maybe I am one; I don't know. If it means a simple guy living a simple life, minding his own business, and ignorant of whatever everybody seems to think I have—no matter what a seven hundred-year-old scroll says about the name I happen to share with that prophecy—then yep, I am a mizmiz. I do believe I have been patient, and I am very grateful for all everyone has done and is doing for me and my family. I know my sister and I would probably be dead by now if it weren't for all of you. Irshad, what I am not is a puppet or stuffed toy that will just sit in the seat and come along for a ride to places I have never heard of in a land to which I never dreamt of traveling. I will not be a dot. I will not sit by completely disconnected and let others go into harm's way on my behalf and not do whatever I can do to help. Now, what are we doing in Göreme?"

Irshad stared straight ahead and continued to grind his teeth. Leyla sat there with her arms folded and also looked out the front window. I moved to see if there was something in front of us that I should know about—nothing that I could see. "My grandmother used to say, 'sharp vinegar only damages its container.' I don't want to be the reason for your extreme frustration," I said quietly.

"Sormak ayip degil, bilmemek ayip'" Irshad said.

Leyla turned to me and translated, "It is not disgraceful to ask, it is disgraceful not to know."

"I apologize, Thad," Irshad said. "It is not personal, but I do not like to be responsible for a life that is not a trained member of our operations team. I realize that is a personal shortcoming, thinking of my concerns when your sister's life is also at stake. We will arrive in Göreme in about an hour. We are to park, just the three of us, in the parking lot of the Chelebi Cave House Hotel. A Hashshashin joke. They all think they are funny. You know, the Celebi family is giving up a treasure at the hotel that has their name. The hotel is run by a local guy and his Japanese wife with no connection to Leyla's family. Leyla will set the relics on the hood of this car and walk ten paces away. You will follow her. Your sister will walk unescorted to the car and get in. Of course, you will visually confirm it is your sister. Someone will retrieve the relics, and you and Leyla will get back into the car and drive away. I don't expect it will be that simple. On the other hand, they really want these relics and may actually behave."

"That does sound simple enough," I offered. "Do you think the Furqaan will try to complicate the exchange?"

"Great question," Leyla said. "My guess is they won't because of the risks on the Hashshashin home turf. I think that is why they made an effort back in Aksaray. I will admit, I didn't really think they would try there either, so I could be wrong."

We drove in silence, each battling with our own thoughts. The outside landscape became more and more otherworldly. Odd-shaped and barren hills dotted both sides of the road. I half expected to see Anakin Skywalker cruise by on a pod racer. I wonder what my sister thought about her travels to and captivity in this place. Was I really going to get to see her in less than two hours? We were in the city before I realized there was even any population center within miles. The first thing I saw was a group of six or seven hot air balloons. Then I started noticing doors and windows carved into the hillsides and fairy chimneys, as Leyla had called them. "Is there a festival going on?" I asked.

"Not that I know of; why do you ask?" Leyla said.

"All the hot air balloons. In the States, that usually is the sign of a festival or big event."

"It is a normal part of the horizon here. The tourists come from all over the world for hot air balloon rides over this land-scape," Leyla explained. "Too bad this isn't the most convenient time to take a ride. Cappadocia is breathtaking from a relaxing hot air balloon."

We drove past the hotel entrance and pulled into the parking lot and parked far away from the buildings and other vehicles.

"We will wait here for Sami and Lydia to report in and for Asr, afternoon prayer," Irshad said. "I am sure we are already under surveillance by the Hashshashin and perhaps the Furqaan as well."

Five minutes later the secure radio vibrated. Irshad left it on the seat but answered without looking down at it. He looked at each of us as he spoke as if he were in conversation with us. "This is Irshad. We are in place. Where are you?"

"We are ten minutes from the town. We will have the perimeter surveillance in place within twenty minutes—five minutes to spare on Asr. Karim will check into the hotel, Lydia will be to the north across the street, and I will be in the car to the south in the parking lot of the Topdeck Cave Restaurant. Two clicks on the radio when we are all in place."

It seemed like thirty minutes when the first sound of the afternoon prayer was announced. I was wondering if Irshad or Leyla were going to get out of the car for prayer, but they didn't. When the call to prayer was over, Irshad said, "Show time!" We all got out of the car, and I realized that I never asked to see the relics. Oh well, probably safer. I watched Leyla leave the cloth wrapped box on the hood, and she joined Irshad and me ten feet from the car.

A little boy, maybe ten years old, walked up to us from the hotel and handed a note to Leyla. Then he ran off. We looked at the note together. It was in another language, Turkish I guessed, because it didn't look like Arabic; I wasn't sure. Leyla translated for me.

"Very good, my dear friends. We witnessed your meeting in Aksaray with those sons of dogs, the Furqaan. We are glad you were able to defend yourselves, not for your survival of course, but for the relics. You would have been forced to hand over the American for his sister to live. If he is becoming tiresome, you are welcome to hand him over along with the relics and the Hashshashin will be in your debt—a very valuable commodity indeed. Due to these circumstances, the Celebi woman and the American are to travel

alone to Özkonak. Wait at the inside entrance to the city, and we will escort you to the exchange. The rest of your team is to keep their distance. We recommend dinner at the Seten Anatolian, but you may feel more at home at the Dervish Cave House here in Göreme. Ask for Ibrahim—excellent waiter. If you are punctual and follow these directions, your group, plus the American woman, will be united in time for dessert. You must leave now."

"I am glad we set our frustrations aside, Irshad," I said as he shoved the note in his pocket.

"I am still tempted," Irshad said with no apparent humor in his voice. "Leyla, I can't let you do this. You will have no protection even if we could get the team to Özkonak. We need to take care of this here and now."

"There is no *here and now*, Irshad," Leyla said. "It is *there and soon*, and you know it. It is still worth the attempt. Notice what was not said in the note?"

"What are you talking about?" Irshad asked.

"They didn't say bring the relics," I said.

"Exactly," Leyla said. "It is implied, but an oversight, one we can use—our protection. You bring the relics by yourself as obvious as you can in a separate vehicle, but not too close to us. One more person does not pose a threat, and I will explain that we understood that was what the note meant. If they can get their hands on the relics, they will let it pass, I am sure." Leyla turned to me and said, "Let's get moving."

Irshad was left in the parking lot smoldering. I said, "You know, Irshad is going to need some dental work if he doesn't stop grinding his teeth." Leyla chuckled despite the serious situation. "How far to this other town?" I asked.

"Fifteen minutes, maybe twenty," Leyla said. "It is a more recently discovered underground town. I have never been there."

We drove in silence for a few more minutes until I said, "So you and Irshad are engaged. That was disappointing to hear."

Leyla glanced at me and smiled a second time since we departed Göreme. "We are betrothed, not engaged."

"Same difference from where I sit," I said shrugging my shoulders.

"Why the directness, Thaddeus? Is this another essential communication before take-off, like wanting me to know your name?"

"I am not trying to be direct or essential, just honest, just real," I explained. "I never finished my theory about dots. Here is the condensed version since we are driving to our death. The world is shrinking because our reach is expanding. Good thing, right? Our collection of knowledge is bigger than ever and growing. Good again? Maybe not. At the same time, this shrinking world is less meaningful because it is a word clip from Wikipedia or a Google search. We have no actual presence in these places. We are not connecting with actual people—at best just a virtual representation of them. We have a vast amount of data at our fingertips, but the lasting things we need to believe in must come from real connections that spark something inside us. Without these connections, life is hollow or becomes a hopeless joke. Life becomes what I call not-real."

"So, your apathetic directness is because life is not real anymore?" Leyla asked.

"No. Life can still be very much real," I said. "But the line between real and not-real is blurring. Meaning is blurring. A person can sit in the comfort of his office only a few miles from his home in American suburbia and operate a drone over Waziristan and launch a Hellfire Missile at terrorists without presence—without *being there*. Does that make it less real? Is it better to put a person at risk of death to prosecute a more just defense of values?"

"There are a lot of issues wrapped up in that question," Leyla interjected. "You note that I am betrothed, and all of a sudden you are talking about the reality of presence. That feels so academic, ironically not real."

"You are right. Sorry. I am surprised how I am expressing myself. Let me use an example of what I am trying to express. We can walk from the bedroom to the kitchen in our house, experiencing the real-real by petting our cat, and then adjust to observed-real where we watch a cat video playing on our smart TV. We pass through real to not-real when we take care of our virtual pet living on a computer chip, or is that fad over now? Anyway, we finally arrive at the refrigerator for the cat food, where we experience not real-real when we toss a super cold strawberry in our mouth that cannot be frozen because of the biotech insertion of a fish gene in the plant. Maybe that fits in the disgusting-real category, except for our cat who now seems to crave strawberries. The bottom line is, not only can we sometimes not discern the real from the not-real, much of the time we don't even attempt to do so. We simply don't care."

As I sat there gathering my thoughts and why I even brought this up, Leyla asked, "I remember your dot theory of connections between people. I am not exactly sure how these thoughts connect. And I am not sure how I connect to any of this."

"Exactly," I said.

"You mean I am part of the not-real?" Leyla asked.

"No, that is the opposite of what I am saying. I want to understand how you are connected. Betrothed. Engaged. Are you connected or not? Is this the same as being liked on Facebook, or are you in an ironclad relationship? Is it real, or some variance of real?"

"Maybe fifty or one hundred years ago, my betrothal was ironclad. This isn't the result of a virtual relationship, or of some twist of what is real. It is what it is." Leyla said, sounding frustrated.

"I think all this relates somehow," I said trying to sound apologetic. "The broader the reach of technology, the less we can connect. In the world of Facebook, Pinterest, LinkedIn, Twitter, and other new media platforms, social equates to anti-social. Presence equates to absence. In the world of the knowledge machine when we can find an answer to just about anything in fractions of seconds, that knowledge becomes a commodity, not a jewel. Why memorize and treasure a scripture verse when it is retrievable in seconds on our phone? The medium becomes more valuable than the content. I think ambiguity drives inter-action and interaction connects the dots. Connected dots create meaning, and meaning is essential to life at the human level. You are my crucial connection to this whole crazy mess. You make it real. I need that to stay focused on the reality of the seriousness that my sister's life hangs in the balance. And I am embarrassed that I am so bothered by the new knowledge that you are betrothed. It is really not my business, but it feels more virtual than real."

"So you are using me like you have been claiming we are using you?" Leyla asked.

"Wow, I don't know. I don't think so. I guess I am trying to say I really like you, and you are the only thing in the past three days that makes any sense at all. Even Hande's heroics and Ahmet's wounds shrink when it compares with you being in my life. Before you say anything, I know, we only met less than a week ago, and I don't have any right to say these things. I am not a nutcase, although I may be a mizmiz—whatever that is, but I don't think I am not letting the extreme nature of the situation cloud my emotions."

Leyla continued driving us to our potential doom in silence. Then she said, "Crybaby."

"What?" I asked as I turned to look at her. There were bantam tears blossoming in those amazing eyes.

"*Mizmiz* means crybaby," Leyla explained. "And betrothed means it wasn't a decision of the two people involved and was the decision taken when Irshad and I were children. Secondly, it means that while there is this promise of marriage, there is no date or certainty to it. That is considerably different than engaged, which means, Mizmiz, we're going to get married."

"We are?" I asked with a leading smile. "Isn't this a little sudden?"

"Ha ha. That is the definition of engaged. Now get serious, we are entering Özkonak. Help me find the sign for the underground city entrance," Leyla said starting to tense up.

"Our death can wait a minute more. Is the real reason Irshad doesn't like me is because he is jealous or because he has such an odd name and mine is—how did you say it when we met? Awesome, I think the word was."

"Get serious, Mizmiz. There is the entrance," Leyla said.

The town looked quaint and quiet. "The sign says Nevsehir, not Özkonak," I said.

"The town above ground is Nevehir. Özkonak is the town recently discovered that is entirely underground. There is only one tunnel entrance to the entire town that once housed a population estimated at sixty thousand. It was entirely self-contained in its day with a ventilation system, tiny tube holes for communication, a winery, wells, storage, and a sewage system. Pretty amazing for an era we consider backward and undeveloped."

"There, I think that sign says something about an entrance." I pointed out.

We parked near a white diamond sign that at the bottom said in English Özkonak Underground City. To the left of the sign was a pink or earth tone cinderblock gateway with a rounded wooden door all by itself in a gravel parking lot. There were no outdoor lights, and it was already dusk. It would be dark when we came out, if we came out.

"What is the next step?" I asked.

Leyla tried the door, and it was unlocked. "Let's go in." Inside we were immediately faced with a small room and a narrow tunnel that led steeply down an incline to a long tunnel. At least this was minimally lighted.

"Do we keep going, or do we wait here?" I asked.

"Keep going, my friends," a male voice said from the black tunnel. "Welcome to the Al-qasr Almkhfyh. For many years, this was the home to the Hashshashin. It is called Özkonak after the person who unfortunately discovered our home. Although some tourists walk these halls, you are our first official guests this century. Well, after your sister, of course, Mr. Allen. Ladies first, right? Ha ha ha! Just keep walking."

"Leyla turned and whispered in my ear, "I am guessing they can't see us, just hear us. Whatever you say, remember they can hear."

Even in the seriousness of the situation, or perhaps partly because of it, Leyla's breath on my ear sent electricity through my body. I was surprised I didn't light up the tunnel. I turned to her and whispered in her ear, "Whatever happens, thank you for all you and your team have done. And, your hair smells nice." I took the lead and began to walk again.

We walked only about ten paces when some kind of liquid splashed behind us. We turned and saw a puddle of something only two feet behind.

"That, my friends, is boiling hot oil," a voice—no, The Voice, I realized, said. "An interesting bit of information about Al-qasr Almkhfyh is, it is the only underground city in Anatolia that has special delivery holes to drop hot oil on unwanted guests. How very exciting to use these holes for their created purpose. Be very careful, and do not try anything that might cause us to use this system."

"You are the one who needs to be careful," Leyla said. "If we are harmed in any way, you will not get the relics. We followed your note exactly as you wrote it. It made no mention of bringing the relics with us to the tunnel. They are in safekeeping with our companion who has stayed behind but should be in the general area by now."

"You had no right to change the agreement!" The Voice yelled. It echoed through the tunnels and sounded ominous.

It reminded me of being a little boy and watching the Wizard of Oz for the first time. *I am the Great and Powerful Oz! Pay no attention to the man behind the curtain.*

"You changed the rules!" I yelled back with equal indignation. I was disappointed my voice didn't echo nearly as ominously. He must have some kind of sound system set up. "We could have easily exchanged the relics for my sister back in Göreme, but you changed the agreement. We could have accomplished this in Istanbul, for that matter, but that wasn't the agreement. We are still willing to complete our end of the bargain. I have seen the relics. Now I want to see my sister."

"So, our quiet American has found his voice. By now you probably also know of our interest in you. We chose the relics over your miserable presence because I don't believe you have any key to finding the Kitab Kabbani, which probably doesn't exist. Thus, killing you and your sister costs us nothing."

"Except the relics which will be destroyed within one hour if we do not exit this cave safely and with my sister with us." I was making things up as I went, but I was done being the feckless bystander of my life and the lives of those I cared for.

"You are not playing fair, Mr. Allen. I like that. You are still not *akil*, wise, as I mentioned in our first conversation," The Voice said with a sneer.

"Nor am I a *jahech*, idiot, that you called me in that same conversation. I have been awarded the title of mizmiz, however, which I proudly will live up to if I don't see my sister right now. Then you will be out three priceless relics."

"Three relics?" The Voice asked.

I couldn't see Leyla very well in the minimal light, but she wasn't hitting me, so I kept going. "Yes, I noticed the box itself is ancient and probably also came from the grandmaster's hands, possibly to your hands, or if you choose, the hands of destruction, forever lost to everyone." I looked above us to see if there was another hot oil hole. There was. I pointed with my finger to the hole and put my finger to lips and then motioned that we step quietly out of the path of more oil. Somehow they knew where we were, but it could have been simple radio beams or just a guess from the noise we were making. I doubted they had low-light or infrared cameras placed in the tunnel just for our visit.

Chapter 10

As quiet as I could, I moved to the side of the tunnel and away from the holes in the roof. Then I called out, "So what would you like to do? It is in your hands…or not."

As I feared, down came the oil onto the very spot we were standing just seconds before. I yelled out as if I had been caught by the hot oil shower. "Aghhh! Enough, enough!" I yelled. "I didn't think you would really do that. Ahhh! Just let me have my sister and the relics are yours. You win."

"Let us leave the tunnel, and I will call to my companion to set the relics at the tunnel entrance," Leyla added. "I will reenter the tunnel and wait for Mrs. Kabbani, and Mr. Allen can leave with my companion. He needs to get medical attention immediately."

"The Hashshashin do not negotiate. Continue to travel forward in the tunnel. We have armed guards at the tunnel entrance. You cannot escape. You are still close enough to the entrance that your cell phone will still work. Call the person with the relics, and have him leave them as close to the entrance as he dares come. You have five minutes. Then I send in the armed guard at the door to finish the job.

Leyla pulled her cellphone out and saw one bar. She speed dialed Irshad's number. "Don't ask questions. Mr. Allen is injured.

Hot oil was poured on him. He will press forward to retrieve his sister, but you must put the relics close to the entrance to the underground city. You have four minutes." She hung up before he could ask any questions.

Leyla and I started forward down the tunnel. We passed several turns and offshoot tunnels, but we traveled the only tunnel that was lit. We came to a large room that had six offshoot tunnels. The room was completely empty.

"That is far enough," The Voice said.

I stood behind Leyla and huddled up, trying to do my best imitation of a hot-oil-in-the-tunnel burn victim. The room was illuminated by a single bulb at the entrance to the tunnel to our left.

We waited only one minute when The Voice announced, "Very good. We are in possession of the relics. Your companion wisely followed your instructions and did his job."

"Where is Anna Kabbani?" Leyla asked. "We need to get Mr. Allen to medical treatment quickly."

To our right, we heard and then saw movement. Suddenly a body lunged forward and fell to the ground. The body moved slightly but made no sounds. The person had a bag on their head, and their hands were tied behind their back. I hoped it was my sister. A second later two additional people entered the cave room. They were very much alive and were brandishing weapons. They yelled at the person lying on the ground in a language I did not understand. Since I only know English, the list is pretty long. I was pretty sure it wasn't Cambodian or Welsh. Leyla sprang to action and ran to the person on the ground. She pulled the bag off the person's head, and I saw that the person was Irshad. He looked like he had suffered a serious beating and was only semi-conscious. The two men approached Leyla, kicked her and pushed her away.

"Oh, I forgot to mention," The Voice said, "we also captured your companion when he dropped off the relics and shared a little Hashshashin hospitality as a reminder not to deviate from your agreement with us."

"You are the one who has no integrity, and you are a coward!" I yelled back.

"Yes, we shall see who the coward is," The Voice said. "Mr. Allen, you will go with my friend to retrieve your sister. Your companions will stay where they are. I am bored with this game, so go quickly or you will be bathed once more in hot oil."

I moved forward slowly, wondering if The Voice could see me and what their plan really was. I began to walk down the dark tunnel I was directed to by the thug dressed in dirty street clothes. He could have at least had on some puffy pantaloons or a turban, something more fitting an assassin. I said as much to my guard to see if he spoke English and whether The Voice could hear me. "You know, you could dress a little more to the part of an assassin." Instead of an answer, or even the push of a hand or kick of the boot, I heard a thud, like a sack of potatoes being dropped.

Within two or three seconds, a hand was around my mouth, and although I had just inhaled, I felt like I was going to explode because I couldn't breathe. My attacker pulled me closer and whispered in my ear, "Thad, relax, it's Badri. I am going to let go, but don't make a sound. They only have listening devices in the entrance tunnel, but let's take no chances."

I didn't make a sound, but I didn't relax. I turned quickly and faced this person who said he was my brother-in-law. It was so dark with only the tiniest fraction of light coming down the tunnel from the room I had just left. I couldn't tell who it was, and my brain screamed, "This cannot be Badri! You are in an underground city in the middle of Turkey. This is the lair of the Hashshashin, for crying out loud." But another part of me recognized the voice, or was that my wishful imagination? Maybe this person had said something entirely different. "Show me," I demanded in the quietest whisper I could create.

The person took his cell phone out of his pocket and let the LED backlit screen glow near his face. I recognized him immediately. I tried to put a surprised question on my face. He put his finger to his mouth and bent down and duct taped the guard's hands behind his back then taped his mouth and finally wrapped his ankles. I noticed Badri had already taken the guard's gun. He motioned me forward farther down the tunnel. I followed with pleasure. We came to a fork in the tunnels, but Badri did not slow down. He took the tunnel to the right. He seemed to know where he was going, and he was in a hurry. Badri was wearing all black: a black ski cap, a black pullover turtleneck, and black pants. He even had on black tennis shoes. Because of that, it was hard to keep track of him, and I bumped into him several times as I tried to gauge his speed. It was probably less than a minute, but it seemed much longer because I had no idea where we were going when we came to another room with a dim light. Badri stopped and pointed to a pit that was about twelve feet in diameter in the middle. "Ancient well, very deep." He warned.

As my eyes came up from the pit, I realized we weren't alone. There was someone strapped to a chair that was hanging by a rope over the middle of the pit. I couldn't see where the rope was connected nor could I tell who the person was. "Anna, your sister," Badri whispered in my ear.

Badri was in a big hurry. Anna was not moving, not even wiggling. That's confidence, I thought. Maybe she didn't know we were there. I began to motion to her, to get her attention. Badri grabbed me and shook his head. "Look closely," Badri whispered. He motioned to a pulley on the ceiling and his finger traced where the rope was connected to the wall. Then he turned my head with both hands back to Anna. He pointed to the chair she was dangling in and pointed below the chair. Finally, I saw what he was pointing to. There was another rope dangling below the chair. No, it wasn't dangling. It appeared to be stretched tight also. "The top rope is keeping her from falling into the pit—a fifty-foot drop to the rocks below. The rope underneath is connected to explosives. Any movement up or down of the rope, and this whole room is blown to Istanbul. There is no passage to the explosives below."

Obviously, he had studied this out, but I whispered in his ear, "Why not just tie a rope to the rope below and the rope above to keep them taut? It is already connected to the wall over there. It isn't going anywhere."

"Hashshashin booby trap. It isn't as simple as that. That pulley up there has a spring tensioner. Anna's weight is keeping the system balanced. If she is removed, the line will be pulled tighter, and boom! If I cut or loosen the rope below the chair, boom! I will explain it later if you want, but we have little time before we are exposed. Here is the plan."

He ran over to the side wall on the other side of the center pit and brought back a backpack that was obviously very heavy. "Hashshashin gold bars to neutralize a Hashshashin booby trap. Badri then grabbed the excess rope from where the rope holding up Anna was tied to the wall. It was about fifteen feet of excess. He pulled the rope to the other side of the room so it was directly under Anna.

Was Badri going to tight rope walk out to Anna? There was no way I could hold the rope taut enough for him to walk on it. Besides, Anna was dangling about four feet above the pit. Neither Badri nor I were tall enough to stand out there and release Anna. Badri motioned for me to come over to him. He pointed to the light fixture. It was in an ancient crevice where people must have placed a torch in the days before electricity. It was about three feet off the ground. They must have been Hobbit height back in the day, I thought. Badri placed his hands in the crevice, one hand over the other. He removed his hands and motioned for me to copy him. I did, feeling a little absurd. He then began to tie the rope around my chest and over one shoulder, adjusting the rope so it was stretched tight when I stood about two feet from the wall.

I then understood his plan. The problem was my hands were not going to be able to hold the weight of Badri, who was maybe a half inch under six feet and solid muscle, plus the weight of Anna. Together that was about 300 pounds, maybe more. I was about to whisper my concerns when I got an idea. I quickly untied the rope that was around me and, like a jump rope, whipped it up and over the chair Anna was hanging in. Then I ran around the perimeter of the room to where the rope was tied to the wall and retied it there, pulling the rope as tight as I could without pulling Anna toward me, thus changing the tension on the rope connected to the explosives. I then took out one of my shoelaces and tied both ends to the rope running from the wall up to the pulley. The shoelace was parallel to the rope and just barely loose.

I then explained to Badri, "You shimmy across on the rope with the backpack. I will do the best I can to apply equal tension to this side of the pulley. I will measure that by the tension on the shoelace. After all, the extra weight just has to be equal on both sides of the pulley. I just hope the attachment on the ceiling holds. Once you are on the end next to Anna, I will need to apply enough tension to match your weight plus the weight of the backpack, then your weight plus Anna. Some of that tension will be delivered by you, since the rope you will be hanging on will pull from both sides. The real trick will be making the switch."

"No time to lose," Badri said. "They planned to kill you and Anna no matter the negotiations. That's why they lured you here. We only have a minute or two before they figure out you are not being led to them and come this way. Hopefully, your companions will keep them occupied, so they lose track of time for even thirty seconds."

Badri put the heavy backpack on so it draped over his chest and stomach, then he carefully started shimmying out over the pit on the rope. At first, I struggled to hold up much of the weight of Badri plus the pack. I did so by standing under the rope and pushing up the rope with my shoulder, all the time watching my makeshift shoestring tension meter. In the middle, I almost didn't have to do anything. As he approached Anna, I had to pull down on my side of the rope going to the ceiling with everything I had. Luckily I had just enough pull to keep my side equal to Anna's side. Badri was untying Anna when I heard some faint muffles down one of the tunnels leading off from this room. I wanted to yell "hurry," but I figured Badri was already doing that and added stress wouldn't be helpful.

Anna was untied and was moving off the chair as Badri, hanging upside down, was attempting to lift the gold bars onto the chair. The voices were getting louder. We weren't going to make it. I thought, well, if we cause an explosion, at least Leyla and Irshad will have a chance to escape alive. Just as Badri had the backpack on the chair, I whispered, "Grab the left rope and hang on tight!" loud enough that I was sure Badri and Anna would hear me. While attempting to maintain equal tension, I pulled the slipknot loose, and Badri and Anna, clinging to his back, fell into the pit. The rope tied to the wall went tight. "Good. Badri and Anna were able to hold on," I told myself. I quickly ducked into another tunnel—not the one the voices were coming from and not the one I came from.

Just as I ducked out of sight, three people entered the pit room. They saw that Anna was no longer in the chair, and they ran toward the tunnel I had come from. It was a fifty-fifty chance that they would choose the side of the room to circumvent the pit where the rope was not taut holding Badri and Anna. Fortune was with us, and they never noticed the taut rope going from the wall to the pit. As soon as they were down the other tunnel, I helped Badri and Anna pull themselves out of the pit.

"I can't believe that worked," Anna whispered as she gave Badri, then me, hugs. My kidnapped and rescued sister looked great, like she had just gotten back from a hike on the beach. Her light brown, almost blonde hair was a mess and a little longer than the shoulder length cut I last remembered, but her blue eyes sparkled, and she looked fit and healthy. "I think I injured my knee as we hit the pit wall. I won't be able to move very fast. For the past eight to twelve hours I have been in that chair—no food or water—so I'm also pretty weak."

"Do you want to rest here while Thad and I help his friends?" Badir asked Anna.

"You are not leaving me here alone!" Anna said. "I will be right behind you."

"Better yet, you will be between me and Thad," Badri said. "Thad, lead out."

I took off down the tunnel leading to Leyla and Irshad without saying a word. I was thinking, "Okay, that sounded like three guys. They are going to discover the duct-taped guard. Then there is the guard with Leyla. Irshad may not be of much help, so it will be two, three if Leyla is in a position to add to the chaos, plus my sister who isn't doing so well, against five Hashshashin. Not great odds." Sure enough, when we got to the place where Badri had pummeled the guard, he was gone, duct tape crumpled on the floor of the tunnel. We stopped short of charging into the room to see if we could hear anything.

"You have sealed your sure death if you don't tell me where Mr. Allen and his sister are. You have thirty seconds to make peace with your maker. Make peace with your maker," The Voice repeated, laughing. This guy had the strangest sense of humor.

I motioned to Anna and Badri to lie down. I didn't have time to explain, so I just ran. I was back to the pit room in seconds. I searched around for a large rock or pole, but couldn't find anything. So I untied the rope from the wall and attempted to keep the tension equal as I made my way back into the tunnel leading to Leyla. When I got to the end of the rope, I let go and dove for the ground. I no sooner hit the ground than the blast from the bottom of the pit filled the tunnels. Luckily there were many exits for the blast, this tunnel being one of them, so the concussion of the blast wave was not so severe. I got up, not waiting to see if the tunnels were caving in, and ran right past Badri and Anna and tackled one of the bodies in my way. They had not expected the blast, so they were more disoriented than me. I picked up the nearest gun on the floor and hit another Hashshashin on the head. Leyla and Badri had sprung to action and were fighting two other guards. I went to help Leyla when Irshad got off the ground and shot at the person fighting Leyla, narrowly missing him. I had miscounted in my hasty attack. One guard had escaped and now held Anna as a shield. He was screaming something in another language. The message was clear: stop or I shoot.

"This little escape plan is at an end," The Voice yelled as he pulled himself up from the ground. I had a small satisfaction that the person I had first tackled was The Voice. He was not very scary really. Maybe five-feet-seven inches, a little overweight, gray hair and balding. He looked pleased. "Your sister will be dead before you can take one step. Drop your weapons!"

Leyla and Irshad dropped their weapons. Badri made a motion to toss his weapon but held onto it. His arm continued the upward motion and shot at The Voice and then hit the guard's hand holding Anna with the hot weapon. The guard was startled, and the 9mm in his hand fell to the ground. Irshad grabbed The Voice, who had not been hit in Badri's attempt, and pulled him away from joining the action. Badri soon overcame the guard holding Anna with Anna helping by slamming the back of her head into the face of her captor. Those neighborhood self-defense classes back in California were coming in handy.

"Time to get out of here," Irshad said, taking command. "Follow me the way we came."

"No, they will be waiting up there," Badri said.

"There is only one entrance," Leyla reminded Badri. "We need to go quickly. Maybe they won't be expecting us."

"There is another way. The way they brought Irshad in. That is how I got in. Come!" Badri commanded. "I will lead. Thad, you take care of Anna for me."

Badri headed out through the tunnel we just came from, but when he came to the fork in the tunnels, he took the left tunnel. Irshad strode past Anna and me, either upset at his command being taken from him or because he wanted to see this new way out. Leyla was covering the rear. I wondered what had happened to The Voice. Knocked out maybe? Irshad had not had time to tie him up. Then I heard the shot. It was a coward's attack. One shot from The Voice and he had run the other way, presumably to get the guards at the entrance.

Anna collapsed to the tunnel floor. She was hit. I picked her up and carried her down the tunnel. I couldn't tell if she was breathing or not. I prayed she was not seriously hurt, but it was too dark, and we had to move, so I kept going.

I have no idea how many turns and stairs we took, but we exited the underground city to an incandescent moon that illuminated the area seemingly like midday after the darkness of the Gotham grotto. We were on another hill far from the entrance we had used. "Great, now what do we do to escape?" I asked. "They will be here any minute. They will have figured out we used this exit by now."

Badri didn't answer but kept walking quickly through the brush and around the hillside. As we all turned the corner, there was a hot air balloon waiting for us. Badri jumped in and helped everyone else in. That is when he realized that Anna had been shot.

Badri fell to the floor with Anna, holding her and no longer in a hurry or concerned about their escape. Leyla sprang to action and hit the gas torch, and the balloon began to rise slowly. Within sixty seconds we looked like just another sightseeing hot air balloon, one of seven that I counted in the moonlit sky. The escape vehicle was ingenious but slow as we watched the terrain lazily drift by. All our thoughts were on Anna. Twenty minutes later, we landed in an open field on the northern outskirts of Göreme. We flagged down a truck and were taken directly to the nearest hospital. Anna had a faint pulse. She had lost a lot of blood and was in shock.

Irshad had called his team, and we had some security in the small clinic as the overworked doctor tried to save Anna's life.

Chapter 11

THE RESCUE HAD HAPPENED TWO days earlier, but it was still a nightmare that kept replaying in my head. Badri had explained to me that he had secretly traveled to Turkey by road and sea to avoid detection by the Hashshashin. This was no easy task due to the refugee situation on the Lebanon-Syria border and the complex issues between Syria and Turkey. He had eventually rented a small fishing boat in Latakia, and dressed as a member of the crew, made his way to Göreme through the port of Mersin. He had apologized profusely to me about leaving me in the hands of strangers to come to Turkey, but he knew that I would be safe until I arrived in Göreme.

"I knew they were demanding you to appear somewhere in Cappadocia, and I had picked up the Hashshashin trail by playing tourist and asking a few well-worded questions," Badri explained. "The trail led me to Anna, but I had no way of helping her escape on my own. I needed to wait for you, Thad, to help her escape. I followed the Hashshashin into the underground city through their unpublicized entrance. I mapped out the key tunnels the night before. I had not found Anna until they brought her there about twelve hours prior to your arrival. You have an incredibly brave sister, Thad. Not once did I hear her complain, cry, or express fear."

Badri and I had both shed a few tears since, for the fate of Anna. True to what Badri said, she never complained or expressed fear, but she fought. The doctor had pronounced her dead an hour after she arrived at the hospital, only to be proven wrong minutes later when a nurse saw her eyes flutter. I had her blood type and was able to give her blood, and after that long night, she pulled through the valley of death.

Leyla had stayed with us while the rest of the team had returned to Konya. It was our plan to travel there as soon as Anna was able to travel. That came three days later. Now we were safely back in Konya in the Al-Ḥujurāt headquarters. My head was still spinning from the information Badri had shared with Leyla and me while we waited for her recovery to travel. He had waited until we were alone, away from the rest of the team, to share his information—enlightening background that explained the Kitab Kabbani and why I was so key to these insane escapades. Much to my embarrassment, he also bragged about my actions in the tunnels to Leyla. I was glad when we got off of that subject and back to the Kitab Kabbani history.

"My family has always been believers in the one God," Badri had begun. We were sitting on the veranda of the Chelebi Cave Hotel in Göreme. The weather was nice in the sun, a little chilly in the shade. The food was outstanding.

"This is the family folklore. How much is fact, and how much has been created to fill in holes, I can't say for sure. An ancient relative of mine was a minor royal in the Court of Darius in the Persian Empire. Only because he was in the center of the civilized world of the day do we have records of his existence. Darius was a leader who did not allow exploitation or slavery, celebrated diversity in the empire, and practiced an early form of local democracy. They believed in one God and practiced

Zoroastrianism. This was about 500 BC. Our family remained in Persia for centuries, until about 100 BC when fortunes had crumbled, and our family became traders.

"We joined with Nabataeean traders of frankincense in the Arabian Peninsula and the Levant. We converted to Christianity shortly after the time when Jesus Christ walked the earth. Because of our wide travels, we celebrated cross-cultural influences, and about 100 AD, the Kitab Kabbani began to take form. It included family folklore from Persia and stories from my ancestors' travels throughout the known world.

"About 300 AD, my direct ancestor had doctrinal disagreements with the inventions and insertions of man into the scriptures and practices of the Church at the Council of Nicea. My family lost their way for a time. Then, on Saturday, 13 March 624 CE, according to the Kitab Kabbani records, a Kabbani was at the Battle of Badr where he fought against the Meccans. This Kabbani witnessed the descent of angels and was beside Mu'awwidh ibn 'Afrā' and Mu'ādh ibn 'Amr ibn al-Jamūh when he killed Abu Jahl. That was a pivotal moment in history, and my ancestor was there.

"The Kabbani clan also traces its lineage directly to the Prophet Mohammed, as our families joined through marriage, and this heritage is supposedly recorded in the Kitab Kabbani and supports other more well-known books and records already in the public forum.

"From this time forward, the Kitab was the repository for family thoughts on such subjects as the dangers of jealousy, the arrogance of aristocracy, and the tendency of power to lead to pride, greed, and all forms of justification to take and keep power. The book is not a hadith, just the words of humble witnesses of power, both godly and evil."

Badri explained that his name comes from this family member who fought at the Battle of Badr. Only after coaxing from Leyla and me did Badri continue. The family story was getting too contemporary for his humble comfort.

"According to family tradition, the Kitab Kabbani was completed sometime around 1100 AD," Badri continued. "We were still traders by profession. Escaping an attack by European Crusaders, my ancestor found himself north of his regular trade routes, in the Sultinate of Rum, not far from here in the general area of Konya. Our family was at the battle of Koseday when the Mongols attacked, and they escaped to Konya. That is where the Kitab Kabbani was loaned to Rumi. This was one of the books that Hazrat Shemsuddin of Tabriz tossed into the water and came out dry."

Leyla interrupted and explained to me that Hazrat Shemsuddin of Tabriz was Shams. I told her I would have simplified my name, too. Leyla then explained to Badri that she had already shared this story with me.

"After that time, the Kitab Kabbani disappeared," Badri continued. "The book was nearly forgotten except in family oral tradition and several ancient documents that record its name. Then with the discovery of the Fahrunissa Scroll, this all quickly became more than simply a family tradition, but I am getting ahead of myself.

"The Kabbani family continued in the traditions of trading and raising up men of letters and leadership. Actually, Leyla, we had several brief periods of Sufi connections and also became leader-servants in the Ottoman Empire. In 1898 'Abd al-Qadir Qabbani was the Chief of the Municipality of Beirut. This was my great grandfather. He was visited by the Emperor William II of Germany, and at one point during the Emperor's tour, my great grandfather paid a visit to the Emperor on his yacht, the Hohenzollern, on November 5, 1898, and presented him with Oriental textiles inscribed with sayings in memory of his visit to Beirut. These sayings, family lore states, came from remembrances of the Kitab Kabbani. This was the topic of the dinner conversation that night, which also included the Empress Auguste Victoria and German Foreign Minister Prince Bernhard von Bülow. The Kitab Kabbani was mentioned by my great grandfather to the considerable interest of the Emperor.

"It is interesting to note the written record of that evening includes the Emperor making clear that the friendship of his father, Frederick William, towards the Sultanate and the people of the Muslim world was strengthened during his journey and the 'delicious fruits' resulting from it. He specifically noted that the two nations which were different in terms of race and religion could hold together through loyalty and mutual support. According to my grandfather, who heard it from his father, the Kitab Kabbani, or at least the memory of its content, influenced the Emperor significantly. In the Emperor's words, I think he said something like, 'I was deeply touched by the feelings and sympathies shared with me by the Ottoman people during my visit.' Those words were spoken in Beirut, to my great grandfather."

"So isn't it very possible that the book, the Kitab Kabbani, was destroyed sometime after it disappeared?" I asked. "I mean, the last time it was seen was over 700 years ago. Hardly anything lasts that long."

"That is very possible," Badri agreed. "That is the feeling of the Kabbani family. It is really just a quaint memory of family history. Yet we have other tangible items of our place in history. The Prophet, peace be upon him, used to give away hairs from his head to his family and closest friends to keep as blessings. Only three recorded hairs are in existence today, one being held by the Kabbani family. In fact, Leyla, you may know that it is held by Shaykh Muhammad Hisham Kabbani. You met him at my wedding, Thad. He is one of the world's most renowned scholars of Islamic Doctrine and the spiritual science of Sufism and is a prominent American Sufi Muslim. Along the lines of the Kitab

Kabbani, he advocates an understanding of Islam described by his supporters as fundamentally based on peace, tolerance, respect and love. Shaykh Kabbani has been an outspoken critic of extremism as well as the Wahhabi doctrine."

"Yes, I remember meeting him," I said. "We had a great talk together, and he made me feel welcome in a world brand new to me."

"The Islamic world?" Badri asked.

"No, having a brother and an extended family," I said.

"What did you two talk about?" Leyla asked. "I have never met him, but I have certainly studied his works. His papers *Illuminations* and *Universe Rising* are classics."

"I don't remember what we talked about. Sorry. Between him and your grandfather, I just remember they were very nice to me."

"My grandfather was a true gentleman. He passed away two years ago," Badri explained to Leyla. "He was the patriarch, the face of the family to the public, and holder of the family secrets as well."

"Yeah, he told me something like that," I said. "He said the day will come when the family will retrace its steps, desperately in search of its secrets, as the Hajj pilgrim retraces Hagar's steps from Safa to Marwa in her desperate search for water."

"I was thinking about our business secrets, you know, what clients order what and when. He never said anything to me about Hajj," Badri said.

"You know how your grandfather always talked in riddles. I doubt he meant anything by it. Having a conversation with him was like going to the carnival blindfolded. You knew you were going for a ride, just not which one."

"Yes, that was grandfather," Badri chuckled.

"Wait," Leyla said. "Do you remember what you were talking about when he said that?"

"Sure. I only spoke with him three times. The first was at Badri and Anna's wedding and next when he called looking for Badri who, along with Anna, was visiting me. I answered the phone, and we had a brief conversation. The last time was when he called me to wish me 'Happy Birthday.' That was just a few weeks before he died."

"So what was the birthday conversation?" Badri asked. "He never called me on my birthday."

"I told him it wasn't my birthday for another month, but he said he had been thinking of me and thought it best to call when he could. I hardly knew him, but since I really didn't have much of a family, I told him I really appreciated the call. He said something about how busy you were, Badri, and the weight on your shoulders. I asked something about business not being so good, and he said no, the Kabbani name carries its own weight, both in abilities and accountability, or maybe it was responsibilities. I said, wow, I didn't realize the power of a name. And that is when he said the day will come when the family will retrace its steps desperately in search of its secrets as the Hajj pilgrim retraces Hagar's steps from Safa to Marwa in her desperate search for water. He told me to remember what he had just said and then he said it again. Then he asked if I had a birthday wish, and I said I hoped to travel to the beach over the weekend. Maybe down to Pismo. He closed saying something like 'safe travels where ever the manure takes me.'"

Leyla was thinking quietly, but I could hear the wheels spinning. Badri was thinking about his grandfather; I could tell because he had that far-off look. Okay. I will admit it, I was thinking about Leyla and wondering how serious she was with Irshad.

"Wherever the manure takes you?" Leyla confirmed.

"I thought the same thing. Kind of a crude thing to say on a birthday call. But that is why I remember it so well. Makes no sense, but it is kind of funny in a sick sort of way."

"He didn't say manure, Thad," Badri said. "He said Mah-Noor. That means the light of the moon—moonlight."

"Hey, that is pretty cool. Do you know what Leyla means?" I asked Badri. "It means night or one who works with night. Maybe it is meant for us to be on this adventure together, Leyla," I said jokingly.

"Leyla and Majnun," Badri said with a smile.

Leyla was blushing. I asked, "What is that?"

"Just an Arabic folktale. That's all." Badri said.

"Right. Joke time is over," Leyla said. "I think there is more to that birthday call than either of you realize. Badri, could your grandfather really be suggesting that Thaddeus retrace the steps of your family history to find the secret, the Kitab Kabbani?"

"That is quite a stretch Leyla," Badri said. "Grandfather believed there was a Kitab Kabbani, but being lost seven hundred years? And why Thad? Why not send me on the quest?"

"Thaddeus is the perfect candidate," Leyla said. "He is smart, well-read about the Middle East, yet he has no presupposed notions. He is guileless and teachable, an open book."

"Ouch, and I'm not? Thad is a great guy, but he would never even have gotten to Istanbul without your help. No offense, Thad."

"Have you watched him over these past few days?" Leyla retorted. "From what I gather, he pretty much saved your wife and showed more resourcefulness than the seasoned members of my team."

"Umm, guys, I am right here," I reminded them.

"Quiet, Thad," Badri commanded. "I know every corner of the Middle East and the Levant. I speak four languages and three dialects of Arabic. I have trusted contacts in every major city in this part of the world. And I have been trained and prepared to lead the Kabbani family."

"Exactly," Leyla said like she just won the debate. "And the Kabbani family has not found the Kitab Kabbani for seven hundred years. It's time to bring in fresh eyes. Let's just assume your grandfather had selected Thaddeus for this duty. He asked him to retrace your family history—to go from Safa to Marwa. I don't think he was suggesting Thaddeus go on the Hajj. He isn't Muslim. What would Safa mean?"

"I have no idea," Badri said. "I think your logic is flawed. He was just talking like he always did."

"Okay, listen, you two," I interrupted again. "Can I be a part of this conversation?"

"What?" Badri and Leyla asked in unison.

"I think we need to go to Iran," I said.

"What makes you say that?" Badri asked.

"You just told me, Badri. That is where your family started. That is where we need to start. I don't believe that just because the name Thaddeus was on a seven hundred-year-old scroll that I have any key or even a clue. Besides, the scroll was discovered after your grandfather passed away. I am also not convinced that your grandfather was passing me clues—why wouldn't he have just said it—go to Egypt, or go to the tomb of some old dead guy? But I know this: that scroll you told me about, Leyla, was written at the same time that the Kitab Kabbani disappeared, and your grandfather didn't really call me to wish me a happy birthday. There really could be a needle in this haystack, and, despite your compliments, Leyla, I couldn't find the needle if I sifted through the stack, straw by straw."

"Iran?" Leyla said. "Safa in Iran? The Safavid dynasty was founded by Ismael 1st. Hagar's son, Ismael, founded the Arab nation. The Safavids originated through the Safaviyya Sufi order. Maybe the Sufis in Konya transferred the Kitab to the Sufis in Iran for safekeeping? Do we go to the Safavid capital Ardabil? Or to Isfahan?"

"No," Badri shook his head. "Safa is just a placeholder. Thad is right; we go to Iran, but to the capital of Darius, the capital where my ancestors lived, Susa. The question is, what would we do there? What are we looking for?"

"Let's ask Lydia," I suggested. "You told me your ancestors practiced Zoroastrianism, right? Lydia is a Zoroastrian and Iranian."

"That's right," Leyla said enthusiastically. "Her father is the curator of the Zoroastrian museum, the Fire Temple Museum, in Yazd. That is a long way, maybe 900 kilometers from Susa, but he is as good a starting point as any. You know, an interesting side point, it was the Safavids who attempted to crush Zoroastrianism and brought Shia to the forefront of Iranian spirituality. I wonder if that has any connection."

"Now you are grasping at straws," I told Leyla. "Thanks again for the compliments, though."

"I was just kidding earlier about the Leyla and Majnun joke, but maybe I hit closer to the mark than I realized," Badri said.

"What is he talking about?" I asked Leyla. "I am not a Majnun, Badri, I am a mizmiz."

"It's a story," Leyla said. "Maybe I will tell it to you later." Leyla got up from the table and walked off blushing.

I was mesmerized.

"Mizmiz?" Badri said. "You pick up the most random words."

Part II: Iran

Chapter 12

I WAS ENTHRALLED, in a trance like the dancers. If this were to be my last day on earth, it would be a good day to depart. I glanced over at Leyla and immediately took that thought back. A kiss from her and then it would be the perfect day. I knew that wasn't going to happen. She was engaged, betrothed, whatever, and she was practically royalty. I was a fast order cook at a truck stop and practically a nobody. Actually, I was an unemployed fast order cook. I would be lucky to get a homeless dog interested in me once I got home—to a house that was completely trashed and the front door probably still wide open. But it was a great day.

Anna, Badri, Leyla and I returned to Konya with a plan. Anna would stay in Konya for the time to convalesce. It would be a month or so for her to safely travel to her home in Beirut or New York. It would be really tough to leave Anna, for both Badri and I, but she urged us to go. The Al-Ḥujurāt team would travel to Iran via different routes. It took us three days to prepare for our travel, and tonight was our last evening together in this refuge from the world. We were treated to an amazing meal, and now we were watching a Sema, the dervish dance. Leyla fulfilled her promise to share this event with me.

"Dance is the oldest form of prayer," Leyla had explained. "A circle is the oldest form of dance. Animals circle to find peace; people circle to find meaning."

"Swirls are a part of nature," I added. "Hurricanes, planet revolutions, fingerprints, flowers and other plants, tree rings. It's a message we are offered every day if we are observant."

Leyla's eyes sparkled, and she whispered, "The Sura Baqara says, wherever you turn, there is the Face of God. Let me know what you observe from this dance."

We watched quietly as the ceremony progressed. I made mental notes, but I got so involved that I am sure I missed a lot. The dance portion of the ceremony took about twenty minutes I guessed, but "minutes of time" was not the right measure for this ceremony. It was too constraining. Then several songs were sung in what sounded like Turkish. I was starting to pick up the difference between Arabic and Turkish. Soon I would be hearing Iranian, or Farsi, as Badri had called it. This still felt completely unreal.

"So, did you like it?" Leyla asked after the last song was completed.

"It almost put me in a trance. It was so relaxing, yet not in a sleepy way. A more meaningful and connected peace," I struggled to explain. "So, the leader?"

"He is called the sheikh, the spiritual master," Leyla said.

"Okay, the sheikh used that red pillow you mentioned before to establish a starting and an ending place. The dancers passed by him and spoke to him three times. Once the whirling started, I noticed that they twirled on the left foot, powered by the right foot. One thing I think that would be really hard to learn would be twirling on the entire surface of the foot. The natural thing would be to go up on the toes and ball of the foot. The hands were in different positions. They never got dizzy."

"Very good, Thaddeus. It is a seven-part dance and symbolizes one's ascent into heaven. They turn toward truth as they strive to abandon ego. The white gown is the burial shroud of ego; the tall hat is the gravestone of ego. The right hand faces palm up to receive the blessings of heaven. The left hand is palm down to bestow blessings on earth."

"I do have another observation, but it's symbolic like the clothes and hat of the dancers." I was glad for the moment I was alone with Leyla. Everyone else seemed to be absorbed in their own thoughts or conversations. I was dancing in the circles that were Leyla's eyes and explained, "It seems in my own life that God prefers to work with me when I am doing, when I am in motion, dancing, rather than when I am motionless. There is a time for quiet meditation, but even that requires work on our part, to let go, to focus, to consider the immediate moment; but life is meant to be lived, not to sit in an inert stupor. In fact, that is a definition of sin I have been playing around with in my mind. Sin is a waste of time. I mean that in two ways. It is a waste of time to consider it, so why not do something better? But I also think that when we waste time, that is a sin. When God sees us in action, it is like an invitation for guidance, for blessings. If we receive and do nothing, that is a sin. If we plan and do nothing, see and do nothing, understand and not apply wisdom, it is a sin. Anyway, that's just a thought your mention of the hand positions reminded me of."

"Thaddeus Allen, you are like a dance yourself, so many discoveries at every turn. You are brave and resourceful, teachable, it appears, and you have a spiritual nature," Leyla said as she shifted her gaze away from me to the dancers who were leaving the room.

I missed her eyes searching my face. I think my body temperature goes up one degree when she is looking at me, and I don't even have to see that she is focused on me. I was never one to crave the center of attention. These selfie pictures, invented long ago by the Japanese, by the way, if they would have been a fad when I was younger…well, mine would have been of the landscape or the wallpaper—like the camera was looking right through me like I wasn't there. I don't have a low opinion of myself, but I don't need to see myself either. I know I am there.

"You know, the event is not yet over," Leyla said, snapping me out of my thoughts. "The dancers will now retire to pray and meditate in private. Doing must not get in the way of listening. Maybe we should do the same. Big day tomorrow. Are you really willing to do this? It could be very dangerous for you."

"What could be more dangerous than running around a human-sized ant farm with people trying to kill you?" I asked.

"Yes, and that is over. Why are you willing to jump back into the fire?"

"Because, like you, I need to see this thing through. Let's prove there is no Kitab Kabbani or find it and share it with the world. Otherwise, I will need to put myself on the endangered species list."

"And what specie are you?"

"*Mizmiz Depereo.*"

"You are not a *mizmiz*, remember. You were officially christened *Majnun* by Badri in Cappadocia," Leyla laughed. "What does *depereo* mean?"

"You tell me the significance of *Majnun*, and I will tell you what *depereo* means," I countered.

"I am not sure I want to let that little secret out yet," Leyla said.

"Very well. My species shall also remain a secret. You are right. It is time for bed. We leave at five in the morning, right?"

"Yes, out the door by five, take-off by seven for you. Sleep well, Majnun."

* * *

I returned to my room and the safety of not having to portray so much confidence in the next stage of this adventure. We had decided the day before that I would travel with Badri by private aircraft to Yazd, about a twelve-hour flight, not counting a long fuel stop and circumventing population concentrations and known military areas. Leyla, Irshad, Lydia, and Hande would travel separately by car, about thirty-three hours, and meet us at the museum in Yazd. We would be traveling as a visiting archeological team with credentials obtained through Lydia's father. As an American, my situation was a little more complicated. I would actually be traveling on a false passport, using my real name, but under South African citizenship. Badri was using his real passport, but we would travel as covertly as possible, but during the day. We planned to stop for the night at a small town called Chaldiran and then cross the border and arrive at Yazd about the same time as the team. This way I had less potential contact with people, and Badri routinely used his plane for business travel. He had the family pilot fly it in yesterday. It was gassed and ready to go. I knew I would live through the take-offs without Leyla to talk me through it, but I wish there were room for her in the plane just the same. The aircraft was an Aviat Husky, a two-person, tandem-seating high-wing aircraft. It cruised at 230 kilometers per hour, but it had good range and could land and take-off almost anywhere. I packed light, easy because I only had a few changes of clothes that Leyla had given me. I just hoped I could get some sleep.

That night I dreamed about Leyla for the first time. In the dream, we were in Badri's plane, but there were only the two seats, and neither of us knew how to fly. We were flying above the desert having the discussion about our flying fears that had taken place over the Atlantic. Then the plane ran out of gas, and we began losing altitude. "Thaddeus," Leyla calmly said in my dream, "*Majnun* means…" and I woke up.

The next morning I approached Hande, my friend and informant on things Middle Eastern, to wish him safe travel. "Hande, stay awake, and be safe on your drive. It sounds like it will be long and tedious."

"Are you kidding me, Thad? I once drove a motorcycle from Istanbul to Sana'a, Yemen in 56 hours. This is a walk in the parking lot."

"That's a walk in the park," I corrected.

"That's what I said," Hande confirmed. "The flight sounds like a lot of fun though, and you don't have to put up with Irshad."

"That reminds me, you know Lydia has a thing for you, don't you?" I asked.

"And why would mentioning Irshad remind you to tell me about Lydia?" Hande asked with a smile.

"Just another trip and it reminded me of the last one when I got to know Lydia a little better. By the way, I've changed names again," I said to change the subject. While Badri, Leyla and I were in Göreme waiting for Anna to get well enough to bring her here, Badri started calling me Majnun. Neither Badri nor Leyla would tell me what it means. I just barely found out what mizmiz means. I hope this isn't worse."

"Leyla and Majnun. I love it! Badri is my kind of guy. Go, Badri!" Hande said. "It's from a story, a folktale told in many parts of the Middle East. I expect Leyla will explain it when she is ready. Now is not the time to get into it. Time to get our game faces on again, my American buddy, I mean my South African mate. I can't wait to take you to the Talaryazd Restaurant. Maybe the best Iranian food in the country. Then, for dessert, we will go to Amiran Paludeh. They make this special saffron ice cream with pistachios and rose water that is unforgettable."

"And this is how you get your game face on? Food?" I asked.

"Yes. Some have a girl in every port; I know the best restaurants in every city in the Middle East. That is very serious business, my fast-food chef."

"I knew I would like you the day you smashed in my window," I said.

"Don't tell the Arabs and Turks in the group," Hande whispered conspiratorially, "but I think Iranian food is the purest and best in the Middle East. But the best restaurants are in Beirut, Lebanon. Now, I must go. Be cautious, watch and pray!"

I watched Hande get in the car with the other team members. I hadn't talked to Leyla since we parted after the dervish dance last night. She was all business this morning, and they left with only a wave as Badri and I hopped in another car driven by Karim, who would take us to the airport. I was sad to be leaving Konya. I knew it was really the people, my sister in particular, but also the companionship with Hande and relax time with Leyla. But I was also excited to be on my way—a little bit because I knew Leyla would be there on the other end of this journey.

* * *

"There she is," Badri said with pride as we pulled up to the aircraft.

"It's small," was all I could muster. It was painted sky blue with some dark blue highlights. It looked like a toy. The only aircraft I had ever flown in were large commercial jets.

"She is small, but one of the best small airplanes in the region. Two hundred horsepower Lycoming O-360 engine, full instrument navigation set, with GPS, and I have the tundra tires on so we can land just about anywhere. You are going to love this experience." Badri was positively beaming with enthusiasm. I was positively shaking.

Within minutes we had our gear loaded, and Badri strapped me in the back seat since the engine-and-navigation panel was only in the front seat. Badri hopped in and started the engine. I could feel the wind from the propeller passing by the open window. Before I figured out how to close the window, we were taxing to the runway. The pilot that had flown the plane to Konya had filed a VFR (visual flight rules, Badri had explained to me) flight plan to today's destination.

"Alright, here we go!" Badri said over the intercom. We hardly started down the runway, and the tail came up, then we were airborne. The view was amazing. I thought I might be afraid of the height, but I felt snug in the airplane, and I loved the view. With the David Clark headset on, it was quiet and actually relaxing. Badri had told me the headset had active noise reduction, so we would be able to talk without raising our voice, or competing with the engine or air. He was right.

"I love this!" was all I said. I didn't want to interrupt as the control tower gave us clearance to depart their frequency. We were on our way.

Chapter 13

OUR FLIGHT TO CHALDIRAN WAS uneventful except for two personal discoveries. I became so addicted to watching the ground—what we were flying over—that I didn't look at what was in front of us. At one point we were circumventing some weather when we hit turbulence and then went into the clouds very briefly, for maybe only thirty seconds. It really scared me. I felt like a leaf in the wind. From then on I glanced forward about every five minutes. I knew Badri was flying, and I was just the passenger, but I didn't like to be surprised.

I also discovered there are no bathrooms in small airplanes. "Well, duh!" was Badri's response when I mentioned there was no way to use the bathroom. So I had to hold it for two additional hours until we landed. Luckily the airport at Chaldiran was a grass strip. I hopped out as soon as we landed and ran to the bushes. Badri had told me there was a good runway in the city of Van to the south, but this was a better place to stay, and there would be no customs when we departed the next day.

"So this town is named after a very famous battle that has significance for the entire Middle East," Badri explained as we rode into town with the airfield manager—which was really just a farmer who made a few extra Turkish Lira when someone landed in his well-kept field. "Some say the battle of Chaldiran in 1514 was a turning point in Turkish history. I believe it was one of those key intersections in Middle Eastern history. Shah Ismail was defeated by Selim 1st. The Ottomans beat the Saffavids. Modern weaponry beat the old ways. Not only would the structure of the Turkish state be different today, but the Shia traditions could have possibly taken precedence over the Sunni. Instead of a Western-leaning Turkey, they may very well have listed to the East. World War One would have had a different list of belligerents from this region; there may not have even been a push to the gates of Europe as there was with the Ottomans. The actual battle took place about ten kilometers from here near the Iranian town also called Chaldiran. Of course, that was part of the Ottoman Empire in the day."

"Do you think the Kitab Kabbani is another tipping point in world history or at least regional history?" I asked.

"I am not sure words speak louder than actions. The Prophet Mohammed, peace be upon him, did say that the ink of the scholar is more sacred than the blood of the martyr, but this little backyard skirmish between Turks really altered reality for millions for half a millennium and counting. Shah Ismail did survive, although he forgot his favorite wife on the battlefield, and she was captured by the Ottomans and went on to nearly eradicate Sunnis from Persia and established the Twelvers movement."

"I know I should be gleaning far-reaching principles from what you just said, but... he forgot his wife on the battlefield? What was she doing there in the first place?" I asked.

"Wars were slower moving, and there was relative safety not that far from the forward edge of the battle. The Ottomans, however, had adopted the use of artillery and rifles. Modern armaments totally annihilated the Safavid Army. What I wonder about is, why didn't the Ottomans continue on into Persia? That could have been just as large a turning point. Shia could have become just another minority offshoot of Islam."

"Spoken like a Sunni, Badri," I said. "But the basis of their belief systems was based on the same book."

"No difference between that and all the Christian wars of the past two millennia," Badri countered.

"Except that Christians have been able to find peace among themselves," I said.

"Spoken like an American," Badri said with a chuckle. "Last time I looked, the European front of World Wars One and Two was fought between Christians. That was only sixty years ago. In my world, that was yesterday, not ancient history."

We got a ride to a small motel called Otel Yeni Çaldıran by a local farmer who didn't say a word to us. It ended up being more like a bed-and-breakfast place. Badri had told me before we left Konya that he had rented a single room. What he hadn't told me was it appeared this was the only room. He said there were other hotels in the town, but this was safe, the food was excellent, and he knew the proprietors. They were an older couple, Tacim and Ajwan, a Kurdish couple in their seventies, I guessed, but maybe they were younger and had experienced a hard life in this frontier area. I hadn't done anything all day except sit, but I was very tired. We enjoyed a meal of kurt kofte, little balls made of bulgur wheat and herbs; sucuk, a kind of Turkish salami; homemade bread and several types of cheese. It was another great meal and possibly my last in Turkey.

As we completed the meal and thanked our hosts, who had quietly eaten with us, Badri said, "You know why I like flying so much? It isn't the flying itself, but being airborne. I ran across a thought once by a Russian priest named Philaret that said it better than I could. It went something like the walls of division and difference do not rise all the way to heaven. When I am flying there are no borders; there is just one earth. The people are so tiny, or invisible if I fly high enough. I like to think that the all-too-human attributes of pettiness, ego, pride and selfishness do not exist."

"I kind of felt that today," I shared. "With Anna and you safe, this has turned into a quest of discovery instead of a race for survival. I hope we find our answers in Iran."

I slept great and was wide-awake as the sun came up. Badri was still snoring. I made enough noise being bored that he finally opened his eyes. We got dressed, and we were ready to go within fifteen minutes. We were given some boiled eggs and a nearly-toothless smile by Ajwan. Badri told me Tacim had left to work in his fields just outside of town before the sun came up. As previously arranged, the farmer who brought us into town last night was waiting for us in his truck when we left the hotel. We were at the airport twenty minutes later, airborne thirty minutes after that. Badri filed a VFR flight plan in Turkish by radio with the control tower in Van.

"That is Mount Ararat to the north," Badri said. "The traditional site where Noah's Ark hit ground as the Great Flood receded. Its elevation is nearly 17,000 feet."

We turned to a 160-degree heading. Three minutes later Badri announced, "Say it all in Persian, even if Arabic is better."

"What is that supposed to mean?" I asked.

"A quote from Rumi, since we just passed the border and are now in Iran," Badri explained. "And also for the follow-on line: *Love will find its way through all languages on its own, to honor the border your heart has crossed.*"

"I don't know what you are talking about," I said with a grin. "We aren't high enough for you to get hypoxia, but you are starting to make me wonder."

"Ah, it is not I, dear brother-in-law; it is you who have hypoxia of the heart," Badri said as he laughed his way southeast through Northern Iran. I didn't take the bait and remained silent.

"We will stay northeast of the major range of the Zagros Mountains to overfly Hamadan, then to Isfahan. We will then turn farther east to Yazd. That is six and a half hours total flying time. If the winds and weather are with us, we can do that non-stop, even with some slight detours or headwinds. We will need to stop in Isfahan for gas. I would rather clear customs in Yazd; but if fuel is low, we will have no choice."

The mountains were spectacular, but the ground looked pretty dry and arid. There were areas of green, but only in the long, thin valleys. As if reading my mind, Badri said, "It is late fall here, and the harvest season is long over, especially in the high country. Iran has a very dry climate, although it is much greener north, by the Caspian Sea. They call that area Shomal, the jungles of Iran. There is only one major river, the Karun River, and several smaller ones in the whole country."

"Those mountains are really impressive," I commented. "I have read about Iran, but that is nothing like being here."

"Iran has mountain borders on every side of the country. Great to keep out the neighbors, of which they have ten. I wonder if that is a world record?" Badri speculated out loud.

"China and Russia have like fourteen or fifteen, I think. But ten, that is a lot. Can you name them?" I asked.

"Armenia, Azerbaijan, Turkmenistan, Afghanistan, Pakistan, Oman, United Arab Emirates, Kuwait, Iraq and Turkey," Badri said without a pause. The mountains also keep out much of the rain; thus, in the center of the country, it is very arid. I think something like only ten percent of the country is arable."

"So there are like seventy million people in Iran. How do they feed themselves?" I asked.

"They do not only feed themselves; they are food exporters, the largest exporters in the world of pistachio nuts, saffron, and pomegranates. They have this ingenious system of qanats. They are underground tunnels that carry the water from the mountains to the desert. They rival the aqueducts of the Romans, but unlike the aqueducts, which are now only of historical interest, the Iranian system is still in use after 3,000 years. I heard there are over 22,000 qanat segments that carry water over 170,000 miles."

"Carrying the water underground is so smart in such a hot climate. I wonder what they save in evaporation costs?" I asked.

"I have never read anything about that, but you are right," Badri said as he navigated the plane through a valley that looked like it stretched on for hundreds of miles. "The qanat system is what made the famous gardens of Iran possible. In fact, your English word *paradise* is derived from the Persian word for these gardens: *pardis*."

"The ultimate desert dwellers," I said.

"Well, I am sure the Bedouin, the Nabateans, the Coy People down in Africa, and others would dispute that, but you are right. I know of no other desert civilization that has worked with what they have like the Iranians. They have a swamp cooler system called *badgir*. That means *catch wind* and is basically a chimney that instead of funneling smoke up and out of the house, sends cool air down, created by a pool of water and simple fountain at the top of the chimney."

"That is the perfect use of the term *air conditioning*," I said, amazed at Badri's knowledge of this country.

"One more amazing invention—and mind you, these are innovations that are thousands of years old—that I want to mention. They have these ancient refrigerators called *yakhchal*. That means *ice pit*. Around 400 BC they learned how to produce ice and frozen delicacies in the most brutal heat of the summer. These systems worked in conjunction with qanats and badgirs. They built shallow troughs for water next to walls in a specific configuration which channeled winds, causing the water to freeze at nights in the extreme desert climate. They also carried ice from the mountains in subterranean storage spaces under the conical structure of the yakhchal. The circular walls were insulated to withstand high temperatures with a thickness of at least six and a half feet at the base. These walls were resistant to heat transfer and also were completely waterproof. The material used to build them is made of a mixture of ash, goat hair, lime, egg whites, clay, and sand in specific proportions."

"I have read some great books on this country, but all that is new to me. How does the gas look? I am getting excited to put my feet on the ground in Iran. Are we going to have to stop in Isfahan?" I asked.

"I don't know yet. I figured our gas levels for specific checkpoints. We are still thirty minutes out from the next checkpoint," Badri explained.

"Being here, I mean in this airplane, helps me realize how immense this country is," I said.

"An Iranian business associate told me it is about the size of Alaska," Badri added. "It is in the top twenty of countries in the world in land mass."

"Are those houses are down there that look like they don't have roofs?" I asked. "Even if they don't get much rain, I would want a roof over me."

"That is another ancient Persian invention. I don't know the name, but they were the earliest known civilization to harness the wind through windmills. What you see down there are the large wheel paddles on the roofs of houses and other buildings," Badri explained. "But lest you think they are all eco-focused, modern Iran has a terrible problem of pollution, deforestation, overgrazing, and soil degradation. Teheran is one of the worst cities in the world for air pollution, and many of the seven million inhabitants of that city suffer from chronic breathing problems."

We flew in silence for a while, me enjoying the scenery and the horizon sprinkled with snowcapped mountains, Badri either thinking about business, Anna, or navigation. I wondered again what we would really find once we got to Yazd and Susa.

My quiet reverie was abruptly interrupted with sputtering jolts of the aircraft. I thought it was a different kind of turbulence that small airplanes experience. Then I realized the engine was making a noise.

"We are going to have to take the plane down. It sounds like we got some bad gas in Çhaldıran," Badri explained, as calm as if he were explaining that we should turn right instead of left. "We won't know if that is the problem until we get on the ground. Fortunately, we can almost glide from here to Hamadan Airport. The trick is to not land at Hamadan-Shahrokhi Airport. It is farther to the north, but at night it is easy to mistake the two. That is an Iranian Air Force base, and I don't think they would smile on our surprise arrival."

I watched Badri turn his radio to 121.5 and begin to call Hamadan Tower. I began to think about trying to be South African. Badri brought us in for a landing at Hamadan in between much larger aircraft coming and going that threatened to flip us over by the wake turbulence, as Badri called it. The runway sloped up on the arrival end and sloped down from the middle to the end, so it was an odd feeling landing. We taxied off at the very first exit, and a truck with a guy waving out the driver's window motioned to follow him. We parked with a bunch of other small aircraft. Badri hopped out and began talking to the guy from the truck. The truck guy nodded, got in his truck and drove off. As he did, another vehicle arrived. "Customs, Thad. Just stay in your seat for now. Hopefully, this will pass without any complications," Badri said.

The Customs official looked dour as he approached Badri. Badri looked confident and greeted the man with a serious smile. They talked in some language that I was sure wasn't Turkish, probably Farsi. Arabic and English were Badri's native languages, but he also spoke French, Turkish and Farsi, and several dialects of Arabic. My English was pretty good. The Customs agent and Badri walked over to me, and Badri said, "Mr. Allen, this is the Iranian government Customs Agent, Mr. Omidzadeh. Could you present your passport to him for processing? I explained to him about our emergency landing."

I didn't say anything but passed over my South African passport. Supposedly, South Africa had better relations with Iran than most other countries where English speakers were common. I guess we would find out. Mr. Omidzadeh took the passport, thumbed through it, said something to Badri, and left in his vehicle. Badri watched him drive off and then came over to the airplane.

"The Follow-Me truck, the guy that brought us to parking, is going to get a mechanic and gas truck out here soon. Customs has taken our passports into his office for processing. I am not happy about that. Typically, they bring their stamp out to the plane. I assume he is either protecting his own backside since we arrived here unannounced or he is demonstrating his importance. When he saw I was from Lebanon, he asked where I lived exactly, which is another way of asking if I am Sunni or Shia, Druze, or Maronite Christian. What a crazy world we live in. I don't think he cares at all that you are South African."

"So besides being tossed in prison for being Sunni or South African, is the airplane issue serious?" I asked, trying to get my mind off of the Customs issues.

"I won't know until we get the gas in the tank tested. That will take an hour or so, once they get out here to take a sample. I am not sure what damage may have been caused. Hopefully it is the gas and not a mechanical problem. If so, we can drain the tank, put in clean gas, do an engine run to clean the system, top off the tank, and be on our way."

"And if it isn't the gas?" I asked.

"Then we have an engine problem which could be a carbu-retor or something more complex, like a fuel pump, a bad fuel line, or who knows what. I have had bad gas problems a few times, but never anything with these symptoms that was from some other problem. If it is really serious, I may consider leaving the aircraft here if I can find someone trustworthy, and we will continue on by car or train."

The maintenance truck returned to the plane a few minutes later. Badri spoke with them for a few minutes. Badri came over to me while the maintenance guy retrieved some equipment from the truck.

"He is going to take a fuel sample and get back to us within half an hour. We are fortunate it is a slow day and that there is an FBO, fixed base operator, at this airport with a qualified mechanic. They use the testing equipment from the local airline, Iran Aseman. We are now in wait mode. You can get out of the airplane and stretch your legs if you like, or take a nap. Thank goodness it is a relatively warm day. It can get pretty cold in this part of Iran this time of year."

I got out of the plane, and I was surprised how stiff I was. I didn't realize how tense I had been sitting there, waiting, won-dering. For some reason, I felt like I had more presence of mind in the tunnels in Turkey than I had lounging on the parking ramp of the Hamadan Airport. It turned out the maintenance guy beat Mr. Omidzadeh back to the plane. The problem was bad gas. It turns out it there was water in the gas, or in the tank itself.

"We will have to drain the tank and check it for moisture," Badri explained. "It could be the gas we got in Chaldiran, or it could be condensation in the tank. We will then need to purge the tank and lines, change the filter and the oil, and do a ground run. Hopefully, it didn't damage the fuel control unit. That should take a couple of hours. Then we can be on our way."

"Assuming we get cleared from Customs," I added.

Halfway through the draining of the gas, Mr. Omidzadeh returned. He said there was some anomaly with Badri's passport and that he would have to accompany Mr. Omidzadeh to their office. I was cleared into the country without fanfare—which was okay with me. Badri asked if it would be alright if I accompanied him since I didn't speak Farsi. Mr. Omidzadeh, with a plastic smile, said "no." He made quick arrangements with maintenance and explained to me that I could accompany the maintenance worker back to their hangar.

"According to the maintenance guy, their office manager is a retired commercial pilot, so he speaks some English. I should be back within half an hour and certainly before the tank is ready to be refilled. I asked our Customs friend if he could drop you off at the hangar, and he told me he does not run a taxi service. So, for a very short time, you are on your own."

"Okay. Our cell phones should still work here, right?" I asked. "Just give me a call if there are complications." I wanted to sound confident—Badri had enough on his plate, and in this situation, I would not be a mizmiz. Badri departed in the Customs vehicle, and I leaned against the fuselage trying to calm myself. Thirty minutes later, the tank was drained and purged. Still no Badri. Another half hour and the oil was changed and the filter replaced. Still no Badri. The maintenance guy, who spoke no English, needed to get back to the hangar, so I went with him.

"Good to meet you, Mr. Allen," the retired pilot said. "I take it Mr. Kabbani has not returned to the aircraft?"

"That is right, sir. I wasn't sure what I should do."

"Oh please, don't call me sir, and sorry for my poor manners. I am Hvovi, Majid Hvovi. Please call me Boos. That means kiss in Iranian, but it is for my ultra-soft landings. I could make a plane kiss the runway in my day."

"Okay, Boos," I said with some doubt and wondering if I was in the Iranian version of a scene from *My Big Fat Greek Wedding*. "Thanks. I suspect that name could get you into some trouble."

"It has, but it has also opened up some wonderful relationships," Boos said with a chuckle. "So, it is getting close to closing time. My suggestion is, let's pull your aircraft into our hangar for safekeeping, and I can drop you off at a hotel close to the airport. It is your best chance for finding people that might speak enough English that you can get by for the night."

"English isn't my only problem," I explained. "My traveling companion has all the money with him."

"Yes, that does present a problem. I would loan you some money if I could, but I only have a few Rials on me right now. I could let you hang out here, but I am not sure the owners would appreciate that; plus, there is nothing here to eat. I expect your friend will be back soon, as the Customs Office is also closing. Can you call him?"

"I tried while I was out at the aircraft, but I got no answer."

"Hmm. That is interesting," Boos said. "Well, I guess the only thing to do is take you home with me."

"If you just drop me off at a hotel, maybe I can work something out. I am sure my companion will be back soon. As you say, it is almost quitting time."

"Nonsense!" Boos said with a broad smile. You are *mehman*, my guest. You are a blessing to my home. We have a phrase, blessed *paa ghadam,* which literally means *footsteps*, but also means *a surprise guest brings blessings into our home*. So come, we must go."

I left a note on the hangar office door, in case Badri returned here instead of trying to call me. I jumped in a nice Peugeot, a model I had never seen before, and we were off. We drove for about ten minutes on Basij Boulevard and merged to the left onto Imam Khomeini Highway. I was surprised that all the signs had English translations. I felt like I was looking at pictures from Arizona or New Mexico out the window. We turned left a minute later onto Nabovvat Boulevard into a neighborhood of quiet, single-family homes that could have been in my hometown of Madera.

"This is Shahid Madani. A small town just north of Hamadan," Boos said as he parked his car on the street. We got out and walked to a quaint little single-family home.

He opened the unlocked door and walked in, saying something in Farsi. A lady in her fifties entered the small living room. She had a kind smile and a welcoming hand, which I shook. She was in a loose fitting dress that went all the way to her ankles. She had dark hair and dark eyes.

"This is my wife, Sepideh," Boos said. "Sepideh, this is my new friend, Mr. Allen. He is traveling through Hamadan on his way to—I never asked. Mr. Allen, what is your destination?"

It is good to meet you," I said to Sepideh. "Thank you so much for your hospitality." Turning to Boos, I said, "Our initial destination is Yazd, and then Susa. And please, call me Thad."

"I have family in Yazd," Sepideh said with some excitement. "There is a Jewish community there, and my father is the rabbi. He is very old now, but he is well respected."

"You are Jewish?" I asked with more surprise than I meant to express.

"That is a story to share during dinner, Thad," Boos said. "You can wash up, and we will eat in about a half an hour."

I cleaned up and felt almost relaxed—only almost because I was still worried about Badri. Dinner was served in the living room, on the floor. There were pillows all around on a beautiful Persian carpet.

"Noosh-e jaan," Boos said as Sepideh brought out the food. "That means 'may it be delicious on your soul,' but it is used more like bon appétit."

"Thank you from my soul," I said.

The food was Chicken and Berberries according to Sepideh, whose English was pretty good for a person who only studied it in school and practiced with her father as a child and with her husband. The food was out of this world. Well, I guess I was out of my world, but it was as good as Hande had said. The berberries were tart, kind of like cranberries, only better. The rice with the chicken was the best I have ever had. We talked about Boos's career flying, first in the Iranian Air Force in the Shah's government, and then as an airline pilot. They were very nice not to pry too much into the reason for my travels or my supposed life in South Africa. I felt terrible about that lie.

"So, please tell the story of being Jewish in Iran," I said to my hosts.

"I am Jewish," Sepideh said. "My husband is Zoroastrian."

"Wow, this is an interesting story," I said.

"Not that interesting," Boos demurred. As he began to explain, Sepideh got up and came back with Saffron Tea and what she called *Kermani Gaz*, sort of a nougat mixed with pistachios and flavored with rose water.

"Like Sepideh said, I am Zoroastrian, and she is Jewish. We initially met because there simply weren't many non-Muslims to date. I am not allowed to marry a Muslim woman, and if Sepideh were to marry a Muslim man, she would have had to convert to Islam. Of course, far beyond the restraints of the law of the land, we fell in love, and the rest is history. Many of her family converted to the Bahá'í faith in the early 1900s and have since immigrated to Great Britain and Haifa, Israel, and a few eventually ended up in the United States. We have three children, and they are a mixed bag. You see, Zoroastrian identity descends through the father's line, unlike Jewish identity, which is defined by the mother being Jewish. So they can, in a way, choose either. Our oldest son converted to Shia, Islam. He lives here in Hamadan and has his own family. Our daughter is Christian and lives in Orange County, California, in the United States. Her husband is from Beirut, Lebanon, and they run a Persian restaurant there. My youngest daughter has chosen to be Jewish and lives in Tehran, where there are more eligible Jewish bachelors, but sadly, not very many."

"How many Jews and Zoroastrians are there in Iran?" I asked.

"Only thirty years ago there were over 150,000 Jews in Iran. Now we are around 30,000." Sepideh said. "Even still, there are more Jews in Iran than any Middle Eastern Country, outside of Israel. There are over 150,000 Zoroastrians in a land that anciently was ruled by Zoroastrians. They are dwindling in numbers, in part because of their laws. You have to be born a Zoroastrian in order to be one; you cannot enter into the faith from outside."

I would never have guessed, what with Iran's policies toward Israel," I said without thinking. "Oh, I'm sorry if that is a political issue that I shouldn't bring up."

"No, that is alright," Sepideh said. "Jews are considered people of the Book. We are generally respected as Iranian patriots who protect the Holy Scriptures. Here in Hamadan are the tombs of Daniel, Esther and Mordecai. It is Persian heritage marked by Darius, Cyrus, and Xerxes I that has protected the Jewish community in Iran. Some even suggest that Xerxes was the son of Esther and therefore Jewish from his mother's lineage.

"There is persecution now and then, but we have lived here for over two thousand five hundred years, and will continue, God willing. Iran is changing, though, so who knows. You know, Iran has over 370,000 "new Christians" from a Muslim background, that is, not counting the 60,000 historical Christians that have lived here for centuries, according to Open Doors, a nondenominational organization headquartered in Santa Ana, California. My daughter in the United States told me that over Skype just last month. I have no idea how they collect this information, so it could be wrong."

"I had no idea Iran was so diverse," I said.

"Well," Boos interrupted, "97 percent of the country is Muslim, and most of that is Shia. I suppose it is hard for any majority to accept anomalies. The Bahá'í have suffered terrible persecution since they are a religion newer than Islam. New anomalies are particularly seen as a threat. But enough of that. Tell us what brings you to Iran."

"That is a little hard to explain. I am on a quest of sorts. I am traveling to Yazd to meet with a Mr. Nabat, who is connected with the Zoroastrian temple there, and then to Susa, I think, along with a small archeological team, in search of an ancient book. It holds some family records of my brother-in-law, Badri Kabbani. We believe his family was connected to the King Darius court, where this book got its start."

"Is that who you are traveling with?" Boos asked.

"Yes, and I am really getting worried about him. He has traveled through Iran numerous times on business, so I am not sure what could be going on."

"I will do some checking if we don't find him at the hangar when we get there in the morning," Boos assured me.

"Sanai, the Persian poet, said, *Know him as a gift from thy Lord when a guest suddenly shows at your door*," Sepideh said with misty eyes.

"I am sorry, did I say something wrong?" I said, worried about the sudden mood change in the conversation.

"I have been praying for you, Mr. Allen."

Chapter 14

"**Y**OU HAVE BEEN PRAYING FOR me?" I asked, not sure what that meant.

"My father is a student of ancient texts," Sepideh continued, "both Jewish and Zoroastrian from the Achaemenid Dynasty, that is, the time of Cyrus, Darius, Xerxes, and Artaxerxes I. That was the time of the Jews release from Babylonia, the rebuilding of the Wall in Jerusalem, and the building of the Second Temple. In many ways, it was the rebuilding of the Jewish nation. It is so ironic that one of the world's experts on that period lives in the country that is obsessively focused on the destruction of the Jewish nation today."

"That is politics, Sepideh," Boos soothed. "That is not the Iranian people. And you know there has been a historical, although quiet, relationship between Israel and Iran."

"Yes. My father, as I mentioned, is very old. His life's work has been the area you mention with the book you seek. He has compiled this work into three notebook volumes, none of which has an electronic backup. He is unable to share this with anyone due to the present political climate. Although no one knows the full content of this work, it is sufficiently known by the government that we are concerned it will soon be confiscated and destroyed. We have been looking for a way to get it out of the country safely."

"And you are thinking I can help?" I asked.

"I am not assuming that, of course, but I would ask you to please consider it. And there is another reason I was praying for you," Sepideh said, now visibly nervous.

"Sepideh, I don't think we should bother Thad with our problems," Boos said.

"No, please, if there is something I can do, I will do it," I said.

Sepideh took a deep breath, considered Boos's caution and continued. "Bebakhshid, excuse me for sharing a personal story. My family is from Yazd. As I mentioned, my father still lives there. My mother passed away about ten years ago. Yazd is not a large place. The city itself now has a population of about 400,000, but when my father was young, everyone knew everyone."

"If you are going to share this with Thad, get to the point, Sepideh," Boos said softly.

"Let me jump to 2005, and then I will fill in the holes," Sepideh said. "In April of 2005, the President of Iran, Mohammad Khatami, traveled to Italy to represent Iran at the funeral of Pope John Paul II. By coincidence, but perhaps not, he was seated near Israeli President Moshe Katsav. Interestingly, both are from the small town of Yazd. The two had a brief conversation, although Khatami denied this for political reasons. Later, photos of the two that show them shaking hands and obviously talking were released in international media. The world has asked what the two presidents said to each other. Pleasantries? The weather? How are things in Yazd? I know what they spoke of. My father."

"Your father was the subject of two world leaders, who were—are—enemies?" I asked.

"Yes. Mohammad Khatami's father was friends with my father, as were the parents of Moshe Katsav. Both men grew up with a healthy dose of my father's philosophy and principles. He was a behind-the-scenes mentor to both men."

"That is very special, Sepideh," I said. "But why the concern in sharing that with me?"

"Khatami's government stood for noble principles, but he made many mistakes as he tried to balance obstruction by hard-line elements in the clerical establishment, people who did not want to see their power eroded with his goals. After the death of Grand Ayatollah Khomeini, Khatami and his Reformist Movement tried to topple the Iranian religious system of government and replace it with a secular one. He failed, and with failure comes retribution by the victors. They are planning to attack and kill my father. Khatami has also started two non-governmental organizations dedicated to building bridges of understanding: The International Institute for Dialogue among Cultures & Civilizations and the Baran Foundation. "Baran" means "rain" and is an acronym in Persian for "Foundation for Freedom, Growth, and Development of Iran, which is domestic in its focus. His enemies cannot attack these organizations directly, but they can attack them indirectly. "Obliquely" is the word my father uses."

"And you want me to get your father out of the country?" I asked.

"If you could talk him into that, yes," Sepideh said, "but I doubt you will be able to do that. The family has been unsuccessful. He is not afraid of dying, and his wife and ancestors are buried here. Iran is the only home he has ever known. I just wanted you to know how it is important to get his memoirs safely out of the country and to get them published. It would be more difficult for the government to have him disappear if his manuscripts were published and shared with the world."

"So, you said you prayed for me. You really prayed for some solution to this important matter," I clarified.

"No, my father said he knew a person was coming soon look-ing for a book, and he would be the one he could trust with his memoir," Sepideh said in reverence. "We have a belief here, Mr. Allen, that the host of a surprise guest will one day be the guest, and the guest will know what it means to be the guest."

"Saadi, another Persian Poet, said it this way," Boos interjected, "Do a good deed and throw it in the Dejleh River, and the Lord will reward you in the desert."

"I am impressed with your ability to quote ancient poets," I noted.

"Actually, it is an Iranian trait," Sepideh said with a smile. "We revere our poets, and their burial spots are huge attractions to all classes of people and across all religious and ethnic backgrounds. Most Iranians can recite lines from many famous poets, such as from the most famous poem in Iran, *Shahnameh* or *The Epic of Kings*."

"That Saadi poem sounds very much like the Bible, the Old Testament, I believe," I shared. "It says something like cast your bread upon the water, and you will find it after many days."

"You are religious, Mr. Allen?" Sepideh asked.

"I didn't think so when I started this trip, but I am beginning to think so now," I said, wondering how I could have plucked from my mind that scripture that I might have read years ago.

* * *

The next morning I was up with the sun, hoping to get back to the airport as soon as possible to see if Badri was there. Sepideh had a light breakfast ready for us, and she gave me a bag of dried fruits and nuts for my trip. We were back to the airport within minutes and did not find Badri there. I began to feel panic rise from my stomach to my throat and constrict my breathing. Boos said, "I will call my son. He is a lawyer that sometimes works with the local government. Perhaps he can find out what is going on."

Twenty minutes later Boos returned to the hangar and explained what he had learned. It seems our good Mr. Omidzadeh is an associate of another lawyer in the firm my son works for. They attend the same mosque in town. This is really a small place when you are talking about the professional class. Omidzadeh was transferred here from Tehran against his wishes and has been attempting to make a name for himself so he can successfully return to Tehran where his family still lives. My son made a few calls pretending to be a lawyer supporting Mr. Kabbani and found out that he is being held at a local facility in town. As we speak, he is going to visit him just to highlight to the authorities that he is known, and his case is groundless. As it turns out, Mr. Omidzadeh followed through on an injunction filed against Mr. Kabbani from a party in Turkey. This injunction has something to do with the stealing of money and kidnapping and has no authority here as it is obviously bogus (according to my son). The person he supposedly kidnapped is his wife. Omidzadeh decided to follow through on it because Mr. Kabbani is obviously a foreign Sunni and therefore suspect. What Omidzadeh did not realize is the multiple trips Mr. Kabbani has made in Iran and his business dealings are not paltry. Additionally, the Kabbani name is well known and respected, as is Badri Kabbani himself, in both Sunni and Shia houses."

"Yes, I was a witness to what was actually the rescue of his wife and my… my friend. This is a plot by some very evil people, the Hashshashin," I said while attempting not to reveal my part in this, "probably to try to find out where he is." "Why did I ever agree to enter this country in a lie?" I silently asked myself again. "Is there anything I can do?"

"No. I don't know about those groups, except the historical Hashshashin. My son was able to achieve Mr. Kabbani's release with the promise that he will clear this up once he returns to Lebanon. You should be on your way as soon as he arrives before anyone here changes their mind. Go straight to Yazd. Contact my father-in-law as soon as you can. As Sepideh said, he is waiting for you. Give my regards to Mr. Nabat in Yazd. He is a dear friend. How is it again you know of him?"

"He is the father of a friend of mine, Lydia Nabat. We are hoping he can shed some light on our search for the book we are looking for," I explained.

"Yes, well, if anyone can, it will be Mr. Nabat or Sepideh's father," Boos said. Travel safe my friend. Someone wants you to achieve your goal. I am honored to have participated in a very small way. Now I must be off to a meeting with airfield management. I am sorry I won't be able to meet Mr. Kabbani and apologize for our poor manners."

"Thank you, Boos. This has been a special experience. I treasure our new friendship, and I will let you know, somehow, how things go in Yazd and Susa."

With that, Boos was off, and I was left to wait and hope for Badri's quick return. I was starting to worry again when Badri finally showed up in a cab. He apologized again and again for leaving me stranded. I told him it was no problem, in fact, it was a great experience. I shared my evening with Boos and his wife, leaving out the key details of Sepideh's father. I was still processing that.

"Well, thank goodness for that man's son. I think I would have eventually been released, but his son expedited the process by many days. What do you say we complete that engine run and then get to Yazd? The team is probably as nervous about both of us as you were about me last night. Maybe Leyla is even more concerned about you than me," he added with a chuckle.

"Don't I wish," I said honestly. "Yes, let's get out of here. I need to get airborne to relax my nerves."

"I like that attitude, Thad. *Yallah!*"

We were airborne an hour and a half later. It had taken longer than we hoped to get clearance to complete the engine run and then get our fuel topped off. After safely departing the airport, Badri said, "We should land in Yazd in about three and a half hours. Why don't you take the stick and fly for a while? Keep the heading on 150 degrees and an altitude of 7,500 feet for now. Use the altimeter. That is only about 1,500 feet above the ground here, but that will be about 3,500 feet above the ground once we get closer to Yazd. You will want to descend subconsciously, so keep glancing at the instruments. We will adjust for winds aloft at the next checkpoint. I need to get some things written down before we get to Yazd. I will want to get that little issue of kidnapping my wife taken care of right away."

At first, I was a little rough handling the airplane, and my corrections made it worse. Badri didn't say anything, either to be nice or because he was concentrating on writing. How he could write with me trying to fly, I have no idea. Within a few minutes, I had the basic flying part more or less under control. A few minutes later I realized I was too tense, and my right arm was starting to cramp up because I was holding the stick too tight. I found that the plane could pretty much fly itself if I let it, so I did. "Is that how it is with people? Let them fly themselves and they can pretty much handle straight and level life? Ask them to turn or ascend and they might need the touch of a master's hand?" I wondered. "Or do we require a firm, uncompromising grip on the stick that ensures our safe arrival at our destination?"

"Badri, mind if I interrupt your thoughts for a second" I asked over the intercom.

"What is your question, Thad? I don't know if Leyla likes you. You will have to ask her yourself."

"Funny, ha ha," I said. "It seems to me Islam is spring-loaded to controlling people's lives. Is that just my outside perspective? I am used to the freedom of choice. Is that so bad? That is certainly not the case as Muslims see life, or am I totally misunderstanding what I have read and what I have experienced here?"

"Wouldn't you agree that there are some aspects of our life which are beyond our will and power? Some people are born healthy, others chronically ill. Some are born in a little village in the Congo, while someone else is born in London's West end. That doesn't make one person better than another, but some things are more within the grasp of one and not the other."

"Okay, I can agree with that," I said. "But it isn't decreed that the ill person cannot be healed, or that the villager can't find a better life somewhere else."

"I don't speak for all Muslims, Thad, but I think I am safe saying we believe that there are some aspects of our lives that are beyond our control." Badri continued. "These matters are predetermined by God. We call that qada, fate, or qadar, divine decree. Why these conditions are set for each person is a riddle with no answer for mere mortals. In Sura 21 of the Qur'an, it says 'He is not questioned about what He does, but they (the people) shall be questioned.'"

"You mean, we should not question our circumstances, just accept them?" I asked.

"We believe there are good, even perfect reasons why everything is as it is. We cannot understand it all; therefore we should not question it."

"But shouldn't we question fate enough to better ourselves? To rise above circumstance? What if our fate is to question our fate? Doesn't Islam put a high importance on knowledge and learning?"

"Yes, of course. Let me put it this way. Think of a watch. Some parts are round, some of the other parts are odd shapes. Each part is made of different materials, like glass, gems, metal, plastic, and so on. It must be this way for the watch to work, to achieve its created purpose. Now, should the minute hand complain that it has to move faster than the hour hand? Should the number 3 complain because it isn't a 12? Of course not. It must be so for the watch to function properly."

"I think I understand what you are saying, but if that is the case, that watch is the only thing allowed; the digital watch would have never been invented, or it would be heresy."

"I think you are stretching my metaphor. Our planning and actions are known as *tadbir*, while Allah's decisions and decrees are known as *taqdir*," Badri said. "We must follow the Law of the Harvest, that is, plant the seed and water the ground if we want to reap the fruit. But we cannot guarantee fruit. The weather is out of our control. Someone may steal the fruit. We may be forced to sell the ground where the fruit is growing. After all we can do, we may still not be able to enjoy the fruit. That is not to lessen the importance of *dua* or the effect and importance of hard work that might or might not lead to a new invention such as a digital watch."

"I am still struggling with the idea of forced conversions, not allowing the proselyting of other religions and the threat of death for choosing to believe another religion," I said.

"That is a difficult subject, as there are many interpretations of Qur'anic verses and *hadith*," Badri said. "Historically, Islam has not just been a religion, but the form of government. Thus, someone who chose to leave Islam became a political enemy as well. It was like committing treason, which is punishable by death, even in the United States. There are some in Islam that are against any form of punishment for apostasy, and they point to verses in the Qur'an to support their argument. They say the sword of death that apostasy wields cuts its own throat before reaching others. The Qur'an does say, 'Let there be no compulsion in religion: Truth stands out clear from error.' There are other verses that suggest punishment for apostasy, but honestly, I can't think of what they are."

"I can see that most religious people will always defend their religion," I said. "A Christian thinks his religion is the best and others are wrong. Jews will also think in the same way, but Islam says that if there is only one truth, and we are that truth, we are justified in forcing the truth or punishing what must be falsehoods."

"Be careful when you say Islam says…" Badri said. "That encompasses a wide spectrum of over one billion people in many lands, ethnicities, and histories. You are starting to sound like the news pundits that spend two weeks in the Middle East and christen themselves experts. I don't have all the answers, and I have lived, studied, and worked here all my life. All I can say is, you know quite a few Muslims, and have you met any more peace-loving, kind, and inclusive people than that group?"

"No. Those that I know personally are of the best people I have ever met. But some would toss in the crazies that have been chasing us."

"I think every religion has those few that use religion for their own selfish purposes or distort what is good into evil designs," Badri said. "There is much upheaval in the Middle East and Muslim world. I make no excuses, but the lingering effects of borders drawn by the British and the French after World War One, decolonialization, the end of the Cold War, the blessings and strains of globalization, power vacuums, and greedy opportunism all are playing a role in the chaos and upheaval that is bringing out the worst in the worst people."

"And the best in many as well," I said.

"Now it is up to the vast and silent, often fearful, majority to take their stand. That will be the test of the ages and of Islam," Badri said. "Not to change the subject, but to your right about thirty miles off our wingtip is Isfahan. We have 125 miles to go to Yazd, about 45 minutes. How are you doing?"

"If you are asking about my bladder, all is well. If you are asking if I am prepared for Yazd and what could happen there, yeah, I think I am ready," I said confidently.

"That isn't the 'can't wait to see Leyla,' thoughts speaking, is it?"

"Never entered my mind," I said laughing. "But if you can make this plane go just a little bit faster, that would be nice."

"Have I ever demonstrated slow fight in this airplane?" Badri asked. "It is amazing. With full flaps down I can fly at 53 miles per hour. With winds aloft often faster than that, I can actually fly backwards."

"Ha ha. Demo that some other time, thanks," I said.

Thirty-five minutes later we began our descent into Yazd. It looked dry and kind of desolate from the air. We crossed a busy highway that ran north-south and then turned to parallel the highway. That is when I saw the runway off to our left. We turned left and then left again, and we were lined up with the runway. I hoped our arrival would be less eventful than our visit to Hamadan. We landed right on the number 31 painted in white on the runway and taxied into parking. The sign on the building said "Safiran Airport Services." We parked and were in the process of tying down the aircraft when a young man walked out to the greet us. Since we had already cleared customs in Hamadan, Badri explained we would be staying for a couple of days and would let the Fixed Base Operator know our plans by tomorrow night. The young man was pleased to have a paying customer and offered to call a cab for us.

The city of Yazd was about six miles from the airport. We were at our lodgings, the Laleh Hotel, in no time. The cab driver made small talk with Badri. The hotel was a simple two-story structure that looked like an Iranian version of a Motel 6. Once we walked in, however, it was beautiful, with a decorative outdoor pool in the center courtyard with all the rooms facing the pool. It was peaceful and relaxing and very tidy. The stained glass windows above the doors and ornate wood and stone work were magnificent. Most magnificent, however, was the group that met us in the lobby.

"Where have you been, Thaddeus?" Leyla asked with worry on her face.

"It is good to be missed," I said, looking into her wonderful eyes. "You know, I left my home in California a little less than two weeks ago. I think I left the front door open actually, and no one is going to miss me. So thanks for that greeting, Leyla. We had a little detour in Hamadan. Bad gas in the airplane. Sorry we didn't call, but Badri's mobile phone was, uh, not available. So do you have the mystery solved?" I asked to change the focus of the conversation. I figured Badri could explain the details if he wanted to.

"No luck yet even talking with Lydia's father," Leyla said. "Lydia is with him now. We are all to dine together tonight, in just a few hours, so you ought to get cleaned up."

"I can clean-up quick. How was your drive?" I asked hoping to keep the conversation going a few more minutes.

"Long, dry, hot," Leyla said with a sound of finality. Her face looked stressed, or maybe frustrated.

I guessed that was the end of the conversation, so I greeted Hande, nodded to Irshad, and found my room. I was ready to go in thirty minutes and went looking for Leyla. I found Hande, but no Leyla. "Hande, can we go for a walk? Is this a safe area to be out in public? I need to stretch my legs, and I don't want to do so by myself."

"That sounds like a great idea. I am still stiff from our little drive," Hande said enthusiastically. He left a note at the front desk for Irshad. "Team protocol," Hande said.

We walked down the street to the right after leaving the hotel and came to an intersection and turned right again on

Basij Street. "I don't want to bring up this subject every time we talk, but could you tell me a little bit about Leyla. I really don't know her, or understand her."

"So you have a thing for Leyla Celebi?" Hande confirmed. "Most who know her are intimidated by her. Irshad isn't. The only thing that intimidates him is the image he has of himself. Leyla is beautiful, she is smart, courageous, and has a name that others treat almost like royalty. Every once in a while she opens the curtain slightly, and I catch a glimpse of the weight she carries, the responsibility of being a Celebi. Sort of like what your brother-in-law must carry as the oldest son of the oldest son in the Kabbani tribe."

"Well, the other side of the coin is, after you take away all the glitz and glamor of being nearly alone in the world, it isn't all that it's cracked up to be either," I said.

"I am not sure I follow what you said, but here is my quick explanation of Leyla," Hande began. "In Mevlana Rumi's family there is a long, some would say sacred, tradition of spiritual strength and wisdom in their women. That is not the Arab or Persian tradition where often women are to be seen in the home, invisible in pubic, and not heard. Rumi's grandmother was the Princess Khorasan. It was she who lit the spark, the quest for meaning in Rumi's father and then in Rumi. Rumi's mother, Mu'mine Hatun, also was very learned and had the spark of the divine in her. Her father was the governor of Balkh, which is now Afghanistan. Anyone who can rule that land has to be part superhero. Rumi's sister, Fatima Hatun, was already married when the Mongol hordes descend from Asia onto Balkh. Rumi's family left for Anatolia, but she decided to stay with her husband. She not only survived the Mongols but became known as one of the wisest women of her day. Many would seek her out for her understanding of legal matters, international diplomacy, and governance. Now that was just the beginning of the legacy of Leyla's female ancestors."

"What is *Hatun*?" I asked. "Another last name?"

"No, it means lady, as in royal birth. Leyla Hatun, Lady Leyla. It can also signify married or betrothed. Even the name Celebi has long been used in Turkish to mean well-bred and refined. In another time you could never be considered for a serious relationship with Leyla because you aren't royal. Today that isn't the case. In a way, we have come full circle because the first royals weren't royal either. They earned it."

"How in the world could I ever earn Leyla's attention?" I asked myself out loud.

"*No'ollohom Tor, ye'oolo iHlibooh*," Hande said. "The literal translation: We tell them it is a bull, they say milk it. In your case, this means something like you are asking the impossible. As much as I wish you the very best with Leyla, she is betrothed, and her family probably has other expectations for her."

"So what about you and Lydia?" I asked. "No interest on your part?"

"She is Zoroastrian, my American buddy," Hande said as if that explained it all. He looked at me and saw he needed more explanation. "She would have to convert to Islam, and I don't want to ask that of her. And even if she did, it would break her parents' hearts. I wouldn't, but additionally, I could not convert to Zoroastrianism. It is forbidden by both religions. Fate has something else in mind for each of us."

"My father was Catholic, and my mother was Protestant," I explained. "In its day that was pretty heretical, but it worked. They built their own fate."

"It doesn't work that way here," Hande said. "Your parents didn't worship two distinct concepts of God, and your mother didn't have to convert to Catholicism."

"Just live your life, Hande. I can understand if there were blessings that you could not partake of unless both of you were under the same religious umbrella, but in this case, it is about missing out on blessings because of the traditions of your fathers. My brother-in-law is a descendant of the Prophet Mohammed, but he married my sister who is a Christian. They are making it work. I admire them both for their courage. Maybe that is their fate, to swim upstream instead of just going with the current."

"For me, it is *or* not *and*. It is Lydia or my religion, not Lydia and my religion. I am not saying Badri's choices are wrong for him; I just know what is right for me."

"Okay. Why don't you both become Christian? Maybe if you defy everything you know, you will find your own paradise island," I said in frustration.

"So, are we talking about me and Lydia, or you and Leyla?" Hande asked. "Besides, I don't think joining another religion for the reasons you suggest is acceptable in any religion. Just as you can't do a right thing for the wrong reason, you should never do a wrong thing for any reason, no matter how right it feels. You should never just run from something, but always to something."

"Obviously, you have thought about this quite a bit. I am not sure I understand what you are saying, and I think I could come up with a good rebuttal, but that is not what you need is it?" I asked.

"Just be a friend," Hande said. "Life is hard sometimes, but life is good. If we are obedient and faithful, life is meaningful and from that comes joy when we need joy and peace."

"I believe in the abundance paradigm that all of you in Al-Ḥujurāt preach," I explained. "I also believe in a God that loves all humankind and doesn't punish someone because of where they were born or who their parents were. And, I think that paranoia, or a Middle East subset of the concept, is in epidemic proportions." We had returned to the hotel and were walking through the lobby.

"Paranoia? Isn't that a mental disorder?" Hande asked.

"Well, yes, I think so," I began. "It means thinking that the world is conspiring against you and even trying to hurt you. Something like that. What I meant was, people here believe they are persecuted because of their situation, and they can't escape because of their acceptance of fate. Society, family, and even God are conspiring against them. Just my theory, but I think there is a thing called pronoia, too. That is a belief that the universe is actually conspiring for our benefit and that there is a plan for our growth that creates the meaning you mentioned in our lives. We are not slaves, but free agents, and we are to act, not accept that we are only acted upon. The output, the precipitate of this plan, is our joy, our understanding, our peace. That puts us in a place where we become part of the plan, and we can touch the lives of others in respectful and meaningful ways. This gets into something I was explaining to Leyla about being a dot. When we accept that we cannot act for ourselves, we disconnect with others. We aren't allowed to make choices. We are betrothed to the choices of others. In a way, we become one-dimensional. Meaning, what we are all looking for—in the little things and in our life in general—you know, why we are here? Where did we come from? Where are we going? Meaningful answers come when we start seeing patterns, connections. It is like a spider's web. First, two points connect, then those connect with other points, and soon a complex pattern is created that connects us and tells us where we fit in life and provides reason and justification for our simple and mundane choices and the experiences we travel through."

"And when were you going to share all this with me, mizmiz?" Leyla said from her seat in the corner of the lobby.

"Oh, hi, Leyla," I said somewhat startled. "Well, I might have shared it with you on the flight from Germany to Turkey, but you didn't make the flight," I joked.

"Are you still mad about that?" Leyla asked. "If you must know, I was getting the Hashshashin off your flight—remember the visit with The Voice in the bathroom? I saw them come out, and they saw me. I attempted to get them arrested as I was sure they had weapons with them. Ever wonder why their pick-up of you failed so badly in Istanbul? It certainly wasn't the brilliance of the Furqaan."

Hande quietly slipped away whispering, "Warpath. Retreat!" and I was left with Leyla. I wasn't sure if that was good or bad. She seemed upset for some reason.

"Sometimes," Leyla continued, "being an actor requires that others, for our own good act in our behalf—they act upon us, for us. "Acting upon" is what a parent does; it is what someone does that cares about others. Being betrothed is not being a slave, it is accepting the love someone else has for you and accepting the meaning that comes from that love and often from a higher vantage point of understanding than you have. Now, it is almost time to go to dinner. It seems Lydia's father is a temperamental man and untrusting of outsiders, so you might want to keep your comments and thoughts silent tonight until we can assure him of our trustworthiness. Remember, the goal is to find the Kitab Kabbani, not to ask impossible questions that create discord within our team. See you out front in about fifteen minutes."

With that Leyla was gone, Hande was gone, and I was left alone. "The spider web had some serious breaks," I thought and wondered why I was even here.

Chapter 15

I FOUND MYSELF ENJOYING THE dinner party with Lydia and her father, Jal Nabat, Leyla, Irshad, Hande, and Badri. Probably at the suggestion of Hande, we were dining at the Talaryazd Restaurant. I had to admit the food was outstanding. Several times Hande had glanced at me and gave me the thumbs up sign as different dishes were delivered to our table. Mr. Nabat, who we found out had a Ph.D. in Ancient Studies, had been a professor at Shahid Beheshti University in Tehran. He was a thin man with gray hair and thick-rimmed glasses. He was dressed in nice clothes that could have used ironing. He also spoke English better than I did. British English. He had happily agreed to keep the conversation mostly in my native tongue, although I had not said a word after uttering, "An honor to meet you, sir." I am not sure what Leyla's warning was all about, as he seemed very friendly to the group. That was until Irshad brought up the reason for our quest. "Aghaye Nabat, we are in Yazd in search of an ancient manuscript or book. We believe the name is Kitab Kabbani, although it may carry a different name in Farsi. Several groups believe this book exists and are out to destroy it. We hope to find it first and preserve it."

"Yes, Lydia explained the whole story to me," Dr. Nabat said, suddenly losing his previous joviality. "I do not deal in rumors. I also do not deal with young people who are here to stir up possible trouble. The Fire Temple only continues to exist at the good graces of the present leadership in Tehran. I have sponsored your visas for archeological research, but I am not interested in aiding or abetting any action that might jeopardize the Fire Temple status." It appeared the discussion was closed. Everyone sat silent. Lydia looked down at her hands.

I swallowed and broke Leyla's request to remain silent. "Bebakhshid, Dr. Nabat, but I wanted to bring greetings from Majid Hvovi, Boos Hvovi as you may know him. He was very excited that I was going to see you and wishes you well."

Everyone stayed silent and just stared at me like I had cursed this distinguished old man. "You are friends with Boos?" Dr. Nabat asked. "He is a very fine man and one to whom I am greatly indebted."

"He mentioned nothing of this, but only that if anyone could help us it would be you. He said he knows no one that is more learned and more insightful in knowledge of the ancients."

"How is Boos? Is he still flying? You know it was his flying during the hard years after the Revolution that kept my family and me alive. He would secret in food parcels in his bags when he would fly through here. Some we consumed, some we traded for other things. This was before Lydia was born, so I have never mentioned him to her."

"He is no longer flying but has managed to stay in aviation. I had dinner with him last night, and he is doing well. He lives in Shahid Madani."

"So Badri, please tell us about Mr. Hvovi," Irshad said, hoping this new door might open up an avenue of cooperation from Dr. Nabat.

"I am afraid, Irshad, I do not know this person," Badri explained, irritated at Irshad's clumsy attempt to direct the conversation away from me. I didn't mind, as long as we were able to accomplish our goal. I really just wanted to share some news between friends, since we were together. "He is a personal friend of Thad."

Everyone turned to look at me with a little surprise in their eyes or fear of what I might say next. Dr. Nabat didn't appear to be phased by the odd conversation. "Yes, I had heard he moved to Hamadan. And his family is doing well?"

I caught him up on the three children and how his oldest son had helped get Badri out of a little pickle with Customs. I did not mention Sepideh by name, but only that his wife was also well. I wasn't sure how Dr. Nabat felt about Boos' marriage outside of his religion. I didn't want to bring another cloud into the room.

"I owe Boos more than I can express. I can see I have forgotten my manners, even after the pleading of my dear daughter."

"Paa ghadam," I said remembering the words from Boos about surprise guests bringing blessings into the home.

"Yes, young man, exactly," Dr. Nabat said. "Exactly. Will you please call me Jal? I do know of one person in Yazd that is more knowledgeable than me on the subject you search. He would not talk with anyone as he, too, is in a sensitive position. He is also quite old, and his health is not good. He may talk to you, however, young man. The night is still early. May I be excused for just a few minutes? I would like to see if he is willing to listen and to consider your request."

Dr. Nabat got up, came over to me and kissed me on the cheek. He had tears in his eyes. "Boos," he said with a chuckle. And with that, he was gone.

Everyone turned to Lydia and asked what her father may be up to. She said she did not know, and this was a side of her father she had not seen since before her mother had died. She looked over at me and mouthed a silent "thank you." I shrugged my shoulders, and my face got really hot. I hoped I wasn't blushing. Leyla was quietly watching me. Hande was watching Leyla watch me in between his own glances at Lydia. He had been trying to be inconspicuous in his study of Lydia all night. Irshad was talking to Lydia and Badri. The time passed quickly, and then Dr. Nabat re-entered the restaurant. With him was an elderly gentleman with a long white beard, a black hat with a brim, a white shirt, and a long black overcoat. He walked slowly and somewhat bent over, and he had a dour face.

"Mr. Allen, this is Avram Halevi. He is the Chief Rabbi of Yazd and a mentor to many," Dr. Nabat said.

"Yes, I know of your influence for good on many," I said.

Dr. Nabat turned to the group and explained, "Rabbi Halevi is a student of ancient texts, both Jewish and Zoroastrian from the Achaemenid Dynasty—that is, the time of Cyrus, Darius, Xerxes, and Artaxerxes. That was the era when the Jews were released from Babylonia, rebuilt the Wall in Jerusalem, and built the Second Temple there. That is where the Dome of the Rock now stands, but I am sure you know that. Of course, in the meantime, they built an empire that matched the greatest the world had ever seen, in size as well as philosophy of government, commerce, and the arts and sciences."

"Yes, yes, my dear friend," Rabbi Halevi said. "And you are at least my rival if not my superior in this area." He turned to look directly at me as if no one else was in the room. He studied me silently and then said, "Jal tells me you bring news."

"I bring the love of Sepideh to your ears, Rabbi. It is my prayer that her words through me can travel to your heart." I had no idea where these words were coming from, but I took the leap and hoped they were not too flowery or placating. I figured I would hear from Leyla or Irshad later if I had overstepped my bounds. I guess I had far exceeded the bounds she had already laid out for me, so I decided to go for broke. "Sepideh has sent me on an errand to collect your life's work and take it to safety and if possible take you to safety. Others may also want to visit you, but not for the same intent as we have come, due to your influence that reaches the good in people like Khatami and Katsav."

"So you are the one?" Halevi asked, now playing the part of the student instead of the teacher. "Are you the trusted one of my night vision?"

"That I don't know. In my most creative imagination, I cannot conceive that to be true. But Sepideh said you would know. I can only share the words of the poet Saadi who said, 'Do a good deed and throw it in the Dejleh River and the Lord will reward you in the desert.' My companions and I may be the Dejleh River." Everyone was looking at me like I was a baby that just spoke adult words. It wasn't that they were impressed, but surprised and a little uncomfortable because they didn't know how to react.

"Jal mentioned the topic of your quest on the drive here. That is partly why I came. You and I must talk in private, but yes, I will meet your group in the morning, and I might be able to shed some light on that which you seek. Jal does not realize it, or perhaps he is just hiding it, but he has insight to share as well. For now, I am an old man, and I must return to my home. I will meet with all of you tomorrow at ten o'clock at the Yazd synagogue. I bid you a good evening." He turned and left with Dr. Jal Nabat supporting the crook of the rabbi's arm. I could feel the wisdom that had just left the room.

"Nicely done," Badri whispered with a slight smile. Hande gave me a thumbs up from the other side of the table, possibly because dessert had just arrived. Irshad left without a word to pay the bill. Leyla was weeping. "What in the world have I done now?" I wondered.

"Leyla, if there is something I have said to upset you, I am truly sorry," I said as I approached her as we gathered our coats to leave. "Sometimes my mouth gets ahead of my brain. I know you asked me to keep quiet tonight. I should have listened to your advice if it has caused you to be so upset."

"It is now that your mouth is wandering into the wilderness, Thaddeus. Thank you for salvaging the evening and our meeting with Dr. Nabat," Leyla said, and with a smile continued, "I guess he is 'Jal' to you."

"Alright everyone," Irshad said as he returned from paying the bill. "Let's head back to the hotel and get some sleep. We will meet at eight a.m. to prepare for our meeting with Dr. Nabat and Rabbi Halevi."

"Before we go," Hande interrupted, "What was that about *Boos*—doesn't that mean *kiss* in Farsi? And then you mentioned a *Sepideh*, someone's life's work, and *Khatami, Katsav*? And where did you pick up that Farsi and quotes from Persian poetry? I thought we were the local experts, but honestly, I felt like I was in grade school tonight watching you, Thad. Maybe the Fahrunissa Scroll got you right. Talk!"

"There is an old American saying: even a blind hog gets an acorn every once in a while. I was just lucky to meet a very nice family. As for Rabbi Halevi, he has compiled his memoirs into three handwritten volumes, and he may want to get them safely out of the country. He has some direct influence on former Iranian President Khatami, who has now started up two non-governmental organizations that have the fingerprints of our rabbi on them and are angering others in the present Iranian regime. Former Israeli President Katsav is also from Yazd, and his parents were influenced by Rabbi Halevi. The incident in Rome of them meeting and talking may also indicate Rabbi Halevi's fingerprints. This has further angered people in Iran and Israel. The rabbi's life may be in danger."

"You got one thing right, Thad, and I ask you to remember it. You are the blind hog here," Irshad said. "You really don't know the society nor its complexities; thus, you are blind. A hog, as you point out yourself to be, is not *halal*, that is, permissible. Some, not this group, of course, consider you *makruh*—disliked, or even *haram*—forbidden. Please do not let your small successes tonight cloud the understanding of who you are and the tenuous situation you are in just being here."

"I was appropriately warned to stay quiet tonight," I began, looking over at Leyla. "I apologize for any problems I may have caused. Truly. It felt like the night was pretty much over and it may have been my only opportunity to pass on the words I shared. My motivation was not to hog the conversation, just to be friendly. And, thank you for your concern for my safety, Irshad."

The restaurant was located in the new part of the city as Badri explained it, to the far north of our hotel. Otherwise, I would have said I would walk back. I walked out the door and hailed a cab. Badri jumped in with me, and we were back to the hotel in about five minutes.

"Don't let Irshad get to you," Badri said as we approached the hotel. "In a rude way, he was right. On the other hand, follow your instincts. You have a natural sense of things that is open, honest, and fresh. People appreciate that. Continue to be you. So are you alright?"

"Yes, I am fine," I said. "Irshad doesn't bother me. I just feel bad that I did something to really upset Leyla. I have no idea what I did either, which means I could do it again and not even know it."

"Yes, I noticed she was a little emotional, but it may not have anything to do with you at all. Get some sleep and I am sure everyone will be fine in the morning."

"Good night, Badri," I said. "Thank you for everything, and honestly, there is nowhere I would rather be than right here, right now, with you watching my back."

"Here with me or with a certain young lady?" Badri asked.

"Irshad can really get obtuse sometimes, but he was right; I am a blind and forbidden hog, and that brings the harsh reality back to any dreams I may have. Good night. See you in the morning," I quickly added to close up the conversation.

I went to my room deep in thought. I changed and put on the pajamas Leyla had given me when we arrived in Konya. "That was a happy day," I said to myself. "I am sure things will be better in the morning, just like Badri said." My thoughts were interrupted by a knock at the door. I expected it to be Badri. I was surprised it was Leyla. The headscarf she had been wearing since we had entered Iran was hanging around her neck. Her hair looked free and fresh, but her beautiful eyes looked bloodshot and tired.

"Leyla," I said, trying to think of what to say next.

"Thaddeus, I know you may feel this is improper, but may I come in?"

"Sure. Of course. I'm an American. I know little of what is proper." I said trying to joke around and failing as I moved to the side so she could enter the room. I shut the door.

"Please, leave the door open. I want to apologize for saying what I said earlier," Leyla began.

I opened the door part way. "What, you mean calling me a *mizmiz* earlier tonight? I did think I had graduated to *Majnun*," I said.

"Well, that too, Majnun. I want to apologize for my explosion about your discussion with Hande about doing, or being compelled to do. I had no business jumping into your conversation. I guess I felt like I was the one being compelled, and I didn't like it, so I supported it. There is probably some psychological term for me."

"Yeah, I think there is," I said solemnly. "It is called being a normal human being. No one likes to be pushed around, not even indirectly through an overheard conversation."

"Well, I wasn't being normal, so I am sorry. I also wanted to apologize for telling you not to speak up at the dinner tonight. I was following Irshad's direction that he asked that I pass on to you, even though part of me was rebelling inside. If it weren't for you, we would have failed completely tonight, and perhaps the entire search would have ended there. As it is, we have more potential for success than any of us could have imagined. You are an amazing person, Thaddeus." Leyla was staring at me with an intensity that made me wonder if I could handle any more apologies.

"Irshad had some very good points. He delivers like a freight train, but I agree with him, even if it hurts a little."

"Irshad is wise in many ways, but he dances on ice like a hockey player," Leyla said. "I also think he is a little jealous of you."

"Is that a quaint Middle Eastern saying? I didn't know hockey was very big here," I said.

"Ha ha. There is a large Middle Eastern community in Detroit and Al-Ḥujurāt travels there often. I have become a Red Wings fan," Leyla explained.

"And the jealous part? Jealous of what?" I asked. "You two are betrothed—compelled in a good way, of course," putting my hands in front of me to counter a possible slug to the midsection. "I am a nobody fast-order cook from a dusty valley over seven thousand miles from here. In a few days if all goes well, I will be out of everyone's life and forgotten in a week. Well, I am afraid Badri is stuck with me."

"Do I know you better after only a few days than you know yourself?" Leyla asked with an increased intensity in her voice that matched her stare. "Do you know that your namesake Thaddeus was the first Christian Apostle to testify directly to a foreign king? He opened up the Christian work in Syria, Armenia and Persia. He was a simple farmer. There was a time, not long ago, I admit, when I thought you were a simple cook living a simple life. Just about every minute since I sat down next to you in that airplane you have proven that you are anything but simple."

"The Apostle Thaddeus had the mantle of the work; he was called to his position," I said. "I am not called to anything. I remain a simple cook. A simple Majnun. But I am good with that. I am not aspiring to anything other than to be the best person I can be. I just want to help you find this book, or confirm it doesn't exist. And except for one thing, I would happily return to my simple life."

"And what is that one thing?" Leyla asked, leaning forward slightly.

"Kebabs and kofte," I said.

Leyla hit me on my arm. "That's two things, Majnun!"

"Fine, I will tell you that one thing if you tell me what *Majnun* means," I said.

"No way," Leyla said. "You already made the agreement that you would tell me what species you are, that *mizmiz desperate,* or whatever you said."

"*Mizmiz depereo,*" I corrected. "Good memory. I guess I did say that. Okay, I will define my specie, and as a bonus, I will tell you that "one thing," if you finally define *Majnun* for me. Otherwise, I promise I will become the biggest *mizmiz* you have ever seen."

Leyla hit me on the arm again. "You already are Majnun. Alright, I will tell you, but," and she lowered her voice, "you have to shut the door for just a minute."

"Oh, a secret. I am really good at secrets." I said trying to keep things light even though I felt like the air pressure had just increased. I tried to clear my ears by swallowing hard.

"*Majnun* is from the epic love story called *Leyla and Majnun*," she explained while her face turned a pleasing cinnabar. "Don't say a word until I finish, please. These two people fall in love, but their romance is star crossed—sort of a Romeo-and-Juliet tale. Their romance was hidden and kept secret. In the Arabic language, the word *Majnun* means a crazy person. In addition, in Turkey to feel like Majnun is to feel completely possessed, as might be expected of a person who is literally madly in love." Leyla continued blushing, and I even noticed a little perspiration above her upper lip. "But the operative concept here is *crazy person*. You are a crazy person, Thaddeus. Who else would follow complete strangers through tunnels in Cappadocia and then risk prison and death traveling through Iran."

"Crazy or not, it fits, and I like it much better than crybaby," I said. "Well, now that we got that settled, I can get a good night's sleep. See you tomorrow." And I started to open the door.

"No way, Majnun. How do Americans say it? Spill the beans?" Leyla moved to block me from opening the door and pursed her lips trying to look as serious as she could.

"It appears we have a theme going," I said as I tried to match the intensity of her stare. I took a deep breath and said, "*Mizmiz depereo*. You know the *mizmiz* part. Literally, *depereo* is Latin for *I perish* or *I die*, but it is most commonly used to mean, well, I don't know many people that commonly use Latin," I said stalling.

"Get to the point, Majnun," Leyla said.

"It means I am utterly, hopelessly, madly in love."

"So you are an in-love crybaby?" Leyla asked with a slight smile.

"A hopelessly, madly-in-love crybaby," I corrected. "And before I talk myself out of it, you, Leyla Celebi, Leyla Hatun, are the only thing that would keep me from happily returning to my simple life." There I had said it. "I know I have only known you for days, not even weeks, but they have been the most significant days of my life. Like soldiers say of battle, it seems time has stopped, or it is running in slow motion. I have experienced every breath and remember every word, every sight, every taste. I know I am probably still your assignment, your project, but you, well, let me put it this way: I once saw a picture of two bullets from the American Civil War or the Crimean War, I don't remember, that had hit each other in mid-flight on the battlefield. They had smashed together hitting each other straight on." I put my hand on Leyla's shoulder, and I felt her tremble slightly. "What a crazy coincidence that their trajectories crossed at exactly that moment in time coming from opposite ends of existence. Those bullets fused into one."

"So, you never exactly said, who is it you love?" Leyla asked.

"Alicia, the lady at the ticket counter in New York. She had this amazing plastic smile," I said.

"That's what I thought. You are totally crazy." Leyla just looked at me, and I thought she might start crying again. Instead, a slight grin was growing on her face.

I couldn't help myself. "No joking, and I am not afraid to say it to anyone and everyone. I love you, Leyla. I love your sandstorm eyes, and I could talk to you for a hundred years and never tire of your thoughts, your understanding, even a few well-deserved slugs in the arm now and then. And I could hold your hand and be happy until the day I die."

Instead of getting upset, or simply leaving, those perfect lips said, "What are we to do, Majnun?"

"I don't know. For the moment, if that speech didn't scare you away, let's follow the Leyla-Majnun story line and keep it hidden, a secret between us. You need to sort out your feelings for me, and we are still in a very dangerous game. I wake up at night wondering if—when—the Hashshashin are going to attack, or when Efe will show up for the party. Al-Ḥujurāt has made the fool of both groups and that only ups the danger."

"Why are you talking business, Thaddeus? What about us? You wondered why I was crying earlier? You wonder why I was so upset with you? I have always been comfortable with my destiny. I love it. And that love was enough until I got to know you. Leyla and Majnun. It's just a story, told in literally hundreds, if not thousands, of variations in every country in the region, but almost all versions include the same basic facts. The father of Leyla refuses to let her marry Majnun. He arranges another marriage for her, and she marries. They both die of heartache."

"That is a story, Leyla," I assured her.

"That is reality, Thaddeus Allen," Leyla countered.

"Let's make our own reality, Leyla. I don't know how that can be, but it will be." I had yet to even hold this woman in my arms, and I could think of nothing else, but something held me back. Leyla seemed to know this and approved. She leaned her head toward my hand on her shoulder, caressing my hand with her cheek.

"Perhaps this is a silly dream. You don't even know me. We are from such very, very different worlds. I could not live in Madera, California, so far from home. And, although you like kebabs and kofte," she said smiling through her new tears. "You could not live in my world for very long without wanting really good Mexican food."

"So you think my world revolves around food?" I asked smiling, knowing full well what she was talking about.

"Yes. You rated *kofte* above me earlier!"

"Well, it is a little simpler to manage that relationship. And it conforms to my world as quickly as it does to yours. Alas, it is a new relationship each time it is consumed, so it is hard to create a lasting bond." I said just using time so she wouldn't leave quite yet.

"No matter what becomes of us, I know now I must find a way to reject my betrothal. You met my father; what do you think I should do?" Leyla asked.

"Just tell him straight out. I don't know any other way to handle the really hard things. Wait, I met your father? When?"

"On your flight from California to New York. Mack is my father," Leyla said. "With the relics exchange, we had a lot riding on you, and it was another stipulation of my great uncle."

"And your mother?" I suppose I met her at a ticket counter? Is her name Alicia, my first love, and that was a stipulation of your great uncle, too?"

"My mother passed away some years ago. I am sure she would have liked you, though," Leyla said.

"Oh, I am sorry for joking around. Your dad seemed like a very genuine guy. What an honor to meet him. Oh, no! He must have a pretty low opinion of me. I really was pretty much a *mizmiz*, a helpless *mizmiz*, as he guided me to the airport. I wish I had known he had the most captivating daughter in the universe. I would have…yeah, I probably would have just been myself. Doomed from the start."

"One of your most enduring qualities is your authenticity, Thaddeus, and your meekness. And by that, I don't mean weakness. I mean your humility and willingness to learn. You don't let pride get in your way or cloud who you are or your understanding of others. You are guileless and without pretense. I have never met anyone quite like you."

"It's my eyes," I explained. "But you have not told me how you feel about me?"

"I honestly don't know," she said. "I feel differently about you than any man I know. Is that love? At this moment I have no idea. I still feel an obligation to Irshad and to my family. I want to get over that obstacle first before I think any farther ahead. Can you be patient until then?"

"Only until I am 85, then I would need to think about moving on," I said.

Chapter 16

LEYLA LEFT MY ROOM WITHOUT another word. We pretended that nothing had happened between us, even though I suspected neither of us got much sleep. With the perspective of the new morning, I was grateful we hadn't kissed or even embraced, which for sure would have led to kissing, at least on my part. My expression of love and Leyla's indirect expression of the same feelings seemed almost comical, except that I still felt it. I had very little to give up and everything to gain—Leyla. Leyla had so much to discard and so very little to gain—me.

"Thad, are you there? Where did you go, buddy?" Hande was saying to me. "You had that million-mile stare, kind of like you were seeing a mirage. We need to talk before going to visit the rabbi. Wake up"

"Wake up, indeed," I agreed. "Sorry, just wondering what I was really doing here. My sister is safe. Maybe I should be back in California trying to get my old job back. Maybe get solar panels installed."

"You are a nut, my friend—crazy." Hande said, laughing.

"Yes, I have been told that," I said, not laughing.

"Well, they spoke wisdom. You aren't upset with our conversation last night are you? Those were deep topics, and answers are hard to come by. Today may shed some light on the questions of the book. I woke up excited and feeling really good about the day. Pronoia, buddy."

"I will accept your excitement with a little trepidation. Last time I saw you smiling this much you had just busted the windows of a moving car—from the outside," I said, starting to catch some of his excitement.

"Here comes Irshad," Hande said with mock reverence. "Let's show the proper respect and get ready for the business of the day. Listen and learn."

Badri, Lydia, and Leyla had also been listening to Hande. Leyla gave Hande a little push but obviously also appreciated Hande's reverent irreverence with Irshad, but it was also apparent they recognized him as the leader and wouldn't let anything get in the way of the respect he demanded.

"Get your game face on, Hande," Leyla said.

"Good point, Leyla," Hande said. "I need some Zam Zam. I can't believe I have been here way over a day and haven't had any."

"Zam Zam?" I asked.

"It's a popular non-alcoholic beer, one of the best soda pop drinks in the country, and it's only made here," Badri explained.

Not to be outdone, or perhaps to lend support to Hande's peculiar way of getting serious, Lydia added, "I haven't had any Douq either. What kind of an operation are we running here anyway?"

I only had to look at Badri, and he explained, "A yogurt soft drink."

"Now that we have the frivolity out of the way, let's get down to business," Irshad said. "We will travel in two cars. I will drive with Leyla and Hande. Lydia, you know the area the best; you drive the lead car with Badri and Thad. Let's keep our distance. I know we feel like we are on holiday, but neither the Hashshashin nor Furqaan have been neutralized and could have found us by now due to the bogus injunction put out on Badri. They would get as far as Hamadan and then follow us here from the flight plan Badri had to file."

"My guess is they will only be watching us," Leyla added, "letting us lead them to the next clue in finding the book."

"Could be, or they are as spun up as the Iranian Revolutionary Guard on 11 February," Hande said.

"11 February?" I asked, highlighting my ignorance.

"February 11 is Islamic Revolution's Victory Day. Mandatory state-sponsored demonstrations in every city," Lydia explained.

"Focus, team. Hande is right; there is a chance they could just try to end the search right here. After all, in the end, if no one is searching for a book that has been lost for seven hundred years, that is almost the same as destroying it. And both groups are not happy with us."

"The feeling is mutual," I said. "Have you ever considered a preemptive strike on them? Why let them do all the choosing of when, where, and how?"

"Not our game plan," Irshad said. "Al-Ḥujurāt is not an offensive strike team. We don't go looking for battles, and we avoid them if at all possible. Thad, you take the lead with the rabbi. We've got your back if you step out of expected custom or protocol. We don't know what we are looking for, so let's just see what Lydia's father and the rabbi have to say. Anyone should feel free to ask questions. We meet back here and sort out what we have learned and whether we stay, return to Turkey, or travel on to Susa if that still appears to make sense. If things go really bad at any point after leaving this hotel, our new rally point will be Dubai, the Marriott Marquis. You know the sign-in account. Badri and Thad, stick with a member of the team. Any questions?"

No one had any questions. Well, I had about twenty, but I didn't voice them. I didn't think I could take anymore Irshad eye rolls. We arrived at the Yazd synagogue within ten minutes of leaving the hotel. It looked quiet, even peaceful. We left Hande to watch the entrance and entered the building. Rabbi Aram Halevi, along with Dr. Jal Nabat, were waiting for us in the rabbi's office. "Father!" Lydia said, surprised to see her dad in the rabbi's office. "How wonderful to see you again so soon. I am feeling guilty that I have now seen you three times and not once actually visited you at home."

"I was asked to be here by the rabbi. He seems to think I can add some insight to your search. I doubt that, but I have learned over the years to listen to Avram."

"You are all very kind to an old man. Would you like some refreshments? I have bottled water, and I seem to remember your father mentioning you like Douq, Lydia. I have some in the refrigerator there."

"Thank you, Rabbi. I will take one to Hande; he is watching the entrance. I will return quickly," Lydia explained.

The rabbi turned to Irshad and said, "Now, young man, I understand you are the leader of this group. Could you explain what it is you are looking for and why you thought to come here to quiet little Yazd?"

Irshad explained the basics of the Kitab Kabbani, the Fahrunissa Scroll, briefly introduced Badri, and the non-violent highlights of the Konya and Cappadocia adventures. As Irshad was about to explain our reasoning for coming to Yazd and our plan to visit Susa, there was a commotion out front. Lydia ran into the room and said, "A car drove by very slow and then began shooting. Hande dove behind our cars and was not hurt, but both cars were damaged, I think."

"We must go," Irshad said. "We need to get you both to a safer place. Dr. Nabat, do you have any suggestions?"

"Slow down, young man," Rabbi Halevi said in a relaxed tone. "They will not return. Not during the day anyway. I predict we will have other visitors soon. All will be well for today."

"Rabbi, I respect your courage, but this was a warning attack for future action," Irshad said in a tone that was anything but respectful. "There are several groups that are intent on either destroying the Kitab Kabbani or keeping it from ever seeing the light of day. They will stop at nothing to achieve that purpose."

"Yes, yes, dear boy. I know this. They have been trying to find the book for centuries. They will not find it before you do," the rabbi said. He studied the startled looks of all of us, including Dr. Nabat, and said, "Oh, the book is very real, and it is within your reach, although it is not here. We will discuss this further after our new guests have departed."

Irshad began to protest when Hande appeared in the rabbi's study with three men carrying Uzi submachine guns. They spoke in Farsi, and Badri quietly whispered a translation. "Rabbi, is everything alright with you? Are these people your visitors or is there a concern?" the senior man asked.

The rabbi answered in Farsi. "Bless you, Daryush, for coming so quickly. These are my friends. Dr. Nabat is hosting a group of distinguished archeologists that will be visiting Susa soon. The good doctor suggested they visit with me before they departed. Interestingly, they are interested in your namesake, Darius I. I suspect the shooting was anti-Semitic but came to no harm. It is hard times we live in."

The senior person studied the group, nodded to Dr. Nabat, and paused on me. He walked over and asked me something in Farsi. I looked at Badri, who said something in reply and then turned to me, "He is asking who you are. I told him you are an archeologist from South Africa. He would like to see your passport."

I handed Daryush my passport I was grateful to have stuck in my back pocket earlier this morning. He studied it and looked at me again. He said in English, "You can't fake those eyes. Welcome to Iran, Mr. Allen. Anyone who is a guest of Rabbi

Halevi is under my personal protection. I wish you all well in your travels to Susa. It is a good time of year to visit there. Not too hot, but not too many tourists." He handed me back my passport, nodded to the rabbi, and left the room without saying another word.

"There, you see, my young friends. Everything is fine. The Revolutionary Guard has a small station just around the corner. I suspected they would have heard the shots. Daryush is a good boy and worries about me too much. Now, would you indulge an old man one further request? I would like to talk with Mr. Allen alone for a few minutes."

"The Iranian Revolutionary Guards carry Uzis and are friends with the local rabbi?" Hande asked out loud.

"Yes, the Israeli machine gun is the weapon of choice of the IRG," Dr. Nabat explained. "There is a strange, but very real relationship between the Israelis and the Iranians. Did you know during most of the Iraqi-Iranian War, there was a contingent of Israeli military personnel stationed here in Iran? Over 45,000 Uzis, along with nearly $100 million dollars in other weapons and spare parts, were flown to Iran, first through the Argentine Air Force, under the guise of the Argentine airline Transporte Aéreo Rioplatense, and then by ship—all facilitated by Israel. Iranian troops were trained by the Israeli Army, and pilots were made combat ready by Israeli pilots. Historically, the United States was also involved, if you remember the Iran-Contra Affair? That was also initially facilitated by Israel. Even the Israeli bombing of the Iraqi nuclear plant was coordinated with Iran. Of course, the Iranian government will deny all of this."

"I had heard rumors of some of this, but how can you speak of this conspiracy theory with such confidence father?" Lydia asked.

"The good rabbi and I were a part of the initial organization of this." Dr. Nabat said.

"Israel saw the Iran-Iraq War as an opportunity to ensure the perpetuation and safety of the One God minorities that had coexisted in Iran for thousands of years," Rabbi Halevi explained. "This included the large Jewish community, the Christians, and, of course, the Zoroastrian Community, which in some ways is the core of Iranian history. Khomeini and his radical ideology put these groups at risk. Israeli clandestine support ensured these groups some level of security and paved the way for eventual immigration of many Jews to Israel. Lest you young people think that this was purely altruistic, Iran is well aware that Israeli support allowed them to survive and even overcome the Iraqi invasion. That was a very dark time for many, however. I would like now to talk of brighter things. Now you must excuse us so Mr. Allen and I can have that private chat, about family."

"Will you need me for translation, Rabbi?" Badri asked.

"No. My English is not perfect, but what I want to talk about is not complex. Thank you, Mr. Kabbani." All in the room were surprised how well informed this ancient rabbi was, even about the identity of Badri. They left the room, and the rabbi motioned for me to sit close to him. He motioned me closer. I could smell black licorice on his breath. Then he took a small pinch of seeds from a small bowl and tossed them in his mouth.

"Anise seeds," the rabbi said. "I started chewing them many years ago when I quit smoking. Now it is just another bad habit. Some say it also increases the male sex drive, but I have not noticed that." The rabbi chuckled and then coughed.

"This is a strange conversation starter," I thought.

"Rabbi Halevi, your daughter, Sepideh, mentioned that you had your memoirs prepared. What can I do to help get them safely out of the country?"

"We will get to that. First, I have a warning for you. The groups after the Kitab Kabbani—there are several—are ruthless, as you probably know, but also far more cunning and treacherous.

Whatever you might have thus far experienced may only be smoke screens for their actual plans. Now, young man, here is the information I wanted to share with you alone. You might find it a little difficult to believe. I know I do." The rabbi looked in my eyes, smiled and continued. "Several months ago I had a dream that you would come to me through my daughter, Sepideh. Not you exactly, but someone would come. I accepted the dream as one of the many strange dreams old men have. I didn't really think anything more about it until last night when I met you. I am still having trouble coming to believe this dream was of actual events to come. I have never had such dreams, but I do know that is a gift to some people. This is all too strange of an experience."

The rabbi was either hesitating for an unknown reason, or he was simply gathering his thoughts, but we waited in silence for at least a minute. "Dear boy, your life is in danger. Unseen evil plots your death. I can't say why, but my dream left me with the impression that the danger comes from inside as well as outside your small group. I don't want this to sound fatalistic. Unlike my well-meaning neighbors who are all too ready to give fate the credit for the happenings of the world, I believe God knows what will happen, but he does not interfere with people's abilities to make choices which will bless them or condemn them. When God does nudge events, it is for the express purpose of blessings. Evil brings evil upon itself. Of course, evil will have its day of judgment and all that was will be plain for all to see. There will be no more lies."

"I accept your wisdom, Rabbi," I said. "I have no reason to fear anyone in this group, and, in fact, they have all labored to protect me in extremely dangerous situations. I still don't understand my purpose in all this. I am just a simple person who has lived a simple life. I do not desire this adventure, and I don't see what I can do to help find this book, if it really exists."

"As I said, young Thaddeus, the book most certainly exists. You will find proof of this in my memoirs, as you call my research papers. It is by the simple that many of the great things happen. David was just a shepherd before he was a king. Daniel was a simple government administrator under King Darius. And this brings me to your concern. Daniel was threatened from within the government by those who did not like the favor the king showed him, and without, if you count some hungry lions. Darius had established an early form of democratic governance, and his subjects had freedoms unheard of anywhere else in the world. Diversity was embraced. Those who wanted to use the power of the king for their own selfish interests saw Daniel as a way to weaken Darius and remove a dangerous rival. An associate of Daniel, a low-level government scribe of the court, began to record his own thoughts about the events he witnessed. Administrators of the day used scrolls of papyrus and leather."

"Papyrus from 500 BCE survived to this day?" I asked skeptically.

"That these could exist is a wonder, but a fact. I have seen and studied several papyri from Darius's and Xerxes's periods of rule. Several of these papyri indirectly reference a certain Zoroastrian scribe whose records shed light on the inner workings of the royal court and his association with Daniel. It became a small hobby of mine to watch for any suggestion or reference of this scribe and his family. There is a blank period in my studies of this family until these scrolls were again referenced in relation to a negotiation with Nabataeean traders of frankincense from the Arabian Peninsula. The reference spoke of Silacus, a commander in Darius's army, who embarked from Bandar Abbas to the Red Sea around 522 BCE. In his company was this scribe. His name was Tahmasp the Scribe. Now in 90 BCE the family of this scribe is referenced as returning to Bandar Abbas as his forefather left. You see, in those days, there were not last names, only Rashid of this town, or Akbar of this father, or Farhad of that trade. Iran didn't officially start using surnames until 1919. I have only been able to keep track of the family through the referenced scrolls. Now in 90 BCE this family surfaces again: Tahmaspzadeh, son of an ancestor named Tahmasp. He was involved in the frankincense trade.

"This is wonderful history, but how does this lead us to the book?" I asked.

"Tahmaspzadeh had the family scrolls. The Bandar Abbas customs report mentions them, in detail. It appears there was some concern about the content of the scrolls because the manifest also includes the note *family history and religious commentary*. I assume in the comings and goings of this family over the centuries, these scrolls were not noted, since they were personal items. Fortunately, we had a zealous customs agent on this date."

"So how do you know this was, or is, connected to the Kitab Kabbani?" I asked.

"Let's share that with the whole group, so they don't feel completely left out of this adventure," the rabbi said. "I have one other piece of information I need to share with you alone. You have asked how you are connected with this book and chain of events. I need to share something with you about your own family. For this, I need to invite Jal Nabat to enter our conversation. Would you please invite him in?"

I went in search of Dr. Nabat and found him talking with Lydia and Hande. I asked him to return with me, and he did so. We were back with the rabbi in minutes.

"My friend, Jal Nabat," the rabbi began. "Could you now share with us what you told me six months ago?"

Dr. Nabat looked at the rabbi and then at me. "What I am going to share with you is to be kept only between the three of us. Not even my daughter Lydia is to know of this. Is that agreed?"

"Yes, Dr. Nabat. I will keep your secret," I said, wondering what I was getting into.

"Very well. As you know, our family has been Zoroastrian for centuries, perhaps a millennium or more. One of the major points of the Zoroastrian doctrine is that a virgin would bear the Saoshant, a man who would save the world. Does that sound familiar?"

"Yes," I said. That sounds like the Christian doctrine of the birth of Jesus Christ."

"Yes, that is what I thought too," Dr. Nabat said. So I started looking at the intersections of belief between Zoroastrianism and the Judeo-Christian history. Judaism and Zoroastrianism lived side-by-side for centuries. My research could not scientifically prove that Zoroastrianism influenced Judaism or that Judaism influenced Zoroastrianism. What I can say is that Abraham and Moses both lived long before Zoroaster, the founder of Zoroastrianism. The Torah that Rabbi Halevi knows so well, the Law of Moses, the Psalms of David, and the scriptures foretelling the coming of the Messiah, and many of the prophets all had written before Zoroaster was even born. Therefore, it is common sense to conclude it is more likely that Judaism influenced Zoroaster than vice versa, at least that has been my recent conclusion.

"Judaism from day one has been monotheistic. Zoroastrianism is dualistic in nature and historically has distant roots in polytheism. In any case, I believe the evidence for the inspiration of the Bible is sufficient to accept it as the authentic and original scripture. I know from my studies that the earliest written record of Zoroastrian scripture was in the fourth century AD. The oldest manuscript we have of the Avesta—the principle scripture of Zoroastrianism—is from the fourteenth century AD, nearly a millennium and a half newer than the Torah and the Christian New Testament, and seven hundred years after the Qur'an. We do have records, however, of three Zoroastrian Magi traveling to Bethlehem in Judea to worship the Christ child, and we have the converting of the Zoroastrian king and thousands of Zoroastrian followers in Persia shortly after Christ's death and resurrection."

"You speak as if you were Christian, Dr. Nabat," I interjected. "Is that the big secret?"

"No, well, yes and no." Dr. Nabat looked at the rabbi with surprise. The rabbi nodded. "I have secretly converted to Christianity—much to the disappointment of my dear friend, Rabbi Halevi," Dr. Nabat said. "Perhaps one day I will convert him."

"When pigs are kosher, my dear friend," Rabbi Halevi said with a smile.

"There is more that I must share with you, however," Dr. Nabat said. "Please do not share my conversion with anyone. It is hard enough to be a Zoroastrian in Iran. That I am involved with the Fire Temple has historical significance that affords a small amount of protection. Also that I have achieved a small level of prominence in my historical studies would make my conversion news that would upset the status quo here in Yazd. Were I to make my conversion public knowledge, it would put my family in great danger."

"Your secret is safe with me, Dr. Nabat," I said.

"Thank you, young man. And thank you for not quizzing me on my conversion. It happened over a long period, and today is not the time to review that part of my history. But this brings me to the second point, the point important to you. The point that must also remain a secret." Dr. Jal Nabat opened a bottle of water, took a long drink, cleared his throat and continued. "In my intense study of early Christianity in Persia, I, of course, came across your namesake, the Apostle Jude, also known as Thaddeus. A fascinating man. A simple farmer, you know."

"Yes, so I have been told," I said.

"He brought Christianity to Persia and converted tens of thousands of Jews, Zoroastrians and pagans. He carried the Sword of Longinus—the spear that pierced the side of Christ on the Cross—to the Armenians before he came to Persia. According to tradition, Thaddeus died a martyr by spear about 65 AD in Beirut, what was then a Roman province of Syria. Some time later his body was taken from Beirut to Rome and placed in a crypt in St. Peter's Basilica. I wanted to share that brief history of your namesake because I have reason to believe he is your actual ancestor."

Chapter 17

"MY WHAT?" I ASKED, SURE I had heard Dr. Nabat incorrectly.

"You, young man, may very well be descended from the Disciple of Christ, Jude Thaddeus," the rabbi said to add his confirmation. "I am not swayed by his message, but Thaddeus of old did exist, and of all the Apostles, his is the only family of which there is a record that continues beyond his death. Many of the Apostles and early leaders of the followers of Jesus had families, and some wives and children even traveled with their patriarchs on their missions. Thaddeus, however, is the only one whose family records were maintained after the Apostles' martyrdoms. I have studied the records provided by Jal Nabat, and I find them convincing."

There was a loud pounding on the door, and Irshad walked in. "Forgive me, Rabbi, for my intrusion, but we must speak with Dr. Nabat so we can be on our way. We have troubled you enough and fear our welcome is far overspent."

"Yes, it has," the rabbi said under his breath loud enough for me to hear, but not for Irshad to hear by the door. "I am so sorry to hold your group up. We are almost through speaking with Thaddeus here. We were just closing our comments. Give us just a few more minutes, please."

"Of course," Irshad said masking his frustration. "We will be ready to leave as soon as is convenient, Dr. Nabat."

"Thank you," Jal Nabat said.

"He means well," I said when the door closed. "He is the group leader, and he doesn't like to be left out of anything. I apologize for his manners."

"Or lack of manners," the rabbi said. "Please continue, Jal."

"We know Thaddeus and his wife, Mary, had at least one child, perhaps more, because we have a record of his grandchildren being summoned by the Roman Emperor Domitian to Rome in 95 AD. Domitian was a pagan and concerned about the growing popularity of this new religion, Christianity. Like a despot earlier, Domitian commanded that all direct descendants of King David should be slain. If you know your Bible history, you will know that Thaddeus was either the half-brother or the cousin of Jesus," Dr. Nabat explained. He picked up a document that had been sitting on the rabbi's desk. "I brought this along to read to you, Thaddeus.

"Wait," I interrupted. "The Apostle Thaddeus was a blood relative of Jesus?"

"Yes, he was, through both his mother and his father, actually," the rabbi confirmed. "He was called the brother of Jesus in the Christian's New Testament. But that requires a little clarification using the Torah. Lot is called the brother of Abraham when actually he was his nephew. Laban is called the brother of Jacob, but he was his uncle. The sons of Oziel and Aaron, the sons of Cis, and the daughters of Eleazar are called brothers, but they were cousins. Thaddeus was the son of Cleophas, who was married to the sister of Mary, the Mother of Jesus. Thus he was directly related to Jesus. Cleophas was the brother of Joseph, the earthly father of Jesus, through which ran the lineage of King David."

"Wow, I didn't know that," I said, not sure what else to say.

Dr. Nabat cleared his throat to read the document he held in his hand. "Hegesippus, a chronicler of the early Christian Church, relates these facts in the following words: *Of the family of the Lord, there were still living the grandchildren of Jude, who is said to have been the Lord's brother [i.e. first cousin] according to the flesh. Information was given that they belonged to the family of David, and they were brought to the Emperor Domitian by the Evocatus. For Domitian feared the coming of Christ as Herod also had feared it. And he asked them if they were descendants of David, and they confessed that they were. Then he asked them how much property they had or how much money they owned. And both of them answered that they had only nine thousand denarii, half of which belonged to each of them; and this property did not consist of silver, but of a piece of land which contained only thirty-nine acres and from which they raised their taxes and supported themselves by their own labor. Then they showed their hands, exhibiting the hardness of their bodies and the callousness produced upon their hands by continuous toil as evidence of their own labor. And when they were asked concerning Christ and his kingdom, of what sort it was and where and when it was to appear, they answered that it was not a temporal nor an earthly kingdom, but a heavenly and angelic one, which would appear at the end of the world, when he should come in glory to judge the quick and the dead, and to give unto every one according to his works. Upon hearing this, Domitian did not pass judgment against them, but, despising them as of no account, he let them go, and by a decree put a stop to the persecution of the Church. But when they were released they ruled the churches because they were witnesses and were also relatives of the Lord. And peace being established, they lived until the time of Trajan [98 A.D.–117 A.D.]."*

I was stupefied and struggled to make any connection at all to me. "So the Apostle's grandchildren lived. What does that have to do with me?" I asked.

"The Christian Church kept very good records," Dr. Nabat said. "These two grandchildren, humble leaders of the early Church, as the record states, and close blood relatives to Jesus Christ, had escaped death and from then on quietly kept their heritage a secret so as not to become a political target like the leaders of the Church were by the time of the Nicene Council. From what my research suggests, they served almost anonymously throughout the centuries. I believe someday many walking the earth will be surprised at their rich spiritual heritage as descendants of early Church leaders and people of the book. They will be asked, what did you do with that heritage? They may have little to say in their defense."

"So you were able to trace my heritage?" I asked.

"Actually, the tracing went the other direction," Dr. Nabat began, "which is typically much more complicated because instead of building a family tree to an ever decreasing number of ancestors, there were literally hundreds of lines going the other direction."

"I don't mean to sound disrespectful, but honestly, I find it hard to believe that you were able to do this. With the death of my parents, I lost all possible links to family history and haven't honestly tried. I can't believe you were able to go the other direction and find me—the proverbial needle in the haystack. Admit it. Isn't it really just a coincidence that a guy named Thaddeus showed up on your doorstep, and you grabbed at this to explain your riddle?"

"We knew before you arrived," Rabbi Halevi said. "Your family has a history of every few generations naming the oldest son Thaddeus. That quickly eliminated most family lines leading out from those original grandchildren. Your great grandfather Thaddeus led us to you. We, of course, didn't know you would ever come here, and actually, it appears to be a miracle that you did. The circumstances in which you found us are more than curious. We did not connect the dream that Rabbi Halevi had a few months ago to this genealogy until last night. After we left, we had a long conversation and reviewed our research. It is a fact that you are here and that we know of your family through the marriage of your sister to Mr. Kabbani in the other room."

Dr. Nabat continued, "Now we can't be one hundred percent certain that we have your pedigree verified, but that your line distinctly continues the use of Thaddeus every second or third generation is significantly unique enough that I believe we have the right family line."

"What does this mean for me?" I asked.

"Nothing really, and everything," Dr. Nabat said smiling. "Every generation must prove itself. Yet, in proving yourself, you add to two thousand years of family history that finds a Thaddeus again in the Middle East, in Iran. It is your legacy and perhaps something you were preordained to do—that is, find the Kitab Kabbani."

"I thought you said you didn't believe in fate?" I asked.

"I do not," Dr. Nabat said. "I said preordained, not predestined. It is your choice to take up the family heritage we have presented to you and the quest of finding the Kitab Kabbani. Now, Thaddeus…I love calling you that name; it connects me to a sacred past. You must keep this probable family connection to yourself for now. There are of course many more descendants of Thaddeus the Apostle, but we have not been able to track many due to the lack of direct information outside of your family line. It may bring additional attention to you that you do not need right now, just as my conversion to Christianity would bring to me. You must also be cautious. There is danger inside your little group. Be careful who you trust."

"Yes," added Rabbi Halevi. "and if my brief study is correct, Saint Jude Thaddeus is known in the Catholic world as the patron saint of lost or desperate causes. When everything seems hopeless, the support of Thaddeus is often sought. That may be the case in this Kitab Kabbani quest," the rabbi quipped with a chuckle.

"Why me?" was all I was able to ask.

"We must call in the rest of the group and provide them with the guidance the rabbi and I have for them. But before we do, let me answer your question through your namesake," Dr. Nabat said. "At the Last Supper, on the night before Christ's crucifixion, Jesus shares these thoughts with his disciples: *He that hath my commandments, and keepeth them, he it is that loveth me: and he that loveth me shall be loved of my Father, and I will love him, and will manifest myself to him.* Thaddeus then humbly asks, *Lord, how is it that thou wilt manifest thyself unto us, and not unto the world?* What a beautiful expression of love and meekness in the question of Thaddeus. He isn't brash or assumes he knows the answer. He is without pretense or guile and can't imagine the world without the knowledge of the Christ or His teachings."

I swallowed hard. Weren't those almost the same words Leyla had used to describe me last night? I quickly washed that thought from my mind. Now I was making connections where I doubted there were any. I focused again on the words of Dr. Nabat.

"Jesus knew the heart of Thaddeus and answered with equal tenderness and compassion."

"He said, *If a man love me, he will keep my words: and my Father will love him, and we will come unto him, and make our abode with him. He that loveth me not keepeth not my sayings: and the word which ye hear is not mine, but the Father's which sent me.* Thaddeus was assured that Christ would offer His perfect example and message to anyone and everyone who loved him. You see, Thaddeus was still viewing Christ's message from the Jewish perspective that the Messiah would come to establish an earthly, political kingdom—something religions of the Middle East had done and continued to do for millennia, that is, aligning religion with power and governance. For perhaps the first time, Thaddeus understood that Jesus was speaking of touching and redeeming the hearts of all those who would welcome him. Thaddeus realized it was not us vs. them, but an abundance concept of ALL, and he set out to share this revolutionary news. Thaddeus faced the mobs and those threatened by his disruptive message. Just before he died, Thaddeus reportedly turned to Simon, the Apostle and traveling companion, and calmly remarked, *I see that the Lord is calling us.* The world stoned Thaddeus to near death, and one person speared him to finish the evil deed." Looking directly at me, Dr. Nabat said, "In other words Thaddeus, it isn't about you at all. It is about what you can do for those around you."

"Now, let's bring in the rest of the group and see if Jal and I can help you find this book," the rabbi said.

I asked the group to come in and turned the meeting over to Irshad to hopefully reduce the tension he had been feeling of being left out of my discussions with Rabbi Halevi and Jal Nabat.

"We are glad you have had time to catch up on your daughter and her family, Rabbi, and your close friend, Dr. Nabat, but we would like to take just a few more minutes of your time," Irshad began. "We have come to you in hopes that your wisdom could lead us to the Kitab Kabbani or provide clear proof that it no longer exists. If you have any information to guide our quest, we would greatly appreciate it."

"Thank you, Irshad," Dr. Nabat said. "We do indeed have some information that might aid you. As you may know, the Yazd Fire Temple is the ninth and newest of the Atash Behram or Fire of Victory. This is a purification fire that has been burning continually since 1934 in the case of this temple. Zoroastrians come to the temple to worship, but the temple is also an educational center and a school that teaches the Dari language, not the Dari of Afghanistan, but of ancient Persia. It is a closed language we do not teach to non-Zoroastrians, and a growing number of

Zoroastrians do not speak it any longer. In this language is a rich heritage of history, and in your case, information that may lead you to the Kitab Kabbani. All those outside of the small circle of Zoroastrian intellectuals are not privileged to have access to this information."

"Enough of an explanation, good doctor," the rabbi said, obviously tired from his discussions with me earlier. "Let's get to the key points that will most interest our young adventurers."

"Yes, you are right, Rabbi," Dr. Nabat said. "I just wanted to highlight why this information has not come to light before now. Could you first share your information, Rabbi?"

The rabbi smiled at Badri, then turned his attention to his papers and began, as he had with me privately just a few minutes before. "There is an interesting transcript in connection with Silacus, a commander in Darius's army who embarked from Bandar Abbas to the Red Sea around 522 BCE. In his company was a scribe. His name was Tahmasp the Scribe. Later, in 90 BCE the family of this scribe is referenced as returning to Bandar Abbas. I have only been able to keep track of this interesting family through the Tahmasp name and several references to some family scrolls. There were many records of political, religious, and business dealings, but very few had the luxury of recording family matters unless you were a king.

"In 90 BCE this family surfaces again—Tahmaspzadeh, son of an ancestor named Tahmasp. He was involved in the frankincense trade at the time and had just returned from the Arabian Peninsula. The Bandar Abbas customs report mentions them, in detail. It appears there was some concern about the content of the scrolls because the manifest also includes the note *family history and religious commentary*. I assume in the comings and goings of this family over the centuries, these scrolls were not noted since they were personal items. Fortunately, we had a zealous customs agent on that particular date."

"And you are suggesting these scrolls are the Kitab Kabbani?" Irshad asked.

"No, but I believe they were the early records that were eventually transcribed into the Kitab Kabbani," Dr. Nabat said. "This particular family of scribes and traders maintained certain habits that made them easier to track through time than most ancients. It was as if they knew they were going to be traced through time and they wanted to help that along.

"This family maintained property in Susa from the time of Darius and was able to maintain ownership through the dynasties that followed. Another Tahmaspzadeh caught the attention of Pacorus II of Parthia, the dynasty of the day ruling much of what is today Iran and Eastern Iraq, who in 87 AD sent lions and Persian gazelles to Emperor Zhang of Han. Pacorus II requested Tahmaspzadeh support this expedition in which he successfully returned with silk, spices from India, and fine leather, which was then purchased by Roman merchants. Tahmaspzadeh may also be responsible for the first caravans traveling through the Parthian Empire to bring Roman luxury glasswares to China. It was this man's son who was christened Kab."

"Christened?" Lydia asked her father.

"Yes, by this time the Tahmaspzadeh family had converted from Zoroastrianism to Christianity. In consultation with Rabbi Halevi, we originally thought the name Kab signified honor or high rank, but we believe it had an additional meaning bestowed by the Parthian court which meant *to drink eagerly*. That is, to drink in knowledge and experience of lands, peoples, cultures and languages. Within a few generations, this family became known as Qabbani, that is, House of Kab. You may know much of this already, Mr. Kabbani, but it is important to your search for the Kitab Kabbani.

"The family may have converted to Christianity in part because the Romans, in fighting the Parthian, began to employ their allies the Nabataeans to wage war not only on the Parthian southern flank but also in disrupting trade. The Qabbani family had long been connected with the Nabataeans and the frankincense trade. The Parthian court did not favor Zoroastrianism, and it wasn't until the Sassanids several hundred years later that Zoroastrianism was again adopted as the official state religion of the empire."

"You are digressing, Jal," Rabbi Halevi said. "Perhaps I will take up the account from here if that is alright with you?"

"A perfect time to take the reins, Avram, as this is about where your research again takes precedence."

"In 313, when Constantine I proclaimed Christianity to be a tolerated religion in the Roman Empire, the Sassanid rulers of Persia adopted a policy of persecution against Christians, yet many Christians held to their faith. It appears that the Kabbani family didn't, but not because of persecution. There is a letter dated 326, a year after the First Nicaean Council where the Kabbani patriarch at the time rejected parts of the Nicene Creed as this new creed did not conform with the Holy Bible. Indeed, many bishops disagreed with key precepts that men had decided in that council. Constantine's son, Constantius II, sided with Arius, for example, that God the Father and Jesus Christ were separate and distinct beings. But now I digress as well.

"This letter hints at the Kitab Kabbani and at one time may have been protectively stored at the Church of St. Mary in northwestern Iran, which interestingly is the second oldest church in Christendom after the Church of Bethlehem in the West Bank of Palestine. Perhaps due to the international trade contacts of the Kabbani family, a Chinese princess contributed to the Church of St. Mary's reconstruction in 642 AD and has her name engraved on a stone on the church wall. Not that it matters for your search, but the Italian adventurer Marco Polo also notes the church in his written history.

"I would send you to this church to find the book, but Susa should still be your destination. It was here that the Kabbani family returned during the reign of Yazdegerd the First who was very supportive of Christians. Susa at this time had a significant Christian population and later was a diocese of the Church of the East between the 5th and 13th centuries. There is a very real possibility that the Kitab Kabbani has returned there, just as the Kabbani family did so many times through history."

"Or," Dr. Nabat interjected, "it will provide the information as to where is the book's final storage place. Remember, as Mr. Kabbani will tell you, he is Sunni Muslim—and a descendant of Islam's Prophet, Mohammed. The rabbi and I disagree on this. I have no proof to back it up, but I believe you will find guidance left in Susa by the Kabbani family as to the actual location of the book."

"Thank you for the history, Rabbi Halevi and Dr. Nabat. Some of that has only existed as family folklore, not proven history, and some of it I have never heard. I will record this for posterity," Badri said with emotion in his voice.

"Yes," the rabbi said smiling. "I would expect nothing less from a Kabbani. It is in your genes."

"So we should go to Susa, but where? Is there a library, or a person we should contact?" Irshad asked somewhat agitated. I don't think history was one of his favorite subjects in school. Actually, I think fighting after school was his favorite subject. I am only guessing at that because I was sometimes the homework in that extracurricular subject.

"Susa was destroyed three different times," Dr. Nabat said. "Once in the 7th century BCE, once in the 7th century AD and once in the 12th century AD. A book housed in an archive would not have survived. One of the few places invaders didn't bother with was the cemetery. Ironically, many of the ancient cemeteries of that area were unearthed by *friends,* and their artifacts now reside in the Louvre in Paris, France—something like two thousand offering and storage pots. Someday you should visit there, Mr. Kabbani. There may be family history there that will shed more light on your ancestors. Luckily, the most recent cemetery that is anything AD is still there.

"I don't understand," Hande said. "How can the dead talk about the future? I mean, they died, but the Kitab Kabbani hopefully lived on. How can they tell us anything about the future?"

"Because cemeteries are as much for the living as they are for the dead," Dr. Nabat explained. "Graves need to be maintained. Most cemeteries in Iran kept very good records of their benefactors. Find the most recent graves of the Kabbani family and trace the records connected to that grave, and you should be able to come up with further names, addresses, and other potentially valuable information."

"So it is as simple as going to the cemetery in Susa and finding the records from the Kabbani family?" Irshad asked.

"Not quite," Rabbi Halevi said. "Records were not correlated by family; they were only kept for each specific grave. In most cases, lists of graves were not kept either. First, you need to find the grave, then you can find records associated with that grave. You may also need to check more than one cemetery. We aren't sure exactly where the traditional land of this family is exactly located. Susa is a region, not just a single ancient city where the town of Shush now exists. There are at least four cemeteries that are potential candidates."

Rabbi Halevi gave Irshad a list and descriptions of the locations of the known ancient cemeteries in the Susa area. He also explained that we would need to find the local caretakers at each cemetery that could direct us to the records of those graves.

"Please give me or Dr. Nabat a call if you run into any records you can't decipher or that simply don't make sense. I wish you all the very best in your travels, especially you, Mr. Kabbani, as you discover more about your amazing family."

"Thank you, Rabbi and Dr. Nabat," Badri said as he shook their hands. "This has already been an amazing and truly wonderful experience. Our family will treasure what you have shared for generations to come."

Lydia rose and gave her father a hug and began to talk with him quietly. I approached Rabbi Halevi and began to ask him about his research books and his own possible travel when Irshad took control of the group.

"Very good team, let's get back to the hotel and collect our things. We will meet briefly to plan our travel. It is obvious someone has found us, so we need to proceed with caution. Whoever found us, it is also clear that they have been following us—how else would they have discovered us here with the rabbi? Let's take separate routes back to the hotel. Same people in the same cars."

"Would it make sense to have our discussion here?" I asked. "If that is acceptable to you, Rabbi," I added. "I mean, we are probably compromised at the hotel, and there is only one change of clothing and a toothbrush for me to pick up there. I assume it is the same for everyone else. We could leave some money with Dr. Nabat to pay our bill later, if that is okay with you, Dr. Nabat, and we could leave directly from here."

"I would be happy to help," Dr. Nabat said. "I could even pick up your personal things and hold them if there is something you want to keep."

"I wouldn't want us to impose on you any further," Irshad interjected. He looked mad at me but was trying to hide it.

"Wait," Leyla said. "Whoever is following us doesn't know where we are going. Maybe we should leave from here and travel different routes. There are areas along the way where it is totally desolate. It would be hard to follow inconspicuously. It might be our chance to get them off our trail."

"Or they could intervene and end this adventure altogether as you suggested earlier, Leyla," Irshad reminded her. "Listen, we need to stick together but have the flexibility of multiple vehicles. It is not a short drive to Shush; that is the modern term for Susa, Thad. At points, as you note, we will be far from safety."

"Thad and I can still fly and keep an eye on the situation. I can file a flight plan for a return to Hamadan or Kermanshah, and then where your route turns south at Khoramabad, I can divert for weather, or some other excuse, to the south. By that time those who want to get a jump on us will be at the wrong place. You can still take both cars and pick us up at the Dezful airport, about forty kilometers from Shush."

"Not a bad idea," Hande said. "But I have another suggestion. Let's go to Ahvaz. It is a much bigger city where we won't be singled out so easily. It has a great airport with excellent security, and the drive is shorter, only ten hours on good roads. I am sure we can get rooms at the Pars Hotel this time of year. Most important, Thad could experience Nezami Street and some of the best fast food in Iran."

"Good, let's do it," Irshad said trying to regain control of the group with a carrot instead of a stick. "Lydia, if you could take care of hotel arrangements before we go, that would be great. We can have an early dinner in Isfahan." He looked at his watch. "We could be at the hotel by ten tonight. Badri, stay with us for the first hour, and then go on ahead. Let's try the secure radios for contact with you airborne while you are in range. Questions?"

No one said anything, just like the last Irshad briefing. And the one before that. Each shared their personal thanks to Rabbi Halevi and Dr. Nabat. Leyla went to the car and retrieved one of the radios and gave it to me and told me to be careful. Her hand lingered on mine as she handed me the radio. Then she was gone.

I approached Rabbi Halevi, and without saying a word, he handed me a cloth shopping bag with a brown paper wrapped package. He nodded. His old eyes were filled with emotion and nearly-formed tears. I knew he would never consider leaving, so I said nothing. As a second thought, he said, "Please, take a pouch of anise to chew. It will give you courage."

"Do I look scared?" I asked.

"You do when you look at that young woman, Leyla," the rabbi said with a slight smile.

"In that case, I will take it. Thank you, Rabbi Halevi." Turning to Dr. Nabat, I said, "And thank you, sir, for everything. You have both given me much to think about. I am honored to know you. If we find this book, we will have you to thank." I turned and left wondering if I would ever see these men again. It felt like I was leaving a trail of my dearest life-long friends at every stop I made along this journey.

Lydia didn't ask about the bag I had with me as we got in the car. Badri motioned in the direction of the airport.

"Can I ask a question of you, Lydia?"

"Sure, go ahead, Thad," she said as we turned north toward the airport.

"I have not seen a single person with a necktie here in Iran. Is that a cultural thing?"

"It is against the law in Iran," Lydia said. "Women must wear the hijab and men must not wear a tie."

"Why?" I asked. "Is it because of the heat?"

"It has nothing to do with temperature. You know, Tehran gets about as much snow as Denver, Colorado, in your country, and where we are going today gets hotter than Phoenix in the summer. No, it is because it is seen as too Western, an encroachment on our moral and ethical foundation. Freedom is an elusive item in Iran. For example, satellite television is outlawed throughout the country, but you will see receiver dishes in plain view on many houses in most cities. The United States is the great Satan, according to the government, but the most popular satellite channels are based in Los Angeles. Banned Iranian pop music, anti-regime propaganda, and even Christian religious programs fill most of the content of these channels.

"You will find that most Iranians love Americans, but they are not allowed to voice those sentiments. Also, Iran is about to launch its own internet and has purchased huge amounts of filtering equipment from China to control this medium. Yet, among Iran youth the World Wide Web is very popular, despite the risk. In fact, Iran is ranked fourth of all nations in terms of bloggers with over 700,000 blogs, and Persian is the second most used language in the entire blogosphere in the world."

"I had no idea," I said out loud. Inside I was thinking about what Irshad had said, that I really didn't know this part of the world and how out of place I really was. I hated it when the betrothed of my beloved was right.

Chapter 18

BADRI AND I FOUND THE plane in good shape, gassed and ready to go. Not that either of us were experts in counterintelligence, but we didn't see anyone following us to the airport. Badri filed his flight plan to Isfahan, which was along our route. He told me he would change that to Ahvaz sometime after overflying Isfahan if the weather was good and there were no headwinds. I had packed the rabbi's research manuscripts in the storage behind my seat, more nervous about getting it safely out of the country than my own well-being. The weather was cool but beautiful as we lifted off and turned northwest following Highway 71. The desert was stark, and the road looked long. It could have been a highway through southern Arizona, except even from the plane I could see the little green signs every few miles that Badri told me were praises to Allah, or Shia exhortations.

I called the team on the radio, and Leyla answered. "We are just passing the exit for Meybod and Ardakan." Hande had also put a strip of black tape on the top of each car. We hoped it would be visible from the air at one thousand feet above the ground.

I checked my map for those towns, and it only took a couple of minutes to find the team's cars. "Okay, I've got you. Looks like more traffic than expected," I said.

"The traffic will be much less after we get through Isfahan," Leyla said. "We plan to pull over to stretch our legs and pretend to check the engine of our car at Naein. That is where Highway 71 turns due west. Let's see if anyone else is with us. Irshad thinks it would be best to see if anyone is following us while we are still in busy traffic, and someone would be less likely to be aggressive. Keep your altitude so no one realizes you are up there. Stay in the sun if you can."

"I will pass that along to Badri," I said, happy to hear Leyla's voice and knowing no one else could hear our whole conversation. It was too noisy in the plane for Badri to hear my part of the conversation from the front seat of the plane, and he had his headset on as well. I had to take one ear off to use the radio. Irshad could only hear Leyla's side of the conversation. At least I assumed that was the case.

"Do you have the radio on speaker? Badri wants to pass along to Irshad that the weather looks good all the way to our destination, and so we are not planning on stopping for gas." I made that up but wanted a plausible reason for asking if Irshad could hear the conversation.

"I will let Irshad know," Leyla said. "I have the radio connected to an earpiece. Do you need me to switch it to speakers?"

"NO," I said a little too loud and quickly. "No, I wouldn't want to distract him from his driving."

"That's what I thought you would say, mizmiz," Leyla said.

I could tell she was trying to keep her voice professional. But I didn't have to. "I thought I was Majnun? I have been demoted back to mizmiz?"

"Yes, that's right," Leyla said. "For this conversation anyway. Can you see the tape on the top of the cars?"

"Way to change the subject. I can almost see your beautiful sandstorm eyes from here, and I am pretty sure I can smell Quelques Fleurs perfume."

"So are those distractions serious, or can you see the tape?" Leyla asked with a little laugh in her voice.

"Oh, they are serious for sure, but yes, I can see the tape. It will be easy to keep track of you."

"Very good," Leyla said slowly. "Are you able to match our speed? The speed limit is 120 kilometers per hour, which I am assuming is a little slow for you."

"We are matching your speed pretty easily. In fact, I would say we are a perfect match."

"You would say that, but at the moment I can't refute you," Leyla replied.

"I wish I could reach out and touch you, or at least sit close enough to you that I could stare at you until you blush."

"Well, that is good news, Thaddeus. Keep up the good work," Leyla said, back to a serious sound in her voice. "Yes, I wish you could, too. Keep your eyes focused there. We have about twenty miles to go to get to Naeim. Let us know if you see anything we should know about."

This was more fun than any walkie-talkie games I had played as a boy. I knew it was time to get serious, though. I started studying the other vehicles on the road. It all looked so simple and safe from up here. That could change in an instant. I watched the two cars pull over and someone get out and open the hood of the lead car. Everyone else stayed in the cars. Traffic seemed to go by without concern. Then someone pulled over and then pulled out again.

"What was that?" I asked Leyla.

"Just a concerned person offering to help. Irshad told him we are fine, and they left."

About a quarter mile up the road I saw a white sedan pull off and then turn around and drive by our team. The car did not slow down. Maybe they forgot to turn off the unauthorized satellite TV at home.

"Leyla, a white sedan just turned around and passed you on the other side of the road. I will let you know if they double back," I transmitted over the radio.

"Thanks," Leyla said. "Yes, I see the car, but they were already too far away to see who was inside."

"Sorry," I said. "I should have alerted you sooner. Okay, this is the real deal! They just turned around again. Coming your way and will be on you in about ten seconds."

"Got it," was all Leyla said. Badri and I watched Irshad go around to the passenger side of the car and lean in like he was talking to the people in the car. The car with Hande and Lydia began to back up. There were probably six or seven car lengths between the two cars when the white sedan approached. I was surprised that it began to slow. "Man, I hope this is another interested person offering to help," I said to Badri over the intercom. I felt so helpless up here.

I couldn't tell exactly what was happening, but I could see an arm, maybe with a gun, poke out the passenger side window of the white sedan. The car with Hande and Lydia began to move, fast. Lots of dust. They drove straight for the white sedan and hit it. Irshad had jumped in the passenger window, and the car began to move almost immediately. Leyla must have moved over to the driver's seat. She turned her car around and created another large dust cloud.

"Two shots fired," Leyla yelled over the radio. I relayed that info to Badri, who turned the plane, so we had a better angle of view. It looked like a demolition derby down there. I was glad Irshad had opted for the full car insurance package at the rental place back in Turkey.

Lydia was using their car to push the right side of the sedan, forcing it back toward the highway. Cars coming from behind were already having to swerve out of the way. Then the car with Lydia and Hande in it stopped. A person jumped out of the sedan window and was obviously firing at Lydia and Hande. Still, their car didn't move. Leyla, with Irshad riding shotgun, was racing toward the man with the gun. The white sedan pulled forward and to the right, blocking Leyla from hitting the man. Their cars collided. It wasn't a hard hit, but I was sure some airbags went off. Hopefully, Leyla was wearing her seat belt.

"Need a distraction!" Leyla garbled over the radio.

I relayed the message to Badri, and he banked hard to the left, and we lost a lot of altitude very fast. We flew over the chaos at about 300 feet. Badri banked hard to the right, and we descended until we were almost on the highway. We were doing 230 knots just above the ground. It looked like we were going to fly into the backseat of the white sedan. The man outside the sedan saw us and began firing in our direction. Badri didn't flinch, and within a few seconds, we were close enough to give him a haircut with our propeller. Badri pulled up ever so slightly, and we couldn't have missed the white sedan by more than a foot or two. Badri then pulled up hard, and before I knew it, we were upside down. We did a half-roll and were right side up again at about 700 feet above the ground.

That must have been enough of a distraction because when we banked to the left, we could see Irshad tackle the man outside the car. The white sedan had backed up and was pulling onto the highway heading south toward Yazd. Badri saw the same thing and pushed the plane forward hard. Even with my seat belt on, I felt like I was going to be flung from the airplane, except there was a ceiling. Before I knew it, we were playing chicken with the white sedan. We were only inches from the highway pavement. We didn't swerve. I thought we were going to hit the car. I had forgotten that we had up, not just left and right, to maneuver. How Badri missed the car is beyond me. The driver of the sedan was probably wondering the same thing. He had stomped on the brakes and lost control of the car, spinning off the road to the right. The sedan didn't move once the skidding stopped.

"Is everyone alright?" I asked over the radio.

"Irshad and I are unhurt. Our car is drivable, but only to get us back to Yazd. We haven't checked on Lydia and Hande yet. We are still watching the sedan, and Irshad has the gunman tied up, but he is still a potential threat."

Over the radio, I was surprised to hear Lydia's voice. "We are fine, but our car is done. The gunman must have hit something that disabled the engine."

"Lydia, glad to hear you are okay," I said relieved. "I didn't realize there was a third radio."

"Yes, there was always a third radio, just not used," Lydia said. "I was going to let you know we were in contact also, but then Hande and I were learning so much from your conversation with Leyla that we didn't say anything."

"Oh, great," I said. "No apologies for my lack of operational radio decorum."

Then, changing the subject, I said, "Are you still in cell coverage? Could you call your father and have him come out here to pick you up? It might be best not to get the police involved."

"Yes," Leyla chimed in. "Best to keep this as an auto accident. I am just not sure what to do with our friends in the sedan."

"Hande is going to check on them now, maybe exchange contact information for the auto insurance companies," Lydia said jokingly.

I watched as Hande and Irshad both approached the sedan on the other side of the highway. Irshad seemed to have a gun in his hand. I wasn't sure if it was his or what he had confiscated from the gunman. I really should know who in this group carries a weapon. I realized there were still many things I didn't know about this group, including why they seem to be making up plans as they went along. It was like counterterrorism improvisation. These people weren't amateurs, but you would think professionals would have better plans. Irshad was still at the sedan. Hande was jogging across the highway to Lydia.

"Two men in the sedan," Lydia relayed over the radio. "The driver is semi-conscious but dazed. It seems his airbag went off when they went into the ditch. There is a guy in the backseat who is injured, but he will live. Hande told me to tell you, Thad, that the guy didn't have his seat belt on. What's that about?"

"First rule of counterterrorism," I said. "Buckle up. Irshad is in charge, but my input is to leave their car where it is so the police can find it and trace it back to them. Let them explain what happened. Take the three men back with you to Yazd for medical treatment and maybe let it slip that our gunman might be the drive-by shooter at Rabbi Halevi's place. Maybe the ballistics will match. What do you want Badri and me to do?"

"I will check with Irshad," Leyla said.

I relayed all this information to Badri, and he suggested we press on to Ahvaz. "It wouldn't be good for you with a false passport to get tied up in any of this. We can wait for the team there and maybe even do a little poking around while we wait."

"Irshad says go on to Ahvaz," Leyla reported a minute later. "We should only be a few hours behind schedule. We will meet you at the hotel, probably around midnight or one in the morning, assuming we have no complications turning the cars in, explaining why the engine stopped, and getting new rentals. Nothing a healthy tip won't solve."

I wanted to stay overhead for the safety of the team on the ground. Who knows whether this car also had a second vehicle as backup? Badri said we needed to head for Ahvaz, or we would need to stop for gas. I relayed our plan, and we departed the area.

Before we were out of our handheld radio contact, Leyla reported, "Irshad says our friends are Furqaan. Safe travels, Majnun."

"Ah, I have re-attained my rightful nickname," I said with delight. "Stay safe, all of you. See you this evening."

I sadly watched Leyla and team fade behind us as Badri turned the aircraft to a 250 degree heading directly to Ahvaz. We climbed to 6,500 feet. It got pretty cold, even with the cockpit heater. It was a quiet flight. Badri was probably thinking about his family history as I was about mine. "Really? Am I a descendant of the Apostle Thaddeus? Of course, that means Anna is also a descendant. I wonder what she will think of that when I tell her? But that was two thousand years ago. What does it matter? Go back that far and everyone is related to royalty, scoundrels, and religious leaders."

I thought of asking Badri about his feelings of being a descendant of the Prophet Mohammad, but decided not to bother him with a deep question. Instead, I said, "Rabbi Halevi told me to be careful, that there was someone in our group that was a danger."

"What was their proof?" Badri asked.

"A dream," I said.

"Well, that is a better justification than emotion, ego, habit, or other less-than-precise reasons for concern. Halevi had the dream?"

"Yes," I replied.

"And Dr. Nabat, what did he say?"

"He wasn't in the room at the time."

"Well, there are certainly a lot of potential threats in this country. Not only do we have the nemeses you have already been introduced to, but there are more criminals and organized crime as well that would love to get their hands on an ancient book. It would bring a huge price on the black market. If it has incriminating or clarifying religious information, it could be used for blackmail, also. Internally, what do you think? Do we have a wolf in sheep's clothing in our midst?"

"Isn't that a Bible verse?" I asked.

"Yes, I believe so, but I couldn't tell you where in the Bible. That saying is about false prophets, though, and the Qur'an also speaks about that subject in verse 2:79. It says, *Woe to those who write the Book with their own hands and then say: 'This is from Allah' to traffic with it for a miserable price! Woe to them for what their hands do write and for the gain they make thereby.* So, do we have a person in the group who has settled for a miserable price?"

"I don't think so, but then I have no facts to back that up. Everyone has put their life on the line, multiple times. Maybe it is a member of Al-Ĥujurāt that we haven't met yet." Badri was quiet, so I added, "It doesn't seem like there is that much crime in Iran. It is practically a police state."

"Iranian society wears its own burka. Underneath, however, there are blue jeans, t-shirts, and sometimes lipstick and high heels," Badri said. "Did you know that nearly 4,000 Iranians have been killed in the past twenty-five years fighting heroin smugglers, whose main trade route to the West passes through the Islamic Republic? And it isn't just passing, though. Iran itself has a major drug problem, with published estimates of over two million addicts."

"Wow, once again Irshad's words that I am a blind hog prove themselves prophetic," I said.

"I never thought I would hear Irshad and prophetic in the same sentence," Badri chuckled. "You know he was totally wrong. You might not know some societal nuances, but Middle Eastern culture is based on attributes that come natural to you, and people see that. Hypocrisy is also easy to see. Be observant and sensitive, honor your word, act with integrity, and dedicate time to the personal issues, not just the job issues, and you will be more Middle Eastern than Irshad. You may not win every battle, but you will be rewarded with long-term success in a part of the world where success is hard won."

"You say that from the perspective of one who knows your world like a mother knows her nursing child. I am childless."

"Well, that's an interesting metaphor. Either this land or Leyla is turning you into a poet. Listen, it isn't always about your manners in a specific situation. Situational awareness is important, but situational ethics brings eventual and guaranteed failure. Who you really are at the core, your love and care for people, being teachable, being grateful, and willingness to sacrifice are not religious or cultural commodities; they are the human essence. They are not characteristics you can select like a pair of shoes that go with the outfit of the day or that you can set on a shelf for use later when convenient; they are essential for personal peace and to bring lasting meaning and connection with others—anywhere in the world. Sure, you don't want to cross your legs and point the bottom of your shoe at an Arab. That is rude. But being dishonest or uncaring once you know it is rude is so much worse."

As if creating a physical metaphor of his words, Badri pulled the airplane higher, to 8,500 feet. Now it was really getting cold. "We will only need to stay at this altitude for about ten minutes, through this high valley between Dehdez to Izeh, and then we can descend to a more comfortable altitude."

The snowcapped peaks of the Zagros Mountains were higher than our altitude. It was worth the cold temperature to share this lofty height with these sentinels of human history. Wow, I sounded poetic. I knew I was probably naively corny too, but felt mostly inspired.

Badri had begun a slow descent and was on the radio updating our flight plan when our engine sputtered and then failed completely. The silence screamed in my ears. After about thirty seconds, Badri asked, "Do you know where oil was first discovered in the Middle East?"

"What? No." I was shocked at Badri's calm and stupefied by the crazy question.

"Masjed Soleiman. Do you know the name of the company that discovered it?"

"Umm, Badri, the engine quit, and we are falling out of the sky," I said trying to hold onto my sanity as we plummeted to the ground.

"It was called the Anglo-Persian Oil Company (APOC). It was founded in 1908. It changed names a few times over the years and eventually became the British Petroleum Company or BP for short. Do you know who one of the founders of the first petroleum company in the Middle East was?"

"No, but please tell me before we die due to that sudden stop that is coming up."

"Abdul Qader Kabbani, my great grandfather. Do you know where Masjed Soleiman is located?"

"Again, I am sure you are going to tell me," I said in resignation.

"Right in front of our noses," Badri said with some awe in his voice. "Unfortunately, the airport is two miles north of the town, and I am not sure we will make the runway. We are passing 6,500 feet, and the runway elevation is 1,500 feet. The airport only has an NDB, a non-directional beacon, no DME, distance measuring equipment. I am guessing we are between 15 and 18 miles out—300 feet per mile with power on, less with power off…"

Badri was doing some calculations in his head while looking for suitable landing spots. I figured my job was to help look and keep quiet. Instead of continuing our descent, Badri pulled the nose up gently, gaining altitude and slowing the airspeed. We slowed from 140 miles per hour to 58 miles per hour, and we were at 7,500 feet. Badri was talking to the airport in Farsi now.

I couldn't tell what he was saying, but he sounded calm and in control.

"Alright, Thad," Badri said on the intercom. "I exchanged airspeed for altitude to give us a fighting chance at making the runway. We will get there a little slower, but the idea is to get there. I am flying straight for the closest point on the runway, so I may need to do some quick maneuvering at the last second. Just stay calm and say a prayer. We should be fine."

Our heading put us at an angle to the runway, and I could see a road perpendicular to the runway, about a football field from the beginning of the runway. "Why not just land on a road?" I wondered. Then I saw the cars and thought back to the game of chicken we played with the white sedan. I would rather not do that again. It was starting to get a little turbulent as we got closer to the ground.

"This is also a military air base," Badri said. "We don't want to do anything that might cause them to get alarmed. Once we land, stay in the aircraft unless we crash or are on fire—which is very unlikely. I know you will do that, but I have declared an emergency, and so they will be sending out the fire truck and probably military security. Sorry for all the drama every time we get in the air. This isn't typical."

"Not a problem," I lied. "I was getting bored back here and am enjoying the change of pace."

I could see two runways now and the military parking beyond the farther runway. I could also see some vehicles driving across the taxiway toward us. Just as it looked like we were going to make it, we hit a down draft. Badri responded by putting down partial flaps. We were down to 53 miles per hour. It felt like we were a tractor stuck in the mud. A buzzing noise started to sound.

"Don't mind that alarm. We are at stall speed. That is when the airplane stops flying. I have practiced this, though, and I know we have a one- or two-knot cushion. We won't have the maneuverability to bank to the runway, though. Banking the aircraft to turn would reduce lift further, and we would plant it right there. I am going to land on the taxiway right off that large civilian parking ramp in front of us. How are you doing?"

"I am doing great, but I think I have had enough aviation adventures for a while."

I had my eyes glued on the runway and our airspeed. Badri lowered the nose slightly to keep the airspeed from going down more. I felt like I could walk this fast. Once we got really close to the ground, I was sure we weren't going to make it, and then we sort of floated.

"What was that? An angel holding us up?" I asked trying to sound relaxed.

"Ground effect," Badri said. "Certainly our angel today." As he said that, the wheels touched down on the taxiway, and we stopped after a couple of hundred feet.

I wanted to shout for joy, but I realized how tense I was and couldn't have even if I thought it was appropriate. Instead, I said, "Nice job, Badri. It was like we were supposed to land here."

"That is what I was thinking." He opened the cockpit window and took in a deep breath.

The emergency was terminated, and the military fire truck and the van returned to the other side of the runway. A pickup truck towed us to the civilian parking ramp. Badri tied down the aircraft, and I got out. It felt so good to stand on the ground.

"It looks like we will need a new fuel pump. I told the airport that it failed. What really happened was, a bullet from our earlier escapade damaged it. Either it just quit, or the lower fuel level created less gravity pressure in the system, or the altitude reduced the pressure, or a combination of any and all the above. This plane won't be going anywhere anytime soon. Grab your stuff, and let's see if we can find a ride into Ahvaz. I think it is about fifty miles from here."

I grabbed my stuff, which only consisted of Rabbi Halevi's books, and we walked to the small terminal. Badri coordinated for the storage of his airplane and told me he would work out getting the new fuel pump later. That would take a qualified mechanic, and there wasn't one in Masjed Soleiman.

"I would consider doing it myself, but it is a long way home. I want to make sure it is checked out and that there aren't other problems."

The only ride we were able to find was in the back of a pickup truck, which actually felt good.

"You know," Badri began once we were seated, "my great-grandfather is credited with founding the first petroleum company in the Arab World in 1909. The British businessman D'Arcy was the official founder of the first petroleum company here at Masjed Soleiman in 1908, but my great grandfather was here. I have often wondered if my great grandfather knew this was an ancestral home of our family, whether he knew of some family lore that suggested oil was here.

"D'Arcy's personal fortune was depleted. The company staff had been released from employment. The driller, a tenacious guy named Reynolds, was told to stop his drilling. He ignored the order and kept drilling. At four in the morning, the drill reached 1,180 feet and hit a gusher that shot over seventy feet into the air. That day the Middle East ceased to be a forgotten corner of the world or just a place to transit.

"In 1912, the Turkish Petroleum Company (later Iraq Petroleum Company) was formed by Germany, Holland and Britain to exploit the Ottoman oil fields of Mosul, now a part of Iraq. Oil was not discovered on the Arabian Peninsula until 1938. My family was standing at the door when this new era was ushered in."

"It seems your family has a habit of being at the door during the pivotal moments in history in this part of the world," I said.

"Yes, that is kind of what I have been thinking about," Badri said. "I knew of my family history, but what door am I supposed to guard, or open? Is it the Kitab Kabbani?"

"You are asking the wrong guy that question," I said. I was going to ask him about the weight of family heritage, but I decided to put my concerns back on the shelf. "Maybe you will discover oil in Lebanon," I offered.

"Surely there are more important doors to guard than carbon fuel. Yet its wealth facilitates so much else in this region and around the world. And this region eclipses all the known oil of the rest of the world by huge factors, and it is mostly easy oil, not sand tar and shale that cost more than twenty times to produce than oil here.

"You know, I just realized that the third largest oil field in the world is called Majnun. It's in Iraq, just across the border from here. It is estimated at thirteen billion barrels. It produces very little right now due to its close proximity to Iran. The Iran-Iraq war is still fresh in both governments' minds. It would be amazing to live to see the day when the Muslim world can live together in peace and live with the rest of the world in some sort of harmony." Badri chuckled and said, "Now I am starting to sound like the idealistic poet."

"This does feel like a very special place," I said, sharing what I really felt. "Maybe my feelings today come from my near-death experience, coupled with a brief history lesson."

"I am sorry about that," Badri said. "So, tell me about Majnun and Leyla. How is that history developing?"

"Nothing to develop. She is still betrothed to Mr. 'I'm in Charge.' She is Muslim, and I am Christian, I guess. The river gets wider and deeper the more I think about it."

"Become Muslim," Badri suggested.

"I don't want to have this come across as insensitive, but I think there is more than what Islam offers."

"It offers Leyla," Badri said with a smile.

"That is true, and tempting," I agreed. "but probably not the reason for which God, Allah, would want me to convert."

"Then you must find a new path," Badri said with great optimism. Masjed Soleyman was anciently known as Parsomash. It was the oldest capital of the Achaemenid Empire—that's the time period Rabbi Halevi and Dr. Nabat spoke of in reference to my family, the time of Cyrus, Darius, Xerxes, Artaxerxes. So, do people flock to Masjed Soleyman for its ancient culture? No. They come here for the mundane and the fleeting riches of oil. The relatively newer capitals of that empire, Persepolis, and Susa, are where the world goes to study the Achaemenid Empire and gain insight and understanding. Susa was carved out of the wilderness by the courage and will of visionary kings. Don't be Parsomash, be Susa."

Chapter 19

WE TURNED ONTO HIGHWAY 45 and traveled for about fifteen miles and then turned onto another unimproved road heading south for ten miles. We joined Highway 39 at a small town called Mollasani. The agricultural presence was everywhere. Recently harvested fields, others lying fallow with still green grass, and large oak trees along the road. It was a stark contrast from the desert landscape of Yazd. The road followed the Karun River, and twenty minutes later we were entering the outskirts of Ahvaz. I was done with travel for the day. A few minutes later we were at the Pars Hotel. It wasn't anything spectacular, like the hotels in Turkey, but all I wanted was a soft horizontal surface with clean sheets.

Badri and I did some quick shopping for clothing and personal items and were back at the hotel by five in the afternoon. I took a quick shower and changed. Then we went out for dinner. I was starving. We ate Cholo Kabab Koubide, which seemed like a lot of syllables for rice with kebabs. Badri also had me try Fesenjan. Oh, wow! It was a meat and beans dish with a walnut sauce that forever more will make my mouth drool in an embarrassing way at the thought of it. I had mine with fried onion on top. I also noticed that the Iranian rice has a unique flavor and texture. It was completely different than Uncle Ben's or even the Japanese rice I really liked back home. By nine that evening I was in bed asleep.

"There are a thousand ways to kneel and kiss the earth," my dream was telling me. "This is the hour to kiss the earth on Nezami Street."

What was my dream talking about? Then I realized somewhere in a corner of my mind my dream had a voice that sounded like Hande. I opened my eyes, and there he was, smiling and full of energy.

"Do you ever sleep Hande?" I asked, pulling the covers over my eyes.

"Not when there is an experience to share. So get up, my lazy American friend. Rise!"

I wasn't the least bit hungry, but I couldn't tell Hande no. We were on Nezami Street ten minutes later. It was like a street bazaar. Shops and food everywhere. No one asked how much we wanted. We served ourselves. No one asked to be paid. It was the honor system, Hande explained. Hande paid for more than we ate, but that is what he loved about this place. He was paying for those who perhaps didn't pay enough, maybe because they couldn't.

"Was that another Rumi quote that got me out of bed?" I asked as we walked back to the hotel.

"Yes, it was," Hande said, smiling. "And it wasn't really about praying through food. That is probably sacrilegious. Although it does have a certain metaphor I like, you know, kissing the earth, eating the food the earth provides. Actually, I wanted to wake you up to tell you Lydia and I really enjoyed your conversation on the radio with Leyla earlier today."

"Ugggh," I moaned. "I forgot about that! I hope Leyla wasn't too embarrassed when she saw you two."

"She didn't show any emotions at all. Like it never happened. I felt like a voyeur, though; but it gave me the courage to say a few things to Lydia. We are kind of in a relationship. Crazy, huh?" Hande was practically bouncing.

"Well, congratulations! Let me know when you get the religious and cultural bridges constructed. Every time I try to start my construction, the whole thing falls into the water and disappears in the current."

"We have nothing figured out. But if we get serious, we will name our first child after you."

"Get some sleep, Hande. We can talk in the morning." I got back to my room and was out again within thirty seconds of hitting the bed.

I felt like I had just gone to bed when there was a knock at my door. It was a quiet knock, and I am surprised I even heard it.

"Just a minute," I said. "If that is you, Hande, wanting to go eat breakfast, go back to bed."

No one answered, so I put on my pants and a pullover shirt. I stumbled to the door and peeked out, thinking it might be a maid wanting to clean the room. It was Leyla. I opened the door, and she rushed in. "Good morning," I said.

"It's not good to have a relationship with someone on the team during an operation," Leyla said.

"I agree," I said. "You should break it off with Irshad at once."

"I did. Yesterday on the drive here."

"Oh, wow, I was joking. I mean, not really. I was serious, but did you do that for the right reasons? I asked with a mixture of shock and euphoria.

"In the middle of that attack by the Furqaan, I started worrying about you. I was being shot at, and you were my only concern. Then I started worrying about you and me. That worry and hesitation could have gotten somebody killed. I was okay on the job with Irshad because I realized I didn't love him and only worried about him as I did the other members of the team. That was not enough on which to base a relationship for life. But with you I find myself wondering and wishing instead of observing, thinking, and acting wisely."

"Let's talk about that in a second. How did Irshad take this? Does he want to kill me?"

"No," Leyla said. "He was surprised, and it was silent in the car for at least a half hour. Then he said he was good with my decision but asked if any final decisions could be put on hold until after this operation. I think he was more concerned about keeping everyone's head in the game than about our relationship. Maybe that is a laudable leadership trait, but it hurt, even though I was happy to be free of the betrothal."

"So, what are you going to tell Mack? Are you going to wait until this is over?"

"I think my dad will be disappointed, but eventually, he will accept it. I am going to wait, though, like Irshad suggested."

"And what about us? Is our relationship something real or just an operational distraction?"

"What are you talking about, Thaddeus? I thought you were going to die when that guy started shooting at the plane. And as close to the ground as you came, you very well could have. But yes, I am afraid our relationship is a distraction, a wonderful, beautiful distraction, but also a dangerous distraction. I can't believe I didn't think about the other radio in Lydia and Hande's car. They must think I am a little school girl with my first crush."

"You shouldn't be embarrassed that others overheard what they have already seen, in your eyes and mine. Hande and Lydia were grateful for our conversation, by the way. It gave them the permission to talk about their own relationship in their car on the way here also. They have decided to make their fraternization more real, more than a friendly companionship among team members, despite the complications. So is this just a school girl crush for you?"

"I am not a school girl, although I am acting like one. It is the first time I think I have passed infatuation or the idea of love to something much bigger and deeper, so I don't know what it is. I don't want to put a label on it yet. Please have patience with me."

Leyla had been looking out the hotel room window. She turned and looked at me, and I was surprised to see tears in her eyes. Her words hadn't sounded like she was crying.

"There is a Sufi version of the Majnun and Leyla story. In this version, the story becomes a symbol of the love of a human for Allah. It is a story of a quest for God, not unlike the old Christian quests to find the Holy Grail—the chalice that symbolizes the love of God. As you know, Majnun goes crazy for his love of Leyla. The goal of the Sufi is *fana*, which literally means something like complete obliteration, but to us means departing from our socially conditioned mind to find God. So, what is my socially conditioned mind, and what is the will of God? In the story, it is Majnun that goes crazy, and Leyla dies of a broken heart. I am afraid it is I that will go crazy, and you will be left with the broken heart."

"It sounds like to me that Leyla symbolizes God and thus has the power to write the story but for some reason does not." I said. "Maybe Majnun is not crazy but does not accept the socially conditioned mind you mentioned. To others, he may appear crazy, but actually he has only chosen a path others don't understand because their mind is closed. I hate to say it, but Irshad might be right that we keep the story of Majnun and Leyla on the shelf for the moment. Let's get through this alive and then sort this out. There are answers because there you are, standing right in front of me, willing me forward."

Leyla blushed and looked down at the floor for a second and then looked up at me with her eyes almost sparkling. She looked serious, but not a mad serious. She said, "There is a part in the Sufi version of the story that goes something like this. *She favored me, drew me toward her, and took me into her precinct,"* Leyla said as she approached within inches of me. I could feel her breath as she spoke, and as I looked into her eyes, I think I could feel the breath of her spirit. She continued, *"Then with words most intimate addressed me."*

Leyla put her left hand on the nape of my neck and gently pulled my head closer to her and said, "Majnun," and then continued her recitation. *"She then came closer."* Leyla's right arm slowly wrapped around me and held me close. I put my arms around her. I couldn't breathe for the feeling of finally holding her. She almost whispered, *"And raised the garment that veiled her from my gaze; she took me out of myself, amazed me with her beauty... She changed me and transfigured me, marked me with her special seal, pressed me to her, granted me a unique station and named me with her name."* Leyla kissed me, marked me with her special seal, and I knew I was hers, and she was mine.

"I really like that version of the story, but I also believe we can write our own version," I said, still holding her. "And if this is putting our relationship on the back burner, I am all for it."

"I know," Leyla said. "I feel the same. What would happen if we just left, and the Kitab Kabbani was either left hidden, or the rest of the team found it?"

"What about the sacrifices you have already made with the family relics you gave to the Hashshashin, the Fahrunissa Scroll, and the dream Rabbi Halevi had?" I asked.

"The relics were freely given to save you and your sister, not the Kitab Kabbani. I don't know what the scroll means anymore. And what dream did the rabbi have?"

"Sit down," I said. "I need to tell you a few things that the rabbi and Dr. Nabat shared with me. They asked me to keep these things a secret, but I can't keep them from you."

I told Leyla the details about Boos and Sepideh in Hamadan, including Sepideh's explanation of her father's connections with important leaders and his research papers. Then I told her about my private conversation with Rabbi Halevi, about the possible danger of a traitor within the team, about Dr. Nabat's conversion to Christianity, about their knowledge of the Kitab Kabbani and the rabbi's research books, about the flight here and Badri's feelings about the Kitab Kabbani stimulated by our nearly disastrous landing at Masjed Soleyman, and about Badri's command that I be a Susa, not a Parsomash. Lastly, I told Leyla about my possible family connection to the ancient Christian Apostle Thaddeus. It all just spilled out like a dam had burst. I was expecting her to comment on the Thaddeus connection or Dr. Nabat's secret conversion.

"So, maybe I am the danger within," Leyla suggested. "Am I the traitor with my suggestion that we just run away?"

I had not considered that, but then I asked, "Is it being a traitor to want to have a happy life and simply live? No. I have been trying to figure out why I am here since the day we met. Maybe the answer is right in front of me. It's you. Is that fate, divine intervention? I don't know. But," I paused, realizing I had just talked myself into a corner, "if either is possible, then so are the reality and authenticity of an ancient scroll and the dream of an old rabbi."

We were interrupted by a knock at the door. It was Badri, Lydia, and Hande. I was glad Leyla's eyes had cleared up and we were now sitting at the table. I thought all appeared pretty innocent and operational. The smirks from all three told me just the opposite. I asked, "Where is Irshad? We could make this a team meeting on today's plan."

"Irshad went in search of a map store so we could split up and hit multiple cemeteries today. If anyone finds anything, we can contact the others. The front desk knew of a place that probably has what we are looking for, so he should return shortly," Lydia explained.

"So, what are you two up to?" she asked with a broad smile. My guess was she was smiling more for her own new relationship with Hande than for any news about Leyla and me.

"We were just reviewing everything we have learned thus far and what the next step should be," Leyla said.

"Lame answer," Hande said. "You are such a terrible liar, Leyla. What were you two really talking about? Tell!"

"She's telling the truth," I said, coming to her rescue. "Just as you knocked, I had completed reviewing again what we had learned from Rabbi Halevi and your father, Lydia. And, I will admit, we were asking ourselves if this operation is really necessary. Several of us almost died yesterday. Should we press on, or return to Turkey and rethink this?"

"We press on," Irshad said from the doorway surprising us all. "There is nothing to be gained by returning to Konya. I think the Furqaan has made their last attempt to stop us. They have so much explaining to do with Rabbi Halevi's friend from the Revolutionary Guard in Yazd that they won't be a threat again until after we find the book. The Hashshashin must still be licking their wounds from our last meeting in Cappadocia. The only lead we have to go on is the cemeteries in this region. We are here; let's get this done. Any questions?"

No one had any questions. Irshad passed out the maps to each member of the team. "Badri, were you able to rent a car this morning?"

"Yes. Ready to go," Badri said with enthusiasm. "How about I go to the cemetery in Susa? I have been there before as a tourist and know the area."

"That works," Irshad said. "Take Thad and also try to visit the site in Dezful. Hande and Leyla, take Shushtar. If you have time, check out Masjed Soleiman. Lydia, you and I will visit the cemeteries here in the greater Ahvaz area. If we come up empty, we can consider visiting the towns of Ramhormoz, Izeh, and Susangerd tomorrow. Keep the group informed, even if you don't find anything of interest. Check in with me once an hour. I won't call to check on you unless I don't hear from you by the two-hour point. Stay safe. No heroics without team backup. Grab something to eat on your own. Good hunting."

Irshad marked the maps from his original that had been marked by the map store, showing most of the known cemeteries. No one remarked on the obvious switch up of Leyla and Lydia.

Leyla gave me a quick smile and was off with Hande as I heard him say, "Did you know, Leyla, that Iran is one of the world's biggest producers of luxury foods. It is the largest source of caviar, and it is also the world's biggest producer of pistachios, as well as saffron. I know this place for breakfast…" and they were too far away for me to hear the name of the restaurant.

Everyone noticed, but pretended not to notice, that Hande gave Lydia a quick hand squeeze before he left. Lydia and Irshad left next, and Badri and I were left in my room.

"So, breakfast before we go, or hit the road and grab something along the way?" Badri asked.

"I'm not really hungry. Hande woke me for a late night food run when they got in. I can go with you if you want something, though."

"Great, let's get going and skip breakfast. I have to admit, I am really excited about today. It's kind of like going home to a home I have never visited. I have traveled the area as a tourist, but never with actual family history in mind."

When we got to the car Badri had rented, I had to laugh. The hotel parking attendant had just finished washing the windshield of a red BMW X6 that looked like it belonged on the *Fast and Furious* rather than a family history research outing.

232

"Where did you find this in Ahvaz?" I asked as Badri tipped the attendant.

"Iranians love beautiful and fast cars," was Badri's only answer. "Ready to go?"

I felt like I was getting into another aircraft, but Badri drove the car carefully and within the speed limit through the town. When we passed the Ahvaz Northeastern Bypass Expressway, Badri said, "Let's not waste any time." We were quickly doing about 210 kilometers per hour, and the one hundred kilometers to Shush went by in a blur.

I was grateful it was a divided highway and there were no potholes, like in town. I expected the other search groups hadn't even finished breakfast yet when we pulled up to the cemetery. It was just off the expressway, just before the Imam Khomeini Boulevard intersection leading into Shush.

"Just across the expressway are the ancient ruins of Susa," Badri explained. "Beyond that is the town of Shush. The town and the surrounding area have a population of about 50,000 people, so there are probably other cemeteries. This is supposed to be the oldest."

Badri walked into the building that guarded the entrance to the cemetery. It had a center archway and eight smaller arched entrances on each side. The roof looked like patina copper, or it was just painted green to look that way. The entrance had a decorative marble floor—very ornate for a small-town cemetery. Badri was back outside in less than thirty seconds.

"No one there. Let's walk around the cemetery. I see a small mosque or mausoleum in the center. Maybe there is someone there."

We walked through the cemetery. The graves had cement or rock slabs as well as gravestones. Some had small makeshift roofs of corrugated metal built over them. Many looked old, but none looked ancient. There were also old trees scattered throughout the cemetery. There were a few signs, but unlike in Turkey, I didn't see any English translations. Badri found a grounds worker, or maybe he was a visitor just cleaning up a relative's gravesite. I saw him point to the south. They talked for a minute more, and Badri returned to where I was standing.

"That gentleman says this cemetery used to have much older graves, but in the 1930s, the town council voted to build a new cemetery over the much older one. About the time of Reza Shah's forced abdication in favor of his son Mohammad Reza Pahlavi, the town got improvement funds from the central government. The town built the football/soccer stadium just to the south of us. In the construction, many ancient graves were discovered and then covered over. The old man told me most of the town doesn't even know there are graves under their games. There are no records of those ancient graves that he knew of. We could go to the city offices, and perhaps they would have more information."

Badri seemed a little disappointed, but I am sure he didn't expect it would be that easy to find seven-hundred-year-old graves by just pulling off the highway at the first cemetery.

I called in to Irshad to check in and let him know what we had found so far while Badri drove to the city center. Irshad was surprised that not only had we arrived in Shush, but that we were already on the second leg of our search. I told Irshad about the red BMW, and he chuckled for maybe the first time since I had met him.

We arrived at the city building after getting directions a few times. I waited in the car while Badri went in. He had been gone about twenty minutes, and I was getting concerned when he reappeared, heading for the car.

"Good news and bad news," he said as he hopped into the driver's seat. "The good news is, I was able to get a good lead on a local expert of ancient gravesites. The bad news is, they had no records of the ancient site under the football stadium and were concerned I even knew about that. They asked for identification, and when I showed them my passport, they told me to leave. I am glad I got the name and contact information on the expert first."

"So, where is the expert?" I asked. "Hopefully not too far away."

"I suppose that falls in the good news category, also. She is in our next assigned town, Dezful, which is only about twenty kilometers up the road."

"Oh, you mean about two minutes from here," I said.

"No, it will be regular driving. The directions I got take us on the Dezful-Shush Road instead of Highway 37, the divided highway we used coming here."

We drove in silence for about ten minutes, enjoying the day. We drove through a traffic circle that had a huge statue of a hand holding a real fighter jet when we entered town. We pulled over, and Badri bought us some honeydew melon that had rose water sprinkled on it. A perfect morning snack that also made me miss Leyla.

"Dezful is a great example of the diversity of this part of Iran," Badri said as we watched people walk and drive by, slowing down to look at the red BMW. "There are Persians, of course, but also many Arabs—we are only maybe fifty miles from the Iraq border. This was a big hot spot during the Iran-Iraq War, as that interesting statue suggested.

"There are also Lors, Qashquis, and the House of Kassir clan. The other side of town is the river that is very turbulent, except in one area where it is very calm. The local lore states that Khawaja Sultan Sayyid Ali Rudband calmed the waters in the 15th century. There is a mosque there now."

I think Badri enjoyed being a tour guide of out-of-the-way places, and it constantly amazed me what he knew. This really was his backyard. We drove a few blocks and turned right on Ferdosi and right again on Keshavarz. We drove one block and pulled over at a quaint home and parked. We both got out and walked to an old wooden door that had several layers of flaking blue paint. There were two door knockers. Badri reached for the larger one but stopped.

He said, "The sound of the handle informs the person inside the gender of the person outside, thus warning a female inside whether to cover herself before answering. In my father's day, women would also put their finger in their mouth when communicating with male visitors as it was considered immodest for strangers to hear a female's natural voice. Happily, for those who used to have to gag themselves to talk, we have grown away from that practice."

Badri used the larger door knocker, and an older gentleman answered the door. He was short, maybe five feet three inches, and had short white hair. Badri introduced us and provided some additional information, which I assumed was why we were there. The old man ushered us into a small sitting room.

We quietly waited for several minutes. A lady in her late sixties entered the room along with the man who answered the door. She wore a blue hijab and a gray one-piece floor length dress. She vaguely reminded me of the nuns from my childhood. She introduced herself, and Badri introduced us.

The older man suggested and motioned for my benefit that we all sit down. We were presented small glass cups of cherry juice. I could have consumed the whole pitcher. It was delicious. The three conversed for some time. I tried to appear involved in the conversation while trying not to let my eyes wander through the parts of the house I could see from where I was sitting. This was a humble home, but the art on the walls was fascinating.

About the time I was ready to completely zone out, Badri turned to me and said, "Thad, this is Mr. Nazari and his wife. Mr. Nazari is a retired chemical engineer and actually used to work at Masjed Soleiman in the oil industry. His wife studied briefly under Fatemeh Sayyah at the University of Tehran in 1947 and 1948 before she married Mr. Nazari. She was studying to be a literary archeologist. She left school before completing her studies to be with her husband in Masjed Soleiman and was not able to complete her education. To keep her interest active and to be productive, she began a study of ancient records in this area of Iran."

"Tell it like it really was, Mr. Kabbani," Mrs. Nazari said in English. "You are too much the gentleman, and I appreciate that, but history must be told as close to the truth as possible, no matter the pain."

Turning to me, she continued, "Fatemeh Sayyah was a feminist leader that captured my imagination and was also involved with Ashraf Pahlavi, twin sister to the exiled king. I was a passionate and very naïve young woman. I got caught up in the movements of the day, which included something I would never have imagined, the coup that toppled Prime Minister Mosaddegh and brought the Pahlavi family back to power as the constitutional monarch.

"Of course, that didn't happen until 1953. Between 1948 and 1953, I was suspect and was not allowed to continue my studies. By the time of the coup, I was a young mother. By the time my children had grown, the Revolution happened, and further constraints were placed on me as a Pahlavi and American sympathizer.

"As your brother-in-law said, in order to stay active and productive, I spent over thirty years searching out, restoring, cataloging, and writing about local ancient records. All my work has been transferred to the University of Tehran, but I kept a copy of most things."

"I am amazed," I said.

"Amazed at my early naiveté, or my years of work?" Mrs. Nazari asked.

"I guessed you were in your sixties. I just did the math, and—and you are quite a bit older," I said, embarrassed. "I am sorry if that thought is poor manners."

"I quite like your manners, Mr. Allen," Mrs. Nazari said. My husband would say I am somewhat vain about my looks." She turned to her husband and shared my comments. He laughed and patted me on the back.

"Now, Mr. Kabbani, let's see if I can help you with the information you seek. My husband does not speak English, so would you keep him company while Mr. Allen and I search my files? And it is acceptable in this house that he is alone with me. I was once a liberated woman, and I find that my age allows some liberation once again."

I followed Mrs. Nazari into a small study that barely fit the two of us. Two walls were lined with old metal file cabinets that looked like U.S. World War Two surplus.

"Please move those boxes for me, Mr. Allen. I think what we are looking for, if it exists, is in this cabinet."

I picked up the boxes one at a time and set them in the hallway. They were heavy with papers, and the cardboard was falling apart. When I came back into the study, Mrs. Nazari was already digging through her files.

"Mr. Allen, come here!" Mrs. Nazari said, not realizing I had already reentered the study. "Go get Mr. Kabbani. I think I have found something!"

I brought Badri to the study, but he could only stand at the doorway. Mrs. Nazari had placed the two chairs side by side and was laying out a map on them.

"Mr. Kabbani, I have some bad news for you. The cemetery where your ancestors were most probably buried no longer exists. Your family may have been in this general area during the Sassanid Empire, as some burial records link back to that time. Here are the records of a cemetery that is now under hundreds of feet of water and sediment due to the construction of the Dez Dam just fifteen kilometers north of here.

"This general area has suffered from floods from the rains and Zagros Mountains runoff for millennia. About 500 CE, or AD if you prefer, Mr. Allen, the Sassanids became expert dam builders and built many dams and qanat systems, underground irrigations systems, along the Dez and Karun rivers. This enabled irrigation of the desert as well as mills run by stable river flow. It is very possible your ancestors, Mr. Kabbani, were involved in this business or at least held water rights in the highlands north of us.

"I don't know of any other reason for a settlement in the mountains north of us. The ancient historian Polybius recorded the plans of regional development under the initiative of the central government in ancient Persia. I have studied his works, and one of the sites he himself studied was this area. His work on the political system of five generations not suffering government taxation to lower the cost of development is fascinating.

"The Dez Dam was not built until 1963, I believe. Before that, you could have visited the site, although I don't know if any actual graves were visible. In some areas, we have found ancient gravestones, however. The Dez Dam project's political importance may have swept this under the rug."

"That is sad news, but the records themselves are what I am in search of," Badri explained. "I am trying to make a connection with other family lines. Do you have any information about who may have paid to upkeep the cemetery, any ancient forwarding address—whatever they may have called it in those days?"

"Yes, yes, I may have something. It would be in this same file. I honestly can't believe I found this so easily. Let's see here…" Mrs. Nazari spent another ten minutes looking through her files and reading copies of an ancient script that didn't look like Iranian to me.

"Ah, here is something. Nothing definitive, but something. It isn't payment records, which I may also have, but it is a certificate of ownership of the cemetery. If I am translating correctly, it says *descendant of Tahmasp*. It is not until much later that this account is connected with the name Kabbani." Mrs. Nazari was disappointed, but then, she didn't have all the family history information we had.

"Does it have any location information for this Tahmasp?" Badri asked, trying to not sound excited.

"It says *descendant of Tahmasp of Gerrha*," Mrs. Nazari said. "I am afraid I don't know that place. I could be translating incorrectly. Would you like a photocopy of this document? It is a copy of the original that is now in Tehran, but it is fairly clear."

"That would be wonderful," Badri said.

On the drive back to Ahvaz, Badri filled me in on something Mrs. Nazari didn't say. "Although she interrupted me with perfect English because I was being too nice about a very ugly time for Iran, that was not the biggest surprise. More surprising was, she didn't mention the huge stigma the overthrow of Prime Minister Mosaddegh had on relations with the West. It's like she knew you were American.

"You see, the Iranian Military, with key assistance from the CIA and British Intelligence, successfully overthrew the democratically-elected Prime Minister and installed a monarch, son of the previous king, in part because the Prime Minister nationalized the oil industry.

"This was also the early years of the Cold War, and there were serious concerns that Mosaddegh was leaning toward the Soviet camp. The years of the Peacock Throne, 1953 to 1979, witnessed many advancements and religious freedom but also brutal repression of Shia clerics, religious conservatives, and Iranian nationalists. The Shah also signed over 40 percent of Iran's oil production to U.S. enterprises. This is not an honorable moment for U.S. ethical leadership and fomented the seeds of America as the Great Satan."

I had much to think about on the drive back to Ahvaz. I wondered if there were any unblemished good guys anywhere.

Chapter 20

I SET MY OWN THOUGHTS aside and made our hourly check-in call with Irshad and reported on what we had found. Irshad suggested that everyone continue their search in their assigned areas since they were already there. Who knew what else might be uncovered?

Badri and I returned to Ahvaz to do some research on Gerrha, as even Badri had only heard of the name but knew little about it. Before the rest of the team returned, we had discovered with a quick online search using the computer at the business center at the hotel, that Gerrha was an ancient city located in Eastern Arabia. Gerrha was probably well known to the ancient civilizations of Persia and Arabia because it was an important city of an Arabian kingdom for nearly 900 years, until 300 AD.

It checked out that this city was ruled by the Sassanids at the time of the document Badri had obtained from Mrs. Navari. The potentially devastating news was, Gerrha was destroyed by the Qarmatians in the 9th century, and all its inhabitants were killed. The other frustrating news was, there were several theories as to where Gerrha was actually located. A final thing I found fascinating was the Greek historian Strabo, who was actually from Turkey, recorded that the inhabitants of this city built their houses of salt and repaired them with salt water. A contemporary of Strabo, Pliny, the Elder, stated that the city was five miles in circumference and its towers were also built with blocks of salt.

By early afternoon everyone was back in town. They had found nothing of note but were in good spirits because of Badri's find. For having just broken off his betrothal to Leyla, Irshad seemed in particularly good spirits.

When the group was gathered in his hotel room, he began, "We have truly been fortunate to have Badri Kabbani along on this operation. He was key in saving his sister and some of this team while we were in Cappadocia. His happenstance landing in Hamadan led to our connections in Yazd, which led us here to the ancient area of Susa. Oh, and along the way here helped us overcome potential disaster with his masterful flying exploits. Today he opened up a very promising trail to our next and possible final destination in our search for the book that holds his name."

This speech was so not-Irshad and embarrassing for us all, especially Badri. I don't know what everyone else was thinking, but I was wondering if he had discovered something about Badri that was good for his, Irshad's, advancement.

Badri was not trying to hide his frown, but even that didn't dampen Irshad's praise of him. "Alright, that is way beyond actual events," Badri said, "and everyone here knows it. Let's get on with figuring out our next step. It won't include my airplane this time. I checked with the airport, and the part has not come in. I am grounded for the time being."

"That's not the way I see it," Irshad continued. "You drive that BMW like a fighter jet."

My stomach was turning. I knew I could turn this love fest around like no one else in the group, so I said, "We are all aware of Badri's magnificence." Everyone chuckled, except Badri. "But we also know he is related to me, so that has to be a minor flaw with him."

I knew Irshad would probably agree with that statement also, so I hurried on to my point. "I know less about Arabia, where I understand Gerrha was located. I need a brief explanation of what we are getting into here. Can I, should I, even travel into Saudi Arabia?"

"Good point, Thad," Irshad said. "That should be a point of discussion."

Before Irshad could continue, Hande spoke up and asked, "Thad, could you first catch us up on your research of Gerrha? I have heard of the place, but I doubt any of us here know much of any use. I assume Sami Mansur will be in the Kingdom and act as our sponsor; he's from Saudi Arabia," Hande said to Badri and me, refreshing my memory, "and it would be great to have Karim Arkoun there. He is also a part of Al Huj, an Ismaili from Tunisia, and our best historian. He heads up our research team back in Konya."

"Also really good points," Irshad said. "I have already arranged to have Sami meet us in Saudi Arabia once we figure out where we are going to start our efforts. He is flying into Dhahran tonight. He could take Thad's place in the group if he heads back to Turkey."

"Give us what you have on Gerrha," Lydia said, trying to slow down Irshad.

I wasn't sure I really wanted to return to Turkey, although it would be great to see my sister, Anna. That made me think of Badri, and although I was no operational expert, whatever that was, I didn't like the thought of leaving him here without me as his sidekick.

I said, "Either way, no matter where you need me, I am in this to the end. As far as Gerrha, here is what I have learned." I caught them up on my research and then added, "All that is known for sure is Gerrha was a city in ancient Arabia, located on the west side of the Persian Gulf."

"The Arabian Gulf," Badri said, "according to our soon-to -be hosts."

"I didn't know that they called it something different," I said, surprised I hadn't come across that in my reading. "An inferiority complex? I mean, the United States calls the body of water to our south the Gulf of Mexico.

"Anyway, there are a few theories where Gerrha was located. One theory is it was located under the present day ruins of the Fort of Uqair. The fort is about 50 miles northeast of the city of Al-Ahsa. That theory is based on some descriptions from the Greek—Turkish—" I said nodding at Hande and Leyla, "historian Strabo. A sub-theory here suggests that the city of Gerrha and the Port of Gerrha were located about twenty miles apart.

"The second popular theory is Gerrha is located near the present day city of Hofuf. This final theory I uncovered suggests Gerrha was most likely the ancient city of Hajar, located in modern-day Al Ahsa itself. This last theory appears to be the most accepted. My only problem with this theory is Al Ahsa is located sixty miles inland, and in the ancient trading days, that was a huge distance from the Gulf to start a trading route. I don't know the geography, though, so maybe there is a reason I am missing.

"There is a fourth theory, but I couldn't find much about it. Basically, some believe Gerrha was in the archipelago of islands comprising the modern Kingdom of Bahrain, particularly the main island of Bahrain itself."

"Al Ahsa is a famous oasis," Badri explained, "but also a region that encompasses what is now Hofuf, Uqair, and Bahrain. They aren't all that far apart. I suggest we also go to Dhahran, see what your teammate, Sami, suggests and go from there."

"Done!" Irshad said with ridiculous enthusiasm. "Any questions?"

Of course, there were no questions. I turned to Badri in quiet conversation while the group broke up into other discussions and asked about my passport and visas. He said, "When we got you your passport, we got you visas for Saudi Arabia and the UAE, but not Bahrain. I am sure we can get you one in Saudi Arabia if we need to. I think you should go. Non-Muslims travel in Saudi Arabia all the time if that is a concern. There are only a few places that are restricted. In fact, there will probably be more Americans where we are going than you have seen the entire trip.

"Fort Uqair is located on a large ARAMCO facility, I believe, which is a tiny slice of America in Arabia. There is even a U.S. Military base nearby. You have heard of the Khobar Towers bombing where the U.S. military was housed back in the late 1990s, right? That was in Dhahran."

"Oh, that makes me feel better," I said.

"That was almost twenty years ago. You really need to see this to the end. And I heard nothing of Leyla leaving. You should be here for her, too."

"I want to be a part of this, but Irshad is increasingly belligerent toward me. And what is this new love he has for you?" I asked.

"I have no idea. Up until tonight, I thought he was not happy with me tagging along either. His motivation will surface soon enough," Badri predicted.

"So, would anyone like to get a bite to eat?" Hande asked, breaking up the separate conversations.

"I would," Lydia said smiling.

"Great," Hande said, also smiling. No one else expressed interest, knowing Hande was just being friendly and really didn't want anyone else to volunteer to go with them. "So is this meeting over then?" He asked.

"Let's meet at eight tomorrow morning for breakfast," Irshad said. "I will work on travel arrangements to Dhahran for some time tomorrow if I can work that out yet tonight. I also need to call Konya and update our finances. I will see you all tomorrow morning." Irshad left without saying another word.

"Okay, which one of you took Irshad and replaced him with this nice person?" Hande asked. Lydia bumped him with her hip. "Let's eat," she said. "I want to get to sleep early tonight."

"You had a question that was not answered," Leyla said to me. "Maybe between Badri and I, we can talk to you briefly about Saudi Arabia over room service food. Would that be good?"

"That would be great, if that works for you, Badri," I said.

"I can stay for a short time, but I would like to call Anna tonight and see how she is doing. I will keep operational security and not tell her where we are going, but I have only talked to her once since we left Turkey."

"By all means," Leyla said. "Why don't you start on the contemporary situation in Saudi Arabia, and then you can take off. I will fill Thaddeus in on any historical issues that might connect with our mission and the contemporary issues you raise."

"Sounds great," Badri said, as Leyla ordered food. "The short story is, there are several modern power centers in the Middle East: Iran, Egypt, and Saudi Arabia. A second group of countries are content maintaining close relationships with one or two of these power centers, but never all three. An example would be Assad's Syria, which is close to Iran. A third group of countries has attempted to become a new power center, but all have failed who tried. An example was Saddam Hussein's Iraq, which launched a war with Iran and later attempted to absorb Kuwait. There is a fourth group that just tries to survive and maintain some semblance of sovereignty. Lebanon, Jordan, the UAE, and Bahrain might be examples of that group. And then there are the wild cards. I put Turkey and Israel in that group."

"Where do you put Palestine?" I asked.

"Poor Palestine," Badri said. "Alas, they aren't yet a country and are the unwanted stepchild of the Middle East one day and everyone's favorite cause the next. They are more often a means to a short-term end for the big three and their circles of influence than an end goal as a secure country with full sovereignty, even from other Middle Eastern supporters.

"So, to get back to Saudi Arabia, I think the Saudis are worried that they're encircled by significant instability in Iraq, Syria, Lebanon, Yemen; even Bahrain is uncertain. They play well with everyone in the region to a certain extent, as they are the guardian of Mecca and Medina, and they are still wealthy enough to maintain internal stability. What they don't want to have to do is work directly with either of the other big three, Egypt and Iran.

"Just recently they sent $4 billion dollars to Lebanon to help that country shore up their defenses due to the threat of ISIL, the Islamic State of Iraq and the Levant. But talk with Iran on this is almost out of the question. And Iran would talk to Israel before they talked to Saudi Arabia about this. Egypt is still a regional powerhouse and a source of Arab pride, but they have so many internal problems, they aren't playing the game at the moment."

"But from what I have seen, everyone in this region is more or less related," I noted. "Good grief, I found out today on the web when I was researching Gerrha that Arabs and Persians even share the same alphabet, with the Persians adding a few letters."

"True, but speakers of Hebrew and Arabic, both Semitic languages, have completely different racial and historical backgrounds than Iranians. The Turks, who used to rule both areas, have yet a different language and heritage," Badri pointed out.

"There are some things all or many in the Middle East share: a few words, foods, historical events, religions, and of course weather, climate, and an elephant in the room that is rarely talked about: water. But for every common element, there are diverse and deep differences. The Middle East is perhaps the most complex area of the world."

"And that complexity is raised to even greater heights," Leyla added, returning to the conversation, "with the influence or direct involvement of external players like the United States, Russia, China, Europe, and India, to name a few. The Middle East represented a few chess pieces during the Cold War, and although the West has mostly moved on, the Cold War here has accelerated into boiling peace in our backyard."

"It may take several more generations for all the perturbations of fifty years of Cold War to fully dampen out in this region," Badri added. "The present wave of change, secularism's failure to deliver on many promises, is sectarianism's claim for hope and glory. Add to that the Arab Spring uprisings, and we have a very volatile environment.

"What this region really needs, as does every area of the world, is even-handed and compassionate leadership. That is maybe where Al-Ḥujurāt comes in. Now I am afraid I must leave you so I can call Anna. If you find a solution to all the problems of this corner of the globe, let me know; otherwise, I will see you both tomorrow at eight a.m." Badri left with a smile on his face.

"So how can he smile after providing that description of his home?" I asked.

"There is much good also, or perhaps he was anticipating his call to his wife," Leyla said. "You have traveled now, a little bit, in this region. Can you not find something to smile about?"

"Yes, I can," I said. "But to be honest…" I paused for effect and tried to put on a dour face, "there is something I would rather do with my lips than make a smile."

"And what is that, Majnun?" Leyla asked with her eyes dancing.

I leaned over to her and gave her a soft kiss.

"I see you have taken the challenge seriously and found a solution to all the problems in this corner of the globe, and you didn't come to tell me," Badri said with even a broader smile. "Sorry to interrupt your geopolitical research. You should probably shut the door. This is a hotel with many guests. I just wanted to offer my car if you two wanted to go for a drive or to get something to eat if room service doesn't have anything of interest. I am turning the car in tomorrow morning." He tossed me the keys and left without another word. He shut the door.

"I should be embarrassed, but I am not," Leyla said. "So what would you like to do? Room service, or eat at a restaurant in town?"

"Let's just try room service, as you suggested earlier," I replied. "The rental BMW is tempting, but I really don't want to go anywhere either. In fact, I am a little melancholy about leaving Iran. The people, the culture, the land, the food; it is intoxicating."

"It is a blessing to the world to have an Iran," Leyla said. "Early Greece, the West's celebrated source of western culture and philosophy, learned much from Persia. In many ways the rule of Cyrus, Darius and Xerxes was more enlightened than the Greek City States. Alexander the Great discovered that anew when he arrived in these lands. He was accused of becoming too Persian. He came to conquer, but Persian ideas and culture conquered him, and so it goes on today for those lucky few that get to experience this land and its peoples. But I am also ready to go home."

"I don't know anymore where home is for me," I admitted. "I live in the Central Valley of California, and that is my comfort zone, but I think I was mostly eating and breathing there. That isn't really living. With you there, it would be, but I think you might suffocate, and I know I am getting way ahead of myself."

"You know," Leyla said, taking my hand in hers, "one of the things I adore about you is your motivations. They are uniquely pure. Getting way ahead of yourself, if you were someone else, you could be trying to get me into that bed over there. This is, I think, maybe the third time we have been alone in a hotel room, and you haven't pushed the limits."

"That doesn't mean it hasn't crossed my mind, but like the other night when we shared definitions of *Majnun* and *Mizmiz Depereo*, I wanted to take you in my arms, but it didn't feel right; it wasn't right. You were betrothed, and it would feel like cheating. I want to be able to say I always have your interests above mine, but sometimes that statement gets a little cloudy."

"Thank you. I am honored to be desired and doubly honored to be respected," Leyla said. "I think it best to change the subject. The constant reminder of denial of a desire often has the same result as no denial. If there is a candy bar on the counter and we pass it all day saying, I will not eat that candy, we will eat that candy. Why? Because we gave it energy all day long. Better to put distance between us, not in physical distance but with protective walls of social and religious boundaries that are there for our protection and long-term happiness."

"I think I read somewhere that what you are describing is paradoxical intention. Some might call what you are describing as observing with indifference, but there is no way I can observe you with indifference, no matter how well you can do so. The challenge I have been battling is, I don't think the human brain can replace something with nothing. As my father used to tell me, nature abhors a vacuum. If we don't replace a negative with a positive, it will get replaced, but perhaps by something even worse. What do I replace you with?"

"You don't replace me with anything. You better not replace me with anything! You replace your short-term desires for long-term, lasting love. Don't toss out the aspiration or the passion, though. You never did eat that MARS Bar I gave you in Konya, did you? You wanted to save it and enjoy it when the time was right. If I had given you a box of MARS Bars, you would have eaten one right then. I knew you were special when I got to know you on the plane. I think I started to fall in love with you when you didn't eat that MARS Bar."

"I will have that MARS Bar bronzed when we get back to Konya," I said. "You wouldn't have liked me if I had eaten the bar and thanked you for the special treat?" I asked, wondering if our relationship really was built on luck, or fate.

"Oh, Majnun, you have no idea, do you? So as I suggested, let's change the topic."

Someone knocked at the door, and room service delivered a light dinner that was fair, but not as good as almost everything else I had eaten here, and certainly not what Hande and Lydia were probably enjoying.

"Do you think Iran has MARS Bars?" I asked suddenly.

"Another subject, Majnun," Leyla said as she poked at the food. After a minute she said, "They sell them in Saudi Arabia. Are you coming with us?"

"Yes," I said. "Both you and Badri want me along, so no matter Irshad's issues with me, I am going."

"You bother Irshad because you are everything he is not. So tell me about your connection to Thaddeus of old." Leyla said, ensuring the subject was shifted to another topic.

"I read some things about him on the internet earlier today. I was surprised the Bible was not filtered from the internet here. He has a letter that is a book in the Bible. It is titled Jude, so I never realized it was Thaddeus. The focus of the letter, as far as I could understand it with just a few readings, was to warn the early Christians to beware of false teachers and not to listen to their erroneous teachings. A thought stood out. I wrote it down. Here," I said, grabbing the hotel notepad I had used, "*be wary of those that replace spirit with the sensual, murmurers, complainers, walking after their own lusts, and their mouth speaketh great swelling words, having men's persons in admiration are stains on our feasts of charity.* That made me first think of me, you know, Mizmiz, the crybaby, but then later tonight of Irshad and his flowery words about Badri. What gives with that speech anyway?"

"I have no idea," Leyla admitted. "That was really weird. I kind of thought he was on something, but I know that wasn't it. It was quite uncomfortable, mostly because it was not authentic."

"That's it, Leyla," I said. "That is what bothers me about Irshad. He isn't authentic. It's not really an honesty issue; it's more like always wondering what the agenda is. Maybe that is what the point is with all the issues swirling around about religion in the world. Authenticity, or the lack of it. God created a wondrous, amazing world. The animals and the flowers know. Even the rocks sit patiently and know who God is. They have no questions, no doubts.

"The goodness and perfection of the creator are only apparent to us if we are reflecting on our own essential goodness. We have choice, and when we use that choice in ways that move us from our own authenticity as creations of God, the more we reject that goodness for short-term gain or long-term strategies of power, evil gain, or subterfuge, the less we can see God in His perfection and goodness. We start to believe God wants us to do terrible harm to those who do not believe what we believe. We convince ourselves that we have been called of God to do evil, even if we don't think of it as evil, and no matter what other word we might use."

"I do believe all humans can, if they want to and try to, feel and see the goodness of God," Leyla said. "And when we do, we can see ourselves as tools in His hands. When that happens, we can better see and act for good."

"Can we be deceived, truly thinking and feeling that we are doing good when we are really doing evil?" I asked. "Can we refuse to accept the clever counterfeits of deception and lies—like the words I just read from Thaddeus's letter, *great swelling words that replace spirit with lusts*?"

Leyla was thinking, so I added, "Sometimes it scares me that I really can be deceived. I am influenced too much by things that later are proven hollow or shortcuts to dead ends. I have been there. I had sort of checked out of life, just making a living and coming home to an empty house because I was afraid of deception. That fear itself was deception."

"Some people think we can figure everything out with our minds, that we are the masters of our world," Leyla finally said. "There is mystery in the world, in our lives, especially if we rely only on ourselves. We can lean on science and dismiss all else as chaos, but that doesn't extinguish the fire of our search for meaning. Because of that mystery, we raise the sands of the desert then complain we can't see our way to the oasis. That gives us the false sense of authority to say we can do anything our power allows. And then power becomes the justifier. That is the mirage. I don't think you were deceived by your fear, but it didn't allow you to progress either. You were in the sandstorm the world creates."

"So, what can we know?" I asked. "The question of the ages."

"There is probably much we will never know, at least as mortals walking the earth, but God has not left us completely alone. He gave us prophets, and He has given us his word, in the Holy Scriptures, the Qur'an, the Bible, perhaps other writings. I believe there is light in many places, but only the Qur'an is perfect scripture. I think God gives us feelings when we are pure enough to receive them. If we have fear, or apathy, or evil design, we cannot accept that spirit."

"It makes more sense to me that the feelings, if they come from God, or is God, wouldn't come to us if we're not prepared or worthy to receive it," I said. "I have always wondered about prophets and now apostles too. If God provided them for us anciently, why not now? It certainly isn't that we have all the answers in this crazy world. There are so many Christian churches that use the same Bible, and so many Islamic sects that use the same Qur'an. I am not asking God to take away the need for faith. It would take faith to follow a prophet, too. And I think I understand that Mohammed was the last prophet in Islam, right?"

"The Holy Qur'an says that Mohammed was the last seal, the last prophet, that is, until the end of days. At that time, Jesus Christ will come, and he is a prophet to us, not the Son of God, as he is for Christians. Many Muslims also believe in the Mahdi, the Twelfth Imam. Shia Twelvers, in particular, believe this Twelfth Imam will be a prophet ranking above all other prophets except for Mohammed himself. He is believed to come at the end of days, also. I, too, wish there was a prophet, but I don't want it to be the last of days."

"When I was young my dad told me that an Apostle is a prophet, but not all prophets are Apostles. Apostles were the supreme office of the Christian Church anciently. Of course, this comes from a Christian and Biblical perspective. Does Islam have Apostles?"

"Well," Leyla said thinking, "the disciples of Jesus were Muslims and were from the Children of Israel. The Qur'an does not list their names, but in general, we accept the Bible's list that says that the disciples included Thaddeus."

"Wow, I didn't know that," I admitted.

"I don't want to scare you, but I believe you were Muslim once," Leyla said.

"You mean like reincarnation?" I asked surprised.

"No, not like that," Leyla said. "Many Muslims believe everyone is a Muslim at birth when we take our first breath. We have this understanding that the one God gave us life and that breath is the newborn's way of submitting."

"So you believe the whole world is Muslim?" I asked. "Don't let the Catholics and the Jews and the Buddhists and the Hindus in on that secret."

"Muslim just means a person who submits to God. In that sense, everyone is Muslim, even atheists, because they live and are subject to death. Of course, many in the world don't accept the doctrine of Islam. To truly be Muslim, you have to follow through with your natural intuition and choose to submit."

"I can see that," I said, "but Islam is also a religion of constraint. You aren't allowed to choose not to be a Muslim, but it is okay to be a bad Muslim. Well, not okay, but being bad is not as terrible as apostasy."

"All religions have constraints," Leyla said. "Zoroastrians are Zoroastrians because their fathers were. You cannot be a Muslim by testing your DNA. It is not a medical condition passed on from father to child, like original sin in the historical Christian belief."

"But you are talking about choices in religion," I said. "What if you want out? Dr. Nabat chose to leave Zoroastrianism. No one is going to arrest him or kill him for that. Islam is like the *Hotel California*; you can check in but never leave."

"Don't compare my religion, a sacred thing to me, to a hotel," Leyla said.

"I am so sorry. I really didn't mean for that to come out that way. I am just trying to figure out a place for you and me in all this. There has got to be more for us—something I can hold onto, that we can hold onto."

"Grandfather Rumi said, *Whoever you may be, come. Even though you may be an infidel, a pagan, or a fire-worshipper, come. Our brotherhood is not one of despair, even though you have broken your vows of repentance a hundred times, come.*"

"Is that the only way for you and me?" I asked.

"I don't know. I really don't know." Leyla said with a tear in her eye. "Maybe Leyla and Majnun is more than just a silly story."

Part III: Arabia

Chapter 21

LEYLA AND I HAD FINISHED off the bland room service food last night with a feeling of despair and frustration after the early excitement of our first kiss. She left for her room giving me a cardboard kiss that matched the food. I laid awake much of the night trying to understand and trying to follow through with the idea of me becoming a Muslim. It wasn't that I didn't see many wonderful and great things in Islam. I loved my brother-in-law, Badri, and Leyla was becoming the most important person in my life, but I had to be authentic, just like I had expressed to Leyla last night, and something in me told me there was more.

I think Leyla had a difficult night also. When she entered the room for our 8:00 a.m. meeting, her sandstorm eyes were swollen, and her face was pale. No one said anything, but it was impossible to miss the change in our countenances.

If Irshad noticed, he didn't let on. "Good morning, people. Good news. I was able to get air passage for everyone, including you, Thad, if your plan is to continue with us. You know it may become an issue where you and Lydia are not able to travel with us if we need to go to areas where non-Muslims are not allowed."

"I'm going, Irshad, to Saudi Arabia, that is," I said. "If I can't travel to certain locations, I am fine with that."

"Then let's pack our bags," Irshad said. "We leave for the airport at 10:30 for a flight at noon. We are all on the same flight with Iran Air to Dubai and then Emirates from Dubai to Dhahran. Rooms are booked at the Al Othman in Khobar. Because of the last minute flights, we have a six-hour layover in Dubai, so we will have time for dinner downtown if you like. Any suggestions, Hande?"

"Absolutely," Hande said. "In Dubai, my choice would be Al Nafoorah, Lebanese food. Henry Debs is the General Manager. I could call ahead and have a table ready for us. There is the Ossiano, but that is more atmosphere than great food. And there is local cuisine at Bait 1971, but we will be in Arabia for a few days, so we will have that opportunity in Dhahran."

"Good enough. Al Nafoorah. Make the call," Irshad commanded. "Obviously, no weapons since we are traveling by commercial air. Sami has set up passive surveillance for known Hashshashin and Furqaan operatives and is watching the hotel in case anyone followed him. Keep your eyes and ears open. The Kingdom is generally safer than Iran, but both of these groups also operate with more comfort in Arabia, in particular, Furqaan, which has many sympathizers there. If there are no other questions, then I will see you at 10:00 in the lobby. Long day of travel."

When Irshad was gone, I asked Hande what passive intelligence meant. He said, "Probably paying some people to make a call to us if any name on a list enters the country. Sometimes there is a call, but mostly not."

I had about an hour to be in the lobby and nothing to speak of to pack, so I asked Leyla if she wanted to take a walk. She said sure, but with resignation, not excitement.

"So, how are you doing?" I asked when we got to the street.

"I didn't sleep well," she said. "Did you?"

"No, I felt miserable all night. I can see why it is a practice of your group not to have any two people in a relationship on an operation together. Of course, Hande and Lydia seem to be doing well."

"And why is that?" Leyla asked. "Is it because in their case Hande is the Muslim, and he can marry outside of Islam, whereas I can't?"

"Or that I don't have plans to convert." I offered, to take the blame for our impasse. "We are not to the level in our relationship that we are talking or planning marriage. Do we blow up the bridge now? It will probably only get more complicated and our feelings stronger. Or do we press forward into the abyss?"

"Wow, that makes this affinity, this bond we have, sound more like a zombie invasion than a blossoming romance," Leyla said, looking all the part of a little girl who has lost her way.

I turned to her and almost encompassed her in my arms until I remembered where we were. Instead, I said, "Leyla Celebi, you are fast becoming the most important person in my life. You encompass the meaning of why I get up in the morning. My last thought at night is how lucky I am to know that you are on this earth the same time as me, that our paths crossed, that I have talked with you and shared my deepest thoughts with you, without fear of my ignorance or lack of understanding and that you have trusted me and shared your feelings with me…"

"Oh, so in between waking up and going to sleep I am nothing to you?" Leyla asked trying to hide a slight grin. "And you don't dream of me? I am crushed."

This was Leyla Celebi. Now how could I nurture these brighter feelings? I had no idea. Before I could say anything, she said, "Heterochromia Iridum."

"That is the second time you have said that and caught me completely off guard," I said.

"I think I also mentioned to you that I knew about your eyes because of a distant relative. Not only am I related to Ottoman rulers, but I am related to one Byzantine Emperor, Anastasius I

Dicorus, through his sister. Anastasius had one blue eye and one black eye. He had no children, so I am as close a descendant of him as anyone. Along with my Ottoman and Sufi roots, I have a tiny bit of Roman blood also. The reason I have not mentioned it is that just before this operation, well, before the Fahrunissa Scroll was discovered, I was studying his life. It was odd to think of myself as Roman, exotic, you know. Anyway, one of the things I discovered about him was he was Christian and believed Christ and God the Father were separate beings. That put him in direct conflict with the Council of Nicea and the European Church."

"Kind of like Badri's family when they were Christians as well," I said.

"This was all just an interesting historical side story to my family history until I met you," Leyla continued. "Then it was an interesting intersection until I got to know you and started having feelings for you. Now it feels like an indictment, like I am the one in our relationship that should consider adjusting what I know is true. I have thought about it all night."

"I know one thing. During the day, I only want to be with you. At night, all I want is a MARS Bar," I said.

"Oh, no!" Leyla said with a tone that I took as frustration.

"Alright, you are done with the MARS Bar metaphor. Sorry, really. I was just trying to lighten the mood," I said quickly.

"Quit taking everything so personal, Majnun," Leyla said. "I am sure I just saw a Hashshashin from our encounter in Cappadocia. I don't think he realized I saw him. Take my hand and pull me back toward the hotel."

"Gladly," I said. "Let's go back to the hotel," I said more loudly and with enthusiasm.

"Don't get us arrested, Majnun. Subtleness is the name of the game here. Just grabbing my hand will garner more than enough attention."

We walked back to the hotel trying not to look around. We entered the lobby and didn't see any of the team members. We went to my room and shut the door. Leyla called Irshad and told her what she saw. They spoke in Turkish briefly, and then Leyla clicked off her phone.

"Irshad wants us to stay here," Leyla said. "He and Hande are going to attempt to do some discrete surveillance, but the plan is still to depart as scheduled. I am not surprised that the Hashshashin have shown up here. Historically, their area of operation was Persia, and their first historically recoded victim was a Persian. The assassin disguised himself as a Sufi mystic and entered the Seljuk court with ease. That happened in Hamadan, I believe."

"So we just sit around until it's time to leave and then let them follow us? We have to wonder if the next knock on that door is a crazed killer or just housecleaning? That's crazy," I said in frustration. "Can't we do something to get them off our trail for just a few more days? What if I stay behind and become the bait while some or all of the team travel on? The team will be gone before these guys know what happened. Sooner or later they will figure it out, but that may be enough time to get to the bottom of this Kitab Kabbani search. From what I see as the naïve new guy, we need to go on the offensive. Be proactive, not always accept the reactive mode because that's just how we do things," I said in my best Irshad imitation.

"You aren't going to be the bait to lure in anyone, Thaddeus. Two weeks ago you were a fast order cook, as you keep reminding me."

"Two weeks ago I hadn't crossed multiple continents, an ocean and a sea, traveled the breadth of Turkey and Iran, fought guys trying to kill me. Two weeks ago I was a dot, but today I am connected with you, your group, and people like Boos, Sepideh, Dr. Nabat, Rabbi Halevi, Mrs. Navari, Mack and your great uncle, and the plastic smile team of Jim and Alicia at the Delta ticket counters."

"You know you are a nut, Thaddeus Allen," Leyla said, laughing despite trying to stay serious. "What would you propose we do to take the offensive?"

"That is a better question for the whole team. You have some really smart minds and cool heads, and one gorgeous head that is both smart and cool," I said.

"So you think I am gorgeous and smart?" Leyla asked.

"Oh, I was talking about Badri, but yeah, you are pretty cute, too," I said.

"Alright, that is it, Majnun!" and Leyla attacked me with both hands swinging.

My immediate reaction was to cover my face with my arms, but then I decided to take my own advice and take the offensive. I grabbed her arms as best I could. She was really strong. I put her in a bear hug and squeezed until she stopped squirming. I could tell she was a tiny bit irked that I had taken control so fast. I was surprised myself.

Then she stomped on my foot with hers. Not hard enough to do any damage, but it surprised me. We fell to the floor, but I didn't let go. I was able to pin her down and waited for her to stop thrashing. Looking at her, I was about to say something when I lost my breath. She could tell something happened to me and stopped playing. "Are you alright?" she asked.

"I'm sorry. I just realized anew, for the hundredth first time, how beautiful you are and so much more than that, you are amazing and alive, and wise. It isn't just a physical attraction I feel for you. It's like a—a core desire to protect you and take care of you. I know you don't need that, but it is what I feel."

"You don't know what I need, Mr. Allen." She pulled herself free from my arms that had her pinned down and pulled me to her. "I need you," she whispered. "I need you to be safe and not go do some crazy thing just because you have survived this adventure so far."

"I want to kiss you, you know," I said still out of breath. "But if I do, I can almost predict the future."

I got up and went to the bathroom and splashed water on my face. I came back into the room, and Leyla was still sitting on the floor. She was studying me.

"I have never met a man like you, Thaddeus. Let's go to Arabia. Today. The Leyla and Majnun story originated in Arabia. As I've shared with you, it is a story of obstacles and expectations. They fulfilled their duty to family and cultural expectations and tried to balance that with their desire to be together, but they could not make their love succeed.

"I see our future, too. Maybe not as clear as you just did, but we must go to Arabia to complete the circle. This is our chance to find a way to overcome the obstacles and expectations and find peace and maybe even happiness together."

I reached for her hand and helped her up. "Let's go find Badri and figure out our next step," I said. "No more alone together in hotel rooms."

"I'm a big girl," Leyla said.

"Yes, you are, and that is what scares me," I said with a smile. "This is what big people do. Make grown-up decisions that keep them from acting like children."

"I know," Leyla said. "I was just testing you." She held my hand as we walked down the hall toward Badri's room.

We found Badri talking with Lydia at the end of the hallway. There was a large window there that looked down at the parking lot three stories below. "See anything?" I asked. Leyla did not let go of my hand.

"No, but I am not sure what we could really see from up here without binoculars, anyway," Lydia said. "It's pretty tough to ID someone this far away." She noticed Leyla's announcement of our relationship and gave her a brief smile and then continued. "Hande and Irshad have the other two handheld radios. Hande has not reported in, but Irshad says he has seen nothing."

"Time to leave for the airport," Badri said looking at his watch. "Let's get into the public eye. They may follow, but we will be safer. This is still Iran, and although it isn't a police state, it isn't South Chicago either. We will be fine."

I ran back to my room and grabbed the rabbi's package, and we all walked down and out of the hotel together. Lydia called both Hande and Irshad and told them we were leaving and we would meet up with them at the airport. We went in two cabs, Badri and Lydia in one, Leyla and I in the other. We were checked in and waiting at the gate by the time Irshad and Hande caught up with us.

"Still nothing to report," Irshad said.

"I didn't see anything either," Hande said.

"I am sorry if I was just seeing things," Leyla said. "I suppose it could have been my imagination." She was sitting next to me in the waiting area with her hand casually touching my arm. No one said a thing.

"This group says more in silence than any group I have ever met," I thought to myself. I wanted to say it out loud or post it on Facebook, something, that I was in a relationship with Leyla Celebi, but I tried to act like it was the normal thing like everyone else.

We boarded our flight, and the only thing out of my ordinary was the incredible—no, unbelievable—sunset we enjoyed as we descended into Dubai. Leyla had done some seat swapping with Badri, and she sat next to me and let me have the window seat.

I have never seen and may never again experience a sunset like that one. It wasn't just yellow, orange, and red; it had colors I never knew existed. Leyla pointed out cinnabar, burnt orange, blue that you could swim in, and a dark indigo that melted into a black starlit heaven.

"I thought you were just being funny when you told me your favorite colors were cinnabar and magenta. Now that I have actually seen those colors in nature, I have to agree; they are much better than banana yellow."

"Welcome to the Gulf. Those sunsets happen more often than not. The best way to view the sunset here is sitting in a Bedouin tent away from the cities, smelling the goat roasting on the fire, and letting the immenseness of the wilderness envelop you."

We transited the airport in Dubai without incident, and everyone went directly to the restaurant except for Badri and me. We made a very quick detour by cab to his bank in Dubai and deposited Rabbi Halevi's research books in a safety deposit box. Badri told me customs in Saudi Arabia might confiscate the books, and this would be much safer for now.

It only took fifteen minutes, and we were at the restaurant. Far from being a fun restaurant visit, I began to see the real purpose of this side trip. Immediately after eating, Lydia and Leyla excused themselves and went shopping. They were back in less than thirty minutes, not with baubles and the latest fashions, but with two long black dresses, *abayas* they called them, and grey-brown scarves for covering their hair. Then the briefing began. Irshad took the lead, of course.

"Mostly for Thad's benefit, but also to remind us all of the local requirements, I want to highlight a few points. Sorry if this is old news to you, Badri, but bear with us," Irshad said in a placating tone.

"Thad, in all cases foreigners entering Saudi Arabia must have a Saudi sponsor. That means someone or a company who will vouch for the visitor's conduct while in the Kingdom. We are being sponsored for our visit by Sami, who maintains a small historical research firm in country for requirements such as this.

Leyla and Lydia have additional restrictions and will be met by Sami and taken to the hotel by a driver he has employed.

"This is your last reminder; no physical contact with the opposite sex. Thad, it is against the law to be accompanied anywhere by a woman who is not your wife or a registered family member. The religious police especially target interracial couples, so don't be caught with Lydia or Leyla alone, ever. That is guaranteed jail time at the least—the punishment is worse for the man than the woman. Sami will act as both ladies' registered male guardian.

"We will not be eating together after tonight either. We will travel separately, with the women traveling with Sami's driver. The rest of us will have rental cars waiting for us. I will drive one and will travel with Hande. Sami will drive the other, traveling with Badri and Thad. The women have purchased their abayas. Sami will have *thobes*, a white robe with sleeves," Irshad explained, looking at me, "and a *ghutra*, headdress, if you want to wear one. Badri, it is our standard procedure to wear the thobe, but do whatever is your practice when you travel here. We do whatever avoids attention.

"If we find ourselves at any archeological dig or historical place, we will be able to work together and will not be harassed. Enjoy the next thirty minutes. As is our practice, when we leave this restaurant, we will be in the Kingdom. For practice at first, but the real thing is just a few hours away. Any questions?"

There were no questions. At the end of one of these briefings, I planned to really shake things up and ask a question.

Badri pulled me aside and said, "Don't take that briefing too seriously. What Irshad said is fact, but both Lydia and Leyla have obviously done this before, and they aren't worried. There are over 28 million people in the Kingdom, not counting the average two million *Hajj* visitors a year, and they live happy and productive lives. It is a different place than anywhere you have ever been, and the rules are seriously enforced, but the people are loving, kind, and like anywhere else, are just trying to simply live their lives."

"It looked like serious desert that we were flying over on the way here. I am more worried about that than I am about holding hands with Leyla."

"Don't be too worried about the desert. This is a great time of year to visit. In high summer the temperature can reach 130 degrees Fahrenheit and less than 32 degrees in the winter months. It will probably be in the low 80s during the day and the low 60s at night. Don't get me wrong; this is one of the most desolate land masses on the globe. They don't call the area just to the west of us *Rub al-Khali*, the Empty Quarter, for nothing. Well, that isn't fair to the land. The literal translation is the *Abode of Silence*, which conjures up a more romantic vision of the largest unbroken expanse of sand in the world. But there are areas that remind me of Arizona and the Grand Canyon, with mountains as high as ten thousand feet and valleys with garden paradise oases that are more memorable and miraculous because of the surrounding land."

"Saudi Arabia takes up something like 80 percent of the Arabian Peninsula," Leyla added as she walked up to Badri and me. "The Kingdom is bordered by Jordan, Iraq, Kuwait, Qatar, Bahrain, the United Arab Emirates, Oman, and Yemen. Flanked by the Red Sea on the West Coast and the Persian Gulf to the east."

"I just love it when you talk geography to me," I said to Leyla. Badri took that as his cue to excuse himself.

"I think you are going to really enjoy your visit to Arabia," Leyla continued. "I wish we could get you to some of the really amazing cities, like Riyadh, Jeddah, and Mecca and Medina. There are literally a thousand restaurants in Riyadh, and Olaya Street is listed as some of the most expensive commercial space on the planet."

"I thought I was restricted from Mecca and Medina?" I asked.

"Yes, but Riyadh and Jeddah are the two fastest growing cities in the world, and it seems a shame to miss those as well."

"Well, if the next week goes anything like the past two weeks, who knows where we will end up," I said. "The only part of the journey I don't think I am ready for is not being able to hold your hand or be close to you. How in the world do young people even meet and get to know each other?"

"Most meetings of youth are arranged and supervised by the parents with the strict plan of marriage. Technology has changed this somewhat. Not many years ago, there were about a million cellphones in the Kingdom; now there are over 15 million. Not only can young people secretly pass on phone numbers and data, but they can get by the filters and police using Bluetooth, which allows high-speed transfers of photos, videos, and messages at a range of about 15 yards. The government tried to shut that down, but gave up, as it was almost impossible to find cellphones without Bluetooth or cameras. Sad, really. Technology in the hands of the naïve is even more dangerous, I think."

"Hmm, maybe we can at least Bluetooth over the next few days, except I don't have a cellphone," I shared.

"Don't worry, Majnun," Leyla said with a smile. "It will all work out. Hopefully, we will get this operation completed, save the world, and figure out how to solve our own challenges."

"I am glad you listed those in descending order of easiness. So can I ask you a very personal question?"

"I think so," Leyla said.

"What do you wear under an abaya? They look like they could increase the heat by twenty degrees."

"Don't get your imagination going," Leyla said. "You men think everyone is running around in scanties. Most women wear comfortable clothing underneath. I usually wear jeans and a shirt.

In the summer it can get kind of hot along the coast where it is also humid, but in dry heat like in Riyadh, it isn't too bad."

"No, honestly I didn't mean anything, um, sensuous. I was thinking more about the layers of clothing and the heat collected by wearing black. It almost seems like a punishment."

"Sorry for assuming. In some ways it is freedom. No one is looking. It is like I disappear, and we don't have to spend hours in front of the mirror…"

"You don't need to spend even ten minutes in front of the mirror. You wake up perfect." I said.

"I take it back; I was correct in assuming your imagination had a hold on you. Just keep thinking that, though."

"I guess we need to get going. It looks like the group has left. Time to find this book." I was trying to get my game face on as best I could.

"You know, we aren't alone in a hotel room, and it will be days before we can even hold hands. Follow me."

I followed Leyla down the hallway of the restaurant. Lydia was standing by a door and turned the other way when we approached. Leyla opened the door, and I followed her into a room of stacked linens and table accouterments. Leyla turned to me as soon as I shut the door and embraced me. We kissed more passionately than we ever had. But no sooner had she started, she stopped. At least it seemed that way to me.

"That, my dear Thaddeus, is for the wonderful person you are and because I want you to know I am worth waiting for. I don't know what you really think about me, but I have only kissed two boys in my life outside of family greetings. One is Irshad, one kiss only, and believe me, that didn't count. The other boy was when I was 17, and I cut my lip on his braces. I had to tell my dad I had a cold sore, and I felt worse about the lie than the secret kiss."

"If we had another thirty seconds, I could share my entire love life," I said, "but let's go get this book search going and done. The sooner we do, the sooner we can invest serious time developing our own history."

I opened the door and let Leyla lead the way. I heard her whisper a "thank you" to Lydia as she passed.

Chapter 22

THE KINGDOM OF SAUDI ARABIA. Just the sound of the name creates vivid pictures in my mind. Ever since I read *Seven Pillars of Wisdom*, by T. E. Lawrence, this land had captured my imagination. The airport in Dhahran did not disappoint me. Men passed by in white flowing robes and various colored headdresses, *ghutra*, I think Irshad called them. Most were also white or white-and-red checkered. Women wore black abayas, but I could already pick out varieties and levels of quality. Not everyone appeared the same even though their clothing at first glance seemed to portray that. I did notice that the abaya and veil tended to accentuate Leyla's amazing eyes to a new level.

There were scents of musk and what Badri told me was *oud*, a fragrant wood that has a musty woody-nutty smell. Without much baggage, we transited customs quickly, and Sami was waiting for us in the next room to take responsibility for our group. We all greeted each other in a professional manner and were out of the airport in minutes. We traveled in the cars Sami had ready for us down the King Fahad Road, which took us through the middle of the city and then south paralleling a few blocks from the waterfront. We got off on Old Airport Road and were at our hotel in twenty minutes from leaving the airport.

"We will meet in the hotel business center," Irshad said. "Get checked in and see you there in half an hour, at eleven. Keep the three handheld radios on." One radio was for Badri and me; one for Leyla and Lydia; and one for Irshad, Hande, and Sami.

Badri and I got to the business center first. We were reviewing the statement I remembered from Badri's grandfather when Sami, Lydia, and Leyla entered.

"The day will come when the family will retrace its steps desperately in search of its secrets as the Hajj pilgrim retraces Hagar's steps from Safa to Marwa in her desperate search for water," I repeated.

"So, if Safa was the Susa region in Iran, our family's first known traditional homeland, what is Marwa? The cemetery records sent us here, but are we on the right track?" Badri asked himself out loud.

"Briefly tell me the story of the two hills again," I requested.

"Hagar, Abraham's wife, needed to feed her young baby, Ishmael," Sami began to review for the group. "She started searching for food and water in the area where Abraham had left her. She traveled between the hills Safa and Marwa in her desperate search seven times. Allah, in response to Hagar's prayers, created a spring of water at Ishmael's feet to fill their thirst. With their thirst quenched, Hagar climbed nearby hills searching for food. Traders stopped in the valley and asked Hagar's permission to water their camels. Over time, the spring became well known, and people decided to settle in the little valley, and eventually the settlement grew into the city of Mecca. Abraham returned from time to time to visit. When Ishmael turned thirteen years old, Abraham constructed the *Kaaba*, a special house of worship."

"So the spring isn't located on either hill?" I asked.

"There is only 300 meters between the two hills. The Well of Zamzam is located 20 meters east of the Kaaba," Sami said.

"Your grandfather told me we would retrace the steps in search of water. If Safa represents Iran and Marwa represents Arabia, maybe we are looking for water?" I suggested.

"I think we can be even more specific," Badri said. "Safa represents the Susa area in Iran, and Marwa represents the Mecca area in Arabia. My ancestor fought in the Battle of Badr. Although my great grandfather is found in the Levant centuries later, I have many relatives even to this day in Arabia. One, my great grandfather's uncle, was the Governor of the Provence of Mecca."

"Good point, Badri. Can we also pinpoint the place of water?" Lydia asked.

"A place of water between Susa and Mecca?" Leyla asked. "Didn't your family also work in the incense trade? Instead of Mecca, perhaps the Arabian end point is Aden or Sanaa."

"Not that many good restaurants in Sanaa," Hande said walking into the center with Irshad. "So what are we talking about?"

"It would be best if individuals waited until the full team was together to support the discussions," Irshad said, raining on our brainstorming parade.

Badri ignored Irshad's remark and explained, "We were relooking at the statement of my grandfather to Thad. If Safa represents the Susa area in Iran and Marwa represents the Mecca area in Arabia, then what would be the Zamzam well, the place of water in between? Or is Mecca the appropriate end point, which would change the location of the water?"

"Why do we need to know this?" Irshad asked. "We have found the cemetery records which have led us to ancient Gerrha. We need to focus there."

"Let's keep the conversation going, but focus on Gerrha," I suggested. "If the first third of the statement by Grandfather Kabbani got us this far, it would be jumping the gun not to consider the rest, even if just to back up our progress. But we do have a solid lead, as Irshad points out. Brainstorming on the statement of a riddle-master when we have hard evidence in hand would not be wise."

"Jumping the gun. You Americans have so many funny statements," Hande said.

"One-third of the statement? I was only thinking of it in two parts," Lydia said.

"Safa and Marwa create a line, and the water that Hagar was looking for, perhaps the book we are looking for, is in between those points on the line. Once we confirm what Marwa represents, that will help us determine where our Zamzam spring is at."

"Following the book's connection to water, this concept also supports what we know from the Fahrunissa Scroll," Leyla added. "The scroll mentions that the Kitab Kabbani was one of Rumi's books that Shams tossed in the water, but came out dry. It fits."

"Alright, alright," Irshad acquiesced. "We can talk more tomorrow. The plan is breakfast by eight and then travel in our three vehicles to Fort Uqair on the ARAMCO facility. It is doubtful we will find anything there, but best to check it off the list first. Sami has obtained a pass for tomorrow only. Lydia and Leyla will be in the lead car with Sami's driver. Badri, you will take Thad and Hande in the second car. Sami and I will leave a few minutes later to see if we have anyone following us. Just wait at ARAMCO guest parking until we get there, and Sami will check us in. Sami's driver knows where. Do you know the facility, Badri, or do you need a map?"

"I know the place. I believe one of my relatives built that part of the facility," Badri said to a few quiet snickers from Lydia and Hande.

"Good, then," Irshad said. "Any questions?"

There were no questions. I got a wink from Leyla, and I noticed Lydia accidentally bumped into Hande, and they exchanged apologies.

I was asleep before midnight and up by seven. I just couldn't sleep. I dreamed of Leyla again. Instead of flying, we were both stuck in quicksand. She was calling out to me, but I couldn't reach her.

"Badri, does the area we are going to have quicksand?" I asked on the way to breakfast.

"The only areas of quicksand that I know of are in the Empty Quarter. The most famous are quicksands of Umm al Samim, which is around the eastern borders of the Empty Quarter and in Oman. Why do you ask?"

"Crazy dreams last night. I must be chewing too much of the anise seeds that the rabbi gave me," I said.

Breakfast was the best I had eaten since, well, since ever. I was never before a breakfast eater, but I will be now, now that I know what I want. Several stacks of freshly baked flat bread were delivered to our table. When the cloth that covered the pile closest to me was lifted, an unmatched fragrance made my mouth salivate. For a brief moment I was glad Leyla wasn't at the table to see me look and act like a ravenous dog. I watched Badri put a salty white goat cheese in the bread, along with various colors and sizes of olives and a kind of crème cheese that he called labnah on a piece of the bread he had torn off and put it in his mouth. I followed suit and gave up Lucky Charms forever.

Dates and some kind of sweet shredded wheat treat called *kanafih* were also served. I had a little piece, but it was too rich for me. I had some fresh orange juice, but everyone else had this thick coffee that looked more like a petroleum product than a drink. I assumed Leyla and Lydia, in a partitioned-off part of the hotel restaurant, had the same thing. I had brief eye contact with Leyla as we all headed for our cars.

We drove out of the city and were soon in the desert on Abu Hadirya Road heading west then north for a couple of miles. There was only a rare plant here and there and a lot of sand and rock. We turned left on Old Abqaiq Road and headed south. We passed signs for the King Abdul Aziz Airbase and an ARAMCO housing area. We turned left on the Coastal Road and headed south. The Persian Gulf, I mean the Arabian Gulf, was on our left, and desolation was on our right.

We passed a sign for Half Moon Village and Alkhaleej Makarim Village and later signs for several beaches, Bodel, Fahad, and some only marked in Arabic. Power plants, a salt factory, and other ARAMCO facilities appeared near the water as the road headed inland. We turned left toward the water at a sign only in Arabic, but soon I saw signs for ARAMCO Beach.

No sooner had we passed that area than I saw signs for Al-Uqair and Uqair Beach. We took this exit and headed straight on this road that ended at a roundabout. From there I could see the fort to the east. We waited in the parking lot for Irshad and Sami, who arrived within a few minutes. In total, the trip took about an hour.

We were told that the fort was open to visitors, but we had to get special passes to be able to view the other buildings. That took another thirty minutes. We were given ARAMCO maps of the old facilities.

An ARAMCO employee who looked like he was from the Philippines explained, "The old fort is of Portuguese and ancient Islamic origin. This used to be a very busy trading port, but the lagoon is shallow, and modern seaworthy vessels cannot use it. The Saudi Tourism Council has long-term plans to make this area into a deluxe tourist destination, but those plans are moving very slow. There are two interesting points about the fort. This is where the Protocol of Uqair was issued in 1922 that established the modern borders of Saudi Arabia. This is also where some studies suggest the ancient city of Gerrha was located."

"Are there any records, ancient relics, or other proof of that claim?" Irshad asked.

"Nothing definitive that I know of. I have worked here for twenty-two years and have seen archeological teams come and go, but it appears the desert has swallowed any evidence. Most of the studies I have read link Gerrha here because of the lagoon and the location of the Al-Hasa oasis. Artesian wells once fed a series of interconnected streams and lakes draining northeastward toward the Persian Gulf just above Uqair, so traders could safely travel deep into the desert from this port. Walls have been found, as well as an ancient salt mine just to the north of us. As you probably know better than me, some Roman and Greek histories say Gerrha was built of salt blocks."

The ARAMCO employee left us on our own as he had other duties to attend to. It appeared there was no one here that had an interest or formal training in archeology.

"Let's find some shade and talk about this," Irshad suggested.

We walked over to the fort and poked around for a few minutes, but it was obvious nothing was there. Inside the ancient and dilapidated walls, two straight staircases led to a second floor where some rooms were still intact. We gathered there for the view and to be away from prying eyes. Leyla sat on the floor, propping her back against the wall. I sat next to her, but not too close, in case we had unexpected visitors.

"I am not sure what I expected, but I don't see how this gets us anywhere," Irshad said with frustration in his voice. "No archived records from here exist from any period earlier than World War One. Other archeological teams must have asked the same questions, because when I was collecting our passes, I spoke briefly with the facilities supervisor, and he said that not even the Portuguese have any records of the fort or what their explorers found when they got here. I guess I was expecting something more like the Susa area in Iran."

"The desert here is more demanding on humankind than across the Gulf," Sami said. "Remember, Susa was located just outside of Mesopotamia, which has been very kind to man since Adam and Eve. No doubt Gerrha was near here and housed riches unimaginable. Records of their wealth and of their warehouses of commodities from Europe and China note this, but the one instance I find most telling is they bought off a single Greek invasion with 500 talents of silver, 1000 talents of frankincense, and 200 talents of 'stacte' myrrh. I don't know how much the frankincense and myrrh would be worth, but the silver alone would be about 50,000 pounds which today would be worth about 25 million Euros, or something like $33 million U.S. dollars. Not bad for a little desert trading post."

"Impressive, until you consider this same area now generates net revenues in excess of $300 billion a year," Hande added. "And that is the petroleum dollars. This little area is also the world's largest producer of dates, with over ten million date trees alone at the Al-Hasa oasis that harvest over half a million tons of dates annually. Not bad for the Empty Quarter."

"Yes, not bad," Irshad interjected. "So, let's get back to finding the Kitab. I doubt there is a Gerrha treasury that we will discover."

"If there was a treasure to be found, this entire desert would have been dug up and Gerrrha pinpointed long ago," Lydia added.

"Help me with the geography of the peninsula," I requested. "The Safa and Marwa discussion from last night still bothers me. If we are right and for the Kabbani family that is metaphorical for Susa and Mecca, then what is in between? Are we on the right track considering the Zamzam well, and what does that represent?"

"The key city between Susa and Mecca at around the halfway point is Ha'il," Sami said. "It is the breadbasket of the kingdom with much irrigation. Historically Ha'il derived its wealth from being on the camel caravan route of the Hajj."

"That certainly makes sense," Irshad said. "But the location of the support for the cemetery came from Gerrha. Is there a theory that Ha'il was Gerrha?"

"No way," Sami said. "We know for sure that Gerrah was in this general area."

"Wait," I said. "Your family was and still are traders, right, Badri?"

"Yes," Badri said, wondering where I was going with this.

"We aren't talking about going back and forth between Safa and Marwa in a religious sense. Hagar was just looking for water and food. That is what Badri's family did for centuries. They made their living on trade. So what were the trade routes of the day?"

"The An-Nafud Desert in the north of Arabia created a natural boundary which took the trade routes through Mesopotamia and down the east coast of the Gulf. The Rub Al Khali Desert, the Empty Quarter, in the south, created another natural border, so the trade routes stayed north of that area," Leyla said.

"And the routes were also to the north of the Jubal Tuwayq Mountains," Sami added.

"So somewhere in the middle of the peninsula, the routes cut across from east to west?" I asked.

"Yes, that is where the Al Hasa Oasis became so important. And remember what the ARAMCO employee said: there was a series of interconnected streams and lakes leading to the oasis," Sami said.

"So what is halfway in between Susa and Mecca along the trade routes?" I asked.

"No, not halfway," Badri said. "I think I am the only one here who has been on the Hajj. The Zamzam well is actually closer to the Safa Hill than the Marwa. Maybe a third of the total distance from Safa and two-thirds from Marwa. I have never considered that important before, but in this context, it might help locate Gerrha."

"Or at least where in the kingdom of Gerrha the book might be," Leyla added. "Remember, it wasn't exactly in the City of Susa we found our first clues, but in the traditional region of Susa."

"Some say Gerrha is the port; some say it is a place away from the port, like Thad outlined for us," Sami said, getting excited. "But Gerrha was not just a city but a kingdom as you say. Ancient mail would not have been so specific because there would have been no need."

"Just as there would have been no need for last names at that time," I added.

Badri had quietly been studying his map and jumped up and said, "I don't believe it! Following the probable routes down from Susa to Mesopotamia and from there down the Arabian Gulf Coast and then across, in between the An-Nafud Desert to the north and the Rub Al Khali to the south, and also to the north of the Jubal Tuwayq Mountains and finally down to Mecca, then cutting that route into thirds, the first third falls near the Al Hasa Oasis. With modern travel, I never realized how wide the Arabian Peninsula actually is."

"That's where we should be today, not here at this broken down fort," Irshad said.

"This is a great place to be," Leyla said. "We are traveling the route that Badri's ancestors traveled. They set foot in this very fort and probably looked out these second-story windows at the view of a bustling harbor laden with their goods, destined to the west for buyers in Medina, Mecca, and Yemen, perhaps farther on to Egypt and North Africa. Or ships or caravans laden with frankincense, myrrh, dates, gold, salt, and gems for Persia, Europe, India, or China. This is the place of legends and fortunes."

"Speaking of legends, the Queen of Sheba went through Al-Hasa on her way to meet with King Solomon in Jerusalem," Lydia said.

"And it is also the traditional burial place of Leyla and Majnun," Leyla whispered to me.

"We are only thirty miles from Al-Hofuf, the main city in the Al-Hasa Oasis region," Irshad said, "Let's go there for lunch and sort out our next step. Hande?"

"Plenty of fast food places, even a couple Mexican places to make Thad feel at home. How about Al Saudi? Good food, local, and quick. The dividers are also low, so we can keep an eye on Lydia and Leyla."

"Right, you mean so we can keep an eye on you cowboys," Lydia said.

We saddled up and drove in a wagon train of three cars. For the first time, I wondered what Sami's driver did while he was waiting for us. Sami explained that if the driver stayed with us, he would become part of the group and thus, not appropriate to be the driver for two females, so he was unfortunately stuck with the vehicle at all times.

We entered Al Hufuf, also spelled Al-Hofuf on some street signs, only twenty-five minutes later. It was crazy to think this was at best two long days of travel at the time of the Kitab Kabbani. The restaurant we ate at was right across the street from a Kentucky Fried Chicken. It was disappointing, and also a little comforting, I will admit, to see the long arm of American franchising in this oasis.

And then I saw it. Just down the street, I saw a Cinnabon shop. I couldn't believe it. I treated everyone to a gooey pecan roll, even though Badri had to pay because I couldn't use my debit card here.

Sami had attempted to coordinate an office for our meeting at King Faisal University in Al-Hofuf, but his friend there was unavailable. Badri made a call, and he took us to the Al-Hofuf offices of his relative's construction company. As we walked through the entryway, I counted office addresses on the wall in twenty-five locations in Saudi Arabia and twenty-three offices in eleven other countries in the Middle East, Germany, and China. Just a small business enterprise.

We were escorted to a conference room on the third floor where it would be appropriate to meet with both men and women. Refreshments were brought in, and we were left alone as Badri had requested.

"Right. We are here," Irshad began. "Where do we start?"

"The Hofuf Museum is in a government building near the Department of Education. It has a lot of antiquities and could hold archives as well," Sami offered. "But if they actually had an ancient book, I am sure it would be on display, or at least the world would know about it."

"The Qasr Ibrahim, also called the Qaser Al-Qubbah, has an archive as well, but I agree it's hard to believe they would have an ancient book and the world know nothing about it," Hande said. "I think the castle was built in the 10th century, so it might have some information about the Kabbani family. Your uncle who owns this company—he wouldn't know anything, would he?"

"I asked when I called to schedule a conference room," Badri explained. "He and his family are out of the country, visiting London before it gets too cold and rainy. He is a very busy man and has not been able to dedicate time to this family folklore project. This company is only one of eight company groups he owns. Besides construction, he has a significant footprint in trading, manufacturing, hi-tech services, telecommunications, real estate, media, and education. He actually lives in Riyadh, and, although probably familiar with the family lore, this has been more a project from my side of the family in the Levant."

"It all makes so much sense, but we are completely at a dead end," Irshad said. "This is the largest oasis in the world. If the book is here, it will be like finding a needle in a haystack."

Chapter 23

"OR WORSE THAN A NEEDLE in the haystack. I wonder if this is only a myth," Irshad lamented. "Maybe it never existed."

"That's entirely possible," Badri said, "but I think it did exist at one time. There is too much evidence suggesting it did."

"This is not a unique instance of an ancient book," Leyla said. "There are many that have been discovered. Some simply survived through the antiquities, even with people trying to destroy them. Like the Encyclopedia of the Brethren of Purity from Basra, originally written in Persian in the ninth century."

"And the Kitab sirr al-asrar, The Book of the Secret of Secrets, written in Arabic about the same time as the Kitab Kabbani," Lydia added.

"There have also been surprising discoveries," Badri continued, "like the Dead Sea Scrolls in 1947 and just a few years ago seventy small metal books that date to 60 AD discovered in some caves in Jordan. Back in 2006, a thousand-year-old Book of Psalms, from the Bible, was discovered in a bog in Ireland where even stone castles hadn't survived the harsh climate there. Even more surprising, just last year on an ancient manuscript of the Old Testament of the Bible, a Greek text from Euripides that had been erased was accidentally discovered using multispectral imaging and dated nearly five hundred years earlier."

"Great," Irshad interrupted, "So it can happen. And it can happen in many different ways. What does that do in getting us closer to the Kitab Kabbani?"

"It means we don't give up," I said. "It means that until we have exhausted every avenue of discovery, we don't quit. What did you think, that the book was just going to be sitting on some forgotten shelf in a museum or that we were going to find a treasure map and dig it up?"

"There is too much riding on this find," Irshad said, staring at me with smoldering eyes.

"Irshad is right," Leyla said seemingly unaware of Irshad's anger. "The world needs the Kitab Kabbani. It needs the light of ancient understanding, a new witness of original purity. Maybe the only way we will find it is with the same feeling with which I hope it was written and borrowing from that future light to guide our path to it."

"You sound like today's fundamentalists," Hande said. "Only nicer and with a less cruel belief of what the ancients might deliver to this generation."

"Actually, what I was thinking about was, maybe we are searching among the branches for what only appears at the roots," Leyla said.

"What is that?" I asked, startled by the thought.

"Rumi," Leyla said. "Just a thought. He tells us to look at the roots, the origins, the inside core. Maybe there is a deeper meaning to what Badri's grandfather told you."

"And know what feels true and follow that to the source," I added almost to myself.

"Let's deal with the facts, people," Irshad said. "What we feel is not going to get us anywhere. I am going for a walk. Let me have one of the radios. Badri, I will call you when I would like to get back into the building." With that, Irshad marched out of the conference room.

I ignored Irshad's frustration but partly understood it. "I am going for a short walk, too. Can I go to the Men's Room unescorted?" I asked Badri.

"Sure. It's down the hall to the right," Badri said.

I massaged my neck as I walked to the bathroom. "The origin, the deeper message," I swished around in my head. I washed my face at the sink and looked in the mirror. "Was Irshad right? Was this hopeless? Did we simply not have enough facts?" I wondered.

I walked over to the window, letting my thoughts wander. Unlike the conference room, which had no windows, the bathroom had a huge window that went almost to the floor. "I guess one must not share corporate secrets with spying eyes, but one can take care of personal business for the world to see." I mused.

My eyes scanned the buildings, and then something caught my eye. It was Irshad across the street in a park talking to someone. He was waving his hands, and the other man had his arms folded on his chest. Irshad stopped waving his hands, and the other man pointed at him, and Irshad only stood there. As they parted, the man turned toward the building I was in, and although I was three stories up, I recognized him. It was The Voice.

I returned to the conference room refreshed but agitated. "Was Irshad the danger within that the rabbi had warned me about?" I wondered.

"Badri, can I speak to you for just a minute?"

"Yes," Badri said getting up from his chair and walking to the door. "You look a little pale. Are you feeling alright?"

Once we got to a quiet place in the hallway I said, "I just saw Irshad talking to the Hashshashin guy I call The Voice. I saw them through the window in the bathroom. I am sure of it. They were in the park across the street."

"Interesting," Badri said pulling me into a vacant office. "I have kept a few thoughts to myself about him. It is easy to pin things on him emotionally because he isn't the most warm-and-fuzzy guy around. But consider this: Irshad completely missed the man you call The Voice when he shot at him in Ozkonak, the underground city, at less than five feet away. He knew of the other tunnel entrance because they had just brought him down that way after presumably being captured, yet he tried to lead us out the way that had the guards. Did he really knock out The Voice? He never even tied him up. I take personal offense to this because he then shot Anna. And how could they keep up on all our movements? They didn't get everything from my flight plans."

"So what do we do?" I asked.

"Nothing for the moment," Badri said. "We need to keep an eye on him, figure out if anyone else is working with him and what is really going on, if we can. Is he being blackmailed, is he one of them, are they partners in some bigger plot? At some point, we don't let this go any further, and we back out of this operation and get out of here."

"Not without Leyla and the other members of the team," I said. "I don't want to leave them with an unknown danger."

"Right. Admit it; you don't want to leave Leyla under any circumstance. For now, let's go back to the conference room and press on like we know nothing of this. I'm guessing Irshad is going to misstep, and we will hopefully be ahead of the game. But don't be a hero. I think he might be armed, and he is certainly willing to harm or even kill if he is in league with the Hashshashin."

We went back into the conference room just as Irshad was exiting the elevator. "I didn't need to call you," Irshad said. "The security guard remembered me and let me in."

"I hope the walk was helpful," Badri said to Irshad. "Thad has not been feeling well, so you didn't miss a thing."

After we were all seated again, I repeated for the hundredth time, "The day will come when the family will retrace its steps desperately in search of its secrets as the Hajj pilgrim retraces Hagar's steps from Safa to Marwa in her desperate search for water." I paused and then asked, "So what are the roots of that statement?"

"Mankind will always be in some sort of survival mode while living on the earth." Lydia offered. "Hagar went back and forth between the hills seven times. Why seven? The number is a symbol. It's more than one, so it represents change and achievement. This number in many religions represent completion, perfection, even eternity."

"During the Hajj, the pilgrim goes around the Ka'ba seven times," Badri said. "As you note, Lydia, there is a requisite seven trips to and from Safa and Marwa. Another Hajj duty is to stone Satan seven times. Also, we are commanded by seven commands. There are seven heavens."

"Joseph of Egypt held the lives and survival of a country in his hands for seven good years and seven bad years," I added.

"So does that mean we will never find the Kitab Kabbani? The search is eternal?" Hande asked.

"It's starting to feel that way," Irshad said, his first input since returning from his walk.

"Probably the way Hagar felt looking for water," I suggested. "Why did she walk between the hills seven times?"

"It was the desert heat," Leyla said. "Mirages of water appeared near the two hills. When Hagar arrived at Marwa for the seventh time, she heard a quiet voice, and she commanded herself to listen with her heart. She heard the voice again and said, 'I hear your voice; have you got something to help me?' And she saw an angel bring water to the place we know as Zamzam."

"And the mountains shall vanish as if they were a mirage," Badri said with a smile. That's Surah 78:20, Thad, from the

Qur'an. We have been guided this far, a little bit by our own wisdom, but mostly by an unseen hand. Several times on this journey I have experienced the still point in a turning world."

"Wow, the still point," I repeated. "Is that from the Qur'an?"

"T.S. Eliot," Badri said. "I think we are at another still point right now. What is the quiet voice, the *ilm al-ladunni,* our *direct inner knowing,* saying to us?"

"This is ridiculous," Irshad said throwing up his hands. "I am as religious as the next person, but we are not going to sit here with no plan and nothing to do except listen for a quiet voice and look for an angel."

I passed a note to Leyla like I was in grammar school. It read, "*I see an angel right in front of me. What I wouldn't give for your quiet voice whispering in my ear, just like in the tunnels of Ozkonak. I need to talk with you, alone, soon. Something very important.*"

Leyla read the note and looked at me quizzically. I raised my eyebrows. Leyla cleared her throat and said, "I agree with Irshad. Let's do something. I am not discounting our inner knowing, but Thad mentions," and she held up the note I had just passed her, "that the quiet voice has accompanied our actions, not our inaction. I suggest we break up into teams as we did in Susa and hit various possible sites where we might find more information about ancient books, about Gerrha, and about any ancient inhabitants here. Let's just assume this is Gerrha and prove it wrong, or right. I will go with Badri and Thad; Lydia, you take Hande and Irshad. Sami, could you go with your driver and get us accommodations for tonight?"

Everyone was quiet, waiting for Irshad to say something. He was studying Leyla and finally said, "You are putting the entire team in danger with this arrangement. Sami is your registered guardian."

"I am aware of that, Irshad," Leyla said. "Sami can provide written permission for us to travel as a professional group, as he had an emergency that did not allow him to continue this evening with our business. It won't keep us from possibly getting stopped by curious religious police, but it may get us out of trouble if we are stopped. You okay with this, Lydia, Hande?"

"We are all okay with it," Lydia said. "We have done this several times in the past with no problems. Like you said, let's get in a productive afternoon and evening and see what we come up with."

"Very well, then," Irshad said. "Your idea, Leyla. Where do you propose we go?"

"You three hit the museum, the university, and anywhere those sources might lead. Another thought has come to my mind. Talking of Hagar reminds me that Gerrha was a Greek alteration of the Arabic word Hagar, which we know today as Hofuf. We will go to the government buildings at Al Hofuf and see if Badri can get us into their archives. It has been a continuously inhabited city for over a thousand years. Who knows how far back records may go? Let's meet up at whatever hotel Sami comes up with at eight this evening."

"Sounds like we have the basis of a plan," Irshad said in frustration. "Keep your eyes out for anything suspicious. Any questions?"

There were no questions. I certainly had a few I wanted to ask Irshad about his friend in the park, but now was not the time. Sami wrote out Leyla's permission slip, and we were off. I rode up front with Badri. Leyla was in the backseat. As soon as the three of us were alone, I told her what I saw, and Badri mentioned the concerns he had been harboring.

"I can't believe it," Leyla said. "He isn't the most social of people, but he isn't a traitor, and especially not Hashshashin. I agree the circumstantial evidence seems to point to him, but I just can't believe it."

"I know what I saw," I said. "But I agree, Leyla, let's not make a judgment. I just wanted you to be aware of the possibility. Now, how do we get to the Al Hofuf government building?"

Badri drove us there in less than five minutes. He found covered parking that was semi-private so that he could leave Leyla and me in the same car. "I know you can take care of yourself, Leyla, but I would feel better not leaving you alone. Thad, you get into the driver's seat. I will be back as soon as I can. I am not sure this is the right place, but this is where all property ownership records are housed. Seems like the place to start."

As soon as Badri was gone, I said, "So I guess it is out of the question for me to get in the back seat for a kiss."

"Out of the question, Majnun," Leyla said. "Sorry, I am not being much of a conversationalist. I am still in shock over the possibility of Irshad working against us. His family and my family have known each other for years. I have been betrothed to him for half that time."

"Past tense," I said. "You were betrothed to him for many years of a painful and depressing, nae, might we better say bleak, existence."

"Don't push it, Majnun, and drop the old English. Yes, it is past tense. Leave it at that." She paused and then asked, "Do you ever get the feeling that it is the circle between Safa and Marwa that this search is stuck in? Maybe all the clues we have followed were just mirages."

"You are not a mirage. If nothing else is discovered, I found you. Although you almost seemed like a mirage when you walked onto the airplane and I first saw you. Too far away and too unbelievably perfect to actually be real. When you sat down beside me, it was like an angel had just created water in the desert for my parched soul. Would it be sacrilegious to call you Zamzam, maybe ZZ for short? They have a soft drink in Iran called Zam Zam, right?"

"Yes, so you want to call me a soft drink? Is that what I am to you, a refreshment?" Leyla asked with false indignation. "I am sure some use that name for a person, but I wouldn't want you to. I wasn't nervous at all to meet you that day on the airplane, you know. I was curious after our research and then Mack's report about you, but it was a job. I was surprised I was nervous when I came back to sit by you after using the restroom. I was actually disappointed you weren't in your seat."

I was about to remind her how I felt when she didn't show up for the next flight, but Badri was already back. He got into the car and explained, "No records here. They suggested trying the Ministry of Education which oversees museums. Let's get Irshad on the radio and ask him to check it out while he is at the new museum."

Leyla did so and said, "He has just arrived. If the museum has nothing, he will go into the Education building which is connected to the museum. What's next for us?"

"On my way out the door, I saw a poster advertising job opportunities at Saudi Commission for Tourism and Antiquities, SCTA. I asked about it, and an office worker explained it was created in the year 2000, and they picked up the responsibility for research and archiving that could increase tourism and job creation. He also told me there is a little turf battle with the Ministry of Education to integrate the Antiquities and Museums Agency into the Supreme Commission for Tourism. There is a regional office located in the Al Malham Trading Tower on the 7th floor in Al Ahsa. I got the directions, and I suggest we go there next."

We drove there in twenty minutes. "All this is one oasis?" I asked. "This is like Palm Springs, California, on steroids. I love all the palm trees and the quiet streets." Again, Badri drove around until he found an out of the way place to park that gave us some privacy. I dutifully moved over to the driver's seat. "So what happens if we ever actually find the Kitab Kabbani?" I asked Leyla after Badri left us.

"We share it with the world, but its ownership is kept in the Kabbani family," Leyla said. I don't know what Badri's family has decided to do with it for safe and secure storage. That conversation happened above me. I think my great uncle talked with the Kabbani Family Organization President, which was Badri up until last year. I am not sure who it is now."

"I don't want to sound like a broken record," I said, "but I think whoever Irshad is working with doesn't want to destroy the book either, but in their case, use it as a weapon. Otherwise, they would have just killed us by now. I also think they are using the same ploy to capture the Kitab Kabbani that they have used historically, just like you explained to me about some of their other historical habits. In order to get rid of anti-Nizari rulers, clerics, and officials they deemed as enemies, the Hashshashin would carefully study the languages and cultures of their targets. Then they would train an assassin who would then infiltrate the court or inner circle of the intended victim, sometimes serving for years as an advisor or servant. At an opportune moment, the assassin would kill the victim with a dagger in a surprise attack, up close and personal."

"You have been thinking about this, haven't you?" Leyla said. "Are you sure you aren't motivated by some latent jealousy? That seems pretty Hollywood to me."

I wasn't able to rebut her because Badri was running to the car. I couldn't tell if he was excited or upset. He hopped in almost before I had time to scoot over to the passenger side of the car, which wasn't easy with a console in the middle.

"I made a breakthrough in our search," he said.

"That's great," I said.

"Tell us," Leyla asked. "I hope it is good news."

"Good news and bad news," Badri said. "The good news is, there was a record of a Kabbani here as late as 1150 AD. The curator of that census data, created in those days for tax purposes, couldn't tell me if I am actually related to this Kabbani, and he didn't want to suggest that this area was the ancient site of the City of Gerrha. He did say that no matter where the city would have been, this was certainly a part of the greater Gerrha region."

"You are right, that is good and bad news," I said. "But that certainly doesn't get us any closer to the Kitab."

"No, that is good news," Badri said. "I haven't told you the bad news yet. First, one more piece of good news. The Kabbani he found kept a residence here, but records show he actually traveled here from Najran, which he claimed as his official residence. The curator said that was probably to keep his taxes lower here."

"Wow, how far is that from here?" I asked. Can we drive there right now?"

"Are we talking the Najran near the Yemeni boarder?" Leyla asked.

"Yes, but I count that as still part of the good news. It's thirteen hours from here, but still in Saudi Arabia. We don't have visas for Yemen, and it is dangerous enough there that we really would have to rethink next steps, maybe return to Turkey and start this again once we were ready."

"Okay," I said. "if all this is good news, do we really want to hear the bad news?"

"Isn't it interesting that I could collect all that information in a twenty-minute visit to an office that not that long ago just became the custodian of all this data?" Badri asked. "I thought it was odd, so I asked a few questions. It turns out someone came in yesterday afternoon asking for this information. They said they were representatives of the Kabbani family and even provided documentation of that claim. Someone is a step ahead of us. Or they were. When they return this afternoon, they will get some misleading information, sending them to the ruins at Thaj, a three-hour drive north of here because there are no direct roads.

"I convinced the person that this other group was not part of our family, nor authorized, and it would become a serious issue if the SCTA was caught up in an ugly fight with the Kabbani Tribe. He was convinced he had also accomplished his duty to deliver the requested information to a Kabbani. I can't guarantee he will keep our secret and really send them north. After he has had time to think about it, he won't want a return visit from the thugs that requested this information in the first place. That means we probably only have a few hours jump on this other group."

"So what do you propose we do?" Leyla asked, but knowing the answer.

"We leave immediately for Najran. We don't tell the rest of the group, at least not right now, that we have left. I don't want them to worry, but if Irshad really is playing the other side, we can't let them know right now. There is an airport at Najran also. I thought about flying there, but with your guardian papers very suspect, I don't want to go through any places that would require official documents."

"You could leave me here," Leyla said. "I want to go, but I don't want to slow this down either. It was my crazy idea to switch the groups anyway."

"You did that because I said I needed to speak with you," I said. "Besides, it would put you in a dangerous situation that we can avoid. If Irshad really is a bad guy, he would want any information you might have on our whereabouts. At some point, he is going to show his true colors, and when he does, I want you close to me, not close to him."

"Then it is settled. We leave immediately for Najran," Badri said. "There is a regional SCTA office there. I have a name and a phone number. We won't be able to meet with anyone until tomorrow morning, but hopefully, that will keep us ahead of the other group, which by the way I am assuming is the Hashshashin."

We gassed up, bought a case of water in bottles, and got some kabsa to go. I was thrilled to find out that kabsa is orange/red colored rice with lamb or chicken and some strong spices, but not spicy like the Mexican food I was used to. It was great. I had the lamb.

We drove for almost two hours on the 522, merged onto Highway 40, and drove for another hour. We talked about more light-hearted things, the growing up years of each of us, education, what we wanted to be when we were little. I really enjoyed getting to know more about both Badri and Leyla. I am sure they found my formative years to be boring and possibly even something to be pitied.

"This is Riyadh, Thad," Badri said. "I wish we had time to show you around. It is the capital city, and a great city by any measure. There are over seven million people in the greater Riyadh area, and it is like very few cities in the world, maybe Mexico City, Tokyo, Shanghai, and a few in Europe in mixing the ancient with the contemporary. We will get gas here because the next leg is long and dry."

We purchased some snacks, used the restrooms—a completely different experience because it had toilet hoses I assume were to be used like a bidet. We were on our way again within fifteen minutes. Even though we were supposed to be using the secure radios, Leyla called Lydia on her cellphone, explaining we were following a lead and wouldn't get in tonight, but that we were safe. We would connect with the group tomorrow. Lydia, of course, had questions, but Leyla said she would explain tomorrow.

It took forty-five minutes to get outside of the greater Riyadh area and back into the desert. It took another forty-five minutes on several highways before it felt like we were truly in the middle of nowhere.

"This is Route 10," Badri announced. "About 750 kilometers to go. With stops, about seven hours. We should be in Najran by sunrise."

"So, if the map in my head is correct, we are skirting the western side of the Empty Quarter?" I asked.

"That's right," Leyla said. "We are between the proverbial rock and a hard place. The Empty Quarter goes on to your left for over 400 miles. To your right is the Jabal Tuwayq Mountains which parallel our course almost all the way to Yemen."

"Is the Empty Quarter really empty?" I asked.

"They say," Badri began, "that the Empty Quarter is a barrier worse than any sea. It has the quicksand you asked me about, seven-hundred-foot high sand dunes that go on for miles, salt flats, temperatures during the day over 120 degrees Fahrenheit, and very cold temperatures at night. It almost never sees rain, and when there is rain, the Bedouin go as quickly as possible to that location, hoping the shrubs have enough green that their camels can eat. The few oases are far apart, and the water is usually undrinkable for humans. The Bedouin have their camels drink it, and then they later drink the camels' milk."

"And the place we are going," I asked, "is it just as desolate?"

"Desolate is a relative term, Majnun," Leyla said.

I liked it that she had shifted to using the nickname with Badri around. Badri made no mention of her use of the term.

"I have been thinking about this," Leyla said. "It seems to fit into your grandfather's riddle, Badri, that he shared with Thaddeus. Najran was certainly a key stopping place on the Incense Road. The oasis there is famous, and certainly, your ancestors, if they worked the frankincense and myrrh trade, had passed through or stopped there. The stonework and the engineering work of the ancient inhabitants was impressive. The

Najranis were Christians in the centuries before Islam, which fits with your family history. The inhabitants also developed a system of dams and irrigation networks that helped farming become a key component to their success. Caravans not only could procure water but food for themselves and their animals. Doesn't that all sound familiar, kind of like what your family was involved in at the other end of their trading route in Susa?"

"I never knew about the ancient dams and irrigation in Narjan," Badri admitted. "I know the largest modern dam in the Kingdom is located there, which also sounds like the Susa region of Iran."

"So, I just wonder," Leyla said, "maybe Najran is the Marwa in the riddle."

"Or," Badri suggested, "It might mean the water, the well of Zamzam. What does Najran translate to?" he asked, sounding like he already knew the answer.

"Thirsty," Leyla answered. "Wasn't that one of the root meanings of kab, a possible origin of your last name?"

"Exactly," Badri said, "although the root of my last name was just one person's theory, but yes," Badri said.

Chapter 24

WE DROVE FOR HOURS, HOURS with not a single light except the stars, which filled the sky. I couldn't decide if I was more amazed by the sunsets here or the night sky. I realized I didn't have to choose. Some things just happen, and we can enjoy it or ignore it. They are free gifts. But who was the gift giver? Islam's Allah? The Christian God? Someone else's god? I knew one thing looking at this wonder; it wasn't just a freak accident of nature. Science could certainly explain what a star is and why sunsets have colors, but how it happened that I was there to see it, comprehend that I was seeing it, and more, feel something about it, was not a matter of a scientific explanation.

We only saw three vehicles going the other way. At one point Leyla took over driving, and then I took a turn. Leyla kept me company in the front seat while Badri slept in the back, not fearing any religious police stopping us in the middle of nowhere. I wished we were in my car, my '62 Chevy Impala, because it didn't have a console between the driver and the front passenger. We did hold hands for a time.

"Two bullets that collided on the battlefield," Leyla said after a long silence. "A billion to one chance of finding each other. I have been thinking about that. Not only did they become one, but they must have saved the lives of the two souls they would have otherwise hit."

I didn't respond immediately but let Leyla's words dance with the stars of the Empty Quarter while we drove through the seemingly endless darkness. "I am not sure who the souls were that might be saved," I finally said. "Irshad? Maybe we are saving ourselves. I need to think more about that. Maybe the metaphor breaks down at that point."

We stopped and got gas at a lonely outpost near the intersection of Routes 10 and 177. The sign said Sultanah, but I didn't see a town. Badri never stirred. We continued our drive, enjoying the quiet solitude of the wilderness. At one point I said, "I can see why prophets have found understanding in the wilderness. I am not a scriptorian, but wasn't it in the wilderness that God spoke to Abraham and Moses, maybe others?"

"Mohammad's first revelation, peace be upon him, happened when he was sitting in the wilderness," Leyla said, "probably on a night like this. The Angel Gabriel appeared to him and commanded him to 'Recite! Recite! Recite!' Mohammad responded 'I am not a reader.' The angel recited three verses to him, and when he awoke, he had these verses, as he said, inscribed in his heart. That night is called the *Laylat-al-Qadr*, Night of Power. It is also where my name Leyla comes from."

"I believe in prophets," I said, "and their role in the life of humankind. If someone believes in God and God is unchanging and cares for his creations, I don't understand how they can say they don't need a prophet. People and their lives certainly change. We can get lost so easy. So God either speaks to man directly or through someone to help us."

"Or both," Leyla said. "We need personal understanding, but there needs to be someone to speak to all of mankind, too."

"If I can feel the awesome wonder of this night," I continued, "I have the capacity to know the spiritual in a way His other creations do not have. That is a blessing and a burden for us. It seems to me that a primary responsibility of a prophet would be to provide God's will to man and to show how and why this is meaningful to us. Then it is up to us to accept or reject.

"I also think there have been inspired people that may not be prophets but who have made a great impact for good on the world: Confucius, Buddha, maybe some Christian reformers. This is where I had placed Mohammed. He certainly brought many great things to light and has touched lives for good. The Qur'an is an amazing book. I had tried to put him in the status of a prophet in my personal studies when my sister married Badri, but I don't know. I don't know. I just wanted you to know, in case you had hopes of my conversion as a solution to our challenge."

"These things are not for the mind to decide," Leyla said. "They are for the heart. I am not talking of emotions that some would blame on the heart. The heart is pure; some emotions are not."

"I think I know what you mean," I said. "Some emotions are a side effect of deeper feelings, not those actual feelings. We can get into a lot of trouble not being sensitive to the difference."

"So it isn't emotions caused by those that may use the Prophet Mohammed's name as justification for their awful deeds that are clouding your thoughts?" Leyla asked.

"I think there is enough blame to go around in any religion for those that use something good for evil purposes. It might even be the hallmark of goodness that some twist it for their own purposes. It's like the abundance mentality you spoke of when we first met and that Al-Ḥujurāt follows. Short-term gains can be made in an abundance mentality world by those who see things as zero-sum. It's not the abundance mentality that is at fault."

"You should read the poem, *Footnotes to the Book of Setback*, by my distant relative Nizar Qabbani," Badri said from the backseat.

"Well, good morning, sleeping beauty," I said. "Who is Nizar Qabbani?"

"I will answer since Badri may be too humble in his reply," Leyla said. "He is perhaps the most revered contemporary poet in the Arab world. He was Syrian, although his family came from Konya, Turkey—like most good things." I squeezed Leyla's hand as she continued. "He died in 1998, I think. His second wife died in Beirut in a bomb attack by some terrorist group; I don't remember which. His poems are just as popular today as when they were first read.

"Some of his work is too spicy for me, but the poem Badri suggests is a classic. It was written when the combined Egyptian, Syrian, and Jordanian forces lost the 1967 War against Israel. It is an attack on the haughty and self-serving words of the Arab leaders at the time, but it is also an attack on those who claim to follow the tenants of Islam but whose actions and lifestyles are something completely different. It also attacks the disunity of Arab nations, which one could transpose to suggest disunity in Islam as well. Was that a fair synopsis, Badri?"

"You don't need me in this conversation," Badri chuckled. "I'm going back to sleep."

"I will definitely add that to my reading list," I said. "So here is another tough question, and it goes for all religions, but I will ask it regarding Islam since I have two captive experts. Are the modern, or progressive, Muslims that justify their actions by a different interpretation of the Qur'an restoring the religion back to its origin, to what God intended, or are they making their own modifications and thus pushing Islam farther from its spiritual core?"

"By modern, or progressive, Muslims, I assume you aren't talking about fundamentalists that are bent on creating some medieval version of Islam that never existed," Leyla clarified.

"I mean those who are recoiling against the growth of fundamentalism, but also their parents' version of some strict practices that they see as more cultural than spiritual," I said. "Like women can't marry outside the faith, but men can."

"Ah, yes, that question," Leyla said. "It's very difficult to separate what is cultural and what is core religion in Islam. We have no single hierarchical structure. We have no single Pope as the Catholics do in Christianity. And then there is the fear of opening Pandora's Box, I suppose. If we allow this, then what could be next? Some may feel it is appropriate for men and women to pray together in the mosque, but would that lead to women giving sermons? Interfaith marriages could lead to same-sex marriages, and so on.

"The boundaries seem illusive and no one wants to discard precious truths, but they also want it their way. They want to be justified in their actions, perhaps in a similar way to the despots that rule in some countries in this region. I can see what you are saying about God and prophets. Where is God in all this? Does he care? Why are there no more prophets? We have many Muftis, but they don't speak with one voice, so which is the voice of God?

"Yes, and what blessings would we be sacrificing for getting what we want?" I asked. "I believe in a God that wants us to be happy, wants us to achieve and grow, and his joy is helping us achieve joy. Surely God knows better than we do how to achieve that…"

With that, we were quiet for a time. The road continued into the darkness like an answer to our questions. Keep going, keep pressing forward into the darkness, and I will allow your headlights to illuminate the road a little farther along your journey.

We pulled off the road just after Route 117 turned into Highway 15. We were only a few miles from Najran. Leyla returned to the backseat, and Badri took over driving. We drove for about ten miles through small villages and pulled into a gas station just after passing the sign that announced our arrival in Najran. We filled up, bought some snacks, used the restroom, and tried to freshen up. With only a few hours of sleep between us, we looked pretty ragged.

It was after morning prayer, so Badri called the number of the SCTA agent in Najran that he was given in Al Ahsa. Somewhat surprisingly, to me anyway, a gentleman answered and arranged for us to meet him at his one-room office in Najran. It was less than a half mile from where we were. We were in the parking lot waiting for him when he arrived fifteen minutes later.

Badri went into the office alone. He came out thirty minutes later and woke us both up. He got into the passenger seat and told me to follow that blue Fiat that was just pulling out of the parking lot. I almost crashed into a bicycle whose driver was luckily more awake than I was.

"Does this guy know we are following him?" I asked, not sure what we were doing.

"Yes," Badri said. "He is taking us to a place that he thinks I might find interesting. He was very interested in my story. I showed him my identification, and he took some notes. He shuffled through some files that didn't appear to be ancient in any way, mumbled something and then jumped up and said, 'Come, follow me.' He said no more as he grabbed his car keys. We walked out of the building in silence. Now you know as much as I do."

"You're sure this isn't a trap or something," I said.

"I'm not sure, but I don't think so," Badri said. "Let's keep our eyes open, but no, I don't believe this is a trap."

We drove for about five minutes through town and then onto Prince Nayif ibn Abudulaziz road. The road paralleled a riverbed and old growth trees for about three miles and dead-ended in some foothills.

Badri said, "You can get out of the car, but stay close to it. I told him you were my driver and that you are my sister, Leyla. Leyla, come with me, but keep an appropriate distance."

We all got out, and Badri and Leyla walked over to the gentleman. I noticed no introduction of Leyla was made. She was simply there. They talked for fifteen minutes. The man made some gestures and handed Badri a paper. Badri kissed his cheeks, and the man left.

Badri and Leyla came back to the car, and Badri laid out the paper on the hood of the car. I realized it was a map. They were in conversation in what I guessed was Arabic. When I approached, they seamlessly switched to English.

Leyla was talking. "I can't believe it! What an amazing blessing for your family."

"I can't believe it either," Badri said. He turned to me and explained, "So this land you see in front of you is Kabbani land. It has been in the family for hundreds of years. It has been held in a trust of sorts. The local government has sent several letters to my relative here, and he has said he would visit but never has.

"In the past, I could not claim or own this property myself because only Saudi Arabian citizens could own property in the Kingdom. In the year 2000, the rules changed, and there may be a way to transfer the ownership to me. If not, at least we can keep it in the family through my Saudi relatives.

"The reason the SCTA is aware of it is that it has several historic buildings on the property the city would like to develop for tourism. If you are both up for it, let's check them out. He said they were just up this path about 300 meters."

"Absolutely," Leyla said. "What do you say, Thaddeus?"

"If you are going, I am going," I said.

We walked up the path that disappeared into scrubby vegetation a few times, but it was pretty obvious where it was leading. I could pick out some buildings partially hidden by palm trees.

"Mohammed, the SCTA agent, also told me we are only a few miles from the Yemen border, so sometimes there are squatters in the area, but they have never had problems with terrorists here."

The first building was a dilapidated mud brick structure that was partly falling down. It wasn't in much better shape than Fort Uqair that we visited yesterday. There was evidence of squatters with some trash and campfires around the building.

As we worked our way past that building, we got a full view of the other structure. It looked like a castle. It was also made of mud bricks, but it appeared to be in pretty good shape. There were no windows on the bottom floor, but the second and third floors had three windows on each side. The top of the structure was trimmed with an ornate fringe of triangles the looked like hollow Christmas trees, all painted white.

In my imagination, I could almost see some Arab long rifles point through the hollow areas chasing off some Bedouin marauders. The walls were slightly inclined inward, and I didn't see any door to get in. The bricks were large, and I guessed the walls were forty feet long and at least that high. The bricks were lighter brown around the windows, making it very beautiful. The ground that this castle sat on sloped in the back and Badri suggested we go around the building to see if there was an entrance there.

We ended up walking completely around the building, still not discovering an entrance. Badri finally found an entrance in the rock-sloped land that led down to the palm trees. We had assumed this door led to a storage shelter, but a large tunnel led into a large room that was the first floor of the building. Badri said this level was most likely for livestock.

We walked up some wooden stairs hewn out of huge hardwood logs. Badri said this would be living quarters as was the third story. I noticed the windows were larger on the third story. It felt brighter and not so musty. The roof was flat with drains leading to pipes for water to escape. I wondered how often it rained here. There was also a small enclosure that held a water basin for maybe one hundred gallons of water and enough room inside this enclosure for someone to bring in water to fill the basin and protect that water from the weather and dust.

The house—castle—was very beautiful in an ancient sort of way and the view was outstanding. I realized as we walked down to the livestock area that the walls were very thick. I wondered if that was for temperature control or protection, or maybe both. I didn't ask. Badri was in exploring mode, and I didn't want to break his focus.

"There is one more building I want to check out," Badri said. "There is a small building up a little higher on the property according to the map. It is marked as a well, but Mohammed said there was also a mosque there."

We walked on a path that was hewn out of rock and around a turn in the hill. Hidden from the other buildings and the approach to the palm trees was another building just as Badri said. It was octagonal and about twenty feet in circumference. It was also made out of mud bricks. Inside the building was a small fountain that still had water coming out of it. It drained into a lower basin at the foot of the fountain and disappeared somewhere because it never filled up and overflowed.

There was an overwhelming peaceful feeling in this little abode. None of the buildings had any furnishings or anything else detached from the walls. I could only imagine what this place must have been like with Chinese silk and Persian rugs, slow burning frankincense in the air, and food being prepared with spices from India and the Spice Islands.

"We don't have cell coverage here," Leyla said, "but we ought to call the team and let them know we are here or at least that we are alright."

"I noticed some small hotels back in Najran where we might be able to get a couple of rooms," Badri said. "I don't like the idea of staying there, however, since we don't have any official documents supporting our guardianship of Leyla. What if I ran into town and picked up some supplies and we stayed here tonight? I could also make a call to the team either by my cell phone, if there is coverage there, or I can find a land line somewhere."

"I like the idea of staying here," I said. "We would be away from prying eyes, and it would give us more time to poke around."

"I don't think there would be any problems in town, but I like the idea of staying here also," Leyla said. "Rustic—no indoor plumbing that I noticed—but I can do rustic."

"Great," Badri said clapping his hands together. "I will be back in an hour or two max. The first thing I will do is let a few people know you are out here, so that if complications arise or I have a heart attack or something, you won't be completely stranded. See you soon."

With that, Badri was gone, and we were left to do some more exploring. First, we checked out the main building more carefully. There was no electricity to the castle, but there was a line that came as far as the palm orchard. I checked out a small pump house nestled in the palms, and when I switched it on, the pump worked, and water from somewhere flowed into the orchard.

In the house, most of the rooms had doors, which was nice, but the windows were open to the outside, with no frames even for glass. It looked like there may have been curtains at one point, but none remained.

While Leyla was checking out the outdoor restroom, I went to the roof to get a better view of the property. I realized Badri had never mentioned how large the estate was. I am sure this whole thing had not yet settled in his mind. It was like discovering you had a rich uncle who had passed away that you never knew existed.

Looking in the direction of the palm trees, I noticed a pickup truck coming slowly up the road. I could see a driver and at least one passenger. The truck stopped short of where we had parked originally. They got out and closed the doors very quietly. Trying to be stealthy, they ran up to the beginning of the palms and crouched down. I didn't like how this looked. I quickly ran down stairs and ran out to where I thought Leyla was. I crashed into her as I opened the underground door.

"We have guests, and they don't look friendly. They may be just curious, but they are sneaking up to the house by the palms," I quickly said.

Leyla ran outside without a word. I thought she was running away, so I started to follow her. Again we collided as she reentered the livestock floor with a shovel and something resembling a pitchfork.

"I saw these earlier. It's all I could find," she said. "Is there any way we can lock this door?

"I am sure there was a way anciently," I said. "I don't see how we can do anything now. We might be able to do something with the door on the next floor."

We checked and couldn't see a way to do anything. "Okay," I said, making a quick decision. "Let's go up the mosque. Maybe they don't know about it, and I think that door is more easily barricaded."

Without a word, we ran out of the house, and as quietly as we could, we ran up the trail and out of sight around the bend in the trail. "You check out the mosque for security. I will keep an eye on the trail. It would be almost impossible to get to that mosque overland. The trail is the only route to us." I said.

Leyla smiled and leaned in and gave me a quick kiss and was off. I watched the trail and saw no one. It was about ten in the morning, and the temperature was still in the sixties. I was starting to get a little chill from my perspiration and not moving.

I heard something and then realized it was Leyla returning. "We can lock the door from the inside with the handle to the shovel. Anything?"

"No, nothing yet," I said. We waited for another ten minutes, and I began to wonder if I had imagined things. Leyla never questioned me and just stood by me silently, watching the trail. Two minutes later we heard a crunch of rock on boots coming up the trial. I motioned for Leyla to go up the trail to the mosque since she was still in her long dress and abaya, making it difficult for her to run.

I watched until the two men became visible. They were walking cautiously which confirmed to me they were not here to be helpful. I ran to the mosque, and Leyla closed the door quietly and slid the shovel handle between two iron loops. I would have felt better with a metal bar, but this hopefully would hold.

Leyla was already walking around the small enclosure checking out angles of view and anything we might have missed. There were tiny slits for windows to let in air and a little bit of light. The walls were very thick, at least two or three feet, so from the outside it was impossible to see much at all inside. I began to study the area by the fountain. The water was cold, colder than the outside temperature. I guessed that meant it was from an underground source.

I went over to Leyla and whispered in her ear, "Just like old times. Your hair still smells great. Come here and help me with this."

She looked at me quizzically and followed. I took the opportunity to whisper in Leyla's ear again to be closer to her. "This fountain plumbing goes through the wall. I wonder if there is an opening for a person also. This is set in a corner, so there very well could be room for a person to hide. Help me look."

There were no statues with buttons on them that opened a secret door like in the movies, but just when I had given up, Leyla motioned for me to come closer to her. She pointed to a stone about eighteen or twenty inches wide by two feet tall. I looked around, and there were two at each corner. This one, however, didn't appear to have any grout around it, and if you place your hand by where the grout should have been and hold very still, you could feel a slight draft of cooler air.

We tried to find a way to pull it open and couldn't figure it out. I pushed at the stone as hard as I could. Nothing. I pulled out my debit card and ran it down the space between the stone and the clay bricks. I hit something halfway down the length of the stone. I slid the card up from the bottom to get an idea how thick this blockage was, and when I hit it, it clicked, and the stone budged. With only finger pressure I was able to pull the stone open. It was on some kind of a metal hinge and inlaid into the stone, so it was flush.

I heard the two men approaching. Not sure if they could see us from the slit across the room, I motioned for Leyla to go in. Braver than me, she did so without hesitation. For all I knew, it was a pit or just a crawl space to reach the plumbing. She completely disappeared, and I didn't hear a scream, so those two scenarios were false. Her arm came out of the darkness and pulled me in. I had to squeeze in at an angle, corner to corner, but I fit. Leyla pulled at a metal handle on the back of the stone, and it swung back into place. I heard a pin fall back into place on the side of the stone.

As the stone was fully back in place, one of the men outside pushed at the door. Then there was a kick. He said something in Arabic and appeared to have walked away. We didn't move for at least five minutes. Then there was a crash at the door, but it sounded like the door stayed closed. We waited another five minutes and didn't hear anything.

Leyla turned around and stared, feeling the walls and the floor. We were terribly cramped in what we thought was a tiny space. Leyla pulled out her phone and turned it on. Our eyes had adjusted to the pitch blackness of our hiding place, so the phone provided a surprising amount of light. We were in the wall of the mosque, and the space extended to our left. Leyla saw a small metal bar on the ground and placed it snugly in the handle that opened and closed the stone door and another metal sleeve on the mud brick wall. It wasn't overly secure, but it didn't have to be because the hinge on the other side of the stone held it in place.

As we squeezed our way down this space, it started to decline into the ground. By the time we would have reached the first slit in the wall, we were below the slit. By the time we were another quarter way around the mosque wall, we were below ground, and the space was much wider and taller. Another few feet and we were in a large passageway that led deeper into the unknown darkness.

"So does everything in the Middle East eventually end up in an underground tunnel with men trying to kill us?" I whispered.

Leyla turned and put her finger to her mouth, signaling for me to be quiet. We continued down for maybe twenty more steps and then came to a hallway wide enough for two people to walk side-by-side. I wasn't sure, but it seemed like this hallway tunnel was curving to the left. We came to a large room, but we couldn't see much.

The tunnel continued on the other side, and we continued following it. We came to yet another large room. In this room was a staircase that spiraled up and up and up. It was narrow, but not as tight as the hollow wall in the mosque. The spiral staircase simply came to a dead end at another wall. The wall was smooth, with no possible way for a door to exist. Then I looked at the ceiling that was only about six feet high and saw a metal square, about two feet by two feet. It had a handle and a locking mechanism. I pulled at the mechanism, and it was rusted shut. I hit it with my hand, but it still wouldn't budge. I pulled on the handle again. Nothing. It looked like wherever this had led, we would need to return and come back with the Arabian equivalent of WD-40.

"Lift me up," Leyla whispered.

I wasn't sure what her plan was, but I was happy to lift her up in my arms. She exhaled onto the mechanism with heavy breath while pulling on it. Within thirty seconds it opened. I let her down but didn't let her go. "I love being in tunnels with you," I said.

"I love getting out of tunnels with you," Leyla said. "Let's see where this leads."

I pushed the door, and it swung up, but neither of us was tall enough to push it all the way open.

"There must have been a stool or something else people used to open this," I said. "Let me hold you up again and you can push it up and open."

I lifted Leyla, and the door opened easily. She crawled out, and I had to pull myself up and out. The door was only about an inch thick, but the marble stone and the metal plate it sat on were heavy enough that I wasn't sure how to open it once it was back in place. Then I realized the stone piece next to it was loose, so all one would have to do is remove the small stone and then lift the door.

We realized it was in the water shed on the roof of the house. "This is amazing!" I said. "I can't wait to tell Badri. But I wonder where our uninvited visitors are?"

On cue, we both heard the noise of several vehicles coming up the road. We could tell several were large trucks.

"I hope this isn't reinforcements for our visitors," I said.

The people from the trucks were standing around the area where they parked, not coming toward the house. They had blocked the pickup truck, but they didn't seem to be concerned about that, nor making any noise. They sounded happy, even jovial. We didn't see the two men in this group. We watched and waited. Within a couple of minutes, Badri drove up and started giving orders to the men who had most recently arrived. Then he strode to the house. We went outside to meet him.

"What is this all about?" I asked as eight men walked by going into the house. "Did you hire an army?"

"I just got a few things in town. They are going to check out the house first and then bring the things in," Badri explained. "Have you died of boredom since I left, or did you do some more exploring?"

We pulled Badri aside and explained to him about the two men, that we had to hide, and that we had something else to show him after these men departed. Badri pulled one of the men aside and explained about the two other men and their pickup truck. There was a discussion among the men and Badri. Then everything went back to normal, and they continued their inspection of the house.

Badri explained, "It seems the two men with the pickup truck are not the friendliest of people. They must have seen us come in and saw me leave. Thinking this was an opportunity to meet the new neighbors, they may have come to see what they could gain by scaring you into some peace offering. The man I hired this morning to deliver my purchases said they will not be any more trouble. He will make sure they know this is a powerful family and that it would not be wise for them to bother us. I know, that is a little dramatic, but it is more of a deterrent than other types of threats. Family has longer arms than law enforcement here."

Within the next hour, bedroom furniture, rugs, couches, chairs, tables, linens, and food were delivered. "A repair group will be here tomorrow to sort out electricity, water, propane gas, etc. I am afraid we will have to rough it tonight."

"I am prepared to sleep on the floor or in the car," Leyla said. "This is far from roughing it."

"Sorry, I got carried away, but I wanted to send a message to the local community. The Kabbani family is here: we buy from the local community, want to be good neighbors, and all boats will rise working with us, rather than trying to take advantage of us." Badri explained. "By now the entire town knows we are here."

"Did you get a hold of the team?" Leyla asked.

"Yes," Badri explained. "I spoke with Hande and then Irshad. I couldn't see how hiding for another day or two would be helpful, so I told them to come down here when they could arrange transportation. They are going to fly into the small airport and then rent a car. They will be here tomorrow about midday."

It was three in the afternoon before all the men had departed, including the men in the first pickup truck. It was quiet and peaceful, and it was time to show Badri our discovery.

Chapter 25

I EXPLAINED TO BADRI THE events of the morning and how we discovered the passageway between the mosque and the house. We went up to the roof and opened the entrance. We brought a kitchen chair with us that I thought would fit through the door to the passageway. It fit, but didn't leave enough room for people, so we left the chair and climbed in one at a time. We each had a flashlight, and Badri also brought a lantern. It was more exciting this time, realizing we were traveling through a hollow wall in the house. Badri kept saying, "This is amazing!"

We arrived at the first room guessing we were just beyond the house above us. "This must have been dug over a thousand years ago," Badri said as our flashlights scanned the room. "According to SCTA records, the house was built between 800 and 900 AD. The land was originally owned by Nabatean traders and sold to my ancestor whose family eventually built a house here. The assumption was they spent part of their time here and part of their time in Gerrha, or Susa, and eventually Mecca and then the Levant."

There was little to see in this room at first glance. It was hewn out of solid rock, and it was about fifteen feet by fifteen feet with a ten-foot ceiling. There was only one passageway leading toward the mosque. We followed the passageway and could now see nooks in the wall where torches had been placed. We entered the second room, and it also appeared to be a simple room of about the same dimensions. I was surprised how dry it was and that the temperature was not that cold. The air was stuffy, but there was no dust or mold.

"It looks like we are the first people to be in this room in hundreds of years," I said.

"Maybe a thousand years, or more," Badri said. "According to the records the SCTA has, someone in our family from Lebanon or Syria paid for grounds maintenance up to about my great great grandfather's time, the early 1800s, but no one had visited, or at least there are no records of visitors for many hundreds of years. That this has somehow stayed in the family and that it is in such relatively good shape testifies to how forgotten this little corner of the world has been and that the people here respect families and ownership through the generations. Our land in Palestine, less than 200 miles away from my home, has been lost forever, but this endures. Amazing."

"Take a look at this," I said. "I believe there is an inscription on the wall. I thought it was just the rock coloration, but it might be writing."

Badri and Leyla came over to look at the possible writing. "This isn't Arabic or Persian," Badri said.

"I think it is Old South Arabian," Leyla said. "There are many old language groups from this region, but Old South Arabian used a derivation of the Phoenician alphabet and was read from right to left. This looks like pictures I studied in school. Many ancient Christian writings were in Old South Arabian. If I had an internet connection, I could probably translate this. I believe there were no spaces between words, and there were no vowels. This language completely disappeared about one hundred years before Islam." Leyla took out her phone and took a picture of the writing.

"Wait," I said. "This writing is on a stone laid into the wall; it isn't part of the stone wall itself. Look at where this stone touches the wall. Mud was used as a grout or to hide the fact that the stone was not part of the wall. Over time, some of it has flaked away. Maybe there is something behind this stone."

Leyla grabbed the pitchfork that we had been dragging with us in case we met another intruder. She used the tong on the side to dig at the mud mortar.

"I doubt that they had this kind of intensity of light with their torches. This would have been easy to miss, even after seeing the inscription," Badri said.

It took nearly thirty minutes to chip away most of the mortar. "I hope the inscription isn't directions on how to remove the stone," I said.

"That wouldn't make any sense," Leyla said. "See how it is set in the wall slightly higher than the floor of the room. Could it also be on a hinge, like the other stones in the mosque and the house?"

I pulled out my trusty debit card and slid it up from the bottom on the right side, and nothing happened. I then tried it on the left side. Still nothing. Finally, I tried the top going left to right and click, it opened. We looked at each other stunned. "Is there a compartment, or something there?" I asked.

"No," Leyla said as she disappeared from view. "This is another tunnel entrance." The aroma of something hit me with force.

"Frankincense," Badri said. Badri followed Leyla, and I followed him. The tunnel only went six feet and opened into another room. Not just any room. It was a room filled with stuff.

"This looks like a—a library," Badri said, barely able to contain his wonder. "I can't believe what we are seeing."

Leyla approached me with tears in her eyes. "I am so glad we were here together to see this, to share this. No matter what is here, it is ancient and a miracle that we found it in so little time. You got us here, Thaddeus." And with that, she gave me a long and passionate kiss. Badri was in such shock that he didn't even notice.

"Wait, don't touch anything," Leyla said. She began taking pictures of each wall and each area. "I hope my charge holds out. Taking pictures with a flash uses a lot of energy."

The room was the same size as the others, about fifteen by fifteen feet with ten-foot ceilings. Three walls had shelves to the ceiling. The wall by the door had bins and some clay pots. A few of the shelves had broken, dumping their contents on the floor, but most were in fair shape.

"Should we look at this stuff, or get an expert to do this?" Leyla asked.

"Let's be very gentle, but get an idea of what is here, before we let anyone else know about this," Badri said.

There was a one-foot-by-one-foot clay bin with frankincense in it. There were several clay pots full of gold coins. A few weapons with inlaid gems leaned against the wall. But mostly there were scrolls, parchment papers, and some bound books.

"I wish Rabbi Halevi and Dr. Nabat could see this," I said.

"That is a brilliant idea, Thad," Badri said. "The rabbi is too old to travel, and I am not sure what the problems would be getting an Iranian Jewish leader into the country, but Dr. Nabat, with his academic credentials, could travel, and he is someone we can trust. Let's keep this room and the passageways a secret, even from the rest of the team for now, at least until I can get the doctor here and we figure out what we are looking at."

We stayed thirty more minutes poking around but didn't want to damage anything with too close of an inspection. We closed up the library, as we were now calling it, and continued to show Badri the passageway to the mosque. When we entered the mosque, the shovel was still lodged in the door. We decided to leave the mosque door unbarred. Better to remove any curiosity by leaving it open. That had worked for centuries.

We went back to the house down the path from the mosque and were met by a warmly lit house that welcomed us with the smell of food. The man who Badri had paid to clean the house, bring in the furniture, and set up the next day's visitors who would work on the electricity, plumbing, cooking gas, and so on, was just leaving with his wife and son. Badri spoke with him briefly, explaining we had been to the mosque to give thanks for this wonderful blessing of returning to this family home. He and his wife had prepared a wonderful meal for us as a welcome to the community.

We enjoyed the food and the cool evening. We did not talk about the library out loud, for fear of who might overhear. We were all exhausted from the long night last night, the long drive and the excitement of the day. We went to bed early and slept contentedly. The workmen who had visited fixed the door before leaving, the only entrance to the house so that it could be locked from the inside. We were in a relatively secure fortress.

I was the first up in the morning. I went for a jog beyond the mosque. There was little to see, no surprise buildings, no view of the house from up above the mosque. The mountains became so rugged that it was impossible to even to walk more than thirty feet from the mosque in any direction except the trail. I also checked out the palm orchard. They were date palms I realized. I had eaten the green and ripe yellow raw dates that Badri had procured from somewhere in California when he and Anna had visited and recognized them.

No one was awake when I got back to the house, so I went down into the tunnel and entered the library. I was looking at the various books, really most were more like notebooks, loosely bound in different ways. One in particular was interesting because the pages were filled with tiny horizontal and vertical lines. I guessed it was some kind of ledger book. I wondered whether the Kitab Kabbani was among these papers. I left everything in place and took a quick cold water rinse down by the palm orchard. Hopefully, the neighbors weren't spying.

Later at breakfast, I mentioned the book with the lines in it to Badri and Leyla. They thought it was curious, but they didn't think much more about it. Badri left for town to see if he could contact Dr. Nabat and to wait for the team's arrival so they could follow him here. Leyla and I visited the library briefly, but there was little we could do there without worrying we would harm something. We went up to the roof, away from possible prying eyes, to talk and to watch for Badri.

Both Leyla's and my cellphones had gone dead yesterday, but we estimated it was about 11:00 in the morning. A group drove up to the palm orchard. They pulled out many tools and were anything but quiet. We went down to let them in, assuming they were the workers Badri had employed yesterday. I stayed out of sight on the third floor, and Leyla spoke to them from a separate room. They were, in fact, the workers Badri had hired, and they went right to work. Most left the house, but two lingered.

When the other workers had departed, these two quickly climbed the stairs, and I heard a muffled scream from Leyla. I assumed they were attempting to attack her sexually, so I ran in the direction of the noise. I ran into the room I had left her in and charged the nearest man. I knocked him over, and his head hit the floor hard. The other man pulled out a gun and held Leyla as a hostage. He was saying something in Arabic that I didn't understand. He yelled at Leyla, who translated.

"Do not come any closer or he will shoot me. He wants the book, the Kitab Kabbani. I told him that we don't have it, that we have given up looking for it."

"She is right. We are done searching. The book doesn't exist, and we are done with this adventure. Done. Let her go and leave. I will not send the workers outside after you."

Leyla translated. The man said in broken English, "No matter. Your friend Efe sends his regards and said, if it were appropriate, to shoot you between the eyes for the infidel you are and for the lives and time you have caused us to sacrifice. Unfortunately, this is not the most convenient time or place."

"So, you are Furqaan?" I asked.

"That is not your business to know, Mr. Allen. I will tell you this. I have been to your home in California, and you will never sleep another night safely until this adventure, as you call it, is over. And by over, that could mean your life. Now, how is it you are going to prove to me that you have not found the book, that it doesn't exist?"

"This was the end of the line, the last clue, the last place," I said. "We found a shell of a house. It has sat here for centuries, victim to every kind of criminal, vagrant, and treasure seeker. It has been stripped of anything of value long ago. What proof more can we provide for a long destroyed or stolen book? That is if it ever existed and if it even made it this far."

This man, who probably ripped up my perfectly good couch in California, was unsure what to do next. He took out his cell phone and saw that he did not have service. He kicked at his fellow terrorist and the man groaned.

"It is good you did not kill him. I am certain those workers do not have guns with them. The four of us will walk out of here quietly, and you both will come with us. If anyone asks, we are going to the village to get food for everyone."

It took another minute for the man I knocked to the floor to fully wake up. He wanted to kill me right there, but his friend reminded him of the many workers in close range. The four of us walked down the stairs together and outside to their car. No one asked us anything.

We just reached their car when Badri and the cavalry arrived. Both Leyla and I instantly became hostages with guns point at our heads. Irshad took control of the situation and explained, "If you let them go, we will let you go."

The man spoke in Arabic, and Irshad replied again in English. "You are not 'good as dead' if you let them go. Who is going to tell your superiors? We aren't. You aren't. Those workers aren't."

The man hesitated and said in English, "You don't know what you are dealing with here. We are leaving, and we are leaving with these two."

The man pushed Leyla into the car. Leyla kept her momentum going and rolled to the other side of the car and opened the door and fell out the other side. I could feel the man I most recently gave a headache to tense up and pull his gun back up. I thought I was about to be shot, so I did the only thing that came to mind—I bent over as fast as I could, hoping my captor that had me in a bear hug from behind went with me. He did, and as I narrowly missed the opening into the backseat, his head hit it hard. I am sure it put a crease on his forehead. He crumpled to the ground, and I took his gun.

The guy that had been holding Leyla wasn't sure what happened. He turned to shoot me, but I was still crouched down and behind the passenger door. I grabbed his lower legs and pulled him down. He still held onto his gun, so I stomped on his wrist as hard as I could and pointed the gun at him. I was grateful when Irshad and Hande came to my aid because I wasn't sure what to do next. Badri and Lydia were helping Leyla.

"Well, my friend, you hardly needed our help," Hande said laughing. "And without firing a shot, which would have significantly complicated matters for all of us here in the Kingdom. Nice job, John Wayne."

Leyla had just come around the back of the car and saw one man unconscious and the other subdued as I handed the gun to Irshad. I could tell she wanted to say something, but several of the workers were running over to us, and she shifted into the background. Irshad stuck the pistols in his jacket, Badri said something in Arabic, and the workers went back to their tasks.

Badri and Sami took the two Furqaan men back to town and turned them over to the local police, testifying that parading as part of the local workforce Badri had hired, they tried to attack those at the house for unknown reasons. They both had foreign passports, so this matter was taken very seriously. Irshad told us upon Badri and Sami's return that they would not be punished and would be sent out of the country since Furqaan had many sympathizers in high places in the Kingdom. I was just happy to see them gone.

"So what were they doing here? Did you find something that caused them to capture you?" Irshad asked.

"I have no idea how they found us. I told them there was no book, that we had hit a dead end, and we were done searching. I had knocked out one of the two earlier, when they attacked Leyla. Maybe that made them even madder. The other suggested they couldn't come back empty handed. I don't know any more than that."

"So that is the next question," Irshad said. "No book, dead-end, giving up?" he spit out in frustrated fragments of thought.

"That's pretty much it," Badri said. "This is a wonderful family discovery, but the place has been picked clean over the centuries. The house is an empty shell."

"Let's talk this through before we just throw in the towel," Irshad said.

He was about to say something else when the local police drove up. They spoke in Arabic with Badri and Sami. Even those who could speak Arabic, that would be everyone but me, couldn't hear because they were talking in quiet whispers. Ten minutes later the police drove off, and Badri explained to the group.

"It seems the two men we handed over to the police were aided in an escape and then killed by the same people that helped them. No police were even injured. They wanted to warn us that we may have stumbled into a black market smuggling ring or a possible terrorist cell. They are concerned for our safety."

"Who would do that?" Lydia asked.

"Hashshashin," Leyla said. "They are here. I don't know how they keep finding us so quickly, but it sounds like them. Glean any information they can and silence the source."

We spent the afternoon in the safety of the house going over possible clues we might have missed. The workers left about three, having run an electrical line to the house, but with no lights or connections. That would take a week they said. It would have taken a month, plus hundreds if not thousands of dollars in fees and code inspections back home. They filled the water basin on the roof and ensured the outdoor restroom was clean and safe. I guessed if the place were under siege back in the day, you either held it or collected it and dumped it off the roof.

We got nowhere in our discussions. I wondered if it was obvious that we had actually found something. Badri pulled me aside and said, "Let's go for a walk."

We walked to the mosque, knowing it was one place we could go where there were no listening ears. "Dr. Nabat is going to be here tomorrow. How do we explain his arrival and hide anything from Irshad?"

"Could we send him on a mission?" I asked.

"Not right away. He is going to need time to poke around here a little to convince himself this place is empty. Hopefully, he won't be as good as you in discovering the library."

"Maybe we just have to take a chance," I said.

"It's better to have a thousand enemies outside of the tent than one inside the tent," Badri lamented. "I don't like it, but I don't have an alternative. I will make the announcement. I will explain the reason for the secrecy was my concern about the workers. Now that they are gone, I can take everyone down to the library and also mention Dr. Nabat's visit."

We walked back to the house, and while Badri pulled everyone together, I ran up to the roof and entered the passageway. I had gotten an idea and didn't have time to explain it to Badri. I got into the library, knowing the group would not be far behind. I grabbed the three most probable books, and then as a last thought, I also grabbed the book with the odd horizontal and vertical dashes. I closed up the library just as I heard voices echoing in the hollow walls of the house. I went the other way and escaped out the mosque entrance. Not an easy task with four ancient books. I now had the house to myself, so I found a couple of ubiquitous plastic bags and put the books in them. Then I put the bags in a duffle bag and placed it in the trunk of the car Badri had been using.

I caught up with the team as they were still in awe with the library room. "I thought you would be down here when I came back from the restroom and everyone was gone. Pretty amazing, don't you think?" I asked.

"You found this in less than an hour after centuries of treasure seekers thought they had picked this place clean?" Lydia asked.

"Well, it was luck and necessity," I said.

"This is the find of the century, my American treasure hunter friend," Hande said. "Those gold coins are worth a fortune alone, but I will bet the Saudi government will want to buy them."

"Well, let's hope the Kitab Kabbani is here, and we can get back to family and a simpler life," I said.

"Yes, let's hope that," Irshad said looking at me with a blank stare.

I didn't know exactly what Badri had told everyone, but they were very careful touching the ancient scrolls and the books remaining. We stayed in the library until it became boring just looking but not touching. There just wasn't that much to do if you couldn't really read the books, and everyone knew it was best to leave things in place until Dr. Nabat arrived. We had some lively conversations but went to bed at an early hour.

We enjoyed a breakfast of dates, figs, cheese and flatbread on the roof and watched the sun come up. Badri and I left at nine to go pick up Dr. Nabat. I imagined Irshad would go down to the library on his own while we were gone if he hadn't already done so last night. I wondered if the Kitab Kabbani was down there still and I had grabbed the wrong books.

Dr. Nabat was excited to see us when he arrived and was quite nervous. "I have never been here before and wasn't sure how an Iranian citizen and non-Muslim would be treated," he explained as he reacquainted himself with the team.

"Since you came on official business, it is more the transportation than the government that is a problem. I am glad you were able to make the flight to Bahrain. Was the bus trip to Damman easy to catch?" Badri asked.

"Yes, no problem, and no problem catching the flight you arranged to bring me here. So tell me more about the find you made." Dr. Nabat said.

Badri explained what he thought might be in the library, but Dr. Nabat was immediately most interested in the inscription on the stone outside the library. He had a phone-text-sized picture of the inscription that Leyla had taken. "Yes, I think you are right; it is Old Southern Arabic. I brought some materials that may help me translate it, but I make no promises. This is not a language I have studied closely."

We were back at the house for lunch. Dr. Nabat was tired from his all night flights and time at airports, but he was also excited to see the find. I think he was mostly excited to see Lydia again and to be of some help to her and her friends. When he saw the library, he was awestruck, like everyone else had been, and promptly forgot what planet he was on. He began cataloging everything. Each piece was brought into a room on the third floor of the house, where it could be more closely examined. It only took two hours to catalog and transfer everything.

"Is there any chance the book we seek is among the books and scrolls you have seen?" Irshad asked.

"Yes, there are a few candidates," Dr. Nabat said. "I will know more within the next hour."

We all waited patiently while the doctor looked through the books and scrolls. "There are some amazing finds here. This is one of the most astonishing ancient libraries I have ever heard of, let alone be the first to study its contents. There are some ancient texts in Persian and Greek, as well as ledgers and inventories, bills of sale, and other business documents that will shed new light on the famed trade routes of the time periods of these documents. For me, personally, there is a Christian document from 200 AD that is amazing. I have not read its full contents—my Aramaic is very bad—but it is absolutely priceless."

"And the Kitab Kabbani?" Irshad asked with a little impatience in his voice.

"No, nothing of the kind. There may be further hints of records that speak of it, but no, nothing appears to be that book. I am sorry."

"Very well then, we have a decision to make, team," Irshad said. "Do we retrace steps, stay here for that off chance we find something new, or do we return and see if our friend Dr. Nabat comes up with new clues for us?"

"It's time to get back home and regroup," Lydia suggested. "If my father comes up with anything over the next two days, we can make a new plan for further searches. I can stay with him, if that is alright with you, Badri."

"I also vote for a pause in the action," Badri said. "I have a wife that I left in the care of others that I need to get back to her. Hande, would I be overstepping my bounds if I asked you to stay here and watch over Dr. Nabat and Lydia? You could also oversee the house renovations, and I would have an open checkbook for your use."

"I can do that," Hande said. He could hardly contain his grin.

Sami, Leyla, and Irshad also said they would return. Irshad never even asked me what I was going to do. Maybe he realized my plan was to follow. He may have thought I would follow Badri, but my plan was actually to follow Leyla. I hoped Irshad would leave before Badri and Leyla so that I would be able to show Dr. Nabat the books I had hidden.

"The one thing remains," Irshad said. "What about the inscription on the stone outside the library?"

"Oh, yes," Dr. Nabat said. "That ended up being very easy. It is an ancient Arabic saying which has survived to this day. It says, Every day of your life is a page of your history. An apt thought for someone's library."

"That almost speaks to the origin of the Kitab Kabbani," Leyla said. "A family journal of their eyewitness accounts, experiences and thoughts through history."

"Yes," said Dr. Nabat. "But we must not read into history what we want to see. It is a well-known thought that may not have anything to do with a single, specific book.

It sounded like this conversation was going to go on for some time. I motioned to Leyla to follow me. I wanted to go back to the roof and watch the stars come out. I also needed to tell her about the books I stashed away in the trunk of Badri's car. When I walked out of the room, I went into the room Badri and I were sharing and grabbed his car keys. Leyla and I were on the roof a few minutes later. Alone.

I grabbed her hand and BAM! There was a huge explosion. We ran to the edge of the building and saw six men running into the house where the entrance door used to be."

"Furqaan again?" I asked. "Aren't they the ones who liked to blow things up?"

"Could be," Leyla said. "We could be of better help to the team at this point by hiding and sorting out what is really going on." I followed Leyla into the hollow wall entrance and closed the door behind me. We didn't have a flashlight or our cell phones. "Dumb," I thought. "We should have left a few at key places."

We knew the layout of the tunnel well enough, but we still had to move slow. When we arrived at the mosque exit, we listened to see if we could hear anyone. We didn't think anyone was there, so we pulled ourselves out, and I grabbed the shovel that had barred the door. We quietly opened the mosque door, and I peeked outside. The immediate area appeared empty. Then I heard movement coming up the path. Could it be a team member, or someone else? It sounded like a single person, and I assumed they were armed.

I motioned for Leyla to crouch down by the rocks to our right. I figured if this guy saw the explosion, his night vision would still be poor. Leyla could never look like a rock, but I doubted he was expecting us to be here at this time. I coiled up and waited for our intruder to come around the corner. I decided it wasn't a team member because they would be running, not walking up the path. I hoped my assumption was right.

I was a batter in the batter's box. Wham! I swung with all my might and missed his head. I hit him in the chest. "A big guy," I thought. "Great." I did hear his gun hit the rocks. I took another swing while he was momentarily stunned. This time, I connected with his head, and he screamed out but was cut out by another dull thud sound. Leyla put him on the ground with the handle end of his gun. I didn't have anything to tie him up with, so I was going to leave him, but Leyla took off her outer dress, tore some strips of cloth, tied him up and gagged his mouth. She had jeans and a T-shirt on under the dress. So that really is what she wears under her abaya.

Chapter 26

WE WERE BACK AT THE house within thirty seconds. We entered the blown apart entrance and crept up the stairs to the second floor and entered the kitchen area. We heard muffled sounds and waited to see if they were coming our way. They were.

I heard a voice I recognized. Irshad. He was speaking in rapid Arabic. Leyla almost got up, but I pulled her back down. I had no idea what he was saying, but it wasn't accompanied by a victory dance. He sounded mad and very mean.

"Thad!" he yelled in English. "I know you are in this house. Show yourself now, or I will kill Badri. I really don't care about you or your silly girlfriend, my former betrothed. The thing is, I don't want to leave any loose ends. You have two minutes to show yourself, or Badri is a dead man." He yelled something in Arabic.

I wasn't sure what to do. I knew he would probably kill us all anyway, but I couldn't just run and let him kill Badri. I knew there was one thing that he wanted more than any of us, the book, and I only had two minutes. I couldn't find anything to write with, so a grabbed the hummus from lunch and smoothed it out on the counter and wrote my message with my finger. I grabbed Leyla's hand and ran out of the kitchen, down the stairs and out of the house.

We ran directly to Badri's car, got in, and I started it up and left. "In the glove box is the radio. See if you can get in contact with Irshad. I need to talk with him."

"I doubt he has it on," Leyla said. "But you are right; it is worth a try."

Leyla tried the radio, but it didn't work. "Do you think he will see the message in the kitchen before he does anything stupid?" I asked.

"I don't know," Leyla said. "Maybe we should go back, or bring back the police. We can't lie to him for too long. He will figure us out."

"Who's lying?" I asked.

"Well, you said in your hummus message that you had the real book, and if Badri or anyone on the team was harmed, he would never see it."

"Yes. I meant it."

"So where is the book?" Leyla asked.

"In the trunk, hopefully," I said. "Try the radio one more time before we are out of range."

Leyla tried again, and we both heard Badri's voice. "Thad, Irshad saw your message in the kitchen. He left us here, with no transportation and a threat to not follow or any one of us would be shot on sight. He is going to kill you. He is Hashshashin. You were right. What is your plan?"

"No plan," Leyla said. "We are on the run, and it sounds like we only have a five-minute head start. Are you sure Irshad doesn't have a radio?"

"For sure he doesn't have a radio. Hande still has his radio, and obviously, I have the other one," Badri said.

Badri's voice was starting to break up. We were almost out of range. "Okay," Leyla explained quickly, "we don't have cell phones right now. We will meet you in Dubai in two days. If we don't make it, we will see you at the Kabbani family compound in Beirut in five days. If we don't make that, we will attempt to contact you somehow."

We didn't hear anything back, so we weren't sure they got our transmission. "Where are we going?" Leyla asked as she put the radio back in the glove box.

"We need to go in the unexpected direction. The Empty Quarter. We are heading out of Dodge and into the abyss. So what direction would that be?"

"That is an American saying I am not familiar with, but I think I understand." Leyla already had the Saudi Arabia road map in her hand. "Head to the town of Sharorah on Highway 15," Leyla said. "That's about 170 miles from here. It won't be hard to miss. It is the first and only town we will see. We will get gas there. It is a long straight road into the darkness. We will know if there is anyone behind us soon."

We drove in silence for about twenty minutes, each with our own thoughts. "One of the men back at Badri's house called Irshad 'Jabal.'" Leyla said, breaking the silence.

"A nickname like mizmiz?" I asked. "What does it mean? No, let me guess, he who casts a shadow of wisdom and whose armpits do not smell."

"Not a bad guess, Thaddeus," Leyla said chuckling. "I have been thinking about it since we escaped. I think it is a reference to Shaykh al Jabal, which means wise man or elder of the mountain."

"Irshad, 'wise man of the mountain'? No, I like my definition better."

"It is a reference to Rashid ad-Din Sinan, the ancient grandmaster of the Hashshashin," Leyla said, settling back into her somber mood.

"So you think he was always Hashshashin, not just a subcontractor?" I asked.

"He is Hashshashin," Leyla said. "Their tactics have always historically been lies and counterfeit. When they were fighting the anti-Nizari rulers, the Assassins would dedicate years to study culture, language, and practices of their target. They would send their agent to infiltrate the inner circles of trust of the intended victim, often serving them for years and proving themselves as worthy of trust. They would forego opportunities to kill the victim until that trust was one hundred percent. Then they would attack. Thus they created more fear and terror into the hearts of their enemies who would see assassins in their most trusted servants and advisors."

"I know you have moved on from Irshad, but I am sorry," I said, "that your entire relationship, and the time you dedicated to it, was a hoax. So he was an assassin grand master secretly infiltrating Al-Ḥujurāt?" In the silence, something else became clear. "Oh, my goodness," I said. "Irshad always seemed like an odd name. It is an anagram for Rashid. Rashid ad-Din Sinan."

"Wow, you figured that out in your head?" Leyla asked. "You know Irshad is a word in Arabic. It means guidance. I have known others with this name."

"Well, I apologize to all the Irshads who have shared a name with this guy," I said. "So his assignment was to infiltrate Al-Ḥujurāt? I just wonder if that is why he was being so friendly to Badri also. Did he think he could get into the Kabbani family as well?"

"We may never know what that was about," Leyla said. "In hindsight I could see maneuvering going on, times he disappeared, wondering what that was all about. My great uncle, the one you sort of met, never liked Irshad, Rashid, whatever his name really is. My dad was no fan either, but my mother's father was close friends with Irshad's father, and they masterminded our betrothal."

"And everyone just went along with it?" I asked surprised. "So either your grandfather was duped, or hopefully, he didn't know Irshad's father as well as he thought."

"Or Irshad picked up this side work as an assassin somewhere along the way," Leyla said. "Maybe I was too boring for him, and he had to find something else to do with his life."

"Are you serious?" I asked. "You are the reason the sun comes up every day, just so it can catch another glimpse of you. The whole world is indebted to you. Let's just leave it with the clear fact that this guy is an idiot, and somewhere his vision got so muddled that he thought his long-term goals were so overarching that you became a short-term sacrifice. He missed out on the greatest eternal blessing, and he will never know it. I, for one, am grateful for his terrible choices."

We again drifted into silence as the sun set behind us. In a long straight stretch of road where I could see for at least two or three miles behind us, I pulled the car over. I ran to the trunk and retrieved the duffle bag with the books. I got back in and continued driving.

"Take a look at what I grabbed. There are four books in the bag. They appeared to be the most likely candidates for the Kitab Kabbani. Who knows, maybe I left the book back in the library, or it is actually a scroll. Of course, it may not exist, or we just didn't find it yet."

"What made you think to even do this?" Leyla asked.

"Just a feeling," I said. "I figured it wouldn't hurt if there was nothing to worry about, but if something did happen, better to have a little insurance."

Leyla opened the bag and took out the plastic sacks that covered the books. "I am glad you thought to protect these invaluable thousand-year-old books," Leyla joked.

"It was a spur of the moment decision," I explained. "I suppose we could test each book by submerging them in water and seeing if any of them come out dry."

"Not on your life. Maybe that really happened, but maybe for that one instance, to teach my grandfather a lesson. These are amazing books. The calligraphy and artwork are amazing. Any of them could be the Kitab Kabbani judging from the age and binding."

"Can you read anything in any of them, or should I have gone back for Dr. Nabat?" I asked.

Leyla carefully opened pages of the first book and said, "This could be it, but I don't know this language, or at least not the writing, at all. The second one is in Arabic, but the script is difficult for me to read. I believe it is a description of trade routes, customers, and product sources. It is divided by geographic areas. It is going to be fascinating to understand, but it is not the Kitab. This third book is also not what we are looking for. It is in Persian, I believe, but seems to be talking about weather, math, sciences and so forth. Perhaps it could be the Kitab Kabbani if we are completely misinformed about what the book really is. This last book is quite odd. I am not sure what to make of it. It just has short horizontal and vertical dashes. It almost looks like cuneiform, but it isn't. Could it be some kind of inventory system?"

"I only grabbed it at the last second as I was rushing out of the library. It was sitting by itself on a shelf, and since I only looked at a couple of pages, I assumed that surely it would have writing on other pages."

Leyla began to study the book more closely to see if there was any writing in it. Reading left to right, she started by looking inside the left cover. There were a few words written in some text she didn't recognize. The very next page began with the odd dashes. She turned to the inside of the right cover. The pages were blank until five pages in, where the dashes ended. A loose leaf of thick paper, no, papyrus we guessed, was tucked into the book here.

"Thaddeus, this is in Greek! I might be able to read it," Leyla said. She grabbed a pen out of the glove box and looked for something to write on. She couldn't find anything, so she used the margins of the car rental agreement. After a few minutes, she read,

But you must remember, beloved, the predictions of the apostles of our Lord; they said to you, "In the last time there will be scoffers, following their own ungodly passions." It is these who set up divisions, worldly people, devoid of the Spirit. But you, beloved, build yourselves up on your most holy faith. Thaddeus

"Do you think this is from the Thaddeus of early Christianity?" Leyla asked. "It sounds like that is what it is. It is beautiful. This could be from your distant ancestor."

"You know, it sounds familiar, like it is something from the Bible that my father used to read. I remember it because he read very, very little. Interesting, the part about setting up divisions by worldly people."

"Could this book be in some kind of code?" Leyla asked, continuing to look through the book. "It is written by different hands and even different types of ink. Some have faded quite a bit; others have stayed bold. On just a few pages spread throughout the book, it appears the person writing changed, and there is a word or two in a script I don't know. You are right; I wish we could have grabbed Dr. Nabat also.

It wasn't too much longer before we could see the little outpost of Sharorah. We stopped just before town, and Leyla got into the backseat and put on her torn abaya. I drove into town and stopped at the service station. We waited at the pump until someone came out. I sat there like a mannequin, and Leyla did the talking from the back seat. She gave the attendant money for the gas, and he brought out six bottles of water and some candy and chips.

She talked for a minute and then kicked the seat, yelling something at me in Arabic. The attendant chuckled. I drove off not knowing where I should even turn. As soon as we were out of earshot, Leyla said, "Turn left here. Stay on this road until we are out of town." I did as she directed. "Turn left here," she said again a minute later.

"So what are we doing?" I finally asked.

"This is the airport. It's almost bigger than the town. I assume it is here as much for national security as actual air traffic. I thought perhaps we could find a phone to make a call. I still know a few of the team cellphones by heart. Irshad, no way, but Hande or Lydia might have theirs on if they were able to get into Narjan. I told the attendant that we were going to the airport to meet our private aircraft and that you were a lazy driver that I had threatened to leave here. I would love to catch a plane here. There are three flights a day to Riyadh. This is the gateway for Yemen into Saudi Arabia. I don't want to take a chance with that, however. You have no papers, and I have no guardian. That attendant could have asked for your registered driver papers. We were lucky."

We drove to the airport. I put the books in the duffle bag, and we walked in as if I were her driver. She asked for a phone to call to see if her husband's aircraft was on its way. She was promptly guided to a public phone. She called Hande and didn't get an answer. She tried Lydia and got an answer. It was Badri.

"Lydia stayed with Hande. I finally made it into Narjan with Sami. Dr. Nabat also stayed with Lydia and Hande. Are you alright?"

"We are fine," Leyla explained in English. "What's wrong with Hande?"

"The radio went dead before we could let you know," Badri began. "Hande was shot by Irshad before he left. It was his warning to all of us not to follow him. Hande is still alive, but he has lost a lot of blood. A doctor is already on his way to the house. I am just finishing up arrangements for another car."

"We are at the airport in Sharorah," Leyla said. "It is way too quiet to attempt to fly out of here. I had considered buying a way onto a flight, but we simply don't have that much cash, and I have no guardian paperwork for Thaddeus. He has his passport, but I don't. Would it make sense to wait for you here? Could you get an aircraft?"

"Not right now. The police want me to stay here to explain about the attempted robbery by Irshad and his men that got Hande shot. If you can hold out until tomorrow, maybe I can get out there and back."

"I don't know. I am really in the open here, and this is a ghost town. I think we will go out into the Empty Quarter tonight and maybe consider coming back into town tomorrow when there are more people around. If I can find a cheap cellphone, I will let you know. Try to be in Narjan at nine tomorrow morning, and we will try to make another call."

Leyla made some complaint in Arabic when she hung up the phone and marched out with her shiftless driver in tow. Once we got outside, she said, "Hande was seriously injured, and there is no way Badri or other members of the team are going to be able to get out here tonight or first thing tomorrow. We need to get out of town for now and go into the desert where it will be safer for the moment."

We drove back through town and toward Narjan. About a mile out of Sharorah, Leyla directed me to turn right onto Road

180 heading toward Al Kharkhir. The sign said Al Kharkhir was 515 kilometers away.

"Al Kharkhir is the end of the road," Leyla said. "That's only one-third of the way to the UAE. Even still, I wish we could drive there, but without an off-road vehicle, we can't make it."

We drove into the night. There were small hamlets or single buildings here and there. Leyla wanted to be completely out of sight, so we kept driving. Finally, we turned left onto Umm Al Melh Road.

"We don't want to go down this road too far. Supposedly there is a secret U.S. drone base out here. At least that is what Wired Magazine reported in 2011. I don't want to explain to the CIA what we are doing out here. My thought was, I don't think Irshad would want to be caught out here either, so this might be safe for us for tonight. Let's pull over and stop for the night somewhere off the road."

Within a mile, we found a suitable place to park that was semi-unnoticeable from the road. I stretched my legs and then got into the back seat with Leyla. We dined on water and potato chips for dinner. We each had a Bounty Bar for dessert. They are kind of like Mounds Bars, but for some reason, these tasted even better.

We got outside and sat on the sand and watched the stars take over the heavens. I think there were more stars than black sky. "I could sleep out here tonight," I said.

I was about to launch into the Eagles song, "Peaceful Easy Feeling," when Leyla rained on my little patch of the Empty Quarter saying, "Until the jerboas, camel-spiders, sand-vipers, and translucent scorpions find you. You will be much happier in the car. It will also get down into the low sixties or high fifties tonight. That doesn't sound very cold, but without a light blanket, it might be more uncomfortable that you imagine.

"Oh, that reminds me, you will also want to drink a full bottle of water tonight. The humidity here is only about two percent. You will be a raisin by morning if you don't keep hydrating. I will use the left side of the car; you can use the right side if you need to relieve yourself."

"How can something so beautiful be so inhospitable?" I asked.

"Are you talking about me again," Leyla asked with a smile.

"No, you are just the opposite," I said.

"Ugly and hospitable?" she asked in mock horror.

"Yeah, right. If you are ugly, the rest of the world is the walking dead."

"Oh, how romantic you are," Leyla said cuddling up to me. "You know the last the town we were at—Sharorah? It is called the Bride of Empty Quarter. Now that is romantic."

"Is that a proposal?" I asked.

"No, Majnun," Leyla said, punching me playfully in the arm. Unless you want to marry a town."

"I know who I want to marry," I said seriously, "And if Alicia the ticket counter lady won't have me, would you consider being my bride?"

That seemed to shake her out of her playful mood. I was about to apologize when she jumped up and said, "Quick, get in the car! Shamal winds."

No sooner had we shut the doors than Mother Nature's sandblaster hit us. It wasn't that the wind was terrible—I guessed it to be only about forty miles per hour—but the sand it carried made it like being in a blender. The noise sounded almost like static on a radio, turned up to 100 decibels.

The sand was leaking through the cracks in the car, and we were soon covered in silt. Leyla had pulled her scarf off from around her neck and given it to me. She had her dress pulled up over her face. We didn't talk. We couldn't have heard each other if we had tried. We just sat there next to each other waiting for the storm to pass. It finally did, several hours later. We couldn't open the car doors, but we weren't completely buried either. We decided to get some rest and wait to assess the situation in the morning. Sometime during the night there was a very brief rain. I thought that would be a good thing.

Before she fell asleep, Leyla explained, "We will need to be very careful when we get out of the car in the morning. In the valley between sand dunes there is silt the Bedu people call sebkha that gets baked and after a rain actually gets brittle. The edges are like broken glass and will cut through anything from tires to flesh. It is pretty easy to stay out of the uruquin, the bottom of these sand dune valleys. In our case, our car and the wind have created an uruquin around us. We are probably surrounded by this sebkha that has just been rained on. We are surrounded by the desert version of barbed wire. For now, get some sleep, and we will take care of this with some light to help in the morning."

I am not a great sleeper sitting up, but I gave the back seat to Leyla, and I took the passenger seat in the front, reclined it as best I could, and tried to sleep. I had thought perhaps it would get cold enough that we would have to hold each other to share our body heat, but it never got that cold. It was just a miserable night.

The morning did eventually come. We found the car was half buried. We tried to drive out of our gritty morass, and the car didn't budge. We couldn't open any doors, so we rolled down the right backseat window and climbed out. We jumped away from the car, in case the silt had created sebkha. We brought the duffle bag with us, the radio, and our two remaining bottles of water. We ate the last candy bars for breakfast. We had no idea how far away the drone base was or if it even existed, so we decided we would need to walk back to the main road and hope for a passing vehicle.

There were areas where we weren't sure what direction the road went because it was covered in sand, but we always saw it in the distance and could walk to that strip of asphalt. Some of the sand dunes we walked by were hundreds of feet high. I wasn't surprised, now that I had walked in this sand, that glass was invented not far from here.

"I am really grateful it is November and not August," I said as we walked away from our only shelter. "At least it won't get to 130 degrees today."

"Don't let the temperature fool you," Leyla warned. "This desert is just as deadly. Once you asked me for some frivolous thoughts, remember? My favorite color. So tell me some of your deepest thoughts, Thaddeus."

I knew she was trying to get my mind off of our present situation, but I took the bait. "I have only just got you started liking me. Why should I take a chance now with my deepest thoughts?" I said laughing. Leyla quietly kept walking, waiting.

"So. I think that we humans are naturally meaning-seeking. We need meaning even more than we need food and water," I began, thinking of our need for food and water. "Without it, we become vegetables on the table of life. Spirituality in part fulfills the need for meaning, that daily input we need, but religion, organized religion, answers the big questions, the meaning of life, why we are here, where we came from, where we are going. Some religions do a more complete job than others. I used to have the concern about whether religion was created to answer our need for meaning or whether we need meaning because we are naturally spiritual creatures. You know, the chicken and egg question."

"And?" Leyla asked.

"I know—and I don't mean I believe—I really know, that we didn't create God to meet our meaning needs. God really exists, and there is a part in every one of us that knows this. God created man, and the chicken, and they were fruitful and replenished the earth. I also think that parts of religion were created for man, not man for religion. We aren't slaves to, but blessed by, obedience."

"But men do create gods," Leyla said.

"They do. Money, power, clothes, sex outside of love and marriage, and hundreds of other counterfeits of the real thing. And that meaning doesn't last. It often creates a bigger need for the real thing. Instead of trying to find the real thing, or accepting it when we do find it, we justify, we self-medicate, we overindulge, we consume, but we don't find peace."

"Exactly. And the real thing is like watching and feeling the sun rise instead of turning on a light bulb," Leyla said. "The real thing creates and nurtures life. The fake illuminates the mundane, the transitory that will soon turn to dust. So tell me what you think the building blocks are."

"Some of this I already shared with you, I think, on our way to Konya. I don't claim to be an expert, Leyla. These are just my thoughts, and if you have concerns or ideas, I would love to hear them," I said as I worked to recall the list in my mind.

"I will stop you if I remember or if you are putting me to sleep. I will tell you why I ask after you are done."

"Oh, so this is a test, and the pressure is on. Luckily there is nothing else going on in our lives, so I don't have to carry the extra baggage of say, survival, and avoiding ruthless killers."

"You are stalling, Thaddeus," Leyla said.

"Okay. Okay. Here goes. We make meaning through iterative sensory inputs. Our sense of smell, sight, sound, touch, taste, but also authority, that is, higher spiritual inputs, provide input supporting a stimulus, a desire, what we care about, and internal or external enticings. Value, purpose, and practice help create trust. Presence, identity, efficacy, context, and self-worth add to final meaning-making.

"Each of these building blocks is a discussion itself, but just the words should start making connections with our own spiritual understanding. Sufism, for example, must speak to who you are—identity, right?—and during some practice of Sufism, you feel a spiritual presence, perhaps during a Sema dance and so on with concepts like purpose, efficacy, and the other concepts I mentioned.

"I have even played around with which ones are necessary, and which are sufficient, and what happens if one or more aren't provided. Like if there is purpose, but no identity, confusion may result. If there is self-worth, but no presence, one might feel lost, kind of like I am feeling right now. How much further is the main road do you think?"

"That's quite a theory, Thaddeus. Thanks for sharing it. I will have to chew on all that," Leyla said. "I don't know how far the road is. I am guessing we have walked over a mile, so it should be coming up soon."

No sooner did she finish the word "soon" than we saw a car traveling down the main highway. It was only about a quarter mile away. The driver must have seen us also, because it immediately sped up and turned onto the side road, accelerating toward us.

"Quick," Leyla yelled. "Get off the road. Let's head into the desert. That doesn't look like help. It must be Irshad."

Chapter 27

WE TURNED AND RAN OUT into the unknown, again. We quickly disappeared from the road over a sand dune. "Remember," Leyla yelled, "stay out of the uruquin, the bottom of these sand dune valleys. It is very possible there is sebkha due to the rain last night." We crested a second dune and saw that the car was stationary, but we didn't see any people.

"You are sure that might not be someone just wanting to help?" I asked. "I mean, wouldn't you rush to someone's aid if you saw them walking by themselves out of the desert?"

"Just keep running," Leyla replied. "I have a bad feeling about this."

"Funny you should mention that," I said, voicing my own strange feelings. "I had a weird dream a few nights ago, and this is starting to feel like déjà vu."

"Good," Leyla said. "Any meaningful guidance, spiritual, supernatural, or otherwise, would be helpful."

"I will let you know if anything comes to mind." I didn't tell her about the dream where we were drowning in quicksand. I just kept going.

We stopped running and laid down to catch our breath and try to see where they were at, staying near the top of the third dune and hopefully out of sight. Our footprints were lost in the ripples of the dunes, but they knew the general direction we had been running.

"Let's run parallel with this dune and then double back. They probably wouldn't look that way for a while. And maybe other vehicles will come by," I suggested.

We ran for another ten minutes, which is serious work in 800-feet-thick sand. We stopped again and watched for who was following us. We didn't see anyone for a few minutes. Then we saw three men only a dune away from us. One was Irshad. He didn't see us, but he knew somehow that we were near.

"Thad! Leyla!" Irshad yelled. "I know you are out there. We can wait all day. We have plenty of water, a comfortable car to rest in. It is time to give up. If you want to live, now is the time to stand up. In one minute, we will continue our search, and when we find you, you will die."

"Right," I whispered to Leyla. "We are dead as soon as we stand up." So what better thing to do than stand up, I thought, to keep Leyla from that fate. "Stay down and guard the books," I whispered. I stood up and said, "How did you find us so fast, Irshad?"

Leyla tugged on my pant leg. I ignored it. The only person I could now see was Irshad. I assumed the other two men were maneuvering to get closer to us by other routes. I started walking to my right, into the sun.

"And how did you make it through the sandstorm? That was pretty crazy. By the way, I have hidden the book, for my own security and that of Leyla."

"So if I kill you and Leyla, no one would ever find the book?" Irshad asked, but it wasn't really a question. "This is such a lonely place to die. But very convenient."

"Lots of ways to die in this desert," I said only loud enough for Leyla to hear. Even quieter I said, "Stay where you are at and guard the books. I do have a plan."

"Right," Leyla whispered. "You unarmed against three armed, mad, and trained assassins. You are nuts."

"That is one of my names," I said. Much louder I said, "So Irshad, what do you plan to do with this book if you do get your hands on it? Maybe I have misjudged your motives. Really, all I want to do is get out of here with Leyla and live a simple life."

I was slowly walking toward a place where the two dunes Irshad and I were on joined. I didn't want him to lose sight of me as I walked toward the point below that combined crest. About ten feet before the point I had in mind, one of the men crested the dune and came toward me. As I was counting on, the shortest point to me was through the valley. As he approached he transited the bottom point of the dune, and just as Leyla had explained, the silt was brittle and began to break up. The sebkha began to shred the man's pant legs and then his shoes, and then his legs, all in about two strides. The more he tried to get out of Mother Nature's razor blades, the worse his situation became. Before Irshad could answer my questions, the man was screaming for help.

I continued to walk slowly past the man, above the area of the sebkha toward a flat area. I strangely knew this area. I sat down and waited for Irshad or his associate to approach me.

"I don't know what game you are playing, Thad," Irshad said, "but I am not in a negotiation mood. I have put up with your stupidity and your strategy to take away the leadership of my team for weeks, and I am done. I pleaded with my superiors to find a way to kill you and blame it on Furqaan or even the Hashshashin, but there was always this concern that you might have further information. I know that you are nothing but an uneducated charlatan that has gotten a few lucky breaks. I look forward to slitting your throat myself, no matter what that does to my chances of finding the book. But I am sure Leyla is carrying the book, and I will deal with her as soon as I deal with you."

I yawned to communicate my boredom with his ranting. I could see he was holding a gun, but I wanted to get him closer before he decided to use it. "I, too, have looked forward to facing you in a fair fight. I didn't think it would actually be out here in the middle of nowhere, and I really never expected it to be fair, but if this is the day and the place, so be it."

"Aggghhh," Irshad yelled. He tucked his gun into his pants and started walking toward me. "It is Badri that has the answers and the power. Leyla was useful to a point in the return of the relics. Badri will eventually find the Kitab Kabbani and be persuaded to unite with our cause; but you, you are an annoying insect that must be smashed. Now."

Irshad was walking, trying to stomp with not much success in this sand, directly for me. I was either a dead man in the next thirty seconds, or I would be rid of Irshad of his own choice. I tried to act calm as I stood up and brushed off my pants. There was a man out there somewhere that was also still a very dangerous threat. The man in the sebkha quagmire was injured badly, but not dying. Then there was Irshad. I would soon see what category he fit in. I was hoping for a third category. The sand under him began to crackle, almost like Rice Krispies breakfast cereal. At first, Irshad continued to try to stomp forward, but it was clear this sand was more than just thick sand. It was quicksand, just like my dream.

"Irshad," I said, now actually sad for him, "you may be right, I might be ignorant and a pest, but I am grateful to you for your arrogance and obstinacy. I may not be the greatest catch in the world, but in comparison to you, I am almost palatable."

"I will kill you," Irshad screamed. "I will leave you for the desert to consume."

"I am afraid it is the desert that is already consuming you," I said.

Not until those words, did Irshad realize what he had stepped into. "How did you…?"

"How did I know?" I said, finishing his question. "Some mirages are not light's twinkling reflection on the heat of the desert floor. Sometimes they are the desert floor that looks safe but demands a sacrifice. Many trusted you, but they should have mistrusted. You could have provided safety, but instead, you were a danger beyond compare. You used others vulnerabilities against them. The desert is playing your game. In my case, well, I was vulnerable enough to become immune to your virus. You would never believe me if I explained how I knew there was a pit of quicksand in this very spot."

"Thad," a seemingly humbled Irshad began. "Get me out of here, and you and Leyla will go free. I promise this. Having the debt of a Hashshashin grandmaster in your pocket is a powerful thing." A wave of fear ran through him, and he struggled not to thrash. He tried to reach the invisible side of the pit. There was nothing to grab onto.

"I don't want your promises, Irshad," I said. "I don't want to be your judge. If I knew a way to get you out, I really would. You chose your course. Call in your other man and perhaps he will have an idea."

With that, Irshad began calling out for his other associate. The man in Mother Nature's paper shredder had finally broken out of the sebkha and was stumbling up to the scene. He was in no capacity to help. He simply sat down and watched.

Within thirty seconds the other man came over a dune to my left holding Leyla in one hand while holding a knife with the other. Leyla had the duffle bag around her shoulder. As he approached the scene, he dropped his hold on Leyla and cautiously walked forward, testing each step as he went. He said something in Arabic to the other man sitting down who replied pointing to his lacerated and bleeding legs.

Leyla quietly backed out of reach of the man who had been her captor. Both of us knew we were still in extreme danger. Irshad could, for another few seconds, pull out his pistol and shoot us. The healthy assassin could also shoot us, if he had a gun, or slash us with his knife. The injured man couldn't catch us, but if he had a gun, he too could, for the moment, injure or kill us. It was a very strange scene.

Leyla took my hand, and we simply began walking. No one stopped us. Within ten minutes we reached Irshad's car. The keys were in the ignition. We briefly discussed the ethics of the situation and decided we could not just leave them there to die, even if that is what they would have done to us without a second thought. We drove as fast as we could back to Sharorah and reported that robbers had descended on us and in the midst of our escape, they got caught in quicksand.

We drove back to the sight, and only the injured man was still sitting there. He was only semi-conscious, due to loss of blood. Irshad and the other assassin were gone. Whether they had both escaped, or one left and Irshad was taken down into the quicksand, we did not know. The injured man was taken to Sharorah for care.

We drove past Sharorah in Irshad's car and kept going. It was already evening, but we had no interest in sleeping in the car in the desert another night. We pulled into a gas station on fumes at the intersection of Highway 15 and Route 1050 that headed south into Yemen. By the time we finally pulled into the parking area by the palms at Badri's house, it was one in the morning.

We were exhausted, filthy, starving, and probably smelled like ancient camel drivers that may have frequented this oasis. We honked the horn and left the headlights on while we pulled ourselves out of the car. Badri and Sami had approached without us seeing them. Once they saw it was us and that we were alone, they ran to us, and we nearly collapsed into their arms.

After some food and cold showers down by the water pump in the palm grove, we shared our story. Dr. Nabat had already taken charge of the four books. We also found out that Hande was near death and that Lydia was with him. He was in too serious of a condition to travel by some life flight means to a larger city with better medical services. There was still a possible threat from Irshad and his associate if they had escaped, so Sami stayed up to keep guard. Leyla and I slept for eleven hours.

I was grateful to wake up in Badri's house once again. Leyla looked amazing after a single night's sleep. I looked like I was twenty years older. Dr. Nabat was very excited with the books that had just been returned to the library. Badri was amazed at my quick snatch job and was certain they would have been lost had they still been there when the Hashshashin arrived.

"The book that intrigues me the most is the book with the dashes. The loose leaf that Leyla translated is actually from the Christian New Testament. It is from the Book of Jude. I don't know if it is an exact copy of the original Greek, but the translation that you stuck in the book caught my attention, and I looked it up this morning. The book itself is a complete mystery."

"What about the words, if they are words, that are inserted here and there in the book?" I asked.

"The first words are in Old Aramaic," Dr. Nabat explained. "Sometime around 500 BC, after the Achaemenid conquest of Mesopotamia, Old Aramaic was adopted by Darius 1st as the single language for official communications. Then, later in the book, I found Dari, the ancient Persian Dari, the same Dari some Zoroastrians still speak. Then later I found Old Southern Arabic, and finally modern Arabic. That alone is fascinating, the progression of languages, but what is really interesting is what these short phrases say. They all can be translated to say the same thing. They all say, 'This is my book.' The last phrase in modern Arabic says hatha kitabi."

Dr. Nabat studied my eyes to see if I had any recognition of what he had just said. Finally, it clicked. "So this book, found in the Kabbani family's ancient library says indirectly it is the Kitab Kabbani?"

"Yes," Dr. Nabat said. "And if there is any doubt about your part in this, I understand it was you who discovered the library in hours, where it remained hidden from practiced treasure hunters for centuries. Then, when it was again threatened, both here and in the desert, it was you who protected it."

"I wouldn't leave Leyla out of this adventure," I said. "Truth be told, Dr. Nabat, I was more concerned about protecting her than the book."

"As it should be, dear boy. And I told you before, please call me Jal. Rabbi Halevi told me he gave you anise seeds to give you the courage to sweep this young lady off her feet. I will have to tell him about your desert experience. He will want to take a small amount of the credit, you know."

"Please tell the rabbi I have done my best to be courageous, but we have not yet figured out how to build a bridge over the gaps that separate us," I said.

"Yes, I know what you mean. By the way, Lydia told me about her and Hande. I don't yet know what my exact feelings are, but I ended up telling her I had left Zoroastrianism for Christianity. It is still our secret as I must travel back to Iran in a week. It seems to have given her some solace in her own bridge building. I pray Hande pulls through."

"I would like to see both Hande and Lydia. Hopefully, I can get into town today."

"First I need your thoughts on the book. You and Leyla have studied it longer than anyone. Do you have any ideas what the dashes mean?"

"Let's bring Badri, Sami, and Leyla into the conversation," I suggested.

We walked down to the second floor where everyone else was eating a late lunch of lamb and rice. We all enjoyed the lunch together, made plans to go into town to get rid of Irshad's car, to see Hande, and to plan our travel out of Saudi Arabia. We then turned our attention to the book.

"So if this is THE book, then these dashes must be some form of communication," I said to get my thoughts flowing. "It doesn't look different in its marks from the first to the last of the book. The people or scribes that made these marks and the inks are different, but it is still very uniform."

"Could it be some kind of cuneiform?" Leyla asked.

"I considered that earlier today, but it doesn't work," Dr. Nabat said. "I don't know of any language that looks like this. Maybe someone made up their own language and passed it down through the family over the ages. Badri says he has never heard of anything like that in family stories or traditions."

"It is a code," I said. "The actual content is hidden as a final protection in broad daylight. It can't be too complex, or how could Rumi have read it?"

"Hmm, a code," Dr. Nabat said, chewing on this thought. "A code that would have been understood anciently and in modern times. That cuts out some of the more technical ways to create code that we might use today. Flexible enough to work with changes in languages and cultures, but stable enough to last the ages and be understood by those who should and would need to know its content."

"What is your estimate on when this may have begun?" Badri asked.

"If we use the language passages as a guide, it could have started around 500 BC," Dr. Nabat said. "But the research I mentioned when you were in Yazd suggests that the first parts of the book were actually scrolls."

"So it is possible that the scrolls are either in the library now, that they were destroyed, or lost?" Badri was asking.

"Or," I interrupted, "they could have been copied and put in this book for easier storage and transport."

"That is possible," Dr. Nabat agreed. "Your family certainly did a lot of traveling. Your ancestors made Marco Polo seem more like a fledgling tourist compared to their constant globetrotting."

We talked for another hour but got nowhere. We wanted to get to town and back before it got dark, so we left our discussion with no real progress made toward understanding the contents.

We found Lydia at the small clinic sitting outside Hande's room with her head in her hands. She looked worse than Leyla and I did on our arrival back at Badri's house. After some brief hugs and condolences, we all walked into the room.

"No change," Lydia said. "He is barely hanging on to life. The bullet wound has not become infected, but we really don't know if there is any internal bleeding or what other parts of his chest are damaged."

I went over close to Hande and whispered,

The breeze at dawn has secrets to tell you.
Don't go back to sleep.
You must ask for what you really want.
Don't go back to sleep.
People are going back and forth across the doorsill
Where the two worlds touch.
The door is round and open.
Don't go back to sleep.

Hande was motionless. Everyone gave him brief words of encouragement and then left the room. Sami brought food back for Lydia even though she said she wasn't hungry. She and her dad held each other in a long embrace, and then we left. It felt so wrong to go, but there wasn't any room at the clinic and nothing anyone could do.

We went to sleep early. Leyla and I still felt like dryer sheets after an hour of tumbling. I didn't have any dreams, and I woke up feeling almost human. Breakfast was wonderful. I was grateful for the little things and hoped I would never lose this morning's perspective. A fresh slice of an orange, a quiet breeze, the aroma of an ancient piece of frankincense from the library sitting on Dr. Nabat's makeshift desk. It was a good day, and it had just begun.

"We weren't meant to find the Kitab Kabbani and have it be unreadable," Sami complained as he sat down to breakfast.

"Patience," Badri offered. "That we found it this fast, in what, three weeks more or less, is nothing short of a miracle. It was only a few days ago that we opened the cover. It will come."

"I know," Sami said. "I just didn't expect it to be a book in code."

"Something I have been wondering," I said, adding to the questions instead of answers, "why was it that we actually found it? Why after hundreds of years was now the time? Why would your grandfather make these hints, when he could have found the book himself at a younger age? In an earlier generation?" I asked Badri.

"It was time, I guess," Badri answered. "We, my family, Al-Ḥujurāt, were waiting for you," he added.

"That's a lame answer," I said. "So if I were killed in a car accident on the way to work two months ago, the book would have remained hidden forever? I doubt it."

"There are a lot of questions I don't have answers to, Thad," Badri said. "But I do know this entire operation would not have happened had you not been along for the ride. How did my grandfather know to contact you and share his little hint months before the name Thaddeus was mentioned in the Fahrunissa

Scroll? For that matter, how did the Fahrunissa Scroll come to be and the name Thaddeus play such a pivotal role?

"Why did Leyla's father and great uncle trust you? I mean, you are a great guy, but only Leyla has had the opportunity to really get to know you. I won't even list all the other key intersections of the last weeks where you have walked through the haze with a clarity none of us have had."

"Oh brother, brother-in-law," I said. "You know me. I am a simple guy from a quiet corner of central California. I have no super powers, and, other than a little reading, this is as foreign as foreign gets for me. I think the question we ought to be asking right now, that we never got to in the past, is *why thirsty?* Why did we need to find this book so badly? Hagar wanted to make sure her baby, Ishmael, survived—the future of the Arab race, the future of Islam in many ways. How does this book play a role, or are we just manufacturing a role for it? And while I have the soapbox, here are some thoughts. Today no one kills more Arabs than Arabs. No one kills more Muslims than Muslims. War, destruction, ignorance, half-truths and full lies are placed at the doorsill of a religion of peace and education. We are hoping for answers with this book. I wonder if it has those kinds of answers."

"That has always been, with all great religions," Leyla chimed in for the first time. "Maybe that is why the book is in code. It says the hard things in an unbiased way. Like Polybius's histories, folklore suggests that the Kitab Kabbani talks of politics, religion, diplomacy, economics, behaviors. If there were someone to emulate in history, it would have been Polybius. Others wrote histories, but most had agendas. Polybius pushed away from the dangers of fables as history. Unbiased truth was his credibility."

"More or less in Polybius's words," Dr. Nabat began. "Previously the doings of the world had been, so to say, dispersed, as they were held together by no unity of initiative, results, or locality. But history has become an organic whole, and the affairs of Italy and Africa have been interlinked with those of Greece and Asia, all leading up to one end."

"Exactly," Leyla said. "The Kabbani book, instead of providing a skewed report— that is, just with the perspective of a victor, provides, I hope, a report of eyewitnesses that could see the forest and the trees—a family of educated and experienced scribes and recorders that had traveled the globe and had the histories of their forefathers on which to build their own under-standings. Instead of one man surveying the world, we may find an entire family who has surveyed history as it happened."

"I have a thought," I said. "Polybius lived during what exact period of time?"

"Around 200 BC to 100 BC. He didn't live to be 100, but that was his general century of experience and activity," Dr. Nabat said.

"He reported on many wars and was active in politics under the Romans," Leyla added. "He wrote of the Seleucid empire that included most of modern Afghanistan, Iran, Iraq, Syria, and Lebanon, together with parts of Turkey, Armenia, Turkmenistan, Uzbekistan and Tajikistan. His works were certainly known by the literate of the day, which surely included the former scribes of the Archimedes rulers who would one day be the ancestors of the Kabbani family. He very well could have been a role model for the first Kabbani scribes."

"Whether he was or wasn't, we won't know until we get this book decoded," I said. I was very excited because an idea was forming in my mind.

"Could it be this easy?" I asked myself out loud. "Didn't he also do a lot of writing about the irrigation techniques of the Persians, Dr. Nabat?"

"Yes, he did actually, now that you mention it," Dr. Nabat said. "How did you know that?"

"Mrs. Nazari," I said, smiling at Badri. "Someone you really need to meet. As Mrs. Nazari explained it to us, Polybius recorded the plans of regional development under the initiative of the central government in ancient Persia. Something like five generations were allowed to work the land if they developed irrigation techniques and dams. He also speaks of some of these techniques migrating from Persia to Arabia.

"What have we learned about the Kabbani family in both Persia and Arabia? They were very much involved in the engineering of dams and developing irrigation, in the Susa area and the Najran area. This also connects them to the migration of technology along the trade routes they plied. I think the ancient Kabbani family, before they were known as Kabbani, could have been sources for Polybius's work."

"Very interesting theory, Thad. I can accept that as a possibility," Dr. Nabat said.

"Yes, I suppose that is plausible," Leyla agreed. "That they knew of Polybius's work was almost a certainty. That Polybius knew of the Kabbani dams and irrigation work is less certain, but possible. It was a much smaller world in many ways in 150 B.C."

"That is what I am playing with in my mind, Leyla," I said. "That they knew of Polybius's work was almost a certainty." I paused to let this process. "So what else is Polybius famous for?" I asked.

"Other histories and his diplomatic service," Leyla answered.

"Oh! I know where you are going," Dr. Nabat said, grabbing a blank sheet of paper. "He is famous for the Polybius Square. Do you think…?"

"Yes, I do think it is a possibility. What if every phrase is the key, that is, when the language changes, it is signaled by the phrase 'This is my book'?"

"I am sorry," Sami interjected. "What are you two talking about?"

"I am no expert on Polybius or his histories. I have never read any of them. I am aware of something he developed while in the diplomatic service Leyla mentioned. Polybius was famous for his square. It is a simple way to create a cryptographic message. He used a five-by-five matrix. The vertical and horizontal margins were numbers. The corresponding matrix boxes were letters of an alphabet. So A in the English alphabet was one, one. This was the basis for the modern tap codes used by prisoners of war for example. If the alphabet was bigger than five-by-five, that is, twenty-five letters, you could group a couple letters in one box, or drop a letter altogether. People, just like today, could figure out the word from the context. And of course in some languages we are potentially dealing with here, we could drop the vowels completely. If the alphabet was really large, a six-by-six matrix could be employed."

"So you are suggesting that the vertical dashes define the X axis, and the horizontal dashes define the Y axis, and the letters inside the matrix are defined by what language is being used?" Leyla outlined.

"Yes," I said. "And not only the language, but which alphabet is being used, since some languages employed different forms of script to communicate it in written form."

Dr. Nabat was already drawing out a matrix for the Old Aramaic that might have been used for the first part of the book. "You know," he said while filling in the matrix with the appropriate script, "this would work really well as languages were forgotten within the family. As new languages became the standard form of communication, the book could be continued without depending entirely on the past."

Leyla had a smile or maybe a smirk on her face. I wasn't sure why or what was on her mind.

Chapter 28

WE LEFT DR. NABAT TO test out this idea, thanks to Leyla bringing up Polybius. I grabbed Leyla's hand and asked her if she would like to go for a walk.

"Better yet, let's go see how Hande is doing," she suggested. I couldn't believe I hadn't thought of that.

Badri drove, and Sami came with us. We found Lydia in the room with Hande. At first, we thought he was still unconscious, but then Lydia put her finger to her lips to keep us quiet as we entered. Hande's eyes were still closed, but he was talking quietly.

"I want to talk to my American friend, Lydia," Hande whispered.

"I'm here, Hande," I said approaching the bed.

He opened his eyes and smiled weakly. "So Lydia tells me you had an adventure without me. I am very mad at you. Explain."

"Sorry, buddy," I said smiling back. "It was actually completely unplanned, and I wouldn't classify it as an adventure. You shouldn't feel bad that you missed this one."

"Irshad got to go. He left me a present, but didn't take me with him," Hande continued trying not to laugh. "Speaking of going, was it you that whispered the words of Rumi that I whispered to you in Konya?"

"Yes," I admitted. "They came to mind as I saw you sleeping when I visited you yesterday. I needed you awake. I count on you to get me out of all the difficult situations I get myself into. And I haven't eaten at a decent restaurant in days."

"Your words came to me as I was actually standing in the doorsill—the doorsill of this world and the next. Your words enticed me to come back. They reminded me of Lydia, of my family, of you, of the important things I could yet do. Thank you."

I was touched beyond words. I squeezed his good shoulder. He winced and then smiled, "Just joking, you serious American," he said.

We could see he was tiring, so we said our goodbyes and followed Lydia into the hallway. She explained that Hande had woken up early this morning asking for water. He had progressively become more aware and interested in eating and talking. "He shared the experience at the doorsill in detail with me. Thank you, Thad." Lydia gave me a hug and shivered. "I had convinced myself that he was gone, and maybe he was. All I know is, he is back, and I know what I would have lost had he left me here.

"The nurse says his vital signs are improving, but it will be at least another week until he can travel to a good hospital to ensure he makes a full recovery. They say it isn't much of a difference flying to Riyadh or to Istanbul, so we are hoping to return to Turkey late next week."

We said our goodbyes, promising to come visit again tomorrow and spend more time. I don't think Lydia and Hande minded being alone, however. I was wrong about it being a good day. It was a very good day.

Returning to Badri's house, I went directly to the third floor, where Dr. Nabat was working on decoding the Kitab Kabbani. This was the real discovery, not finding the physical book itself. The treasure was in the content, not the cover and the papyrus, vellum, and paper. I instantly felt guilty for my expectations of his progress. He had foregone traveling to see his daughter and probably future son-in-law to test out the Polybius theory.

"I have interesting news," he said looking up at me as I walked into the room. "It appears that your idea of the Polybius Squares was correct. I have tested the first page of the book and the last page. It will take me some time to decode the Old Aramaic. The Arabic will go much faster. With the Old Aramaic, I was at first puzzled on how to employ the Polybius Square. You see, there are only twenty-two letters in Old Aramaic. I assumed two letters were included in a square with a closely pronounced letter, like qop and kap for example. But that created a four-by-five matrix, or a five-by-four matrix. Neither seemed to work.

"Then I considered the fact that the Aramaic alphabet was derived from the Phoenician script. That means all the letters represent consonants. This script is actually the antecedent of most of the alphabets of the Middle East. The Hebrew alphabet is the closest to Aramaic script. That is one of the reasons Rabbi Halevi and I met each other. Our research worked with the same ancient language forms. The Nabataean script was also derived from the Aramaic, which eventually evolved into the Arabic script, replacing older scripts of Arabia, such as the Old South Arabian that is on the entrance stone to the library.

"Sorry, I am wandering. An interesting innovation in Aramaic are the small marks that represent select vowels, a, i, and u. That's twenty-five and works with the traditional five-by-five Polybius Square. I just had to figure out where the vowel boxes in the matrix fit."

"So have you been able to come up with any actual words or sentences?" I asked, impressed that he was able to accomplish this much since we traveled to town and back.

"I first wanted to test out the theory before attacking actual text, so I went to the end of the book and tried the modern Arabic. That also proved complicated since Arabic has 28 letters in its alphabet. I tried again the five-by-six or six-by-five matrix, but I couldn't find any set of six horizontal or vertical dashes, so I ruled that out. I then considered the addition of vowel marks, but again, I found no dashes for six, so I ruled that out. That left me with putting more than one letter in three boxes or completely dropping a letter or more."

"And?" I asked, happy about his decoding adventure, but wanting to get to the bottom of his discovery.

"Well, I believe instead of combining more than one letter in a box of the matrix, the creator simply dropped three letters, letters that are rarely used. When those letters do come up in words, they can be assumed from the context. The letters I eventually dropped were *ghayn*, *dād*, and *ta*. Now I had a five-by-five matrix, and I filled it in from right to left and tested it. It worked!"

"So do you have any content decoded yet?" I asked, excited for his progress.

"No," Dr. Nabat said. "I have tested out a few words in different parts of the text, but as you will note, there is no space between words, just the dashes continuing page after page. There are times when I can tell a new addition was made to the book, and I can start there to begin the decoding and then the translation work. It will be weeks before I can have any sure context and months or even a year or more to have the whole book decoded and then translated into English, Arabic, Farsi and Turkish."

"Wow, I didn't realize it would be so complex," I said, trying not to sound disappointed.

"Something I have been thinking about, Doctor: would you be willing to relocate to Lebanon while you take charge of this work?" Badri asked. "I was considering putting two or three people on staff, plus a supervising expert on this project. That might mean immigrating, as I don't know what we could work out with your government for temporary travel that could extend, as you say, into months. I want to keep the book at our family compound where it would be safe and if that becomes difficult with local security and political issues, perhaps setting up something in Turkey or Cypress where my family has secure housing."

"Much to think about, Mr. Kabbani," Dr. Nabat said. "I have some relatives in Iran. Also, my friendship with Rabbi Halevi is important to us both. I am not sure I could leave him."

"Wait," I said. "You don't need to leave your home, that is, if you don't want to. All you need are copies of the pages, which would be better anyway. I doubt you want to open these ancient pages constantly. I would think we could make a very good copy, and you could travel home with it. No one in customs would question it. Of course, we could also digitize it, and you could access it on any computer."

"Yes, we could let the whole world access it, and they could make their own decoded translations. Complete transparency would add to the credibility of the message," Badri said. "Dr. Nabat, I would be honored if you, Rabbi Halevi, and Mrs. Nazari would form the core research team to head up this project. That all three of you are located in Iran might be problematic, but in the short term, no one needs to know about this project."

"I am honored, Mr. Kabbani," Dr. Nabat said. "As I mentioned, much to think about, and I am only speaking for myself, of course. I have considered, as will others, that there may be multiple layers of meaning in this code, that is, other words that could change the content and context. For example," and Dr. Nabat wrote out a string of letters that read hearthandfeast. "That could be read heart hand feast or hearth and feast. Very different."

Leyla had been unusually quiet during this conversation. She motioned for me to leave the room with her. We excused ourselves and ended up walking up the trail to the old mosque. We hadn't said a word on the trail, but we held hands, and that was enough for me. We entered the ancient building and sat down, leaning against the wall. We left the door open for the light, which was fading.

"Our adventure is about over, Thaddeus," Leyla said. "Yes, there is much yet to do, but our part in this is coming to a close."

"Not everything has to come to a close, Leyla," I said. "Where do you want to go from here?"

"Home," Leyla said.

"And with us?" I asked, clarifying my original meaning of my question.

"This adventure, this operation has been amazing," Leyla began. "Never has Al-Ḥujurāt done anything like this that I know of. In the recent past, we have delivered secret messages between leaders of tribes or even countries, we have rescued people, we have supported archeological research, and at times we have had to work with some threats to our lives, but never have we had the kinds of relentless attacks we have experienced in this operation. Never have we had to unravel so many riddles. And we have done so with seeming ease. It doesn't work like that normally, but it did in this case for some reason I have yet to understand. That has taken us all to new heights of excitement and confidence."

"I am grateful to have been along for the ride," I said.

"You have been more than a body in the passenger seat, but where I am going with this is, you and I have been able to ride this wave of exhilaration, and I am afraid it has clouded our understanding and judgment of our own relationship."

"Wait, Leyla," I began.

"No, please, let me say what I need to say," Leyla said. "As I listened to Dr. Nabat just now, I heard the message that the Kitab Kabbani is now in the hands of its rightful owner, Badri Kabbani, and that the experts will need time to get the content published. Reality has set in. As Dr. Nabat explained his amazing progress, we were flying high, and all seemed clear. Now I see that understanding the Kitab Kabbani will take some time. Like my enthusiasm, I think we got too close to the sun, and our wings are melting. And like Icarus, I fear you and I will fall into the sea."

I sat there quietly while I collected my thoughts. Leyla must have taken this as giving up and agreeing with her bleak assessment of our future together. I heard her begin to weep softly.

"Icarus flew, Leyla," I finally said. "Sure, the story goes that Icarus's father made him wings and told him not to fly too close to the sun. He was disobedient and plunged to his death. One moral to take away is: be obedient, listen to experts, play it safe, do what dad says. What we don't think about is Daedalus also told his son not to fly too close to the ocean because the water would also ruin his wings. That is exactly what Majnun and Leyla did, and they also met a tragic death. Flying too low is more dangerous than flying too high, because it feels safer, but it isn't."

"Yes, but," Leyla began to protest.

I kissed her lips quiet and said, "Now it's my turn to say what must be said. Icarus flew! I know this is just a story, but follow it through with me. Before that day, he had never flown. His comfort zones had to shift. Conformity told him not to fly, but he did. He chose the courageous path. For a time, he conquered and owned something that before that day was unthinkable.

"The world will always have their *I-told-you-so* triumphs that assuage their fears and justifications. 'I knew that marriage wouldn't work.' 'I knew that leader was a crook.' 'He should have known better.' Whatever. It isn't the fall, Leyla; it's the flight. That doesn't mean we are free to take drugs, or get drunk, or do something really stupid, just for that momentary high. We still need to align our values with eternal principles. We still need to be obedient to those principles. That is really what Icarus did in order to fly. He harnessed principles that allowed him to escape the bonds of earth."

"You are a storyteller," Leyla said, smiling through her tears. "You tell the old stories as a healer would. You tell them in a new way, while not changing the traditional information offered. I am not sure of the new reality your telling suggests, though."

"I don't see it as changing the story to a new reality; it is just completing the story. I have always felt bad for the young rich man in the Bible story. My dad read that story to me many times when I was disobedient. This young rich man is basically a good person and meets Jesus Christ's basics standards of obedience and goodness but is asked to give up his riches and join with Christ. The young man turns away. Perhaps Jesus knew this young man's heart and the love he had for his riches. But that is where the story ends. The failed young rich man.

"I often thought about him and hoped he repented and with his second chance took up the mission Jesus Christ invited him to join. That isn't changing the story but choosing the best that is in every one of us. Why not? It doesn't break any rules or principles; in fact, it celebrates them."

"Muslims are familiar with a similar story from the Bible. It is the story of Joseph of Egypt. He runs from Potiphar's wife who seeks his love, who we call Zuleika. She is reviled as a sinner, and that is where the tale ends. In Sufi stories, though, Zuleika's love for Joseph is a symbol of the soul's deep longing for God, not the base love of an adulterer. Muslims believe that Zuleika, after many years of suffering, repentance, and spiritual conversion, either ends up marrying the Prophet Joseph, or in another version, the wife that Pharaoh gives Joseph, Asenath, was, some scholars suggest, really Zuleika's daughter. Either way, there is a reconciliation of sorts."

"I wonder if this is where the writer of the film *The Graduate* got his ideas?" I said out loud. Before Leyla had a chance to ask what I was talking about, I changed the subject and said, "I have been doing my own research, with Badri's help. I could be completely off base here, but I could only find two instances where the Qur'an talks about marriage to non-Muslims. I pulled these off the internet back in Iran when I was doing the Gerrha research."

I pulled the worn sheet of paper out of my pocket and read, "Quote, *And do not marry polytheistic women until they believe. And a believing slave woman is better than a polytheist, even though she might please you. And do not marry polytheistic men to your women until they believe. And a believing slave is better than a polytheist, even though he might please you.* Unquote. That is from Sura 2, verse 221."

"Yes, I know that verse," Leyla said.

"Here is the other one, from Surah 5, verse 5. Quote, *And lawful in marriage are chaste women from among the believers and chaste women from among those who were given the Scripture before you, when you have given them their due compensation, desiring chastity, not unlawful sexual intercourse or taking secret lovers.* Unquote.

"The way I see it, there is a difference made between non-Muslim People of the Book, that is those of the Judeo-Christian faiths, and non-Muslim polytheists. These verses say that both men and women are not permitted to marry outside of believers in God. Okay, so that is pretty clear. The next point is that men are permitted to marry chaste Muslim, Jewish or Christian women. I certainly put you in that category."

"Thanks, Majnun," Leyla said. "I think you are missing a key point of the context of these verses."

"Maybe so, but here is my thought on the context I believe you are going to raise. You read from these scriptures that though Muslim women are not directly addressed, if Muslim men are given permission to marry Muslim women, then naturally, Muslim women can marry Muslim men. That's it. The Qur'an doesn't offer any further guidance on whether Muslim women can marry men, quote, *of the Book,* unquote."

I thought I had explained my case well, and angels would sing, and a light would shine, and Leyla would fall into my arms. Right.

"Traditionally," Leyla began, "the practice has been that no, the reverse is not accepted for Muslim women. There is exact permission for Muslim men to marry women who are People of the Book. Women must also be given exact permission, and they are not. There is much justification for this decision, and all major Muslim sects accept this as doctrine.

"Basically, it comes down to preservation of what we call *Ummah*, the Muslim Community. It is the man that establishes the religion of the family. Our legal system is based on this practice, and tradition holds this standard in terms of not only religion, but language, culture, customs, and values. Women marry into a family, not the other way around. The same is true in Christianity as I understand it, even if in the western world it is not practiced as it used to be."

I wasn't ready to give up yet. I said, "But isn't Islam a belief? You said yourself it isn't a genetic gift. Deciding to follow the father's beliefs is a decision of the children. Women are the primary nurturers of the children. There is a British saying, *the hand that rocks the cradle rules the world*. I would think religion and spiritual belief would spring from the mother. Islam says there is no compulsion in religion, but it sure feels like there is in practice." As soon as I said it, I felt bad about my last statement. "Sorry, that is mostly emotion speaking, not my true feelings."

"I don't have answers for your questions," Leyla said. "Sometimes things are just what they are. Who are we to say we know more than the combined wisdom of our ancestors? Who are we to think we have new answers to the same old questions?"

"Who are we not to consider these questions? I agree we need to respect the wisdom of the past and the doctrine of the present, but we are the intersection to the future. If we don't do our best—which might mean completing the story—we are cheating those who come after us. I know we are still in the early stages of our relationship, and all this talk about taking serious steps toward marriage is probably premature, but not far into getting to know you,my goal became quite serious. Let's try again to put this tough subject on a shelf for now."

"I would like to know what is in the Kitab Kabbani," Leyla said. "Somewhere along the way it became, in my mind, a potential answer to our challenges. It became personal, not just a voice from the past about religion, culture, politics and common identity of this region."

"It will come," I said. "Another month is not too long to wait for something that has been waiting for hundreds of years to speak to us."

We returned to the house to find everyone at dinner. We joined in without any questions being asked of us. News arrived by a driver from Lydia that Hande had been approved for travel, and he would fly directly to Istanbul. The visiting medical doctor suggested he be moved as soon as possible and not wait the week suggested earlier. The note explained that Hande and Lydia would leave midday tomorrow. Lydia requested that her father visit this evening if possible. The discussion over dinner was whether Leyla and Sami should also go to ensure no complications with Lydia and Leyla's departure. The team had morphed into a group of friends over the past few days, so Leyla agreed to travel with Sami.

Badri would stay in Najran to arrange for the care and support of his new house and property there and for the preservation and gifts to Saudi Arabia of much of the library content. He would arrange for the quiet shipment of the Kitab Kabbani and a few other family relics to Beirut. He estimated that would only take a few days, and by then one of his family solicitors would be in the country to arrange for all else.

I would stay with Badri, and then we would travel to Dubai to pick up Rabbi Halevi's research. From there we would travel to either Beirut or to Turkey. Badri was anxious to get Anna safely to Beirut or perhaps to their property in Jubayl, where she could convalesce further.

We all agreed to travel into town tonight for a team meeting with Hande and Lydia. Badri would also find a place where we could make a copy of the Kitab Kabbani for Dr. Nabat. The page count was 517 pages, some of which were quite delicate. Badri had decided to have pictures taken of the pages and put on a small flash drive. This technique would be much kinder to the pages and easier to decipher in its original state than a black and white copy.

"*The Kitab Kabbani holds great secrets that will not find light until there is great darkness,*" Badri repeated to the team at our ad hoc meeting in Hande's room. The team had turned to Badri as their new unofficial leader for this last gathering. "Those are the words of the Fahrunissa Scroll. That seems to suggest that there is something that will shed light on this darkness in the Kitab.

"I have asked Dr. Nabat to share the basics of the few pages he has been able to decode and translate as an offering of closure to this operation. That will happen tomorrow morning at breakfast in this room. I will offer whatever resources are needed to completely decode and translate the Kitab as quickly as possible. Dr. Nabat's work, for now, is to be kept secret. After his work, hopefully with Rabbi Halevi's and Mrs. Navari's help, is completed, we will post the work on the internet for the world to see and for their own decoding and translation efforts."

"We will do our very best," Dr. Nabat said. "And perhaps one day I will be able and ready to migrate to be closer to Lydia, and I hope, Hande."

"I am probably out of the Al-Ḥujurāt operations business, according to the doctor," Hande added. "I may start my own restaurant in Konya or Istanbul. I would be honored to have your presence nearby. Lydia says you are a great cook in your own right. And you, my American buddy, what are your plans?"

"I have none at the moment," I explained. "I have always been either the captive audience or just along for the ride. Now that the ride is over, I am not sure what is next for me. I need to return home if for no other reason than to clean it up and take care of obligations there."

"The Fahrunissa tomb scroll also predicted, *one sharing the same name as the Brother of Jesus the Prophet will be the bearer of the key to reclaiming the Kitab Kabbani,*" Leyla said. "We all know you have been the key many times to the success of this operation and its continuing success of bringing to book to the world. And far from being captive, you have captured all of us."

"To that end," Badri interrupted, "I want to announce that I have offered to Thad to relocate to our family site in Jubayl. It may be known to some of you as Byblos, the ancient Phoenician port village. Byblos, one of the oldest continually inhabited cities in the world, has been closely linked to the legends and history of the Mediterranean region and the Middle East for thousands of years. According to Phoenician tradition, it was founded by the God El, and even the Phoenicians considered it a city of great antiquity.

"Byblos is also directly associated with the history and diffusion of the Phoenician alphabet—the precursor to many present phonetic alphabets, some of which are found in the Kitab Kabbani. It was the Greeks, sometime after 1200 BC, who gave the name "Phoenicia" to the coastal area now known as the Levant. They called the city "Byblos" (Greek for papyrus) because this commercial center was important in the papyrus trade—the key element of ancient literary communication.

"Much of the books that filled the shelves of the great Library of Alexandria were made of the papyrus from Byblos. English vocabulary includes words from this root, such as Bible, bibli-ography, bibliophile, and in other languages, such as biblioteca, Spanish for library.

"And as you probably already know, Jubayl is derived from the ancient Canaanite word for the town, Gubal, meaning well or origin. Byblos-Jubayl is nearly synonymous with writing, books and source. The history and meaning of this place, recognized by the United Nations as the oldest continuously inhabited city in the world, suggests it ought to be the home for the Kitab Kabbani and research center for this and similar works from around the world."

"It would be an honor to have you in the neighborhood," Lydia said, smiling at me.

"And maybe you could cook me a genuine American ham-burger when I visit," Hande added.

"I leave it to you to talk Thad into this new adventure," Badri said. "I have talked to him, as well as his sister about it, but he has not yet been swayed. Either way, the Kitab Kabbani will have a new home soon, and you are all invited anytime."

Leyla locked eyes with me. She had said nothing to persuade me as the others had. A storm was brewing in her eyes, but I couldn't tell if that was good or bad.

Chapter 29

Badri, Sami, Leyla, Dr. Nabat—I just couldn't bring myself to call him Jal—and Lydia, who was persuaded to get a good night's sleep before her travels tomorrow, and I all drove back to the Kabbani house in good spirits. I was mostly play acting, but I didn't want to bring down the good feelings of everyone else. Since Leyla rode back with Sami and Lydia, I didn't have a chance to speak with her. I really wanted her input and wasn't sure I really wanted to be a neighbor, as Lydia had put it, if Leyla was only to be a distant friend. I went to bed with many thoughts on my mind but happily fell asleep. About two in the morning, however, I woke up and couldn't get back to sleep. I had no dream to ponder and didn't want to wake Badri, so I went up to the roof to watch the stars and consider my future.

I was surprised to find Leyla there with Lydia. "Lydia, you were supposed to come back to the house so you could get a good night's rest," I said.

"I couldn't sleep," Lydia offered. "I was just telling Leyla I was going to give it another try. Maybe you can keep her company for a few minutes. See you both in the morning."

"You having trouble sleeping, too?" I asked.

"I don't know," Leyla said. "I haven't tried yet. Lydia and I were just comparing notes on these last thirty days. Usually, we would have a full team debrief on what we did right and mistakes we need to correct, processes that need improvement, and so on. With Irshad gone, it never happened."

"So what did you do right and what mistakes do you need to correct?" I asked her.

Leyla looked at me trying to decide what to say. I could tell she knew what I was asking, but it didn't look like she was going to risk going there.

"You know, another possible origin for the port town of Jabayl is from the Arabic Jabal, which means mountain."

"Is Jabayl also on a mountain?" I asked, willing to let her talk about anything on her mind.

"It is near Mount Lebanon. It provides an additional meaningful reason for the Kitab Kabbani to be located there. In the Qur'an, Surah An-Naba, that's chapter 78, it says, *About what are they asking one another? About the great news—That over which they are in disagreement. No! They are going to know. Then, no! They are going to know. Have We not made the earth a resting place? And the mountains as stakes?*"

"Wow, that almost sounds like it is talking about the Kitab Kabbani and the resting place of this great news," I said.

"It does. But I suspect that Badri didn't mention this connection because these verses are most likely talking about the Qur'an itself and its message, not the message of a book written by scribes, not prophets."

"I see what you mean," I said. "The Kitab Kabbani, no matter its message, is just a book, and no one ever claimed it to be more."

"Mountains, I believe," Leyla continued, "protect the earth's surface from the molten inner core and from the storms on the surface."

"I have read," I said, "that science suggests that if the surface of the earth were smooth, the air would punish the surface with relentless winds which would make the surface we live on too hot and uninhabitable."

"We have talked about a verse later on in this same Surah, *And the mountains are removed and will be but a mirage.* I have seen that happen on this operation more than just a few times. I am still amazed at this entire effort. It really had no complex plan and just happened."

"Since I have nothing to compare it with, I had just assumed you and your team were miracle workers all the time," I said.

"We are good at what we do, but we never do this. And it wasn't us that did it. That is what Lydia and I were talking about. It was you mostly, with some help from Badri, but mostly you that made this happen."

I chuckled and wanted to refute her, but then a thought came to mind that I had been playing with in my mind, and I could now try to put into words. "It wasn't me, Leyla. That isn't humility speaking, but simply the truth. We started out thinking there was Al-Ĥujurāt, the good guys, and at least two teams of bad guys, Furqaan and the Hashshashin. All along there was another team at work here. I don't know if it was God, angels, jinn, or who, but we were guided, and this was handed to us. We all made sacrifices, you most of all, giving up your relics, but it was a small price to pay, I think."

"You think?" Leyla asked.

"Yes, it still depends on what is in the book and on what will come of its message. People died, some very bad people, but they were people just the same. My sister almost died. Hande and I almost died. I don't know what is worth the price of you especially, Leyla."

Leyla stared at the heavens and the thousands of stars twinkling just to be in her presence. "You know, there is another verse, just after talking about the mountains as stakes. Verse eight. It takes quite a turn in subject matter, but there have been times over the last month that it feels like the perfect completion of the Kitab Kabbani search and rescue operation. This is the other thing Lydia and I were talking about."

"Sorry, I don't have any idea what you are talking about."

"Yes, you do," Leyla said. "It begins to explain the future of this earth, or in this case, the post-Kitab Kabbani adventure. It says, *And We created you in pairs.*"

"We?" I asked. "Was there more than one creator?"

"Allah and angels," Leyla said.

"Oh," I said. "So were we created as a pair? Is that what you are asking?"

"I wasn't asking anything, just thinking out loud," Leyla said. "Lydia and Hande have been to death's doorsill together and are going to get married, and with Lydia's father's blessing. I don't know how Lydia's relatives or Hande's family will take this announcement, but they are moving forward with their plans. Lydia also told me the secret you have known for some time and that you shared with me confidentially, that Dr. Nabat converted to Christianity. Don't worry; the secret is still safe with me, and I will tell no one."

"That appears to be an entirely different situation as I understand the rules," I said, trying to get to the heart of the matter. "They could jump across the stream whereas it appears you and I have to construct a mammoth bridge across a raging river where death is a possible outcome."

"Yep, something like that," Leyla said shaking her head with a slight smile. "Following your happy summation of our situation, sometimes I see you and me as Majnun and Leyla, doomed to an unfulfilled relationship where love dies a slow death by a cancer that is the dictates of tradition and doctrine. In this scenario, we treasure our fidelity until we meet again on the other side of life, in the eternal heavens.

"Then I wake from that dream, or nightmare, and think, yes, there is a certain freedom in that, turning our backs on the carnal and the worldly, for something great in the world to come. I would even accept what that would mean for us, but I am always left with a lingering feeling that there is more we are meant to do, together, here in preparation for there. And of course, none of this back and forth conversation I've had includes you, the important other half of this reality."

"Thanks for thinking of me," I said taking her hand casually. "I am just as guilty of my own one-way conversations about us. I have been thinking of our relationship in terms of the Kitab Kabbani. They run parallel tracks right through the landscapes, histories, and people of this part of the world. We can look at our relationship through the eyes of Leyla and Majnun, Parsomash and Susa, or as the Kitab Kabbani—a mysterious harbinger of great promise but still unknown. The Kitab Kabbani will be published one day. It is potentially a great historical document, but we have scripture, the Bible, the Qur'an, possibly other guidance from deity, and what does the world do with that? They squabble and use these words for their own designs. The story of Leyla and Majnun is a story of earthly injustices and pain for the obedient, if that is what you want to see. Majnun can represent mankind and Leyla the divine female where the mortal cannot reach the immortal, if your weakness is the fleeting feelings of spiritual love in the carnal soul. It can define for us what we may desire in the moment, or it can bring some clarity to you and I and our future, if that is what our hearts or our spiritual natures dictate.

"It will be the same with the Kitab Kabbani. It may be another voice to some of the truths that they already accept or are on the fence about. To others, it will be a book of significant connection between the world and the heavens, the carnal and the spiritual. It will be what people want it to be."

"And it may be enough of a clear voice to some to entice them to make changes or choose a new path that could change the course of history," Leyla added.

"Exactly," I said. "And where are we on this path? Is there more? Do we sacrifice now for something to come? I don't mean do we sacrifice this life for happiness in the world to come, but rather, do we sacrifice pieces of present doctrine because it feels like there is more, much more to come if we find it and face it together?"

"I have never considered it that way," Leyla admitted. "You are painting a picture of us being cast out of the Garden of Eden, aren't you?"

"I don't believe Adam and Eve actually sinned. They were like little children, not fully knowing the good from the evil. Eve transgressed the law, and Adam, wanting to fulfill the other laws, chose also to transgress. Once they partook of the fruit of the knowledge of good and evil, they were fully aware and became co-creators of mankind with God.

"I am not saying we are as elect as our first parents—well, maybe you are, but I'm not—but what I am saying is, we have experienced God's hand in the many events we have shared over the past many days. I don't think we ought to toss that aside with our dirty laundry, promising we will clean it and wear it on the other side of the veil of this life."

"And you aren't sharing these deep thoughts just so you can have me in this life? You want me now for reasons that transcend the now?" Leyla asked.

"You know the answer to that, Leyla," I said looking into her eyes. "We both know we could have made that choice for the wrong reasons several times over the past weeks. I can't say that I am perfect, that my heart is fully pure, or that I don't desire to be with you, but if that were all, I would have either followed through with that desire, or I would have walked away knowing my motivations were simply base desires. So is it you or Alicia, the ticket counter lady?"

I got a really good sock in the arm for that, but it felt great not to be so bound by seriousness that we couldn't even smile.

"The sun will soon be up," Leyla said. "How about I sleep with you right now?"

"What?" I asked in shock.

"I meant exactly what I just said, nothing more, just sleep," Leyla said smiling. "Hold me. I have been up all day and now nearly all night, and I am going to collapse and get an hour of sleep before the sun rises. Maybe answers will present themselves in the light."

I leaned against the wall of the roof fortress and took Leyla in my arms. We were both asleep within a minute or two. My last thought was how wonderful her hair smelled.

We were awakened by Badri at seven in the morning. "I thought you two had eloped or something. I couldn't find you anywhere. Breakfast in thirty minutes, then we are off to the clinic. I don't know about you two, but I can't wait to hear what Dr. Nabat has been able to decode and translate from the Kitab."

Everyone was excited to be together one last time while still in the Kingdom. We were all going different directions, some within hours, some within a few days. I would be glad to be an honest man again. I really hated being in another country on a false passport. I couldn't wait to travel to the Gulf again on my real passport. I promised myself I would never travel again with false identification. If I couldn't go as who I am, I simply wouldn't go.

Hande was looking pretty healthy. Lydia and Leyla looked like they had only gotten an hour of sleep, which I think was pretty close to the facts. Badri was positively beaming. He had discovered an ancient home, family treasures, many of which he was prepared to donate to the Saudi government in gratitude for not confiscating a home he never knew he had and so he could quietly take out a few historical relics he planned to keep in the family holdings.

Dr. Nabat seemed nervous but also excited. He had gone from a wary and even negative support to Lydia and her friends to a trusted member of Al-Ḥujurāt and soon world-renowned decoder and translator of the Kitab Kabbani—that is once he safely immigrated to another country.

"It is time for us to go our separate ways," Badri began. "Dr. Nabat has been working very hard, sacrificing time he could have dedicated to spending time with Lydia, to decoding and roughly translating a few small sections of the Kitab. I now turn the time over to the doctor for a brief summary of what he has discovered."

"Thank you for this opportunity to share a few minutes with you. I have always been worried about my Lydia since she left home to go work for this mysterious research agency in Turkey. I knew she was not accomplishing human resources reports for commercial companies in Istanbul, but I never imagined she would find herself in this exciting environment with such quality people and that I would have the chance to participate in some small way with her."

"Not a small way father," Lydia said smiling brightly. "You are bringing meaning to all our efforts. Thank you."

"I may have a skill set you need at the moment, but I have to say before I start that I only added my efforts to yours because of curious turns in my own research that led me to Mr. Thaddeus Allen, long before I actually met him. That is a story for another day, however. It is an honor, in many ways only you and I understand, to know you, and then, of course, Badri Kabbani and all of you."

Dr. Nabat took a drink of water and then opened his notebook. He cleared his throat and began. "First, a few sentences from the early pages of the Kitab. I am assuming these were transcribed from the original scrolls. The first sentences read: *Recently returned from inspection of the Nile Canal, ordered built by the King of Kings, Darius. Ships now cross from Egypt to Persia in trade and commerce. I come away from my tour with varied, but intertwined interests. I believe I can harness the power of water at home with a catch and archive of the melting snow. I am considering entering my first son in the venture of commerce as my duties at court allow. I will begin a record of the viperous*—I think he was trying to express the concepts of dangerous and revolutionary—*concepts of the King of Kings Darius. No king demands dignity and leniency, tolerance and respect for the unprivileged as he does.*

"Then he adds a statement I believe he attributes to Darius, but I will need to understand the full context better to be sure. It reads: *I will not tolerate that the weak shall suffer injustices brought upon them by the mighty. I am mightier than the mighty and what is just pleases me. …You, my subjects, must not assume what the powerful undertake as sublime. What the common man achieves is much more extraordinary.*"

With that, Dr. Nabat looked up at the group and said, "This is extraordinary."

"In those brief lines," Badri said, nearly choked up, "is the trajectory of my family speaking from the dust of over two thousand five hundred years ago. How could he have ever imagined…"

"I have just a little bit more from the middle and near the end of the book, if you would like me to share it," Dr. Nabat offered.

"Oh my, by all means," Badri said.

"These are just fragments of statements, so we shouldn't read into them too much of our own expectations or understanding. These statements, I am guessing, run between the early years of Christianity, the apostasy from Christianity following the Nicean

Council era, and the early days of Islam. First a few lines from the early Christian pages."

"Traveled to Susa to hear a messenger of Jesus of Judea. I understand the heart of the gospel of Jesus is the condescension of the Lord for all men everywhere, not just those Jews of that land. The atonement gives power to the name of Christ. The hands of the gospel is our sacrifice. Our sacrifices, that which God asks of us, gives power to our faith. If we sacrifice according to charity, they are no sacrifice at all, but an exchange for the highest blessings."

"And this from the Nicean Council era I am guessing," Dr. Nabat continued. *"The Council of the learned men in Bithynia brings news of much to think about. There should be no compromise with principles, yet I see some values taking precedence over principles, palatability and politics swaying values. Short term unity at what cost eternally?"*

"This last piece is from the final pages of the book and was a little easier for me to decode and translate. I can't help but wonder if these words influenced Rumi, that is, if shared before they were put into code to be hidden until this time." Dr. Nabat shuffled to the last page of his notes and began,

"At the core of Islam there is only the Love of God, not us against them, nor that feeling or announcement that we have truth and they do not. We must love all human beings and all of Allah's creations. This is the original and true message of Islam, that we are all God's creations, no matter those of another belief, another religion, another culture, another language, another color, another kingdom.

"The only real difference between men lies in their conduct and actions, the values they display, not just preach, and their faith in God, and determination to live that faith. When we all look to God and not to each other, then men are one, with no differences. No one but God is perfect. All men must treasure the good as best as we can understand it and shake off the dust that is remaining. We cannot

make others follow us, but we must be the light that they will turn to and choose to follow.

"The Prophet Muhammad is not a basket of goods that we can choose from and discard others, but neither is he the only basket and not the last before the end of the world. We must wash away our complacent pride, our conceit and our feelings of select superiority to become one again. That is true Islam. Once we lay the kalimah on the altar of our hearts, we will never again see or treat anyone as different from us."

"Is recitation of the Kalimah or the outward practices of the rituals of Islam enough to keep someone a Muslim, regardless of the deeds and beliefs of that person? NO, Allah says."

"And there is manifest to them of God what they had not expected to see, the Qur'an says. Even the mighty in spirit and the pure in heart have not yet seen the full plan of Allah for his creations."

"That is all I have had time to decode, and I may have translated incorrectly or taken a statement out of context, so please forgive me if I have presented something extremely wrong or distasteful in my choice of words.

"I find it interesting," Dr. Nabat continued, "that there are themes running through these citations even though I am fairly certain the writers of later inputs into the Kitab could not understand the earlier inputs in the previous ancient languages. Each generation must have been schooled in the coding structure and recording process, but I doubt they would have been taught the ancient languages; otherwise I think this book would be in only one language.

"I hope this has been helpful, and I am very excited to complete the full decoding and translation. Oh, and I have come to my personal conclusion and humbly suggest that the initial translation be made into Arabic since it appears that a full quarter or more of the book is already in Arabic. The secondary translation should be in Farsi, and the third translation should be in English, but by someone much more skilled than me in that language."

"Thank you," Badri said. "These past thirty days have been an incredible experience for all of us. You are always welcome at my home anytime, and I hope we have many opportunities to see each other in the future. As the Kitab Kabbani shows, time is relentless and continues to move forward, despite our best efforts to dissect it and slow it down. The very best we can do is fill it with friends, service, and love, and maybe some great meals, I add for Hande."

Badri turned to look at me and then at Leyla, Lydia, Hande, Dr. Nabat and Sami. "God bless you all in your travels, your future, and your weighty decisions. What you do with your time may not be recorded in a book like this," he said pointing to Dr. Nabat's notes, "but they will be recorded; that, I am sure of." Badri gave everyone a hug and personal words of thanks and encouragement. We each followed suit with brief words and long hugs. With that, it was over.

We stayed at the clinic until Lydia, Hande, and Leyla left with Sami for the airport. Badri drove Dr. Nabat, who would leave in the morning for Yazd, and me back to his ancient castle home. The house seemed empty without the rest of the team. To be honest, it felt like the Empty Quarter without Leyla there.

"May I offer some unsolicited advice?" Dr. Nabat asked me as we reentered the house.

"Of course," I said, wondering what was on his mind.

"I have made some very difficult decisions in my life, none more complex for me than my acceptance of Christianity. I use that word, acceptance, very carefully. I see it as more than submission. It is putting my will on the altar and taking up God's will, to be sure, but it is also a partnership of sorts. I do all I can, and I have faith that God will make up where I fall short. Don't you be afraid to do the same. It is not fate that directs us, but we can allow chance and circumstance to rule us if we let it. We can't have everything we desire, but we can choose everything we really need. You know, I have failed at what I didn't want to do but did it because I thought I had to and because it seemed like the safe path. My advice to you is to take a chance to succeed at what you love. He that endureth to the end shall be saved."

"Those words sound really familiar," I said.

"They are from the Bible," Dr. Nabat said. "And I have come to believe that to endure is not to accept and suffer, but live fully, love always, and be grateful. Abundance mentality, which is the campfire the Kitab Kabbani seems to dance around, and a guiding principle of Al-Ĥujurāt is part of that. But take it from this old man, gratitude is the gateway to abundance. The more we focus on being grateful for what we have, for what we have been given, the more we realize our abundant life. Those who concentrate on what they don't have more easily slip into the zero-sum game of in order for me to win, you must lose.

"Your relationship with Leyla Hatun is not a zero-sum relationship. As well, the world's religions are not a zero-sum calculation either. I do believe there is one true religion, and we will have the opportunity to choose it or reject it in this life or the next because God loves us and what does not get taken care of in this life, will be on our schedule in the next life. Just don't wait until the next life if treasures of our heart present themselves here."

"Thank you, Jal," I said. "Lydia is a very fortunate young lady to have you as her father. I will take your words to heart, but I can only speak for me, of course."

"Trust without reservation," Dr. Nabat said with a kind smile, "then act, my boy. It is the reason behind the action that justifies choice. People cannot be compelled to believe or not believe. We all have to choose. It is the core of all religions to submit, but submission to God does not mean that man is no different than cattle or sheep—that they must be coerced into the corral, or lured in by some base need, like food or water. We cannot be forced to believe against our will. That is not submission. That is a kind of slavery. Spiritual submission is inside then out; slavery is outside and then in, if we allow it to enter.

"You will be fine, my young friend. Many people have confidence in you. I do. The rabbi does. The Al-Ḥujurāt team does. Your brother-in-law does. And I suspect from what Lydia told me, Leyla Hatun's family does. That does not mean they do or don't acquiesce to your desires, but that they know you will make the right decisions."

Totally confused, I returned his smile and excused myself to try to sort out his words, my thoughts, and the paths I could choose to take. Only one thought that I have come to believe brought me peace as I exited the house for the little mosque up the trail. I suspect that life really is perfectly fair. It just appears not to be because of two reasons: first, we are not perfect judges and second, because life does not end where our vision does. I knew that no matter where the path I chose led, if I did my best all would work out, eventually.

The next morning Badri and I drove Dr. Jal Nabat to the airport and saw him off to Yazd. We hoped we would see him and his family permanently in Lebanon one day soon. We returned to a truly empty house and decided it was time we pack up and leave as well. Badri coordinated for a caretaker to live at the house, and the last of the library relics and treasures were removed and securely transferred to a bank vault in town. The Saudi government would take possession of most of these items in a few days and transfer the rest to Badri once reviewed. Badri would carry the Kitab with him in a specially created box.

We departed the next day for Dubai by private aircraft. I picked up Rabbi Halevi's papers, and we flew directly to Beirut. Badri and I had decided to add the rabbi's works to the research center if he would give his permission to do so. Anna, who had just returned to Lebanon herself, met us at the airport with a driver and took us to the Kabbani home in Ras Beirut. It was peaceful, and it was great to be with my sister and Badri, but I didn't feel any closure from the last month like I should have.

The next day we drove thirty minutes north to Jubayl to review plans for the Kitab Kabbani Research Center. It was a wonderful day, and I began to really see myself living in this amazing little town. Of course, my mind was somewhere else, and Badri knew it.

"I think it is time you and I take a trip to Turkey," Badri told me that evening.

I didn't want to be the reason he was pulled away once again from his wife, but I did want to eat some more kebabs, kofte, dolma, and borek.

Part IV:
da-i-ra,
Full Circle

Chapter 30

IT TOOK A COUPLE OF days for Badri to complete a few business deals that needed his immediate attention after a month of vacation, as he termed our adventure to his business associates. That also gave me time to catch up with my sister and get my thoughts in order. Anna arranged the travel and also coordinated with Leyla to get the Al-Ḥujurāt team to Istanbul. It turned out that Lydia and Hande were already scouting out locations in Istanbul for their restaurant. Sami had returned to Saudi Arabia to see his family, so it was only Leyla who planned to travel from Konya for the reunion.

Badri and I arrived at Sabiha Gökçen International Airport on a crisp morning of about 45 degrees. It didn't seem like the same airport, but I was on a similar mission to save a life, this time, mine. "Was that a selfish thought?" I wondered. "Is a suffocating man's struggle for breath selfish?" my reason answered.

We took a taxi to the Pera Palace Hotel where we had planned to meet. "This hotel was originally built in 1892 to cater to passengers who arrived in Istanbul on the Orient Express," Badri explained. "There are more chic hotels and some opulent palaces that Leyla's ancestors used to inhabit that have been converted to stops for the rich and famous, but this is my favorite. It is East meets West," Badri explained as we entered the lobby.

"Anatolia has been regarded as the bridge between East and West," Leyla said as she walked up to us. She was stunning, and the entire hotel lobby seemed to pivot around her. "My country, and this city, in particular, connects two worlds. It is where the garment that covers the earth meets and is buttoned together. It is no wonder this is the home of the Dervish dance today."

Leyla took my arm, wiggled her fingers to Badri as a way of saying goodbye, and we were out the door I had just entered. Without even a hello, Leyla continued, "In the sema where you witnessed the dance, there were a few things you missed in your excellent observations. We speak of the *Qutb*, which literally means the pivot point. It also represents celestial movements, and it is the Sufi spiritual leader that has a divine connection with God. He is not known to the world, and there is only one at a time on the earth. He is only revealed to a select few, so I wouldn't put him in the category of prophet that we spoke of before."

"It's really good to see you, too, Leyla," I interjected.

"According to Ismailis, the Qutb's presence on earth is deemed necessary for the existence of the world," Leyla continued. "I do not know the Qutb, nor is his presence central to my faith. What I do believe is, we each need qutb in our lives, just as the world will one day need to bridge the widening gap between the Orient and the Occidental.

"In the dervish dance, we speak of the alchemical marriage that takes place. You might have missed that. This marriage is between heaven and earth. The dancer had one hand turned up and one hand turned down as you observed. The dancer is the qutb, connecting both with his body. You also noticed that the dancers turned left. The clockwise turn to the right represents the journey, the adventure into the world—not unlike the adventure we just completed through Turkey, Iran, and Saudi Arabia, and then back to Turkey. Interestingly, a clockwise travel pattern.

"The left-hand, counterclockwise pattern of the Sema is the quest for the soul, Thaddeus. This is the real journey we have taken, the search for truth, the journey to our inner hearts." Leyla paused and turned to look at me as busy pedestrians walked by and cars that never heard of catalytic converters passed by on their way to their next stop.

I had no idea where Leyla was leading, if she was leading, so I said, "I guess connection has to do with your reference point. The United States is also a qutb of sorts. On its east horizon, Western Europe. On the coast I know best is the horizon of the Orient. Could it be that we have taken different journeys to the truth and to our inner hearts?"

"Not if there is a universal truth," Leyla said as her eyes misted. "Not if there is to be any hope for humankind other than continued misunderstandings, zero-sum gamesmanship, and bloodshed."

"Not if there is to be any hope for us," I added the thus far unspoken.

"The final transformation of the Sema," Leyla said, with tears now streaming down her face, "where truth is found, is the alchemical marriage. When the dancers retire to meditate, that is the *Shebi Arus*, the final transformation, the wedding night as Mevlana called it. Is there to be a marriage and final transformation for us?"

"I want there to be," I said. "First, I need to return to California and close out my life there and return to Lebanon. I hope to do that in two weeks' time. When I return, let's each have whatever answers we have come up with ready to share, and we will go from there."

"Don't give up on us, Majnun. Mevlana, Rumi, said, *Dance, when you're broken open.*

"Dance, if you've torn the bandage off. Dance in the middle of fighting. Dance in your blood.

"Dance, when you're perfectly free. Struck, the dancers hear the tambourine inside them, as a wave turns the foam on its very top, begin. Maybe you don't hear that tambourine, all the tree leaves clapping time. Close the ears on your head that listen mostly to lies and cynical jokes. There are other things to hear and see: dance, music and a brilliant city inside the soul." Leyla squeezed my hand and turned and walked down the street.

I returned to the hotel empty-handed in a sense. It was a great gathering of friends, and Hande took us to a great restaurant. He conspiratorially whispered to me that he had already hired the chef at this place who would be coming to work with him in a month. No one asked me about Leyla. Maybe they already knew her plan to skip the dinner meeting. Badri reviewed the plans for the research center and its non-political, non-religious focus. I could tell that the Al-Ḥujurāt members were very interested in the overlap with their own research efforts. Would this be competition or a partner, they wondered. I smiled as I had already talked with Badri about this, and we had a great plan in place.

I flew out the next evening for California. My car was still parked where I left it, although it cost me several hundred dollars to leave parking. I was just grateful my debit card worked even though it was a little scuffed up. I found my home in semi-clean shape and solar panels installed on the roof. I had a one-day yard sale of my furniture and found a realtor to put it on the market.

I drove to Mable's Table Truck Stop, suggested some Turkish menu changes that I thought might be big hits with the Punjabi truck drivers, and bought a gooseberry pie that I had hard frozen. I said my goodbyes to my co-workers, neighbors and the friendly missionaries that happened to stop by. They gave me some things to read which I tossed in my bags.

Before leaving, I pulled out Mack's business card and gave him a call. I thanked him for his help getting me out of New York and explained my plans. Within one week of arriving in California, I was on an Air France flight to Paris with a connection to Beirut. The only thing I would really miss would be my car, but I was confident the new head cook at Mable's Table Truck Stop would take good care of it.

I was embarrassed, but grateful, when I got to the ticket counter in Sacramento, finding that I had been upgraded to first class all the way to Beirut. When I got to my seat, I was handed a note by a very nice flight attendant named Vivienne.

The note read, "Thank you for watching over my little girl this past month. I got a full report. Her great uncle also thanks you and said it was a pleasure to meet you. I didn't realize you actually met him. You know, there is a reason my last name is Albright and not Celebi, so I share the words of Rumi as one gringo to another. *You are a volume in the divine book, a mirror to the power that created the universe. Whatever you want, ask it of yourself. Whatever you're looking for can only be found inside of you.* Mack."

Additional works on sale by this author:

Media in the 21st Century:
Meet-Up or Meltdown in the Meaning Marketplace
Published by Byblos Media, June 2010; 583 pages
ISBN 978-0-9746003-6-9

The Seeds He Planted
Published by Byblos Press, December 2007
ISBN 978-0-9746003-2-1

Nahum's Story
Published by Byblos Press, December 2007
ISBN 978-0-9746003-3-8

Conversations Among Butterflies
Published by Byblos Media, August 2015
ISBN 978-0-9746003-7-6

Chinese Circus
Six novellas of mixed genres and styles that consider
contemporary themes of interest, interwoven into one book.

Published by Byblos Press, January 2016
ISBN 978-0-9746003-9-0

For more information:
www.mike-mitchell.com/

Sign up for the author's mailing list at:
www.eepurl.com/bviacf

Or scan the QR code:

www.ingramcontent.com/pod-product-compliance
Lightning Source LLC
Chambersburg PA
CBHW060342260626
47160CB00006B/2181

* 9 7 8 0 9 7 4 6 0 0 3 8 3 *